D0393471

Puffin B

I LIKE THIS STORY
A Taste of Fifty Favourites

I Like This Story is a very special book – it's the 2,000th Puffin to be published! And what better way to celebrate than to dip into fifty marvellous stories and experience the delight of discovery. Some stories you might know, others will be new to you: fantasy and reality, humour and drama – everything is here for the taking. From *The Dolphin Crossing* to *Tom's Midnight Garden*, from *Little House in the Big Woods* to *A Wizard of Earthsea*, from Leon Garfield to Arthur Ransome, and Jan Mark to Clive King, there is something for everyone!

Kaye Webb became Editor of Puffin Books in 1961. During the 1960s and 1970s her instinct and flair resulted in the addition of many outstanding titles to the Puffin list, and in 1967 she launched the highly successful Puffin Club. She is widely known for her remarkable contribution to the world of children's books, and was awarded the M.B.E. in 1947. She retired from Puffin in 1979. With this book she celebrates her twenty-fifth year of involvement with children's books. Also edited by Kaye Webb is *I Like This Poem* (Puffin 1979), a collection of poems chosen by children *for* children, which is already one of the best-loved poetry books of all time.

I LIKE THIS STORY

A Taste of Fifty Favourites

* * *

CHOSEN BY KAYE WEBB

Illustrated by Anthony Kerins

PUFFIN BOOKS

Puffin Books, Penguin Books Ltd, Harmondsworth, Middlesex, England
Viking Penguin Inc., 40 West 23rd Street, New York, New York 10010, U.S.A.
Penguin Books Australia Ltd, Ringwood, Victoria, Australia
Penguin Books Canada Limited, 2801 John Street, Markham, Ontario, Canada L3R 1B4
Penguin Books (N.Z.) Ltd, 182–190 Wairau Road, Auckland 10, New Zealand

This selection first published 1986

This selection copyright © Kaye Webb, 1986
Illustrations copyright © Anthony Kerins, 1986
Copyright information for individual extracts is given on pages 383–5
which constitute an extension of this copyright page
All rights reserved

Typeset, printed and bound in Great Britain by
Hazell Watson & Viney Ltd,
Member of BPCC
Aylesbury, Bucks
Filmset in Linotron Bembo

Except in the United States of America,
this book is sold subject to the condition
that it shall not, by way of trade of otherwise,
be lent, re-sold, hired out, or otherwise circulated
without the publisher's prior consent in any form of
binding or cover other than that in which it is
published and without a similar condition
including this condition being imposed
on the subsequent purchaser

CONTENTS

*For all members of the Puffin Club,
past, present and future*

INTRODUCTION

The fifty stories I'm telling you about are some of my favourites, but I've left out other more famous ones because I'm almost certain that you'll have already discovered them for yourselves. So what you will find here are either treasures that are a bit rarer, or just one example from an author who has written many rewarding books which I'd hate you to miss.

It hasn't always been easy to find pieces which can stand alone like little stories, so mostly I'm offering 'cliff hangers', which I hope will intrigue you so much you won't be able to wait to discover what happens next.

One of the special charms of books is that they can give you so many different kinds of pleasure. Some will increase your knowledge about the world in general (as well as telling a cracking good story), some introduce you to fantastic places and characters which set your imaginations whirling. Others are reassuring and comfortable; showing you everyday people coping with the kind of difficulties that you can imagine happening to you. But the very best thing is that you can enjoy them anywhere, at any time – they become your private world which no one can invade or disturb.

Perhaps you should know what special qualities I had in mind when I settled on this final fifty: firstly, they are all books that I believe you could read *at least* twice, and find

something new in them each time; next, they are all books
that use words interestingly and so help you to express exactly
what you want to say. Finally, I hope they will widen your
horizons and help you understand the world you are growing
up in.

I hope you will enjoy them as much as I do.

K.W.

Richard Adams

WATERSHIP DOWN

As a rule, a paperback editor only gets to choose books from ones that have already appeared in their first, hardback form (that is, with hard covers and a proper binding), and so have already been read and judged by a lot of people: reviewers, booksellers and often teachers and librarians. But occasionally we get a chance to discover something good which has not appeared anywhere else, and that can be terrifically exciting.

This happened to me when I was sent a printer's proof of *Watership Down*. It was enormous – 478 pages – so I took it home to read in bed. I didn't go to sleep until 5 a.m., and by then I knew it had to become a Puffin.

What made this book seem particularly special was that it felt so absolutely *new*. At least, I'd never read a book about a community of rabbits (some of them talking and behaving rather like civil servants) escaping from their threatened warren and journeying many miles in search of a new home. It is not only their adventures which make them so original and compelling, it's that they are so individual. My favourite is Hazel, the born leader who is full of good sense, but there's a lot to be said for courageous Bigwig, and what would any of them have done without Fiver, with his special gift for scenting danger? Here is just one episode, when the group think they have found some very soft lodgings and want to stay, but Fiver senses evil just in time.

* * *

Hazel woke. He was in the burrow. He shivered. Why was there no warmth of rabbit bodies lying close together? Where was Fiver? He sat up. Near by, Bigwig was stirring and twitching in his sleep, searching for warmth, trying to press against another rabbit's body no longer there. The shallow hollow in the sandy floor where Fiver had lain was not quite cold: but Fiver was gone.

'Fiver!' said Hazel in the dark.

As soon as he had spoken he knew there would be no reply. He pushed Bigwig with his nose, butting urgently. 'Bigwig! Fiver's gone! Bigwig!'

Bigwig was wide awake on the instant and Hazel had never felt so glad of his sturdy readiness.

'What did you say? What's wrong?'

'Fiver's gone.'

'Where's he gone?'

'Silf – outside. It can only be silf. You know he wouldn't go wandering about in the warren. He hates it.'

'He's a nuisance, isn't he? He's left this burrow cold, too.

You think he's in danger, don't you? You want to go and look for him?'

'Yes, I must. He's upset and over-wrought and it's not light yet. There may be elil,* whatever Strawberry says.'

Bigwig listened and sniffed for a few moments.

'It's very nearly light,' he said. 'There'll be light enough to find him by. Well, I'd better come with you, I suppose. Don't worry – he can't have gone far. But by the King's Lettuce! I won't half give him a piece of my mind when we catch him.'

'I'll hold him down while you kick him, if only we can find him. Come on!'

They went up the run to the mouth of the hole and paused together. 'Since our friends aren't here to push us,' said Bigwig, 'we may as well make sure the place isn't crawling with stoats and owls before we go out.'

At that moment a brown owl's call sounded from the opposite wood. It was the first call, and by instinct they both crouched motionless, counting four heart-beats until the second followed.

'It's moving away,' said Hazel.

'How many field-mice say that every night, I wonder? You know the call's deceptive. It's meant to be.'

'Well, I can't help it,' said Hazel. 'Fiver's somewhere out there and I'm going after him. You were right, anyway. It *is* light – just.'

'Shall we look under the yew tree first?'

But Fiver was not under the yew tree. The light, as it grew, began to show the upper field, while the distant hedge and brook remained dark, linear shapes below. Bigwig jumped down from the bank into the field and ran in a long curve across the wet grass. He stopped almost opposite the hole by which they had come up, and Hazel joined him.

* enemies

'Here's his line all right,' said Bigwig. 'Fresh, too. From the hole straight down towards the brook. He won't be far away.'

When raindrops are lying it is easy to see where grass has recently been crossed. They followed the line down the field and reached the hedge beside the carrot-ground and the source of the brook. Bigwig had been right when he said the line was fresh. As soon as they had come through the hedge they saw Fiver. He was feeding, alone. A few fragments of carrot were still lying about near the spring, but he had left these untouched and was eating the grass not far from the gnarled crab-apple tree. They approached and he looked up.

Hazel said nothing and began to feed beside him. He was now regretting that he had brought Bigwig. In the darkness before morning and the first shock of discovering that Fiver was gone, Bigwig had been a comfort and a stand-by. But now, as he saw Fiver, small and familiar, incapable of hurting anyone or of concealing what he felt, trembling in the wet grass, either from fear or from cold, his anger melted away. He felt only sorry for him and sure that, if they could stay alone together for a while, Fiver would come round to an easier state of mind. But it was probably too late to persuade Bigwig to be gentle: he could only hope for the best.

Contrary to his fears, however, Bigwig remained as silent as himself. Evidently he had been expecting Hazel to speak first and was somewhat at a loss. For some time all three moved on quietly over the grass, while the shadows grew stronger and the wood-pigeons clattered among the distant trees. Hazel was beginning to feel that all would be well and that Bigwig had more sense than he had given him credit for, when Fiver sat up on his hind legs, cleaned his face with his paws and then, for the first time, looked directly at him.

'I'm going now,' he said. 'I feel very sad. I'd like to wish you well, Hazel, but there's no good to wish you in this place. So just goodbye.'

'But where are you going, Fiver?'

'Away. To the hills, if I can get there.'

'By yourself, alone? You can't. You'd die.'

'You wouldn't have a hope, old chap,' said Bigwig. 'Something would get you before ni-Frith.'*

'No,' said Fiver very quietly. 'You are closer to death than I.'

'Are you trying to frighten me, you miserable little lump of chattering chickweed?' cried Bigwig. 'I've a good mind –'

'Wait, Bigwig,' said Hazel. 'Don't speak roughly to him.'

'Why, you said yourself –' began Bigwig.

'I know. But I feel differently now. I'm sorry, Bigwig. I was going to ask you to help me to make him come back to the warren. But now – well, I've always found that there was something in what Fiver had to say. For the last two days I've refused to listen to him and I still think he's out of his senses. But I haven't the heart to drive him back to the warren. I really believe that for some reason or other the place is frightening him out of his wits. I'll go with him a little way and perhaps we can talk. I can't ask you to risk it too. Anyway, the others ought to know what we're doing and they won't unless you go and tell them. I'll be back before ni-Frith. I hope we both shall.'

Bigwig stared. Then he turned furiously on Fiver. 'You wretched little black beetle,' he said. 'You've never learnt to obey orders, have you? It's me, me, me all the time. "Oh, I've got a funny feeling in my toe, so we must all go and stand on our heads!" And now we've found a fine warren and got into it without even having to fight, *you've* got to do your

* noon

best to upset everyone! And then you risk the life of one of
the best rabbits we've got, just to play nursey while you go
wandering about like a moon-struck field-mouse. Well, *I'm*
finished with you, I'll tell you plain. And now I'm going back
to the warren to make sure everyone else is finished with you
as well. *And* they will be – don't make any mistake about
that.'

He turned and dashed back through the nearest gap in the
hedge. On the instant, a fearful commotion began on the
farther side. There were sounds of kicking and plunging. A
stick flew into the air. Then a flat, wet clot of dead leaves shot
clean through the gap and landed clear of the hedge, close to
Hazel. The brambles thrashed up and down. Hazel and Fiver
stared at each other, both fighting against the impulse to run.
What enemy was at work on the other side of the hedge?
There were no cries – no spitting of a cat, no squealing of a
rabbit – only the crackling of twigs and the tearing of the
grass in violence.

By an effort of courage against all instinct, Hazel forced
himself forward into the gap, with Fiver following. A terrible
sight lay before them. The rotten leaves had been thrown up
in showers. The earth had been laid bare and was scored with
long scratches and furrows. Bigwig was lying on his side, his
back legs kicking and struggling. A length of twisted copper
wire, gleaming dully in the first sunlight, was looped round
his neck and ran taut across one fore-paw to the head of a
stout peg driven into the ground. The running knot had
pulled tight and was buried in the fur behind his ear. The
projecting point of one strand had lacerated his neck and
drops of blood, dark and red as yew berries, welled one by
one down his shoulder. For a few moments he lay panting,
his side heaving in exhaustion. Then again began the strug-

gling and fighting, backwards and forwards, jerking and falling, until he choked and lay quiet.

Frenzied with distress, Hazel leapt out of the gap and squatted beside him. Bigwig's eyes were closed and his lips pulled
back from the long front teeth in a fixed snarl. He had bitten
his lower lip and from this, too, the blood was running. Froth
covered his jaws and chest.

'Thlayli!' said Hazel, stamping. 'Thlayli! Listen! You're in
a snare – a snare! What did they say in the Owsla?* Come
on – think. How can we help you?'

There was a pause. Then Bigwig's back legs began to kick
once more, but feebly. His ears drooped. His eyes opened
unseeing and the whites showed blood-shot as the brown
irises rolled one way and the other. After a moment his voice
came thick and low, bubbling out of the bloody spume in his
mouth.

'Owsla – no good – biting wire. Peg – got to – dig out.'

A convulsion shook him and he scrabbled at the ground,
covering himself in a mask of wet earth and blood. Then he
was still again.

'Run, Fiver, run to the warren,' cried Hazel. 'Get the
others – Blackberry, Silver. Be quick! He'll die.'

Fiver was off up the field like a hare. Hazel, left alone, tried
to understand what was needed. What was the peg? How was
he to dig it out? He looked down at the foul mess before him.
Bigwig was lying across the wire, which came out under his
belly and seemed to disappear into the ground. Hazel struggled with his own incomprehension. Bigwig had said, 'Dig.'
That at least he understood. He began to scratch into the soft
earth beside the body, until after a time his claws scraped

* The group of strong or clever rabbits surrounding the Chief Rabbit in a
warren.

against something smooth and firm. As he paused, perplexed, he found Blackberry at his shoulder.

'Bigwig just spoke,' he said to him, 'but I don't think he can now. He said, "Dig out the peg." What does that mean? What have we got to do?'

'Wait a moment,' said Blackberry. 'Let me think, and try not to be impatient.'

Hazel turned his head and looked down the course of the brook. Far away, between the two copses, he could see the cherry tree where two days before he had sat with Blackberry and Fiver in the sunrise. He remembered how Bigwig had chased Hawkbit through the long grass, forgetting the quarrel of the previous night in the joy of their arrival. He could see Hawkbit running towards him now and two or three of the others – Silver, Dandelion and Pipkin. Dandelion, well in front, dashed up to the gap and checked, twitching and staring.

'What is it, Hazel? What's happened? Fiver said –'

'Bigwig's in a wire. Let him alone till Blackberry tells us. Stop the others crowding round.'

Dandelion turned and raced back as Pipkin came up.

'Is Cowslip coming?' said Hazel. 'Perhaps *he* knows –'

'He wouldn't come,' replied Pipkin. 'He told Fiver to stop talking about it.'

'Told him *what*?' asked Hazel incredulously. But at that moment Blackberry spoke and Hazel was beside him in a flash.

'This is it,' said Blackberry. 'The wire's on a peg and the peg's in the ground – there, look. We've got to dig it out. Come on – dig beside it.'

Hazel dug once more, his fore-paws throwing up the soft, wet soil and slipping against the hard sides of the peg. Dimly, he was aware of the others waiting nearby. After a time he was forced to stop, panting. Silver took his place, and was followed by Buckthorn. The nasty, smooth, clean, man-smelling peg was laid bare to the length of a rabbit's ear, but still it did not come loose. Bigwig had not moved. He lay across the wire, torn and bloody, with closed eyes. Buckthorn drew his head and paws out of the hole and rubbed the mud off his face.

'The peg's narrower down there,' he said. 'It tapers. I think it could be bitten through, but I can't get my teeth to it.'

'Send Pipkin in,' said Blackberry. 'He's smaller.'

Pipkin plunged into the hole. They could hear the wood splintering under his teeth – a sound like a mouse in a shed wainscot at midnight. He came out with his nose bleeding.

'The splinters prick you and it's hard to breathe, but the peg's nearly through.'

'Fiver go in,' said Hazel.

Fiver was not long in the hole. He, too, came out bleeding.

'It's broken in two. It's free.'

Blackberry pressed his nose against Bigwig's head. As he nuzzled him gently the head rolled sideways and back again.

'Bigwig,' said Blackberry in his ear, 'the peg's out.'

There was no response. Bigwig lay still as before. A great fly settled on one of his ears. Blackberry thrust at it angrily and it flew up, buzzing, into the sunshine.

'I think he's gone,' said Blackberry. 'I can't feel his breathing.'

Hazel crouched down by Blackberry and laid his nostrils close to Bigwig's, but a light breeze was blowing and he could not tell whether there was breath or not. The legs were loose, the belly flaccid and limp. He tried to think of what little he had heard of snares. A strong rabbit could break his neck in a snare. Or had the point of a sharp wire pierced the wind-pipe?

'Bigwig,' he whispered, 'we've got you out. You're free.'

Bigwig did not stir. Suddenly it came to Hazel that if Bigwig was dead – and what else could hold *him* silent in the mud? – then he himself must get the others away before the dreadful loss could drain their courage and break their spirit – as it would if they stayed by the body. Besides, the man would come soon. Perhaps he was already coming, with his gun, to take poor Bigwig away. They must go; and he must do his best to see that all of them – even he himself – put what had happened out of mind, for ever.

'My heart has joined the Thousand, for my friend stopped running today,' he said to Blackberry, quoting a rabbit proverb.

'If only it were not Bigwig,' said Blackberry. 'What shall we do without him?'

'The others are waiting,' said Hazel. 'We have to stay alive. There has to be something for them to think about. Help me, or it will be more than I can do.'

He turned away from the body and looked for Fiver among the rabbits behind him. But Fiver was nowhere to be seen and Hazel was afraid to ask for him, in case to do so should seem like weakness and a need for comfort.

'Pipkin,' he snapped, 'why don't you clean up your face and stop the bleeding? The smell of blood attracts elil. You know that, don't you?'

'Yes, Hazel. I'm sorry. Will Bigwig –'

'And another thing,' said Hazel desperately. 'What was it you were telling me about Cowslip? Did you say he told Fiver to be quiet?'

'Yes, Hazel. Fiver came into the warren and told us about the snare, and that poor Bigwig –'

'Yes, all right. And then Cowslip –?'

'Cowslip and Strawberry and others pretended not to hear.

It was ridiculous, because Fiver was calling out to everybody. And then as we were running out Silver said to Cowslip, "Surely you're coming?" And Cowslip simply turned his back. So then Fiver went up and spoke to him very quietly, but I heard what Cowslip answered. He said, "Hills or Inlé, it's all one to me where you go. You hold your tongue." And then he struck at Fiver and scratched his ear.'

'I'll kill him,' gasped a low, choking voice behind them. They all leapt round. Bigwig had raised his head and was supporting himself on his fore-paws alone. His body was twisted and his hind-parts and back legs still lay along the ground. His eyes were open, but his face was such a fearful mask of blood, foam, vomit and earth that he looked more like some demon-creature than a rabbit. The immediate sight of him, which should have filled them with relief and joy, brought only terror. They cringed away and none said a word.

'I'll kill him,' repeated Bigwig, spluttering through his fouled whiskers and clotted fur. 'Help me, rot you! Can't anyone get this stinking wire off me?' He struggled, dragging his hind-legs. Then he fell again and crawled forward, trailing the wire through the grass with the broken peg snickering behind it.

Joan Aiken

THE WOLVES OF WILLOUGHBY CHASE

The first Joan Aiken book I read made me want to stand up and cheer, because it was exactly the kind of outrageous fantasy that I enjoy most. It's not fantasy in the ordinary sense of 'other worlds', it's just that in many of her books Joan takes this world, puts it back a few centuries and then turns it upside-down so that the wrong king (a Stuart) is on the throne, and there are terrible Hanoverian plots to overthrow him.

The characters she writes about are either monstrously wicked or tremendously nice, and she manages to weave some of them in and out of quite different stories. For instance, Dido Twite, a sharp little Cockney, is left for drowned in *Black Hearts in Battersea*, but turns up again on the deck of a whaler in *Night Birds on Nantucket*, where she has been lying asleep for ten months.

In another of her stories, *The Cuckoo Tree*, Joan has the Houses of Parliament put on rollers and due to be drowned in the Thames on Coronation Day, except that Dido turns up with an elephant to haul it back again! Now you see the kind of book I mean. One of her own favourites, *Midnight is a Place*, is very different, about the dreadful lives lived by young child workers in the Lancashire carpet mills, but of course there's a good plot and a happy ending. But if you are discovering Joan Aiken for the first time, you might start off with her first novel, where the chief enemy, Miss Slighcarp, a bogus governess to Bonnie and Sylvia, is left in charge when Bonnie's parents go away.

* * *

The governess, who had been examining some books on the shelves, swung round with equal abruptness. She seemed astonished to see them.

'Where have you been?' she demanded angrily, after an instant's pause.

'Why,' Sylvia faltered, 'merely in the next room, Miss Slighcarp.'

But Bonnie, with choking utterance, demanded, 'Why are you wearing my mother's dress?'

Sylvia had observed that Miss Slighcarp had on a draped gown of old gold velvet with ruby buttons, far grander than the grey twill she had worn the day before.

'Don't speak to me in that way, miss!' retorted Miss Slighcarp in a rage. 'You have been spoiled all your life, but we shall soon see who is going to be mistress now. Go to your place and sit down. Do not speak until you are spoken to.'

Bonnie paid not the slightest attention. 'Who said you could wear my mother's best gown?' she repeated. Sylvia, alarmed, had slipped into her place at the table, but Bonnie, reckless with indignation, stood in front of the governess, glaring at her.

'Everything in this house was left entirely to my personal disposition,' Miss Slighcarp said coldly.

'But not her clothes! Not to wear! How *dare* you? Take it off at once! It's no better than stealing!'

Two white dents had appeared on either side of Miss Sligh-carp's nostrils.

'Another word and it's the dark cupboard and bread-and-water for you, miss,' she said fiercely.

'I don't care what you say!' Bonnie stamped her foot. 'Take off my mother's dress!'

Miss Slighcarp boxed Bonnie's ears, Bonnie seized Miss Slighcarp's wrists. In the confusion a bottle of ink was knocked off the table, spilling a long blue trail down the gold velvet skirt. Miss Slighcarp uttered an exclamation of fury.

'Insolent, ungovernable child! You shall suffer for this!' With iron strength she thrust Bonnie into a closet containing crayons, globes and exercise books, and turned the key on her. Then she swept from the room.

Sylvia remained seated, aghast, for half a second. Then she ran to the cupboard door – but alas! Miss Slighcarp had taken the key with her.

'Bonnie! Bonnie! Are you all right? It's I, Sylvia.'

She could hear bitter sobs.

'Don't cry, Bonnie, please don't cry. I'll run after her and beg her to let you out. I dare say she will, once she has reflected. She can't have known it was your mother's *favourite* gown.'

Bonnie seemed not to have heard her. 'Mamma, Mamma!' Sylvia could hear her sobbing. 'Oh, why did you have to go away?'

How Sylvia longed to be able to batter down the cupboard door and get her arms round poor Bonnie! But the door was thick and massive, with a strong lock, quite beyond her power to move. Since she could not attract Bonnie's attention, she ran after Miss Slighcarp.

After vainly knocking at the governess's bedroom door she went in without waiting for a summons (a deed of exceptional bravery for the timid Sylvia). Nobody was there. The ink-stained velvet dress lay flung carelessly on the floor, crushed and torn, so great had Miss Slighcarp's haste been to remove it.

Sylvia hurried out again and began to search through the huge house, wandering up this passage and down that, through galleries, into golden drawing-rooms, satin hung boudoirs, billiard-rooms, ballrooms, croquet-rooms. At last she found the governess in the Great Hall, surrounded by servants.

Miss Slighcarp did not see Sylvia. She had changed into what was very plainly another of Lady Green's gowns, a rose-coloured crêpe with aiguillettes of diamonds on the shoulders. It did not fit her very exactly.

She seemed to be giving the servants their wages. Sylvia wondered why many of the maids were crying, and why the men looked in general angry and rebellious, until she realized that Miss Slighcarp was paying them off and dismissing them. When the last one had been given his little packet of money, she announced:

'Now, let but a glimpse of your faces be seen within ten miles of this house, and I shall send for the constables!' Then she added to a man who stood beside her, 'Ridiculous, quite ridiculous, to keep such a large establishment of idle good-for-nothings, kicking their heels, eating their heads off.'

'Just so, ma'am, just so,' he assented. Sylvia was amazed to recognize Mr Grimshaw, apparently quite restored to health, and in full possession of his faculties. He held a small blunderbuss, and was waving it threateningly, to urge the departing servants out of the great doors and on their way into the snowstorm.

'What a strange thing!' thought Sylvia in astonishment. 'Can he be recovered? Or was he never really ill? Can he have known Miss Slighcarp before? He seemed so different on the train.'

At that moment she heard a familiar voice beside her, in the rapidly-thinning crowd of servants, and found Pattern at her elbow.

'Miss Sylvia, dear! Thank the good Lord I saw you. That wicked Jezebel is paying us all off and sending us away, but she needn't think *I'm* going to go and leave my darling Miss Bonnie. Do you and she come along to the little blue powderroom, Miss Sylvia, this afternoon at five, and we'll talk over what's best to be done.'

'But Bonnie can't! She's locked up!' gasped Sylvia. 'In the schoolroom cupboard!'

'She never has . . .! *Oh*, what wouldn't I give to get my hands round that she-devil's throat,' muttered Pattern. 'That's because she knew Miss Bonnie would never stand tamely by and let her father's old servants be packed off into the snow. Let her out, Miss Sylvia! Let her out of it quick! She never could endure to be shut up.'

'But I can't! Miss Slighcarp has the key.'

'There's another – in the little mother-of-pearl cabinet in the ante-room where the javelins hang.'

Sylvia did not wait. She remembered how to find her way to the little ante-room, and she flew on winged feet to the mother-of-pearl cabinet. She found the key, ran to the schoolroom, opened the door, and in no time had her cheek pressed lovingly against Bonnie's tear-stained one.

'Oh, you poor precious! Oh, Bonnie, she's wicked, Miss Slighcarp's really wicked! She's dismissing all the servants.'

'What?' Bonnie was distracted from her own grief and indignation by the tale Sylvia poured out.

'Let us go at once,' she exclaimed, 'at *once*, and stop it!' But when they passed the big schoolroom window they saw the lonely procession of servants, far away, toiling across a snow-covered ridge in the park.

'We are too late,' said Sylvia in despair. Bonnie gazed after the tiny, distant figures, biting her lips.

'Is Pattern gone too?' she asked, turning to Sylvia.

'I believe not. I believe she means to hide somewhere about the house.' Sylvia told Bonnie of Pattern's wish to meet them that afternoon.

'Oh, she is good! She is faithful!' exclaimed Bonnie.

'But will it not be very dangerous for her?' Sylvia said doubtfully. 'Miss Slighcarp threatened to send for the constables if she saw any of the servants near the house. She might have Pattern sent to prison!'

'I do not believe Pattern would let herself be caught. There are so many secret hiding-places about the house. And in any case all the officers are our friends round here.'

At that moment the children were startled by the sound of approaching voices. One of them was Miss Slighcarp's. Sylvia turned pale.

'She must not find you out of the cupboard. Hide, quickly, Bonnie!'

She relocked the cupboard door, and pocketed the key. As there was no time to lose, the two children slipped behind the window-curtain. Miss Slighcarp entered with the footman, James.

'As I have done you the favour of keeping you on when all the others were dismissed, sirrah,' she was saying, 'you will have to work for your wages as never before.'

The blue velvet curtains behind which the children stood were pounced all over with tiny crystal discs encircled with seed-pearls. The little discs formed miniature windows, and, setting her eye to one, Bonnie could see that James's good-natured face wore a sullen expression, which he was attempting to twist into an evil leer.

'First, you must take out and crate all these toys. Put them into packing-cases. They are to be sent away and sold. It is quite ridiculous to keep this amount of gaudy rubbish for the amusement of two children.'

'Yes, ma'am.'

'At dinner-time bring some bread-and-water on a tray for Miss Green, who is locked up in that cupboard.'

'Shall I let her out, ma'am?'

'Certainly not. She is a badly-behaved, ill-conditioned child, and must be disciplined. She may be let out this evening at half-past eight. Here is the key.'

'Yes, ma'am.'

'The other child, Miss Sylvia Green, may lunch in the schoolroom as usual. Plain food, mind. Nothing fancy. From now on the children are to make their own beds, sweep their own rooms, and wash their own plates and clothes.'

'Yes, ma'am.'

'After dinner I wish you to see to the grooming of the horses and ponies. They are all to be sold save four carriage horses.'

'The children's ponies as well, ma'am?'

'Certainly! I shall find more suitable occupations for the children than such idle and extravagant pursuits! Now I am going to be busy in the Estate Room. You may bring me a light luncheon at one o'clock: chicken, oyster patties, trifle, and a half-bottle of champagne.'

She swept out of the room. The moment she had gone James went quickly to the closet and unlocked it, saying in a low voice, 'She's gone now, Miss Bonnie, you can come out.'

Nina Bawden

CARRIE'S WAR

Some authors have a special gift for making their characters so vivid and alive that you feel you know them intimately. Nina Bawden is brilliant at this, and she also invents marvellous stories that are full of suspense and excitement and yet are about quite ordinary people. I love all her books, especially *The Peppermint Pig*, and one of her latest, *The Finding*, which is about young Alex, who was found lying in the arms of the Sphinx on the Victoria Embankment in London, and whose adoptive parents celebrate his birthday on his 'finding' day. Alex's life gets more and more complicated when he inherits a fortune and can't bear the publicity.

But if you haven't discovered Nina Bawden's stories yet, *Carrie's*

War is a good one to start with. Carrie and her brother are wartime evacuees in Wales. They are billeted with Mr Evans, a mean bully of a shopkeeper (who makes them walk on the edge of the stairs so that they don't wear out the carpet), and his scared sister, Auntie Lou, who isn't allowed to give them enough to eat.

This is a scene from the beginning, when life does seem pretty hopeless, but they do find friends eventually and then Carrie does something absolutely dreadful to try and lift the ancient curse which hangs over the house at Druid's Bottom.

* * *

Nick had been born a week before Christmas. On his birthday Auntie Lou gave him a pair of leather gloves with fur linings and Mr Evans gave him a Holy Bible with a soft, red cover and pictures inside.

Nick said, 'Thank you, Mr Evans,' very politely, but without smiling. Then he put the Bible down and said, 'Auntie Lou, what *lovely* gloves, they're the best gloves I've ever had in my whole life. I'll keep them for ever and ever, even when I've grown too big for them. My tenth birthday gloves!'

Carrie felt sorry for Mr Evans. She said, 'The Bible's lovely too, you are lucky, Nick.' And later, when she and Nick were alone, 'It was kind of him, really. I expect when he was a little boy he'd rather have had a Bible for his birthday than anything else in the world, even a bicycle. So it was kind of him to think you might feel like that, too.'

'But I didn't want a Bible,' Nick said. 'I'd rather have had a knife. He's got some smashing knives in the shop on a card by the door. A Special Offer. I've been looking at them every day and hoping I'd get one and he knew that's what I was hoping. I looked at them and he saw me looking. It was just mean of him to give me a rotten old Bible instead.'

'Perhaps he'll give you a knife for Christmas,' Carrie said, though she doubted it, in her heart. If Mr Evans really knew Nick wanted a knife, he was unlikely to give him one. He thought it was bad for people to get what they wanted. 'Want must be your master,' was what he always said.

Carrie sighed. She didn't like Mr Evans, no one could, but Nick hating him so much made her dislike him less. 'He's getting us a goose for Christmas,' she said, 'that'll be nice, won't it? I've never had a goose.'

'I'd rather have a turkey!' Nick said.

*

The goose was to come from Mr Evans's older sister who lived outside the town and kept poultry. Nick and Carrie had never heard of her until now. 'She's a bit of an invalid,' Auntie Lou said. 'Bed-fast much of the time now. Poor soul, I think of her but I daren't go to see her. Mr Evans won't have it. Dilys has made her bed and turned her back on her own people, is what he says, and that's that. She married Mr Gotobed, the mine-owner, you see.'

The children didn't see but didn't like to ask. It made Auntie Lou nervous to be asked direct questions. So they said, 'Gotobed's a funny name, isn't it?'

'English, of course,' Auntie Lou said. 'That upset Mr Evans to start with! An Englishman *and* a mine-owner, too! She married him just after our dad was killed down the pit – dancing on our father's grave, was what Mr Evans called it. The Gotobeds were bad owners, you see; our dad was killed by a rock fall that would never have happened, Mr Evans says, if they'd taken proper safety precautions. Not that it was young Mr Gotobed's fault, *his* father was alive then, and in charge of the mine, but Mr Evans says all that family was tarred with the same brush, only thinking of profits. So it made him hard against Dilys. Even now her husband's dead, he's not willing to let bygones be bygones.'

Though he was willing to accept a goose at Christmas, apparently. 'They're always fine birds,' Auntie Lou said – as if this was sufficient reason. 'Hepzibah Green rears them. She's good with poultry. Fine, light hand with pastry, too. You should taste her mince pies! Hepzibah looks after Dilys *and* the place best as she can. Druid's Bottom was a fine house once, though it's run down since Mr Gotobed passed on and Dilys took bad. Needs a man's eye, Mr Evans says, though he's not willing to give it, and Dilys won't ask, of course.' She sighed gently. 'They're both proud people, see?'

'Druid's *Bottom*,' Nick said, and giggled.

'Bottom of Druid's Grove,' Auntie Lou said. 'That's the cwm where the yew trees grow. Do you remember where we picked those blackberries up by the railway line? The deep cwm, just before the tunnel?'

Nick's eyes widened. He said, '*That dark place*!'

'It's the yews make it dark,' Auntie Lou said. 'Though it's a queer place, too. Full of the old religion still, people say – not a place to go after dark. Not alone, anyway. I know I'd not care to, though I wouldn't let Mr Evans hear me say it. Wicked foolishness, he calls that sort of talk. There's nothing to be afraid of on this earth he says, not for those who trust in the Lord.'

Carrie was excited; she loved old, spooky tales. 'I wouldn't be afraid of the Grove,' she boasted. 'Nick might be, he's a *baby*, but I'm not scared of anything. Can I come with you, Auntie Lou, when you go to fetch the goose?'

*

But as it turned out, she and Nick went alone. On what

was, perhaps, the most important journey they ever made together.

They were due to go to Druid's Bottom two days before Christmas, but Auntie Lou was ill. She coughed all morning and her eyes were red-rimmed. After midday dinner, Mr Evans came into the kitchen and looked at her, coughing over the sink. 'You're not fit to go out,' he said. 'Send the children.'

Auntie Lou coughed and coughed. 'I thought I'd go tomorrow instead. Hepzibah will know I'm not coming now it's getting so late. I'll be better tomorrow.'

'I'll want you in the shop, Christmas Eve,' Mr Evans said. 'The children can go. Earn their keep for a change.'

'It'll be a heavy goose, Samuel.'

'They can manage between them.'

There was a short silence. Auntie Lou avoided the children's eyes. Then she said, uneasily, 'It'll be dark before they get back.'

'Full moon,' Mr Evans said. He looked at the children, at Nick's horrified face, and then at Auntie Lou. She began to blush painfully. He said in a quiet and ominous voice, 'You've not been putting ideas in their heads, I do hope!'

Auntie Lou looked at the children, too. Her expression begged them not to give her away. Carrie felt impatient with her – no grown-up should be so weak and so silly – but she was sorry as well. She said innocently, 'What ideas, Mr Evans? Of course we'd love to go, we don't mind the dark.'

*

'There's nothing *to* mind,' she said to Nick as they trudged along the railway line. 'What is there to be scared of? Just a few old trees.'

Nick said nothing; only sighed.

Carrie said, 'All that queer place stuff is just Auntie Lou being superstitious. You know how superstitious she is, touching wood and not walking under ladders and throwing salt over her shoulder when she's spilled some. I'm not surprised Mr Evans gets cross with her sometimes. She's so scared, she'd jump at her own shadow.'

But when they reached the Grove, Carrie felt a little less bold. It was growing dusk; stars were pricking out in the cold sky above them. And it was so quiet, suddenly, that their ears seemed to be singing.

Carrie whispered, 'There's the path down. By that stone.'

Nick's pale face glimmered as he looked up at her. He whispered back, 'You go. I'll wait here.'

'Don't be silly.' Carrie swallowed – then pleaded with him. 'Don't you want a nice mince pie? We might get a mince pie. And it's not far. Auntie Lou said it wasn't far down the hill. Not much more than five minutes.'

Nick shook his head. He screwed up his eyes and put his hands over his ears.

Carrie said coldly, 'All right, have it your own way. But it'll be dark soon and you'll be really scared then. Much more scared by yourself than you would be with me. Druids and ghosts coming to get you! Wild animals too – you don't *know*! I wouldn't be surprised if there were wolves in these mountains. But *I* don't care. Even if I hear them howling and snapping their jaws I shan't hurry!'

And she marched off without looking back. White stones marked the path through the yew trees and in the steep places there were steps cut in the earth and shored up with wood. She hadn't gone far when she heard Nick wailing behind her, 'Carrie, wait for me, *wait* . . .' She stopped and he skidded into her back. 'Don't leave me, Carrie!'

'I thought it was you leaving *me*,' she said, making a joke of it, to comfort him, and he tried to laugh but it turned into a sob in his throat.

He hung on to the back of her coat, whimpering under his breath as she led the way down the path. The yew trees grew densely, some of them covered with ivy that rustled and rattled. Like scales, Carrie thought; the trees were like live creatures with scales. She told herself not to be stupid, but stopped to draw breath. She said, 'Do be quiet, Nick.'

'Why?'

'I don't know,' Carrie said. 'Something . . .'

She couldn't explain it. It was such a strange feeling. As if there was something here, something *waiting*. Deep in the trees or deep in the earth. Not a ghost – nothing so simple. Whatever it was had no name. Something old and huge and nameless, Carrie thought, and started to tremble.

Nick said, 'Carrie . . .'

'Listen.'

'What for?'

'*Sssh* . . .'

No sound at first. Then she heard it. A kind of slow, dry whisper, or sigh. As if the earth were turning in its sleep. Or the huge, nameless thing were breathing.

'Did you hear?' Carrie said. 'Did you *hear*?'

Nick began to cry piteously. Silence now, except for his weeping.

Carrie said, dry-mouthed, 'It's gone now. It wasn't anything. There's nothing there, really.'

Nick gulped, trying hard to stop crying. Then he clutched Carrie. 'Yes there is! There is *now*!'

Carrie listened. It wasn't the sound she had heard before but something quite different. A queer, throaty, chuckling, gobbling sound that seemed to come from somewhere above them, higher up the path. They stood still as stone. The sound was coming closer.

'*Run*,' Carrie said. She began to run, stumbling. The big bag they had brought for the goose caught between her legs and almost threw her down but she recovered her balance, her feet slipping and sliding. She ran, and Nick ran behind her, and the creature, whatever it was, the gobbling *Thing*, followed them. It seemed to be calling to them and Carrie thought of fairy tales she had read – you looked back at something behind you and were caught in its spell! She gasped, 'Don't look back, Nick, whatever you do.'

The path widened and flattened as it came out of the Grove and she caught Nick's hand to make him run faster. Too fast for his shorter legs and he fell on his knees. He moaned, as she pulled him up, 'I can't, I *can't*, Carrie . . .'

She said, through chattering teeth, 'Yes you *can*. Not much farther.'

They saw the house then, its dark, tall-chimneyed bulk looming up, and lights in the windows. One light quite high up and one low down, at the side. They ran, on rubbery legs, through an open gate and across a dirt yard towards the lit window. There was a door but it was shut. They flung themselves against it.

Gobble-Gobble was coming behind them, was crossing the yard.

'Please,' Carrie croaked. 'Please.' Quite sure that it was too late, that the creature would get them.

But the door opened inward, like magic, and they fell through it to light, warmth and safety.

Betsy Byars

THE EIGHTEENTH EMERGENCY

It was hard to choose which of Betsy Byars's books I should tell you about. They are all so good at understanding children's lives, and yet each one is quite different. If you enjoy this, then you should have a go at *The Pinballs*, which is about a family of foster children, or *The TV Kid* or *The Midnight Fox*.

But, for the moment, meet Benjie (known as Mouse) and his friend Ezzie, who have worked out seventeen ways of dealing with all sorts of emergencies, such as *'Emergency Four: When attacked by a crocodile, prop a stick in its mouth', 'Emergency One: If caught in quicksand, lie down'*. But neither of them can think of the right way to deal with the school bully . . .

* * *

As soon as he saw Mouse, Ezzie got up and said, 'Hey, what happened? Where'd you go after school?'

Mouse said, 'Hammerman's after me.'

Ezzie's pink mouth formed a perfect O. He didn't say anything, but his breath came out in a long sympathetic wheeze. Finally he said, '*Marv* Hammerman?' even though he knew there was only one Hammerman in the world, just as there had been only one Hitler.

'Yes.'

'Is after *you*?'

Mouse nodded, sunk in misery. He could see Marv Hammerman. He came up in Mouse's mind the way monsters do in horror movies, big and powerful, with the same cold, unreal eyes. It was the eyes Mouse really feared. One look from those eyes, he thought, just one look of a certain length – about three seconds – and you knew you were his next victim.

'What did you do?' Ezzie asked. 'Or did you do anything?'

At least, Mouse thought, Ezzie understood that. If you were Marv Hammerman, you didn't need a reason. He sat down on the steps and squinted up at Ezzie. 'I did something,' he said.

'What?' Ezzie asked. His tongue flicked out and in so quickly it didn't even moisten his lips. 'What'd you do? You bump into him or something?'

Mouse shook his head.

'Well, what?'

Mouse said, 'You know that big chart in the upstairs hall at school?'

'What'd you say? I can't even hear you, Mouse. You're muttering.' Ezzie bent closer. 'Look at me. Now what did you say?'

Mouse looked up, still squinting. He said, 'You know that big chart outside the history room? In the hall?'

'Chart?' Ezzie said blankly. 'What chart, Mouse?'

'This chart takes up the whole wall, Ez, how could you miss it? It's a chart about early man, and it shows man's progress up from the apes, the side view of all those different kinds of prehistoric men, like Cro-Magnon man and Homo erectus. *That* chart.'

'Oh, yeah, I saw it, so go on.'

Mouse could see that Ezzie was eager for him to get on to the good part, the violence. He slumped. He wet his lips. He said, 'Well, when I was passing this chart on my way out of history – and I don't know why I did this – I really don't. When I was passing this chart, Ez, on my way to math –' He swallowed, almost choking on his spit. 'When I was passing this chart, Ez, I took my pencil and I wrote Marv Hammerman's name on the bottom of the chart and then I drew an arrow to the picture of Neanderthal man.'

'What?' Ezzie cried, '*What?*' He could not seem to take it in. Mouse knew that Ezzie had been prepared to sympathize with an accident. He had almost been the victim of one of those himself. One day at school Ezzie had reached for the handle on the water fountain a second ahead of Marv Hammerman. If Ezzie hadn't glanced up just in time, seen Hammerman and said quickly, 'Go ahead, I'm not thirsty,' then this sagging figure on the steps might be him. 'What did you do it for, Mouse?'

'I don't know.'

'You crazy or something?'

'I don't know.'

'Marv Hammerman!' Ezzie sighed. It was a mournful sound that seemed to have come from a culture used to sorrow. 'Anybody else in the school would have been better. I would rather have the principal after me than Marv Hammerman.'

'I know.'

'Hammerman's big, Mouse. He's flunked a lot.'

'I know,' Mouse said again. There was an unwritten law that it was all right to fight anyone in your own grade. The fact that Hammerman was older and stronger made no difference. They were both in the sixth grade.

'Then what'd you do it for?' Ezzie asked.

'I don't know.'

'You must want trouble,' Ezzie said. 'Like my grandfather. He's always provoking people. The bus driver won't even pick him up any more.'

'No, I don't want trouble.'

'Then, why did you –'

'I don't *know*.' Then he sagged again and said, 'I didn't even know I had done it really until I'd finished. I just looked at the picture of Neanderthal man and thought of Hammerman. It does look like him, Ezzie, the sloping face and the shoulders.'

'Maybe Hammerman doesn't know you did it though,' Ezzie said. 'Did you ever think of that? I mean, who's going to go up to Hammerman and tell him his name is on the prehistoric man chart?' Ezzie leaned forward. 'Hey, Hammerman,' he said, imitating the imaginary fool, 'I saw a funny thing about you on the prehistoric man chart! Now, who in their right mind is going to –'

'He was right behind me when I did it,' Mouse said.

'What?'

'He was right behind me,' Mouse said stiffly. He could remember turning and looking into Hammerman's eyes. It was such a strange, troubling moment that Mouse was unable to think about it.

Ezzie's mouth formed the O, made the sympathetic sigh. Then he said, 'And you don't even know what you did it for?'

'No.'

Ezzie sank down on the steps beside Mouse. He leaned over his knees and said, 'You ought to get out of that habit, that writing names and drawing arrows, you know that? I see those arrows everywhere. I'll be walking down the street and I'll look on a building and I'll see the word DOOR written in little letters and there'll be an arrow pointing to the door and I know you did it. It's crazy, labelling stuff like that.'

'I never did that, Ez, not to a door.'

'Better to a door, if you ask me,' Ezzie said, shaking his head. He paused for a moment, then asked in a lower voice, 'You ever been hit before, Mouse? I mean, hard?'

. . . . . .

'Benjie, come up now,' his mother called again.

'I'm coming.'

'Did you tell your mom about Hammerman being after you?' Ezzie asked.

'Yeah.'

'What'd she say?'

He tried to think of the most impossible statement his mother had made. 'She said I'll laugh about it in a week or two.'

'Laugh about it?'

'Yeah, through my bandages.'

Ezzie's face twisted into a little smile. 'Hey, remember Al Armsby when he had those broken ribs? Remember how he would beg us not to make him laugh? And I had this one joke about a monkey and I would keep telling it and keep telling it and he was practically on his knees begging for mercy and –'

Mouse got slowly to his feet. 'Well, I better go,' he said.

Ezzie stopped smiling. 'Hey, wait a minute. Listen, I just remembered something. I know a boy that Hammerman beat up, and he said it wasn't so bad.'

'Who?'

'A friend of my brother's. I'll find out about it and let you know.'

'All right,' Mouse said. He did not allow himself to believe it was true. Sometimes Ezzie lied like this out of sympathy. If you said, 'My stomach hurts and I think I'm going to die,' and if Ezzie really liked you, he would say, 'I know a boy whose stomach hurt worse than that and *he* didn't die!' And if you said, 'Who?' Ezzie would say, 'A friend of my brother's.' Ezzie's brother had only one friend that Mouse knew about, and this friend would have had to have had daily brushes with death to fulfil all of Ezzie's statements.

Still, it made Mouse want to cry for a moment that Ezzie would lie to spare him. Or maybe he wanted to cry because Hammerman was going to kill him. He didn't know. He said, 'Thanks, Ez,' in a choked voice. He turned and walked quickly into the apartment building.

John Christopher

THE GUARDIANS

John Christopher has written three books about a time in the future when mankind is ruled by machines. These are known as the *Tripods* trilogy, and each one has, for its hero, a rebellious boy who isn't satisfied to lose his individuality by being 'capped'. His struggles to restore man's humanity make the stories almost unbearably exciting. The book I have chosen here is in many ways the forerunner of the *Tripods*, and is worth reading first.

The story is set in the future. Rob, the hero, was born in the noisy, mindless Conurbs where everyone lives in crowds, all think alike, and books are denounced as 'dangerous'. Rob's father dies mysteriously, and Rob is put into a frightful State Boarding School.

He decides to run away and cross the terrifying no man's land into the County where, instead of the desolation he expected, people are living elegant, harmonious nineteenth-century lives. But he is a runaway who would have no future if it wasn't for the young 'aristocrat' who befriends him. Even then he discovers that this pleasant life has its sinister side. This extract is from the beginning of the book, when Rob is trying to get through the fence into the County.

* * *

Rob slapped himself into something like life – he was tired and cold, hungry again, and aching from sleeping on ground which made the hard mattresses of the Boarding School seem like plastifoam. He went to the fence and looked at it. It ran as far as he could see in either direction, straight to the east, curving inwards and out of sight to the west. The mesh was in a pattern of half-inch diamonds, the metal supports several inches thick and sunk in concrete blocks. The bottom of the fence disappeared into the ground. Electrified? He did not feel like touching it to try.

He looked through the mesh. It seemed no different there – open grassland and trees in the distance. The ground rising to a near horizon. Farther off, featureless hills. He decided he might as well walk on, to the west since it looked less depressing than the long line of fence to the east.

He came to a part where there were more trees on this side, some growing quite close to the fence. If there were one right up against it which he could climb . . . Or if, for that matter, he had one of the long flexipoles used by jumpers in the Games, and the skill to vault with it, he could get over very easily. But there wasn't, and he hadn't. He checked, glimpsing something, a small flash of movement, on a branch of a tree ahead of him. A small brown shape. Something else known only from the Zoo: a squirrel.

It stayed on the branch for several seconds, sitting up with its paws to its face, nibbling something or washing itself. Then it whisked back towards the trunk and down to the ground. Rob lost sight of it when it disappeared into grass. Not long after, though, he saw it again, this time racing up and over the fence! That solved one problem. He put a finger, tentative still, against the mesh. It was cold harmless metal.

He still had to find a way of getting over it. He was no squirrel. The small-gauge mesh and the smooth poles offered no kind of toehold. There was nothing for it but to carry on walking. At least it helped him forget how cold it was. The sky behind him was pale blue, beginning to flush gold with the invisible sun. But it was cold enough. There were places where the grass crackled with frost.

He found the answer at last in a minor landslip. The hill had crumbled slightly, above and below the fence, and rain had washed the loose soil down. It did not amount to much but the steel mesh instead of running down into the ground showed a gap underneath. It was no more than an inch or so, but it gave him the idea. He squatted down and set to work enlarging it. The ground was friable but it was not easy: his finger-tips burned with cold. He kept at it. Bit by bit he dug earth away until there was a gap he thought he could wriggle through. But he had been too optimistic and had to go back to digging.

The second time he made it. He scratched himself on the sharp base of the mesh and had a moment's panic when he stuck half way, but he managed at last. He stood up shakily. He was in the County.

*

The slope still shortened his horizon to the north, but the brow was no more than fifty yards away. It should offer a vantage point. Rob climbed it, and climbed into the warmth and brightness of the rising sun. A bird was singing far up in the sky; he looked for it but could not find it. All was blueness and emptiness.

He stood at the top of the rise and looked around. There were hills on either side, the sun's orb just clear of one to the east. He was dazzled by sunlight and had difficulty taking in the landscape before him. It went down in a gentle fall and was not wild but patterned with fields and hedges. To the left a cart-track led in the distance to a lane. To the right . . . He dropped to the ground. A man was staring towards him.

He was sure he had been spotted: the man was no more than thirty yards away and he must have been outlined against the sky. But the man did not move as seconds passed. Rob's eyes, growing accustomed to the bright sunlight, took in details. A face that was not a face. Where legs should have emerged from old-fashioned black trousers there were sticks. A scarecrow, in fact. He had read of them in an old book.

It stood in the centre of a ploughed field. He went across and looked at it. Turnip face with eyes and mouth roughly cut, a worn black suit stuffed with straw. The trousers were badly holed, the jacket torn under the sleeve but otherwise in fair condition. Rob fingered the cloth and then undid the front buttons and pulled it off. Straw fell round his feet. He shook dust and insects from it. When he put it on it felt cold and damp but he reckoned it would soon warm up. It would make a difference the coming night if he were still sleeping out. It was too big, of course. He turned the sleeves back inside which improved things, though it bagged round his chest. The scarecrow looked sadly naked – solid to the waist but above just a turnip head supported on a stick. Rob looked closely at the head. A bit mildewed but it might be edible. He decided he was not quite hungry enough for that.

He went roughly north-west. There were different crops in the fields. In one big field there were rows of small green-leaved plants with tiny purple flowers. Would they bear some kind of fruit in due course? They would have to be very small. He pulled at one and it came up with white oval things hanging from its roots. Potatoes, he recognized. He could not cook them, but filled the pockets of his jacket in case he found a means later.

His feet were tired and aching from the unaccustomed walking but he pressed on, leaving the fence as far behind him as possible. He rested from time to time, and once while doing so heard a new sound. It grew louder and clarified into something which he had at least heard in historical epics H V – the thudding of horses' hooves.

Rob took cover behind a nearby hedge. It had a view of the lane and soon the horsemen appeared, riding to the west. There were half a dozen, in red tunics with gold buttons and gleaming leather straps and belts. They rode with careless arrogance; he heard them calling to one another and laughing. A couple of big dogs, one yellow, one white with black spots, lolloped alongside, their mouths open, red tongues hanging from between white teeth. And the horsemen had swords: the scabbards rattled against their high brown leather boots.

They did not look his way. The cavalcade rode on, disappearing behind high hedges, the sound of their passing gradually fading on the morning air. The King's Musketeers must have looked something like that, riding through the summer fields near Paris on their way to a brush with the Cardinal's men. It was more story-book than real; fascinating but scarcely believable.

Not long afterwards he saw the first house inside the

County. It had outlying buildings, a small pond, and poultry pecked the ground near by. A farmhouse. There would be food there, but he dared not approach. Smoke rose from a chimney and as he watched a figure came from one of the outbuildings, crossed the yard, and disappeared inside the house. Going to breakfast, perhaps. Rob felt in his pocket and brought out one of the tiny potatoes. Friction had rubbed it clean of earth. He bit into it. It tasted unpleasant in so far as it tasted of anything, but he managed to chew it and get it down. It quenched his thirst a little too. He ate three or four more.

The day wore on. During one of his rests he took off the jacket and rolled it up as a pillow for his head. He fell asleep and woke with the sun burning his face. It was high in the sky, almost at the zenith. He chewed more potatoes and went limping on his way. His feet were hurting him. A mile or so farther on he stopped at the edge of a field and took off his shoes and socks. His feet were blistered and some of the blisters had burst, exposing raw flesh.

He realized he could not go on indefinitely like this, but did not know what else to do. Field had succeeded field, with little change. There were animals in some which he knew were cows. One obtained milk from cows, but how? And anyway the sight of them made him nervous. In other fields there were men and machines. He could not tell precisely what the machines were doing because he had given them as wide a berth as possible. They were silent, presumably powered by fuel cells. He had also kept clear of houses, not that there were many. The emptiness of this land, which had been surprising and troubling, was becoming monotonous, mind-wearying. Rob looked at his swollen feet. He wondered if it would be better to lie up in the shade. But would he be any better able to go on later in the day?

And what was he hoping to achieve? He had come here spurred by hatred of the school, and by the discovery that his mother had been born and lived her early life in the County. He had had this idea of farmlands as places that produced food, but it was not turning out like that. All he had found – all he looked like finding – was a few small raw potatoes.

He might as well, he thought miserably, give himself up. He would have to do that eventually, or starve.

Someone called in the distance and he looked up quickly. There was a man on horseback in the gap at the end of the field. The call had been to Rob. There was a way through to another field on the left, and a wood not far off. If he could only reach it . . . The horseman had started to come forward. He decided that he had no time to put on socks and shoes. He grabbed them and ran.

The field into which he emerged was long but narrow – it was only twenty yards or so to a high hedge separating it from the next field which in turn was bordered by the wood. There was no gap, but Rob saw a place where it looked thin enough for him to squeeze through. He made it, with thorns tearing at him, and thought he was safe: the horseman would have to find a longer way round and by the time he did Rob would be in the wood. He could surely dodge a man on horseback there. His feet were hurting horribly but he disregarded that. Thirty yards to the wood, perhaps less. He heard another call and glanced over his shoulder. Horse and rider were in mid-air, clearing the hedge in a jump.

He tried to squeeze extra strength out of his legs. Twenty yards, ten, and hooves thudding in his wake. He would not reach the sanctuary. He wondered if the horseman would ride him down, or slash him with his sword. Then his left foot turned under him and he crashed to the ground. The impact dazed and winded him. He lay gasping and heard the sound of hooves slacken and cease. The horse was snorting quite close and above him.

Rob looked up. The sun was behind the rider's right shoulder and he could not see him properly for the glare. There was an impression of fairness, of a blue shirt open at the neck. He looked for the sword but could not see one.

The horse moved, jigging, and the rider checked it. The light fell at a different angle and now Rob could see him clearly. He was not a man but a fair-haired boy, not much older than himself.

Susan Cooper

THE DARK IS RISING

If you had a lovely time reading all C. S. Lewis's Narnia Chronicles (*The Lion, the Witch and the Wardrobe*, etc.) and want more of the same, then this series of five books – *The Dark is Rising* is only one of them – will give you what you want, although they are of sterner, more frightening stuff. Will, the seventh son of a seventh son, discovers on his eleventh birthday that he is the last of the Old Ones, whose mission it is to keep the Powers of Darkness from enveloping the world.

He has some fearful experiences and terrible decisions to make as he slowly collects the Six Signs which, when they are joined, will banish the Dark Rider and his cronies. In this episode the

Powers of Evil invade even the church, where Will is celebrating Christmas with his family.

The other four books in the sequence are: *Over Sea, Under Stone*, *Greenwitch*, *The Grey King* and *Silver on the Tree*.

* * *

'O ye Frost and Cold, bless ye the Lord, praise Him, and magnify Him for ever,' sang Will, reflecting that Mr Beaumont had shown a certain wry humour in choosing the canticle.

'O ye Ice and Snow, bless ye the Lord, praise Him, and magnify Him for ever.'

Suddenly he found himself shivering, but not from the words, nor from any sense of cold. His head swam; he clutched for a moment at the edge of the gallery. The music seemed to become for a brief flash hideously discordant, jarring at his ears. Then it faded into itself again and was as before, leaving Will shaken and chilled.

'O ye Light and Darkness,' sang James, staring at him – '*are you all right? Sit down* – and magnify Him for ever.'

But Will shook his head impatiently, and for the rest of the service he sturdily stood, sang, sat, or knelt, and convinced himself that there had been nothing at all wrong except a vague feeling of faintness, brought on by what his elders liked to call 'over-excitement'. And then the strange sense of wrongness, of discordance, came again.

It was only once more, at the very end of the service. Mr Beaumont was booming out the prayer of St Chrysostom: '. . . who dost promise, that when two or three are gathered together in thy name thou wilt grant their requests . . .' Noise broke suddenly into Will's mind, a shrieking and dreadful howling in place of the familiar cadences. He had heard it before. It was the sound of the besieging Dark, which he had heard outside the Manor Hall where he had sat with Merriman and the Lady, in some century unknown. But in a church? said Will the Anglican choirboy, incredulous: surely you can't feel it inside a church? Ah, said Will the Old One unhappily, any church of any religion is vulnerable to their attack, for places like this are where men give thought to matters of the Light and the Dark. He hunched his head down between his shoulders as the noise beat at him – and then it vanished again, and the Rector's voice was ringing out alone, as before.

Will glanced quickly around him, but it was clear nobody else had noticed anything wrong. Through the folds of his white surplice he gripped the three Signs on his belt, but there was neither warmth nor cold under his fingers. To the warning power of the Signs, he guessed, a church was a kind of no man's land; since no harm could actually enter its walls, no warning against harm should be necessary. Yet if the harm were hovering just outside . . .

The service was over now, everyone roaring out 'O Come, All Ye Faithful' in happy Christmas fervour, as the choir made their way down from the gallery and up to the altar. Then Mr Beaumont's blessing went rolling out over the heads of the congregation: '. . . the love of God, and the fellowship of the Holy Ghost . . .' But the words could not bring Will peace, for he knew that something was wrong, something looming out of the Dark, something waiting, out there, and that when it came to the point he must meet it alone, unstrengthened.

He watched everyone file beaming out of the church, smiling and nodding to each other as they gripped their umbrellas and turned up their collars against the swirling snow. He saw jolly Mr Hutton, the retired director, twirling his car keys, enveloping tiny Miss Bell, their old teacher, in the warm offer of a ride home; and behind him jolly Mrs Hutton, a galleon in full, furry sail, doing the same with limp Mrs Pettigrew, the postmistress. Assorted village children scampered out of the door, escaping their best-hatted mothers, rushing to snowballs and Christmas turkey. Lugubrious Mrs Horniman stumped out next to Mrs Stanton and Mary, busily foretelling doom. Will saw Mary, trying not to giggle, fall back to join Mrs Dawson and her married daughter, with the five-year-old grandson prancing gaily in gleaming new cowboy boots.

The choir, coated and muffled, began to leave too, with cries of 'Happy Christmas!' and 'See you on Sunday, Vicar!' to Mr Beaumont, who would be giving only this service here today and the rest in his other parishes. The rector, talking music with Paul, smiled and waved vaguely. The church began to empty, as Will waited for his brother. He could feel his neck prickling, as though with the electricity that hangs strongly oppressive in the air before a giant storm. He could feel it everywhere, the air inside the church was charged with it. The rector, still chatting, reached out an absentminded hand and turned off the lights inside the church, leaving it in a cold grey murk, brighter only beside the door where the whiteness of the snow reflected in. And Will, seeing some figures move towards the door out of the shadows, realized that the church was not empty after all. Down there by the little twelfth-century font, he saw Farmer Dawson, Old George, and Old George's son John, the smith, with his silent wife. The Old Ones of the Circle were waiting for him, to support him against whatever lurked outside. Will felt weak for a moment as relief washed over him in a great warm wave.

'All ready, Will?' said the rector genially, pulling on his overcoat. He went on, still preoccupied, to Paul, 'Of course, I do agree the double concerto is one of the best. I only wish he'd record the unaccompanied Bach suites. Heard him do them in a church in Edinburgh once, at the Festival – marvellous –'

Paul, sharper-eyed, said, 'Is anything wrong, Will?'

'No,' Will said. 'That is – no.' He was trying desperately to think of some way of getting the two of them outside the church before he came near the door himself. Before – before whatever might happen did happen. By the church door he could see the Old Ones move slowly into a tight group, supporting one another. He could feel the force now very strong, very close, all around, the air was thick with it, outside the church was destruction and chaos, the heart of the Dark, and he could think of nothing that he could do to turn it aside. Then as the rector and Paul turned to walk through the nave, he saw both of them pause in the same instant, and their heads go up like the heads of wild deer on the alert. It was too late now; the voice of the Dark was so loud that even humans could sense its power.

Paul staggered, as if someone had pushed him in the chest, and grabbed a pew for support. '*What is that*?' he said huskily. 'Rector? What on earth is it?'

Mr Beaumont had turned very white. There was a glistening of sweat on his forehead, though the church was very cold again now. 'Nothing on earth, I think, perhaps,' he said. 'God forgive me.' And he stumbled a few paces nearer the church door, like a man struggling through waves in the sea, and leaning forward slightly made a sweeping sign of the Cross. He stammered out, 'Defend us thy humble servants in all assaults of our enemies; that we, surely trusting in thy defence, may not fear the power of any adversaries . . .'

Farmer Dawson said very quietly but clearly from the group beside the door, 'No, Rector.'

The rector seemed not to hear him. His eyes were wide, staring out at the snow; he stood transfixed, he shook like a man with fever, the sweat came running down his cheeks. He managed to half-raise one arm and point behind him: '. . . vestry . . .' he gasped out. '. . . book, on table . . . exorcize . . .'

'Poor brave fellow,' said John Smith in the Old Speech. 'This battle is not for his fighting. He is bound to think so, of course, being in his church.'

'Be easy, Reverend,' said his wife in English; her voice was soft and gentle, strongly of the country. The rector stared at her like a frightened animal, but by now all his powers of speech and movement had been taken away.

Frank Dawson said: 'Come here, Will.'

Pushing against the Dark, Will came forward slowly; he touched Paul on the shoulder as he passed, looking into puzzled eyes in a face as twisted and helpless as the rector's, and said softly: 'Don't worry. It'll be all right soon.'

Each of the Old Ones touched him gently as he came into the group, as if joining him to them, and Farmer Dawson took him by the shoulder. He said, 'We must do something to protect those two, Will, or their minds will bend. They cannot stand the pressure, the Dark will send them mad. You have the power, and the rest of us do not.'

It was Will's first intimation that he could do anything another Old One could not, but there was no time for wonder; with the Gift of Gramarye, he closed off the minds of his brother and the rector behind a barrier that no power of any kind could break through. It was a perilous undertaking, since he, the maker, was the only one who could remove the barrier, and if anything were to happen to him the two protected ones would be left like vegetables, incapable of any communication, forever. But the risk had to be taken; there was nothing else to be done. Their eyes closed gently as if they had gone quietly to sleep; they stood very still. After a moment their eyes opened again, but were tranquil and empty, unaware.

'All right,' said Farmer Dawson. 'Now.'

The Old Ones stood in the doorway of the church, their arms linked together. None spoke a word to another. Wild noise and turbulence rose outside; the light darkened, the wind howled and whined, the snow whirled in and whipped their faces with white chips of ice. And suddenly the rooks were in the snow, hundreds of them, black flurries of mal-evolence, cawing and croaking, diving down at the porch in shrieking attack and then swooping up, away. They could not come close enough to claw and tear; it was as if an invisible wall made them fall back within inches of their targets. But that would be only for as long as the Old Ones' strength could hold. In a wild storm of black and white the Dark attacked, beating at their minds as at their bodies, and above all driving hard at the Sign-Seeker, Will. And Will knew that if he had been on his own his mind, for all its gifts of protec-tion, would have collapsed. It was the strength of the Circle of the Old Ones that held him fast now.

Helen Cresswell

THE NIGHT-WATCHMEN

One of the chief reasons I like Helen Cresswell's books is that she's good at new ideas – and at making sly little jokes. I chose this one because, in a way, it's a joke from beginning to end, and also it's about tramps, and I think most people find them fascinating (even if it's only wondering which ones live rough for pleasure and which for poverty).

Now, here are two particularly interesting ones who do it for pleasure. They are brothers, Josh and Caleb. A boy, Henry, finds them in the park and then discovers that they like his town and are planning to stay for a while. You'll see how they do it. They are a very practical pair and everything's very ordinary until the mysterious train comes to rescue them from the men with the green, glassy eyes who are seeking them out.

It won't take you long to read, but I bet you'll remember it for ages (especially Caleb's wonderful cooking), *and* afterwards you'll take a much closer look every time you encounter one of the gentlemen of the road . . .

* * *

At the end of an hour the hole was finished to Caleb's satisfaction. The water main lay smooth and shining at the bottom and Josh ambled over to the barrows and came back with a red flag, which he hammered into the side of the hole.

'Just puts the finishing touch,' he remarked. 'We've never had anyone fall into any of our holes yet, have we, Caleb?'

Caleb was looking over Josh's shoulder.

'Public,' he said briefly.

Henry knew his cue. He stuck his hands in his pockets and wandered off along the embankment. When he had gone a little way he stopped and searched for a few stones. He began to toss them idly into the water. As he did so two young women with prams passed him, talking and laughing. Henry waited till they had gone a hundred yards or so, then turned and strolled back to the bridge. By then they were out of sight. The danger was past.

'Can't be too careful,' remarked Josh as Henry rejoined them. 'As long as you don't *draw* attention, you don't get it.'

'Not many people come down here anyway,' said Henry. 'There's nothing to come for.'

'That was what we reckoned,' said Josh. 'We always look over the bridges when we're ticking, and this was the best by a long stretch. The minute I set eyes on this bridge I could picture it with a hole under. Seemed made for it. I like a bit of green as well, and a bit of water.'

'Now then,' said Caleb briskly, 'what about the hut?'

'Hut next,' agreed Josh. 'And a bite of dinner, p'raps?'

'I was thinking of an omelette . . .' said Caleb.

'Perfect,' said Josh. 'One of them with the herbs . . . that French one you do.'

'The Normandy,' nodded Caleb. 'But there's a snag.'

'Snag?' queried Josh. He was collecting the tools and now carried them over to the barrows, where the others followed him.

'Eggs,' explained Caleb. 'No eggs. I shall have to 'ave a bit of a shop round, first. Do with some butter, too. And cheese.'

'I can't put up this hut singlehanded,' pointed out Josh.

'And pepper,' went on Caleb. 'We're clear out of that. And the anchovy essence is down to the last drop, and haddock's nowhere at all without anchovy, do what you will with it.'

Josh was looking up over the roofs of the wharf-houses.

'It's a wet-looking sky up there,' he observed. 'And with this wind it'll be the kind of wet that gets right in under bridges. Once the rain gets a bit of a slant on it there'll be no keeping dry under this bridge. Hut first, shops later.'

'All right,' said Caleb, huffy now. 'There's no *need* to have an omelette. There's no *need* for me to go fiddling for hours on end with dishes you'd be lucky to get even if you was king. There's no *need*. Beans on toast'll do me if it'll do you.'

Josh looked miserably first at Caleb, then at the sky.

'I'll do the shopping,' offered Henry.

They looked startled.

'If you just give me a list and the money it won't take long. I'll do it quicker than you would – I know the shops. Then you can get the hut up before it rains.'

Caleb looked dubious but tempted. Josh was overjoyed.

'There!' he cried. 'There's an offer for you! Hut and dinner both! Have your cake and eat it!'

He began to rummage in his barrow, took out a box and from it produced a makeshift pad of odd pieces of paper threaded together on a string. He took a pencil stub from his pocket, lifted a larger box from the barrow, sat on it and waited – evidently for Caleb to begin dictating.

'Butter, you said,' he murmured, writing. 'Eggs, pepper . . .'

'Anchovy sauce,' said Caleb. 'Mushrooms, a sprig o' parsley, a pound of tomatoes and watch they don't give you the soft 'uns, a small –'

'Hold on, hold on!' cried Josh, scribbling furiously.

'A small chicken,' continued Caleb relentlessly.

'Shall I get a frozen one?' asked Henry.

Now Caleb *did* stop. His white face drew itself into an expression that was by now becoming familiar to Henry. It was a sort of *shrunk* expression.

'Pardon?' he said, very distinctly.

'I said – shall I get a frozen one?' repeated Henry.

'In so far as I know,' said Caleb, 'there is no such thing as a frozen chicken. Chickens is either alive and laying eggs, or dead on the table. That's nature, that is. But as to frozen –'

'My mother always gets frozen ones,' said Henry.

He was dimly beginning to perceive that he must either stand up to Caleb in the early stages of their acquaintance or else be trodden on for evermore.

'She says they're just –'

He broke off. Josh, seated behind Caleb, was pulling the most extraordinary faces, which coupled with vigorous shakings of the head left no doubt at all of what he was trying to convey.

'Well, all right, then,' said Henry. 'An ordinary chicken.'

Caleb nodded, mollified.

'He got strong views on cooking, you see,' explained Josh apologetically. 'That all, then, Caleb?'

'Do for now,' said Caleb. 'Did we *ought* to let him go, Josh? What if he don't come back?'

'He'll come back,' said Josh. 'Liked the look of him first time I saw him. More or less counted him as a sign.'

Henry was by now used to being discussed as if he were not there. He could even understand Caleb's point of view.

'Don't worry,' he said. 'I'll come back. I should like to see anyone stop me.'

Josh beamed.

'There you are!' he said. 'You've got no trust in human nature, Caleb, that's your drawback. Now here's the money, here's the list and here's a carrier bag. Watch the handles, one of 'em seems a bit shaky. Going to be useful you are, young feller. Nice there being three of us for a change.'

Caleb said nothing. All the way along the embankment Henry could feel his pale suspicious eyes boring into his back. He did the shopping as quickly as he could, but it was nearly an hour before he turned on to the canal road again and with enormous relief saw that they were still there. Even now he could not feel quite sure of them.

As he drew nearer he could see that a kind of hoop-shaped canvas hut had been erected in his absence. It sat snugly under the middle arch on the narrow strip of green, and Henry could see Josh and Caleb nearby busy with their unpacking.

Caleb pounced on the carrier bag the minute Henry set it down and swiftly checked off the items, examining each with care if not actual suspicion. He even opened the bag of tomatoes and felt them, one by one. Henry was glad he had remembered to ask for firm ones. He would not have liked to see Caleb confronted by a pound of squashy tomatoes.

'That's all right, then,' said Caleb, satisfied at last. 'Any change?'

Henry handed it over and Caleb counted it and handed it to Josh saying, 'Yours, Josh. I'll get the stove lit.'

He disappeared into the hut. Henry, left alone with Josh, decided to ask some of the questions he had thought of during the past hour.

'What are you going to do with the hole now that you've dug it?' he began.

Josh looked up from his sorting. Henry noticed that the boxes seemed to contain paper, mostly.

'Oh, the hole's done with now it's dug,' he said. 'It's just a bit of background, as you might say. It'll just stop there till it gets filled in again.'

'And when will that be?' asked Henry.

'When we flits,' explained Josh. 'When we've finished.'

'Will it be very long?' persisted Henry.

'Can't say. But I liked the way this town ticked, or we shouldn't have gone to the trouble to dig a hole in the first place. We should've stuck it out for a few nights in the park.'

Henry considered this. Light began to dawn.

'You mean you've dug a *hole* so that you can put up the *hut*!' he cried. The whole amazing pattern was beginning to fall into shape.

Josh lowered his voice.

'You see, if we was to go putting up huts all over the place, there'd be questions asked. There'd be police and Authority on us before we'd so much as got the stove lit. But a hut with a *hole*, ah, that's a different matter!'

Henry, delighted, could see that it was.

'It blends in with the background natural, d'ye see,' Josh went on. 'Just dig a hole and put up a red flag and you could camp till doomsday and not a question asked. Worked it out a few years back, we did, the summer Caleb got pneumonia park-sleeping.'

'It's marvellous!' cried Henry. 'Absolutely marvellous!'

'It's beating 'em at their own game,' said Josh, 'that's the way we look at it. Dozens of holes we've dug, the long and broad of England, and not so much as the bat of an eyelid. You could dig one outside the Houses of Parliament, if you'd a mind to, and as long as nobody fell in it there'd be no questions asked. That's what you got to watch. If anyone was to fall in you'd have the Authorities on you and the game *would* be up.'

Henry saw his opening.

'What game?' he asked. 'What do you do?'

'Do?' said Josh. 'I wouldn't rightly say that we do anything. It's more a matter of what we *are* than what we *do*.'

'What are you, then?' pressed Henry desperately.

Josh hesitated. Then:

'Night-watchmen,' he said at last. 'That's what we are. Night-watchmen.'

Henry stared at him.

'Among other things,' added Josh.

As Henry opened his mouth Caleb's thin face poked from the hut.

'*He*'s not stopping, is he?' he said. 'There ain't enough herbs for three.'

Henry, startled, looked at his watch.

'Dinner!' he cried. 'I'm late! Back this afternoon!'

He had gone only a few yards when he heard Josh. He turned.

'Supper!' called Josh. 'Come to supper! Seven sharp!'

Henry nodded. Somehow he would manage it.

Roald Dahl

THE B F G

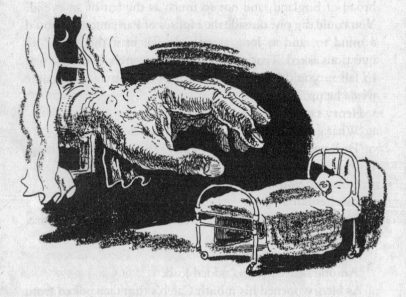

I thought my favourite Roald Dahl book was *James and the Giant Peach* until he wrote this one, which really earns my top marks.

You might think that stories about giants are something that you've grown out of, but not this one. He's not only friendly, but very funny, and I'll be surprised if you don't find yourselves using some of his favourite words, such as *whoppsy* and *fizzwiggler*, *rotrasper* or *whizzpopping* and *swizzfiggling*. Not that *whizzpopping* is something you'll undertake lightly, especially if you have tea with the Queen as the BFG manages to do. He can also hear 'all the secret whisperings of the world'.

His companion in these adventures is an orphan called Sophie whom he plucked out of the orphanage window while he was out and about, catching dreams . . .

Here he is explaining to Sophie why he collects people's dreams.

* * *

Back in the cave, the Big Friendly Giant sat Sophie down once again on the enormous table. 'Is you quite snuggly there in your nightie?' he asked. 'You isn't fridgy cold?'

'I'm fine,' Sophie said.

'I cannot help thinking,' said the BFG, 'about your poor mother and father. By now they must be jipping and skumping all over the house shouting "Hello hello where is Sophie gone?" '

'I don't have a mother and father,' Sophie said. 'They both died when I was a baby.'

'Oh, you poor little scrumplet!' cried the BFG. 'Is you not missing them very badly?'

'Not really,' Sophie said, 'because I never knew them.'

'You is making me sad,' the BFG said, rubbing his eyes.

'Don't be sad,' Sophie said. 'No one is going to be worrying too much about me. That place you took me from was the village orphanage. We are all orphans in there.'

'You is a norphan?'

'Yes.'

'How many is there in there?'

'Ten of us,' Sophie said. 'All little girls.'

'Was you happy there?' the BFG asked.

'I hated it,' Sophie said. 'The woman who ran it was called Mrs Clonkers and if she caught you breaking any of the rules, like getting out of bed at night or not folding up your clothes, you got punished.'

'How is you getting punished?'

'She locked us in the dark cellar for a day and a night without anything to eat or drink.'

'The rotten old rotrasper!' cried the BFG.

'It was horrid,' Sophie said. 'We used to dread it. There were rats down there. We could hear them creeping about.'

'The filthy old fizzwiggler!' shouted the BFG. 'That is the horridest thing I is hearing for years! You is making me sadder than ever!' All at once, a huge tear that would have filled a bucket rolled down one of the BFG's cheeks and fell with a splash on the floor. It made quite a puddle.

Sophie watched with astonishment. What a strange and moody creature this is, she thought. One moment he is telling me my head is full of squashed flies and the next moment his heart is melting for me because Mrs Clonkers locks us in the cellar.

'The thing that worries *me*,' Sophie said, 'is having to stay in this dreadful place for the rest of my life. The orphanage was pretty awful, but I wouldn't have been there for ever, would I?'

'All is my fault,' the BFG said. 'I is the one who kidsnatched you.' Yet another enormous tear welled from his eye and splashed on to the floor.

'Now I come to think of it, I won't actually be here all that long,' Sophie said.

'I is afraid you will,' the BFG said.

'No, I won't,' Sophie said. 'Those brutes out there are bound to catch me sooner or later and have me for tea.'

'I is *never* letting that happen,' the BFG said.

For a few moments the cave was silent. Then Sophie said, 'May I ask you a question?'

The BFG wiped the tears from his eyes with the back of his hand and gave Sophie a long, thoughtful stare. 'Shoot away,' he said.

'Would you please tell me what you were doing in our village last night? Why were you poking that long trumpet thing into the Goochey children's bedroom and then blowing through it?'

'Ah-ha!' cried the BFG, sitting up suddenly in his chair. 'Now we is getting nosier than a parker!'

'And the suitcase you were carrying,' Sophie said. 'What on earth was *that* all about?'

The BFG stared suspiciously at the small girl sitting cross-legged on the table.

'You is asking me to tell you whoppsy big secrets,' he said. 'Secrets that nobody is ever hearing before.'

'I won't tell a soul,' Sophie said. 'I swear it. How could I anyway? I am stuck here for the rest of my life.'

'You could be telling the other giants.'

'No, I couldn't,' Sophie said. 'You told me they would eat me up the moment they saw me.'

'And so they would,' said the BFG 'You is a human bean and human beans is like strawbunkles and cream to those giants.'

'If they are going to eat me the moment they see me, then I wouldn't have time to tell them anything, would I?' Sophie said.

'You wouldn't,' said the BFG.

'Then why did you say I might?'

'Because I is brimful of buzzburgers,' the BFG said. 'If you listen to everything I am saying you will be getting earache.'

'Please tell me what you were doing in our village,' Sophie said. 'I promise you can trust me.'

'Would you teach me how to make an elefunt?' the BFG asked.

'What *do* you mean?' Sophie said.

'I would dearly love to have an elefunt to ride on,' the BFG said dreamily. 'I would so much love to have a jumbly big elefunt and go riding through green forests picking peachy fruits off the trees all day long. This is a sizzling-hot muck-frumping country we is living in. Nothing grows in it except snozzcumbers. I would love to go somewhere else and pick peachy fruits in the early morning from the back of an elefunt.'

Sophie was quite moved by this curious statement.

'Perhaps one day we will get you an elephant,' she said. 'And peachy fruits as well. Now tell me what you were doing in our village.'

'If you is really wanting to know what I am doing in your village,' the BFG said, 'I is blowing a dream into the bedroom of those children.'

'*Blowing a dream?*' Sophie said. 'What *do* you mean?'

'I is a dream-blowing giant,' the BFG said. 'When all the other giants is galloping off every what way and which to swollop human beans, I is scuddling away to other places to blow dreams into the bedrooms of sleeping children. Nice dreams. Lovely golden dreams. Dreams that is giving the dreamers a happy time.'

'Now hang on a minute,' Sophie said. 'Where do you get these dreams?'

'I collect them,' the BFG said, waving an arm towards all the rows and rows of bottles on the shelves. 'I has billions of them.'

'You can't *collect* a dream,' Sophie said. 'A dream isn't something you can catch hold of.'

'You is never going to understand about it,' the BFG said. 'That is why I is not wishing to tell you.'

'Oh, please tell me!' Sophie said. 'I *will* understand! Go on! Tell me how you collect dreams! Tell me everything!'

The BFG settled himself comfortably in his chair and

crossed his legs. 'Dreams,' he said, 'is very mysterious things. They is floating around in the air like little wispy-misty bubbles. And all the time they is searching for sleeping people.'

'Can you see them?' Sophie asked.

'Never at first.'

'Then how do you catch them if you can't see them?' Sophie asked.

'Ah-ha,' said the BFG. 'Now we is getting on to the dark and dusky secrets.'

'I won't tell a soul.'

'I is trusting you,' the BFG said. He closed his eyes and sat quite still for a moment, while Sophie waited.

'A dream,' he said, 'as it goes whiffling through the night air, is making a tiny little buzzing-humming noise. But this little buzzy-hum is so silvery soft, it is impossible for a human bean to be hearing it.'

'Can *you* hear it?' Sophie asked.

The BFG pointed up at his enormous truck-wheel ears which he now began to move in and out. He performed this exercise proudly, with a little proud smile on his face. 'Is you seeing these?' he asked.

'How could I miss them?' Sophie said.

'They maybe is looking a bit propsposterous to you,' the BFG said, 'but you must believe me when I say they is very extra-usual ears indeed. They is not to be coughed at.'

'I'm quite sure they're not,' Sophie said.

'They is allowing me to hear absolutely every single twiddly little thing.'

'You mean you can hear things I can't hear?' Sophie said.

'You is *deaf as a dumpling* compared with me!' cried the BFG. 'You is hearing only thumping loud noises with those little earwigs of yours. But I am hearing *all the secret whisperings of the world!*'

'Such as what?' Sophie asked.

'In your country,' he said, 'I is hearing the footsteps of a ladybird as she goes walking across a leaf.'

'*Honestly?*' Sophie said, beginning to be impressed.

'What's more, I is hearing those footsteps *very loud*,' the BFG said. 'When a ladybird is walking across a leaf, I is hearing her feet going *clumpety-clumpety-clump* like giants' footsteps.'

'Good gracious me!' Sophie said. 'What else can you hear?'

'I is hearing the little ants chittering to each other as they scuddle around in the soil.'

'You mean you can hear ants talking?'

'Every single word,' the BFG said. 'Although I is not exactly understanding their langwitch.'

'Go on,' Sophie said.

'Sometimes, on a very clear night,' the BFG said, 'and if I is swiggling my ears in the right direction,' – and here he swivelled his great ears upwards so they were facing the ceiling – 'if I is swiggling them like this and the night is very clear, I is sometimes hearing faraway music coming from the stars in the sky.'

A queer little shiver passed through Sophie's body. She sat very quiet, waiting for more.

'My ears is what told me you was watching me out of your window last night,' the BFG said.

'But I didn't make a sound,' Sophie said.

'I was hearing your heart beating across the road,' the BFG said. 'Loud as a drum.'

'Go on,' Sophie said. 'Please.'

'I can hear plants and trees.'

'Do *they* talk?' Sophie asked.

'They is not exactly talking,' the BFG said. 'But they is making noises. For instance, if I come along and I is picking a lovely flower, if I is twisting the stem of the flower till it breaks, then the plant is screaming. I can hear it screaming and screaming very clear.'

'You don't mean it!' Sophie cried. 'How awful!'

'It is screaming just like you would be screaming if someone was twisting *your* arm right off.'

'Is that really true?' Sophie asked.

'You think I is swizzfiggling you?'

'It *is* rather hard to believe.'

'Then I is stopping right here,' said the BFG sharply. 'I is not wishing to be called a fibster.'

'Oh no! I'm not calling you anything!' Sophie cried. 'I believe you! I do really! Please go on!'

The BFG gave her a long hard stare. Sophie looked right back at him, her face open to his. 'I believe you,' she said softly.

She had offended him, she could see that.

'I wouldn't ever be fibbling to you,' he said.

'I know you wouldn't,' Sophie said. 'But you must understand that it isn't easy to believe such amazing things straightaway.'

'I understand that,' the BFG said.

'So do please forgive me and go on,' she said.

He waited a while longer, and then he said, 'It is the same with trees as it is with flowers. If I is chopping an axe into the trunk of a big tree, I is hearing a terrible sound coming from inside the heart of the tree.'

'What sort of sound?' Sophie asked.

'A soft moaning sound,' the BFG said. 'It is like the sound an old man is making when he is dying slowly.'

He paused. The cave was very silent.

'Trees is living and growing just like you and me,' he said. 'They is alive. So is plants.'

He was sitting very straight in his chair now, his hands clasped tightly together in front of him. His face was bright, his eyes round and bright as two stars.

'Such wonderful and terrible sounds I is hearing!' he said. 'Some of them you would never wish to be hearing yourself! But some is like glorious music!'

He seemed almost to be transfigured by the excitement of his thoughts. His face was beautiful in its blaze of emotions.

'Tell me some more about them,' Sophie said quietly.

'You just ought to be hearing the little micies talking!' he said. 'Little micies is always talking to each other and I is hearing them as loud as my own voice.'

'What do they say?' Sophie asked.

'Only the micies know that,' he said. 'Spiders is also talking a great deal. You might not be thinking it but spiders is the most tremendous natterboxes. And when they is spinning their webs, they is singing all the time. They is singing sweeter than a nightingull.'

'Who else do you hear?' Sophie asked.

'One of the biggest chatbags is the cattlepiddlers,' the BFG said.

'What do they say?'

'They is argying all the time about who is going to be the prettiest butterfly. That is all they is ever talking about.'

'Is there a dream floating around in here now?' Sophie asked.

The BFG moved his great ears this way and that, listening intently. He shook his head. 'There is no dream in here,' he said, 'except in the bottles. I has a special place to go for catching dreams. They is not often coming to Giant Country.'

'How do you catch them?'

'The same way you is catching butterflies,' the BFG

answered. 'With a net.' He stood up and crossed over to a corner of the cave where a pole was leaning against the wall. The pole was about thirty feet long and there was a net on the end of it. 'Here is the dream-catcher,' he said, grasping the pole in one hand. 'Every morning I is going out and snitching new dreams to put in my bottles.'

Suddenly, he seemed to lose interest in the conversation. 'I is getting hungry,' he said. 'It is time for eats.'

Lionel Davidson

UNDER PLUM LAKE

When Barry, who tells this story, first meets Dido in a cave in Cornwall, he thinks he is an ordinary boy like himself – but he is wrong. Dido belongs to Egon, a world beneath the sea, where people live for hundreds of years and spend their lives quite differently. They aren't cruel or greedy, they never feel pain and they get their pleasure out of physical things like racing sharks through magical waters, sky-diving in kites or whizzing on special skis or toboggans down the power slopes of switched-on mountains, and they have timeless caverns where they can stop their lives and relive any moment they choose.

This is a an exciting and memorable book, full of ideas as well as excitement. It is really a package of fantastic experiences. The author said he had rewritten it eleven times and wouldn't mind doing it again as he keeps thinking about it.

Here is Barry being taught to toboggan on the switched-on mountain.

* * *

He did two runs, very carefully, without trying anything. He pointed out every detail to me. It's power tobogganing. The power comes from the mountain. The toboggan just has the controls. You sit one behind the other, tightly strapped in. You toboggan up the mountain as well as down it. There's an up-track and a down-track. You go up quite slowly. The toboggan grips the track like a magnet. Coming down, it still grips it tightly, but you're going faster. If you switch off, you're going much faster.

That's the trick. You go as fast as you dare before switching on again. They have the same procedure, a starter on top and a judge below. But this way, it's pure speed. You get from top to bottom as fast as you can, in any way you can.

He didn't tell me the various ways you could do it. He just did the first two runs nice and steadily.

He showed me how you worked the toboggan. The front person worked the controls. The back person helped steer, leaning out sideways or backwards when the toboggan rounded a bend or leaped a hump.

He gave me good warning when I had to do it. He'd yell 'Right!' or 'Left!' and I'd lean out to right or left, and we'd swish round the bend without the rear end wobbling. Or if a hump was coming, he'd yell, 'Back!' and I'd lean out backwards and we'd sail over and land flat without the nose scooping. (The toboggan is heavier at the front because of the controls.)

At the sharper bends there was a red sign, to give advance warning. But at some of them I saw a yellow sign, with an arrow pointing outwards from the mountain, and I asked why.

He pointed over the side. 'Lower track,' he said. 'You can take a short cut.'

Below, I could see the track zigzagging down the mountain.

Second time round, he showed me the short cut.

Turning sideways at the yellow arrow, you could leave the track, grip tightly to the mountain with power on, and descend to join the next stretch of track below. You could save seconds that way.

He told me when we were going to do it. He yelled, 'Back!' and I stretched back as far as I could and we took a slow dive vertically down the mountain.

My head swam.

I was standing upright.

We were stuck like flies to the side of the mountain. I felt my eyes glazing, my body rigid. Yet the moment we hit the lower track and he switched power off and we were whizzing away again, it felt like colossal fun. We did it four or five times, and by the end I was yelling, 'Whee!' and laughing as gleefully as he did.

His eyes were shining behind his goggles as we went up for the third run, and he said something to the starter.

'We'll do a timing now,' he told me.

I'd forgotten about the timing. He hadn't asked for a timing before.

He started off fast right away, and he didn't even bother putting power on at the first wide bend, just yelled, 'Right!' and I swung out and we lurched round the bend at speed.

I felt my heart beginning to thud. I could see the red sign

ahead for a hairpin bend. It came rushing up in a sickening blur, and he still didn't put power on. He began yelling, '*Left! Left!*' without slackening speed for an instant. I saw, without believing it, that he didn't mean to put power on at all. We were going racing into the hairpin bend. He was leaning out to left himself. I leaned out as far as I could. I leaned so far my head brushed the snow on the banking as we swished in a jackknife curve round it, and levelled out into a wild dangerous wobble, racing from side to side of the icy track as he hurtled down it, not losing speed for an instant.

I could hear him cackling in front. I could see another red sign coming up, with a yellow one.

'Dido!' I yelled. 'Slow down!'

He couldn't hear me. The wind snatched my words away. I could hear him, though. He was yelling. '*Back!*'

Back? He meant left. I had to bend *left* again. Another tight hairpin was coming. It was almost here.

'*Back!*' he yelled. '*Back!*' and started straining back himself, so I did, too.

He didn't turn into the bend. He followed the yellow arrow. He went full speed off the mountain.

I thought my heart had stopped.

We were in the air, off the mountain.

Just as we lost contact, he snapped power on. I felt the magnet clamp tight. We fell and hit the lower track hard, and the instant we did so, he let power off, and we were still going at terrific speed.

I couldn't bear it. I wanted to get out. I wanted to get off.

He was cackling like a lunatic in front.

I followed blindly whatever he said. '*Left!*' '*Right!*' '*Back!*' We skated madly round the banking. We flew through the air over humps.

We came to another arrow.

'*Back!*'

Again we flew off the mountain. I wanted to close my eyes, but daren't. I was straining back, waiting for the thud of power to come on. It came on, and I clenched my toes, waiting for the thump. There was no thump. Almost immediately, he let power off again. The lower track sailed past us, and we were still dropping. He let one track, two tracks, flash past, before bringing on power, and we landed on the third. He switched power off just as we landed, but we did it with such a thud we leaped clear in the air, a good five feet, still scudding down at breakneck pace.

I'd practically given up now. I wasn't even sure when it ended. We were stopped. People were jumping and yelling. The judge was checking the figures. He was checking them again. I hadn't even got out of the toboggan. I was still strapped in.

'Well. Not bad,' Dido said. He'd shoved his goggles up, and was grinning. 'Second best time for eighty years. What do you say to that?'

I didn't say anything.

'Barry?' he said. He seemed to be looking at me closely.

Then I was in a hut, and he was giving me tigra.

'Are you all right?' he said.

I still couldn't speak.

'Barry?'

I sipped the tigra. I felt better every second.

'Didn't you like it?' he said.

'I hated it,' I said. 'Don't do it again. Never do *anything* like that with me again.'

He just blinked at me.

'Have a nap,' he said. 'It's time for one now.'

*

I asked him about it later. I asked about the danger. I asked if it wasn't possible to be killed in Egon.

He said of course you could be killed. If you smashed yourself badly, you were killed.

So he knew. He knew what could happen.

Meindert DeJong

THE HOUSE OF SIXTY FATHERS

Sometimes you can care so much for a character in a book that you actually weep with joy when the story comes to a happy ending. That's what this story did to me. When the Japanese invaded China in the last war, eight-year-old Tien Pao, and his pet pig, Glory-of-the-Republic, got separated from his father and mother and set out on an impossible journey to find them. Scaling cliffs, crossing rivers, walking with his pig for hundreds of miles, hiding from enemy Japanese, starving until he saves a shot-down American airman, at last he is befriended by Chinese guerrillas, and finally adopted by his sixty American Fathers – and it's all based on a true story.

* * *

From behind a tall bush at the side of the path stepped a man. Tien Pao heard the soft step. He jumped to his feet, froze there. He had heard but one soft step, but he and the airman and the little pig were inside a ring of armed men. The airman stirred and moaned, but he did not know what was going on.

A tall, bearded man, who must be the leader, pointed with his gun to the airman. 'Who is he? And what are you doing with him?' he asked in Chinese.

Tien Pao opened his mouth, but no sound would come. Fear choked his throat. He stood staring down at the helpless figure of the airman. What must he say? Anything he said might be all wrong. It must be best to tell the truth.

Tien Pao looked up from the airman to the bearded man, and somehow he found courage and words, and when he began he talked as he never had talked in his life. He told about the battle he had seen from the high cliff, and that this was the airman who had killed all the Japanese on the road. He told how he had called out a warning from the cliff. The men listened silently. At last the leader nodded. 'You have spoken the truth. We, too, know of the great battle of this brave warrior, but we marvel that you found him. We could not find him, nor could we find you.'

'It is more that he found me,' Tien Pao said hastily. And then he looked earnestly up at the man. 'Please, my lord,' he begged. 'Please, Sir Bandit, do not kill him, for this warrior airman has greatly helped our people.'

The men chuckled, the leader stroked his beard in amusement. 'Ah, we may look like it, but we are not bandits. We, too, fight the Japanese. We are the Chinese guerrillas of the mountains. We come out at night to kill and destroy the Japanese. But we shall do well by you and the airman.'

To Tien Pao's astonishment, the leader made the soft cuckoo call. Down the path there was an answering sleepy call. Two men came silently through the dark; between them they carried a rough, hurriedly-made stretcher. Without a word they laid the feverish, muttering airman on the stretcher and trotted off down the path. Some of the guerrilla band went with the stretcher-carriers as guards, but the airman knew nothing of what was happening to him.

After the airman was gone, the leader took Tien Pao on his shoulder. 'The pace we set, and the shape you're in – we'll do it this way.' When Tien Pao looked back, a guerrilla trotted on behind with Glory-of-the-Republic under his arm as if he weighed no more than a chicken. They set off through the night, deeper into the dark mountains, away from the guiding sound of the river.

The guerrillas moved swiftly and silently through the black mountains, down beaten paths, but also over many secret trails that must be known only to them. They walked as surely as if it had been daylight. No one spoke a word. Tien Pao still marvelled at the sudden happening. 'Often I heard the sleepy cuckoo call these many nights, but I didn't know,' he whispered down to the guerrilla.

The guerrilla chuckled. 'We are in all the mountains,' he said softly. But then he laid a warning finger on his lips. They were going down a broad, well-worn mountain path – Tien Pao was to talk no more. The guerrilla who was carrying Glory-of-the-Republic had one hand around the little pig's snout. Glory-of-the-Republic was sound asleep. His ears hung limp.

Suddenly there was the hushed cuckoo call. The little procession melted from the path and into the shadows of the rocks. In one moment the trail lay empty, except for the man with Glory-of-the-Republic. Now he set the little pig down in the middle of the path, gave the sleepy pig a sharp, mean jab, and then he was gone from the path, too. Glory-of-the-Republic let out a long, loud squeal. Bewildered and alone, the little pig stood on the path. He raised his nose to snuffle for Tien Pao. He grunted a sharp question.

Down the steep path a Japanese soldier came stealing, gun in hand. For a moment the bayonet on his gun flashed in the dark as he lunged at the unsuspecting little pig. The guerrilla leader clamped a hand over Tien Pao's mouth to keep him still. Tien Pao struggled. But as the leader held him hard, guerrillas slid out of the shadows behind and to either side of the charging Japanese. Suddenly the Japanese soldier charged no more. A black cloth came down from nowhere over his head. Strong hands pinioned his arms. There was a muffled scream, the gun clattered to the rocky path. It bounced up and landed beside the startled little pig.

One muffled, short scream and then the Japanese had vanished down the mountain between two guerrillas. The remaining guerrillas took up the march again. They were silent. Ahead walked the scouts. Far behind, trailing along, each man by himself, came the rear guard. Thus they were protected on all sides from any surprise by the Japanese. But the rest of the night they did not meet a single living thing. Nor did the cuckoo call again.

Toward the morning the party at last halted. A little mud house loomed up; it clung to the side of a cliff. There was no one in the little house but an old, withered, toothless crone. At a word from the leader she silently began cooking rice over a ready fire. Tien Pao looked around the little room crowded with the men. 'But the airman, where is he?' he demanded wildly. 'Where is the American?' Nobody answered. Only the old crone looked at him. The guerrillas were gathered close together, whispering.

Tien Pao was bewildered. 'But where then is the Japanese soldier?' he asked in confusion. 'Did you kill him?'

'Oh, no. Oh, no,' the guerrilla chief said at last. He was mightily pleased with the work of the night. He was examining the rifle taken from the Japanese. 'It is a good gun,' he said. He ran his fingers over the ammunition belt. It was full except for one bullet. The soldier had evidently intended that for Glory-of-the-Republic, if he couldn't run the little pig through with the silent bayonet. 'Oh, no,' the chief said. 'If we had wanted to kill the Jap, we wouldn't have tricked him with your pig. Alive he is worth far more, alive we can question him.'

'But where is the airman?' Tien Pao asked again.

'Not here,' the leader said briefly. It was clear he did not want to answer the question.

'What did you do with him?' Tien Pao persisted. 'I must know. He is my friend.'

The guerrilla shook his head. 'Your white friend is safe, that is all you need to know,' he told Tien Pao. 'And do not ask any more. It is far better that you do not know how we are taking him back to the American lines. You are still more than a day's journey inside Japanese territory, and you might still be captured. And then you would talk. Oh, yes, you would talk! But if you do not know, you cannot tell.'

Tien Pao nodded sombrely. The words filled him with sick horror. But the food had begun cooking, and Tien Pao forgot everything for the heavenly odours of the rice and greens. He almost fainted over the bowl of steaming rice that was handed to him. All the men were hungry. They ate hurriedly and silently. Tien Pao wolfed his bowlful. He was holding out his bowl for more when at a whispered word from the leader the men arose. The journey was to go on even by day. The guerrillas wanted to get Tien Pao out of Japanese country as fast as the airman. They knew only too bitterly well what happened to those who helped American pilots to escape.

At a nod from the leader, the old woman went to a secret hole in the wall and took out buckets and carrying-poles and hoes. Tien Pao was to carry two buckets. 'Now remember this,' the guerrilla chief told him, 'during the day we do not fight the Japanese. We are now farmers. If we meet Japanese on the path, do not run, no matter how scared you may be. When the warning comes, get off the path as soon as possible and go to the nearest rice paddy with your buckets. But do not run! Act exactly as if it were your father's rice paddy. Do you understand?

'Another thing,' the leader said. 'Today I am your father, Huan. You will trot at a respectable distance behind me with your buckets. Your name is Tsu, and you are not too bright. If we are questioned by the Japanese, let me do the talking. If they speak to you directly, act the fool, and don't be alarmed if I abuse you and even slap your face for your stupid answers. Now repeat our names, and remember them.'

Tien Pao repeated the names.

'One more thing,' the guerrilla said, 'if any of the Japanese that pass us order you to work — work for them. Do not show that you hate them, work for them willingly — it is at night that we kill them.'

One of the guerrillas had fitted a false bottom with air holes into one of Tien Pao's buckets. Glory-of-the-Republic had been trussed up, legs and snout. The old woman had brought a little pile of old, wet straw and litter. Now Glory-of-the-Republic was lowered into the bucket, the false bottom was pounded over him, and the rubbish and straw were spread over the false bottom. The second bucket was filled with heavier litter. The buckets were now balanced on the carrying-pole, and both looked equally full and heavy. It was hard to see Glory-of-the-Republic trussed up and shoved into the bottom of a bucket, but Tien Pao realized they could not travel by day in Japanese-occupied territory with a pig.

'Son, Tsu, we must go,' the guerrilla leader ordered. He threw a hoe over his shoulder.

'Ready, honourable father, Huan,' Tien Pao said meekly. He braced his shoulders under the carrying-pole and started to lift the buckets.

'A moment, please,' the old crone mumbled apologetically to the guerrilla leader. With a toothless smile for Tien Pao she hastily brought him a second bowl of rice.

The guerrilla impatiently lowered his hoe, but he said nothing.

'Because of the heavy load and the starved lad – the journey will go much better for a second bowl of rice,' she apologized. 'A child must eat. And . . . and I love a child.'

The guerrilla smiled a little, and Tien Pao hastily wolfed the rice. 'Ready,' he said with his mouth full of food, and shouldered his loaded buckets. He trotted out behind his so-called father. But outside the door he turned, and said with all his heart to the old crone: 'And I love you.'

It was a lovely smile her old mouth gave him in their parting.

Peter Dickinson

THE DANCING BEAR

Here is what is officially described as a historical novel, but like all
Peter Dickinson's books, the people are so vivid and believable that
the historical side slips in unnoticed. This story begins with the
horrifying sacking of the Christian city of Byzantium by the barbarians, in AD 558. From then on it is the story of how Silvester,
a young slave, who is custodian of Bubba the dancing bear, sets
out to follow the Huns and rescue his mistress and old playmate,
the Lady Ariadne.

On his long and fearful journey into a lawless land, Silvester
takes the bear and Holy John, the holy man who wants to bring
Christianity to the heathens.

If you haven't discovered Peter Dickinson's books before, I also recommend his earlier trilogy, *The Changes*, about a time when Britain is struck by a strange malady which causes everyone to hate and fear all machinery.

This scene in *The Dancing Bear* is at the beginning of the blood-thirsty raid on the palace, when Lady Ariadne is carried off.

* * *

Silvester slept in the women's wing with the eunuchs, on the floor below the women. He had a little cell on his own, smaller than a cupboard. If he had been free-born he would already have been sent to sleep on the opposite side of the courtyard, in the men's wing; but slaves, even valued ones, were treated without thought, as if they were almost women themselves, so he expected to sleep in this cell until My Lord chose one of the slave-girls as a wife for him.

In his dream he rode a horse along a dreary and endlessly winding river towards the Akritas estate where the Lady Ariadne was waiting for him with toothache, but the horse melted and he was trudging with tired legs and the estate when he came to it was an empty hovel and the dentist's tools which he held in his hand had become the Lord Celsus's seal-brooch and there was Holy John sitting at the next bend on a juniper bush and shouting at him for the sin of stealing it.

The shouts woke him and he lay sweating in the dark.

It took him some moments to be sure that the shouts were real, and not part of the dream. Then he thought that some quarrel had broken out between the Celsus and Akritas famil-ies, and the betrothal would not take place – Addie would like that. Slowly he realized that the shouts consisted of sounds no Greek would ever utter; and then the orange glare of burning began to stain the dark. He threw his fur aside and stumbled to the window. Other heads were already craning out on

either side, and a shrill screaming wail rose as the servants
of the house saw the armed savages below and the flames
beginning to show against the wall. The street front of the
house was built of imposing stone, but the wings and back
of the courtyard were mostly timber. Silvester withdrew
from the window, pulled his tunic on back to front and ran
up the private stair to his mother's room. She had a candle lit
and was sitting on the edge of her bed cradling the Lady
Ariadne in her arms.

'It's the Huns,' he said. 'I saw them in the harbour. Or the
Khan's come.'

'Nasty vicious types,' said Nonna. 'I wouldn't trust them.'

'Why's Addie here?'

'She came to sleep with me after the feast. And *you* must
call her the Lady Ariadne.'

'I know. Will they come up here?'

'If they do they'll get the rough edge of my tongue.'

Silvester tried to pull himself together. Nonna was talking
like that – old-servant's chatter – thinking the ordinariness of
it would comfort the Lady Ariadne. Nonna adored her, but
had never understood her.

'We must hide,' he said.

'They'll look under the beds,' said Nonna. 'I know the
type.'

Her voice was shaking now. She was really frightened.

'Will Bubba let us into her den?' whispered the Lady
Ariadne.

Nonna cheered at once, and became her sturdy self.

'That's a notion,' she said, easing the Lady Ariadne upright.
'You go with Sillo, darling. Sillo and Bubba will look after
you.'

Once he'd been given his orders Silvester felt quite confi-
dent of carrying them out. It was acting on one's own that was

hard for a boy brought up to be a slave. He took the Lady Ariadne's hand – she was still in her green nightgown – and led her out into the chaos of the corridor. Through the sharp stink of smoke crowds of servants were jostling along, some of them still screaming, and some trying to drag chests of their belongings away from the fire towards the back of the house, although there was no way out there. It took him several minutes to struggle the few yards to the private stair, and when he reached it he found why – the eunuchs were trying to climb up from below, and so jamming the corridor. He shouted Lady Ariadne's name at Symmachus, who stared at him with unmeaning eyes but whose body somehow obeyed the habit of deference and squeezed to one side to let them pass. Nobody else was trying to go down; the panic of fire and sword swept through the house, each man's madness infecting the next. If the Lady Ariadne's hand had not been twined into Silvester's so tightly that it hurt he too might have joined in the madness. But now he was obeying his orders.

The lowest flight of the stairs was a well of dark peace, with panic above and murder outside. They stood panting and listening behind the door but heard only uninterpretable noises. Carefully Silvester eased the door open and stepped into the deep shadow of the fig tree that stood beside it. The far side of the courtyard, including any Huns, was hidden by the stream of smoke from the burning wing, and above the smoke, lit by flame, stood Holy John on his pillar with such a look of happiness on his face that he might have been drunk. The children slipped across the small gap to the cage. Silvester fumbled with the familiar catch and let them in, but only pulled the door to in case the smoke became unbreathable and they had to leave in a hurry.

Bubba greeted them with a deep, nervous growl. Stupid

though she was she knew that something unfamiliar was happening out in the courtyard. Silvester crouched by the stone arch of the den.

'It's all right, my beautiful,' he whispered. 'Nobody's going to hurt you. We'll look after you.'

Bubba grunted when she heard his voice. Her straw rustled as she lumbered towards him.

'Stay still, Addie,' he whispered. 'She'll want to smell who it is.'

He crawled into the total blackness and let himself be snuffled at; then he called Addie in for similar treatment.

'It's fresh straw yesterday,' he whispered. 'Bubba sleeps in that corner, so we'll . . .'

He was interrupted by a prod on his chest with blunt claws.

'No,' he whispered crossly, 'not now. We haven't come to play games, just to borrow your straw.'

Bubba growled.

'Oh, all right,' he said. 'Get into a corner, Addie, and keep out of the way.'

Wrestling with an affectionate bear who weighs four times what you do is an art; the important thing is to go limp if you find yourself being rolled on. Silvester had never tried it in the dark and his head was singing with buffets against the stone walls of the den before Bubba tired of the game as suddenly as she had demanded it. He tickled her arm-pits briefly and then she sneezed, dug herself into her straw, sneezed several times more and began to snore.

'Where are you?' he whispered.

'Here. I'm cold. There isn't any straw.'

'She's probably taken it all into her own corner. She does that. But she's asleep now, so she won't mind us coming too.'

Carefully he eased enough straw away to make a nest for

her against the warm bear-hide, helped her to find her way in, then heaped the straw back on her. There wasn't enough straw for another nest, nor any reason why a slave shouldn't shiver provided his mistress was warm. He sat with his back against the wall and his knees drawn under his chin and tried to guess what was happening by the noises outside and the changing light under the low rim of the arch. Now only a few of the guttural shouts of the attackers reached him, and the screams of the household seemed to be lessening, but the steady, coarse roaring of burning timber rose and rose. Twice, though, there were shouts that seemed to come from outside the cage; then he heard the flap of bare feet running. Sometimes the entrance went almost black, and at other times was strong orange with enough light reaching inside the den to pick out glitters from the straw. The racing of his heart and the gulping in his throat lessened. No one had found them yet. They would be all right.

The bright arch deadened and became dark. The air in the den, which had hitherto been sharp with burning but breathable, thickened. He gasped and lowered his head to the floor. Bubba coughed in her sleep, coughed again and woke growling.

'It's all right,' he choked. 'It'll go away. It's all right.'

She growled again.

'Sillo. I can't breathe. Where . . . What's happening?'

'The house is on fire. I haven't heard any Huns for some time, but we'd better stay here.'

'Where's Nonna? Mother?'

'Run away, I expect. They're all right.'

'I can't breathe. What's happening?'

She was still half held by her shocked sleep, but Silvester could hear the beginnings of panic in her voice.

'I must look,' she said.

'I'll go.'

'No. Stay there.'

He obeyed, as he had been trained to. He heard the sudden rattle of straw as she left her nest and groped for the entrance of the den. In any case, he thought, there was no danger in all this smoke – but the wind must have shifted for suddenly he saw her shape sharp against the orange arch of the den. He was going to shout a warning, but then the arch blacked out completely; Bubba, moving with a bear's silence, had followed the Lady Ariadne and now squatted growling in the entrance of the den. Beyond her the Lady Ariadne began to scream.

'Help! Sillo! Help! Help! Help!'

Silvester kicked and pummelled at Bubba's unfeeling back until with a harsh grunt she edged forward into the cage. Silvester rushed out. The Hun who had the Lady Ariadne by the arm was backing away from the bear, not realizing that Bubba was just as alarmed by him. Silvester flung himself at the man without thought, hitting at his body and kicking at his legs but from too close to do him any harm. It was like trying to fight a tree-trunk. For a moment he saw a hairy arm in front of him, so he bit hard at it and tasted blood. The man bellowed, and then Silvester found himself hurtling across the cage and crashing into the wall of the den. He collapsed to his knees, sick with black pain, but managed to struggle up, shaking his head. As his vision cleared he saw the Hun stoop to pick something off the floor, a kind of satchel; the man had never let go of the Lady Ariadne, so he had no spare hand for his weapons. Silvester steadied himself against the wall for another useless attack but at that moment Bubba gave a deep growl, rose on her hind legs and lurched forward. Tethered to the rails of the cage two of the Lord Celsus's town horses reared and plunged with terror. With a desperate quick movement the Hun swung his satchel at the bear. Silvester heard a heavy thud and saw Bubba collapse backwards, put her paws to her snout and start weeping. Once again he rushed forward, hoping at least to give Bubba time to recover from that lucky blow on the only place where she could be hurt at all – after that she'd be really dangerous to the Hun. He saw, beneath the bead-fringed turban, the man's face grinning with the lust of an easy fight, but he never saw the satchel looping back to hit him on the return stroke. For an instant, in a pain-filled and tumbling world, he noticed the top of Holy John's pillar through a rift in the smoke, empty. 'That's all wrong,' he thought. Then the dark took him.

J. Meade Falkner

MOONFLEET

A boy I know asked that his tenth birthday treat should be to visit Fleet, in Dorset, the place where *Moonfleet* was written. So we went. We found the church where John Trenchard was trapped in the vault with the smuggler's loot and the broken coffin of the giant Blackbeard (said to contain a certain great treasure), and we walked on the cliffs where John made his escape from the Revenue-men after a desperate shoot-out. Later we went to the Isle of Wight and found the well in Carisbrooke Castle where the diamond was supposed to be hidden. And that's just the beginning of one of the best stories of smuggling, imprisonment, slavery and shipwreck ever written. It's also the story of a wonderful friendship between John and Elzevir, the dour innkeeper, who shares all his adventures.

Here's John, remembering the time he was trapped in the vault.

* * *

They must have found glasses, though I could not remember to have seen any in the vault, for a minute later fugleman Ratsey spoke again –

'Now, lads, glasses full and bumpers for a toast. And here's to Blackbeard, to Father Blackbeard, who watches over our treasure better than he did over his own; for were it not the fear of him that keeps off idle feet and prying eyes, we should have the gaugers in, and our store ransacked twenty times.'

So he spoke, and it seemed there was a little halting at first, as of men not liking to take Blackbeard's name in Blackbeard's place, or raise the Devil by mocking at him. But then some of the bolder shouted 'Blackbeard', and so the more timid chimed in, and in a minute there were a score of voices calling 'Blackbeard, Blackbeard', till the place rang again.

Then Elzevir cried out angrily, 'Silence. Are you mad, or has the liquor mastered you? Are you Revenue-men that you dare shout and roister? or contrabandiers with the lugger in the offing, and your life in your hand? You make noise enough to wake folk in Moonfleet from their beds.'

'Tut, man,' retorted Ratsey testily, 'and if they waked, they would but pull the blankets tight about their ears, and say 'twas Blackbeard piping his crew of lost Mohunes to help him dig for treasure.'

Yet for all that 'twas plain that Block ruled the roost, for there was silence for a minute, and then one said, 'Ay, Master Elzevir is right; let us away, the night is far spent, and we have nothing but the sweeps to take the lugger out of sight by dawn.'

So the meeting broke up, and the torchlight grew dimmer,

and died away as it had come in a red flicker on the roof, and the footsteps sounded fainter as they went up the passage, until the vault was left to the dead men and me. Yet for a very long time – it seemed hours – after all had gone I could hear a murmur of distant voices, and knew that some were talking at the end of the passage, and perhaps considering how the landslip might best be restored. So while I heard them thus conversing I dared not descend from my perch, lest someone might turn back to the vault, though I was glad enough to sit up, and ease my aching back and limbs. Yet in the awful blackness of the place even the echo of these human voices seemed a kindly and blessed thing, and a certain shrinking loneliness fell on me when they ceased at last and all was silent. Then I resolved I would be off at once, and get back to the moonlight bed that I had left hours ago, having no stomach for more treasure-hunting, and being glad indeed to be still left with the treasure of life.

Thus, sitting where I was, I lit my candle once more, and then clambered across that great coffin which, for two hours or more, had been a mid-wall of partition between me and danger. But to get out of the niche was harder than to get in; for now that I had a candle to light me, I saw that the coffin, though sound enough to outer view, was wormed through and through, and little better than a rotten shell. So it was that I had some ado to get over it, not daring either to kneel upon it or to bring much weight to bear with my hand, lest it should go through. And now having got safely across, I sat for an instant on that narrow ledge of the stone shelf which projected beyond the coffin on the vault side, and made ready to jump forward on to the floor below. And how it happened I know not, but there I lost my balance, and as I slipped the candle flew out of my grasp. Then I clutched at the coffin to save myself, but my hand went clean through it, and so I came to the ground in a cloud of dust and splinters; having only got hold of a wisp of seaweed, or a handful of those draggled funeral trappings which were strewn about this place. The floor of the vault was sandy; and so, though I fell crookedly, I took but little harm beyond the shaking; and soon, pulling myself together, set to strike my flint and blow the match into a flame to search for the fallen candle. Yet all the time I kept in my fingers this handful of light stuff; and when the flame burnt up again I held the thing against the light, and saw that it was no wisp of seaweed, but something black and wiry. For a moment, I could not gather what I had hold of, but then gave a start that nearly sent the candle out, and perhaps a cry, and let it drop as if it were red-hot iron, for I knew that it was a man's beard.

Now when I saw that, I felt a sort of throttling fright, as though one had caught hold of my heartstrings; and so many and such strange thoughts rose in me, that the blood went pounding round and round in my head, as it did once afterwards when I was fighting with the sea and near drowned. Surely to have in hand the beard of any dead man in any place was bad enough, but worse a thousand times in such a place as this, and to know on whose face it had grown. For, almost before I fully saw what it was, I knew it was that black beard which had given Colonel John Mohune his nickname, and this was his great coffin I had hid behind.

Nicholas Fisk

TRILLIONS

Almost all Nicholas Fisk's stories have a science-fiction theme, either strange beings from outer space invade our planet, or we are summoned into theirs, as in *Space Hostages* (the first of his books printed in Puffins).

Grinny is about a sinister old lady who turns up at the front door of a perfectly normal household and hypnotizes everyone into believing she is a lost aunt. However, Nicholas Fisk is a great believer in clever children, so it's almost always a bright boy with a scientific mind who works things out.

I was torn between showing you an extract from this or another of his books, *A Rag, a Bone and a Hank of Hair*, but the plot of that is so complicated that I'm not sure any extract would give you a proper picture of the story, so I can only recommend it.

The book I *have* chosen is also full of ingenious surprises. It begins when millions and billions of diamond-like pieces of grit suddenly invade, first one small town, then turn up all over the world. They appear to be indestructible and have extraordinary powers. They build on each other so that they can make walls or cities, or such trivial things as bracelets – indeed, they can follow any pattern that is set them. The army regards them as enemies, and 'Icarus', an ex-space explorer, is mystified, but one boy, Scott, discovers he can actually communicate with them mentally. Here he is having his first go at it.

* * *

Icarus limped away, fast. Scott was left wondering.

He stayed wondering all day and continued wondering in bed that night.

'We'll never understand, never!' Icarus had said. What had he meant? Could you 'understand' a honey-bee? Perhaps he had meant, 'We'll never get through, establish contact, be useful to each other.' Honey-bees were useful to humans, so humans made themselves useful to honey bees. Give a hive, take some honey.

The trouble was that Trillions had nothing to offer us and we had nothing to offer them.

And yet, thought Scott, Trillions 'try'. They imitate, make shapes, appear to want to play our game. While all we do is talk about them, write about them, make big newspaper and TV stories about them. Trillions try: we don't.

Scott got into bed and looked around him. There was a dusting of Trillions on the window sill and a powdering of them on the floor. He got out of bed and opened the window. The window ledge was coated inches deep with Trillions. He scooped them up with his hands and put them on the sheet of drawing paper on his table. Soon he had a big heap of Trillions. He sat on the edge of his bed staring at them.

Aliens.

There was a scrawling mark on the paper. Some Trillions were busily beginning to reproduce the mark. Scott watched for a little while, sighed and went back to his bed. The Trillions puzzled him, Icarus puzzled him. He got into bed and turned out the light.

In the darkness, he thought he could just hear the very faint scratch and scrabble of the Trillions as they linked and climbed over each other. Scott turned over in bed and tried to ignore the tiny sounds.

Ah! he thought, I am falling asleep. Gratefully, he allowed the familiar fall-asleep processes of his brain to take over. Colours, pictures, snatches of rhyme came into his head from nowhere. He welcomed them. Soon the screen of his brain would go dark and he would sleep.

> Charlie Chaplin went to France
> To teach the natives how to dance

said his brain. Children skipping. Rope twirls, skinny legs jump.

> First he did the rumba
> Then he did the kicks
> Then he did the turnabout
> Then he did the splits

said his brain. But Scott found himself replying, 'No!' He turned over again and his eyes opened. What was wrong?

'Kicks' and 'splits' did not rhyme.

He started another rhyme.

A,B,C,D,E,F,G
That's what teacher said to me

ABC! Teacher! He sat up in bed, wide awake; switched on the light and went to work.

It took him a week to teach the Trillions their ABC. A week that seemed endless. A week that made Scott think that if the Trillions had any intelligence, they were very clever at hiding it.

His method was simple. He wrote an A and the Trillions 'formed' to imitate it. When they were half-way to completing their imitation, he wrote more A's. This confused their purpose. Some Trillions would break away from the A already half-formed to enlist in the armies making new A's. They became so confused that often A's would be formed without the Trillions following a pattern. Eventually, he could write one single small A, watch too many Trillions queueing to form it, scatter the heap and stand back: within minutes, there would be small A's everywhere.

The B's, C's, D's – all the letters of the alphabet. By the end of the week, they could form words. Scott would write WORD once: the Trillions would swarm around the writing: then disperse themselves into groups to make WORD WORD WORD WORD WORD WORD WORD, all over the floor.

At this stage, Scott collected more Trillions from the streets and tried to make them perform the same trick. They could not at first. They had to blend themselves into the mass of trained Trillions. Then they could perform.

'So my trained Trillions are different from just any old Trillions,' thought Scott. 'They can learn. The trouble is, they have no idea of the meaning of what they've learned. They can write WORD without knowing what a Word is. How can I teach them that?'

*

School routines were broken up. School in the morning: Trillions in the afternoon. Each day Scott's team spent three hours in the noisy streets, where the loudspeakers were always pouring out their mixture of soothing music and barked commands and the trucks roared by and the soldiers worked at nothing in particular and the journalists and TV crews went about their mysteries.

This was all wasted time.

More of Scott's hours were taken up with eating, sleeping, being a member of a family. This was wasted time too. All Scott wanted was to get back to his Trillions spelling-bee and to the problem of making the Trillions understand what writing was *for*.

He found the answer by accident.

During one 'lesson', he had the radio on. He worked so long and late that by the time the lesson was finished, the station had closed down. All that remained on the air was a single whining note. He turned the radio off. The sound annoyed him.

Immediately, the Trillions slowed down. He tried to get them working again, but it was as if they were on strike.

He turned on the radio. The whistling note sounded. The Trillions busily returned to work.

Excited, Scott got out his xylophone – a good toy instrument he had never wished to throw away. He found the note on the xylophone that corresponded to the note sounding from the radio; turned the radio off; and played the xylophone note instead.

The Trillions were happy with it. They went on working, making R's.

Scott bent down and busily destroyed all the R's with his hands. The Trillions were now just so much dust, all over the floor. Then he sounded the xylophone note and kept sounding it. Slowly at first, then faster and faster, the Trillions began to form R's.

His mother appeared in the doorway, half asleep and wearing her nightdress. 'Scott . . . What *are* you doing? For goodness' sake, it's long after midnight . . .'

'Sorry, Mother, I was trying something out.'

'Well, try it out tomorrow! Whatever it is, it can't be so important that –'

'It is important, very important –' Scott blurted out. And immediately wished he had not.

She stood looking at him, uncertainly. His face seemed to her suddenly older, and unfamiliar. What *was* he up to?

'You can't carry the whole world on your shoulders, Scott . . .'

'Of course not, Mother. Goodnight.'

*

Had anyone been able to carry the world on their shoulders at this time, he would have found it an uncomfortable burden. Trillions fell and 'formed' their strange, often frightening, shapes: the world got in a temper, partly from fear but mostly from habit. Primitive tribes squatted on the ground, made sacrifices and blamed their gods. Grown-up nations sat round tables, made speeches and blamed each other for all kinds of things having nothing to do with Trillions.

In Harbourtown, still more Trillions fell – a great storm shower of them. And the Major announced over the loudspeakers a major offensive against the Trillions, centred on an Exterminator – a machine that was to destroy the Trillions fed into it. Meanwhile, all Trillion truck teams were to report for duty, immediately. So Scott could not start until evening.

He took his sheets of white paper and scattered Trillions over them. Some of the Trillions shifted and moved without purpose.

He sounded the note that meant R on the xylophone. The Trillions formed R's. Scott scattered them before the letters were formed, then sounded the note again.

'It all depends on whether they *like* work,' he murmured to himself. Once again, the Trillions were forming the letter R. As long as the note sounded, they worked fast and hard. Scott scattered them again. 'R means the note – the note means R. Go on, blast you! R means the note – the note means R.'

There was silence. Scott would not sound the note. The Trillions would not form.

'Go on, go *on* . . .!' grated Scott. He sounded the xylophone, then muted the note with his finger. Some Trillions moved, then subsided. It went on like this for an hour, for two hours. Scott found his jaws were aching: he had been clenching his teeth in the effort to force his will on the Trillions – to point a ray from his mind, almost, at the little glittering heaps.

At last they obeyed. Though Scott had sounded the note only in his mind, there was a sudden scurry of movement on one piece of paper. Some Trillions were forming. Scott craned towards them, growling 'Go on, go on, go on! R! R!'

The Trillions formed an R. Scott let out a great shout of 'Whoopee!' Then 'thought' the note harder still.

All the Trillions formed, furiously. There were R's everywhere! Scott tried to reach his own shoulder to pat himself on the back. He couldn't, and giggled instead. Then he sat down to work out the next steps in the Trillions' education.

'They like work,' he said to himself. 'They want a master – someone to tell them what to do. They've learned. Fine. And now . . . what?'

Leon Garfield

SMITH

Every one of Leon Garfield's books is bursting with action. Many people think his first one, *Jack Holborn*, is as good as *Treasure Island*. My two favourites are *John Diamond* and *Smith*. I've chosen to tell you about *Smith* chiefly because he's such an endearing fellow.

In fact, he's a twelve-year-old pickpocket living in London in the nineteenth century. His best friend is a highwayman, and his favourite 'business' spot is Ludgate Hill, where coaches, carriages and curricles are locked from morning to night in such horrible confusion that sometimes wealthy travellers (Smith's natural prey) get out to walk to their destination.

One morning Smith sees two men murder one of his victims,

and discovers that all he stole was a document which he cannot read and which lands him in such horrors as Newgate Gaol. But here he is at the start of his troubles actually doing a good deed!

* * *

'Watch out! Watch out! Oh! Oh! Ah!'

At the very moment Smith had turned into the alley a gentleman had come out of it. They met and, though the gentleman was tall and stout and huge beside Smith, he was struck with such speed and force that he fell with an angry, frightened cry.

Smith struggled to his feet, was about to rush on, when a hand grasped at his ankle.

'Let go!' he shouted.

'Damn you, no! Help me, first –'

Smith glared wildly down. He saw the gentleman's face, grey as a puddle. His eyes were sunken and dark: no spark of light in them.

'Help me up! Help me, I say! For pity's sake, sir! Can't you see I'm blind?'

'A blind man!' gasped Smith. 'Oh Gawd! A mole-in-the-hole!'

The gin's tempest dropped abruptly away and left a glum wreckage behind, bleak and forlorn in the freezing night.

A boy – a child, thought the blind man, uneasily. Most likely a young thief. Most likely he'll rob me and run off – frightened out of his miserable wits. Oh God! How am I to get home?

'If you let go me ankle,' muttered Smith, 'I'll help you up; that's if you're really blind. Can you see me?'

The gentleman shook his head.

'What am I doing now?' asked Smith, pulling a hideous face.

'I don't know – I don't know! I swear I'm blind! Look at my eyes! Any light in 'em? Look for my smoked spectacles. They're somewhere about. Look for –'

'What am I doing now?' demanded Smith pulling another, even more monstrous face; for he'd help no one who didn't need it.

The blind man loosed his hold on Smith's ankle and heaved himself up on one elbow. He'd lost his hat and his wig was awry, but otherwise he'd suffered no harm. He began to feel the adjacent cobbles for his possessions. Smith watched him and his face returned to normal, but as a last measure he fished inside his coat and pulled out the document.

'What have I got in me hand?' he asked gruffly.

The blind man sighed. 'My life, my boy . . . my life's in your hand.'

Smith scowled and put away the document. 'Here you are, Mister Mole-in-the-hole! Here's me 'and, then! Up with you! Up on yer pins! And 'ere's your 'at and stick and black spectacles . . . though why you wears 'em foxes me! My, but you're a real giant of a gent! Did you know it?'

This last as the blind man stood up and fairly towered over the helpful Smith.

'Thank you, boy. Now – tell me if I'm in the street or the alley and I'll give you a guinea for your pains.'

'You're on the corner.'

'Facing which way?'

'The Lord knows! I've been sick meself.'

'Fever?'

'Half a pint o' gin.'

Suddenly, Smith felt a strong desire to confide in the blind man. After all – it could do no harm.

'Smith,' he said, and held out one hand to be shook while with the other he guided the blind man's hand to meet it.

'Smith. 'Unted, 'ounded, 'omeless and part gin-sodden. Smith. Twelve years old. That's me. Very small, but wiry, as they say. Dark 'aired and lately residing in the Red Lion Tavern off Saffron 'ill. Smith.'

Helplessly, the blind man smiled . . . and his questing hand grasped Smith's firmly.

'Mansfield,' he said. 'Blind as a wall for these past twelve years. Well-to-do – but not much enjoying it. Mansfield. Residing at Number Seven Vine Street under the care of a daughter. Mansfield. Believe it or not – a magistrate!'

'Gawd!' gasped Smith. 'Oo'd 'ave thought I'd ever be shaking 'ands with a bleeding Justice?'

If Mr Mansfield heard he was too gentlemanly to remark on it. Instead, he fumbled in his coat for the promised guinea.

'And now, just point me toward the church that should stand at one end of the street and the guinea's yours, Smith, with my deepest thanks.'

Smith obliged – and took the guinea.

'Seems a lot for a little,' he said.

'Good night, Smith.'

'Same to you, Mister Mansfield, J.P.'

He watched the blind man tap his way down the street, bumping, here and there, into the posts – and sometimes raising his hat to them and mumbling, 'Sorry, good sir . . . couldn't see you . . . so sorry.'

Smith smiled indulgently and was about to make off, when a strangely familiar feeling of pity stirred in him. He had been reminded of the murdered old gentleman. He scowled at his own indecision, stuck his ancient pipe defiantly in his mouth, and hastened in the blind man's wake.

'That you, Smith?'

Smith grunted.

'Didn't expect you –'

'Going the same way meself.'

'To Vine Street?'

'Thereabouts.'

'Glad to hear it, Smith.'

Smith grunted again. 'Oh well – 'ere's me 'and, then . . .
you old blind Justice, you! Just tell me where to turn and
where to cross and I'll see you 'ome safe an' sound. After all –
I ain't done much for that guinea.'

Mr Mansfield found the offered hand and, once more,
grasped it. He sighed and reflected in his heart (which was far
from being as blind as his eyes) that it was an uncanny thing
to be the cause of kindness in others.

Vine Street lay about twenty minutes away. Mr Mansfield
had strolled far that night, having a troublesome problem
that gnawed him. But now, holding Smith's thin hand, the
problem sank somewhat.

'Were it a sickness?' asked Smith after a while.

'My blindness, d'you mean? No. Lost my sight when a
house burned down. Lost my wife as well. A costly fire, that!'

'Oh.'

'Take the next turning on the left, Smith.'

'What's it like – being blind?'

'Dark, Smith. Very dark. What's it like having eyes?'

'The moon's gone in again – so we're two of a kind, Mister
Mansfield, you an' me.'

The blind magistrate felt somewhat taken down – but was
cautious not to show it. Twelve years of his misfortune had
taught him that a bland face was the best security for one in
his situation and that, for a blind man to frown, scowl or
laugh, even, was like a fool discharging his pistol wildly in
the night. The Lord knew who'd be hit by it.

'If you can see a new-built church with a round tower,
cross in front of it and walk with it to your right.'

Smith obliged. Hand in hand they passed by the church –
a very curious pair indeed: small Smith, half a pace ahead,
and huge, stout Mr Mansfield walking somewhat sideways
and behind – for Smith tended to pull, rather.

'Vine Street is the next street that crosses this one. My
house is to the right. I'll be safe enough now, Smith.'

'No trouble. I'm going the same way. To the door, Mister
Mansfield.'

They came to Vine Street. Said Mr Mansfield: 'If you've
nought better to do, will you come in and take a bite of late
supper with me, Smith?'

'Don't mind if I do, Mister Mansfield.'

'Care to stay the night, Smith?'

'Don't mind if I do, Mister Mansfield.'

'Any family, Smith?'

'Sisters. Two of 'em.'

'Likely to worry?'

'Not much.'

'Then it's settled?'

'Just as you say, Mister Mansfield.'

'Anything else I can do for you, Smith?'

Smith sighed ruefully. The only thing he really wanted,
Mr Mansfield was unable to provide.

'No, thank you, Mister Mansfield. You done all you can.'

They came towards the door of Number Seven. In spite of
himself Smith grinned at the irony of his situation. Of all the
men in the town to bump into and befriend, he'd lit on the
one who was blind and so could never teach him to read!

Alan Garner

ELIDOR

Alan Garner's first book, *The Weirdstone of Brisingamen*, was so
compelling that everyone wanted to rush off and visit Alderley
Edge, where the story told of a band of knights sleeping in the
caves of Fundindelve, waiting to be summoned to save the world
from the malice of Nastrond. But I've chosen this, his third book,
because in it he's managed to combine the ancient and modern
worlds so very convincingly.

Elidor is a condemned, lost world. Roland, Helen, Nicholas and
David discover it while exploring a ruined church in Manchester,
and they bring back to their own world four treasures, knowing
that Elidor may be saved if they can keep these safe – but how can

they? Is it just static that makes the television set howl? Are the patches on the attic wall only damp, or are they sinister shadows, and how can shadows stand alone in the middle of a garden anyway?

Any of you who like a little chilling fear with your fantasy will want to read this book to find out the answers. Here is Roland having his first meeting with King Malebron.

* * *

It was a man with yellow hair. He wore a golden cloak, a golden shield on his arm. In his hand was a spear, and its head was like flame.

'Is there light in Gorias?' he said.

'Help me,' said Roland. 'The glove.'

'Is there light?' said the man.

'The glove,' said Roland. 'Helen.'

He could think of nothing, do nothing. His head rang with heartbeats, and the hill spun. He lay on the turf. And slowly a quietness grew, like sleep, and in the quietness he could hold the glove so that it was not a grappling hand. The man stood, unmoving, and the words came back to Roland as he had heard them before the table of the cloth of gold. The table: the castle: and the man – nothing else showed the colour of life in all this wasted land.

The man's face was slender, with high cheekbones, and the locks of his hair swept backwards as if in a wind.

'Who are you?' whispered Roland.

'Malebron of Elidor.'

'What's that?' said Roland.

'Is there light in Gorias?'

'I don't understand,' said Roland.

The man began to climb the hill, but he was lame. One

foot dragged. He did not look to see whether Roland was following.

'Are you hurt?' said Roland.

'Wounds do not heal in Elidor.'

'There was a fiddler,' said Roland. 'He'd got a bad leg. I had to help him –'

'Now that you have come,' said Malebron, 'I need not skulk in beggar's rags again. Look.' They were at the top of the mound. He pointed to the distant ruined keep.

'There is Findias, Castle of the South. And the forest, Mondrum: the fairest wood in Elidor.'

'It was you?' said Roland. 'You? Then you must have been watching me all the time! You just dumped me by the cliff – and left me – and what have you done with Helen? And David and Nick? What's happened?' shouted Roland.

But his voice had no power in the air, and Malebron waited, ignoring him, until Roland stopped.

'And Falias, and Murias,' he said. 'Castles of the West and of the North. There on the plain beneath.'

He spoke the names of castle and wood as if they were precious things, not three black fangs and a swamp.

'But Gorias, in the east – what did you see?'

'I – saw a castle,' said Roland. 'It was all golden – and alive. Then I saw the glove. She –'

'You have known Mondrum, and those ravaged walls,' said Malebron: 'the grey land, the dead sky. Yet what you saw in Gorias once shone throughout Elidor, from the Hazel of Fordruim, to the Hill of Usna. So we lived, and no strife between us. Now only in Gorias is there light.'

'But where's –?' said Roland.

'The darkness grew,' said Malebron. 'It is always there. We did not watch, and the power of night closed on Elidor. We had so much of ease that we did not mark the signs – a crop

blighted, a spring failed, a man killed. Then it was too late –
war, and siege, and betrayal, and the dying of the light.'

'Where's Helen?' said Roland.

Malebron was silent, then he said quietly, 'A maimed king
and a mumbling boy! Is it possible?'

'I don't know what you're talking about,' said Roland.
'Where's Helen? That's her glove, and the thumb's stuck in
the rock.'

'Gloves!' cried Malebron. 'Look about you! I have endured,
and killed, only in the belief that you would come. And you
have come. But you will not speak to me of gloves! You will
save this land! You will bring back light to Elidor!'

'Me!'

'There is no hope but you.'

'Me,' said Roland. 'I'm no use. What could I do?'

'Nothing,' said Malebron, 'without me. And without you,
I shall not live. Alone, we are lost: together, we shall bring
the morning.'

'All this,' said Roland, 'was like the golden castle – like you
sang? The whole country?'

'All,' said Malebron.

'– Me?'

'You.'

Findias . . . Falias . . . Murias . . . Gorias. The Hazel of
Fordruim . . . the Forest of Mondrum . . . the Hill of Usna.
Men who walked like sunlight. Cloth of gold. Elidor –
Elidor.

Roland thought of the gravel against his cheek. This is true:
now: I'm here. And only I can do it. He says so. He says I
can bring it all back. Roland Watson, Fog Lane, Manchester
20. What about that? Now what about that!

'How do you know I can?' said Roland.

'I have watched you prove your strength,' said Malebron.

'Without that strength you would not have lived to stand here at the heart of the darkness.'

'Here?' said Roland. 'It's just a hill –'

'It is the Mound of Vandwy,' said Malebron. 'Night's dungeon in Elidor. It has tried to destroy you. If you had not been strong you would never have left the stone circle. But you were strong, and I had to watch you prove your strength.'

'I don't see how a hill can do all this,' said Roland. 'You can't fight a hill.'

'No,' said Malebron. 'We fight our own people. Darkness needs no shape. It uses. It possesses. This Mound and its stones are from an age long past, yet they were built for blood, and were supple to evil.'

Roland felt cold and small on the hill.

'I've got to find the others first,' he said.

'It's the same thing,' said Malebron.

'No, but they'll be better than me: they're older. And I've got to find them, anyway.'

'It is the same thing,' said Malebron. 'Listen. You have seen Elidor's four castles. Now each castle was built to guard a Treasure, and each Treasure holds the light of Elidor. They are the seeds of flame from which all this land was grown. But Findias and Falias and Murias are taken, and their Treasures lost.

'You are to save these Treasures. Only you can save them.'

'Where are they?' said Roland. 'And you said there were four Treasures: so where's the other?'

'I hold it,' said Malebron. 'The Spear of Ildana from Gorias. Three castles lie wasted: three Treasures are in the Mound. Gorias stands. You will go to Vandwy, and you will bring back light to Elidor.'

Jean Craighead George

JULIE OF THE WOLVES

There are two different kinds of animal stories: those where animals are made to talk and behave like people (anthropomorphic, if you fancy exact descriptions), and those telling about animals as they really are, like the famous *Tarka the Otter*. I have many favourites like this, including *Joe and the Gladiator* by Catherine Cookson, *The Otter's Tale* by Gavin Maxwell and *Break for Freedom* by Ewan Clarkson. This one, though, is unlike any other I've ever read, and it says something so important about our attitude to animals that I want everyone to know about it.

Julie's Eskimo name is Miyax. She is only twelve, alone, lost and starving in the Alaskan tundra – her only hope lies in being accepted and fed by a wolf pack. But this means days of patience, watching their ways and learning their body language. This story is about how she survives for nearly two years; how the great black leader wolf, Amaroq, takes her under his protection, how she learns to make herself a sleigh out of frozen caribou skins, to trap the baby lemmings for food, 'sing' wolf songs and even sew up the wounds of Kapu, her wolf-cub friend. Every chapter, every page, tells us something new and fascinating about Eskimo legends and wolf-lore, and although the end is not quite as happy as one could wish, it will be impossible not to feel liking and admiration, not only for Miyax but for the wolves who care for her.

Here is just one of the exciting adventures and dangers which happened to her every day.

* * *

She cut the rest of the caribou leg into bite-size chunks and stored them in her sled. Then, adjusting her mittens in the darkness, she took a bearing on the North Star and started off.

Her icy sled jingled over the wind-swept lakes and she sang as she travelled. The stars grew brighter as the hours passed and the tundra began to glow, for the snow reflected each twinkle a billion times over, turning the night to silver. By this light she could see the footsteps of the wolves. She followed them, for they were going her way.

Just before sunrise the wolf prints grew closer together. They were slowing down for the sleep. She felt their presence everywhere, but could not see them. Running out on a lake, she called. Shadows flickered on the top of a frost heave. There they were! She quickened her stride. She would camp with them and do the dance of the-wolf-pup-feeding-the-lost-girl for Kapu. He would surely run in circles when he saw it.

The shadows flattened as she walked, and by the time she reached the other shore they had turned into sky and vanished. There were no footsteps in the snow to say her pack had been there and she knew the Arctic dawn had tricked her eyes. 'Frost spirits,' she said, as she pitched her tent by the lake and crawled into bed.

*

By the yellow-green light of the low noon sun Miyax could see that she had camped on the edge of the wintering grounds of the caribou. Their many gleaming antlers formed a forest on the horizon. Such a herd would certainly attract her pack. She crawled out of bed and saw that she had pitched her tent in a tiny forest about three inches high. Her heart pounded excitedly, for she had not seen one of these willow groves since Nunivak. She was making progress, for they grew, not near Barrow, but in slightly warmer and wetter lands near the coast. She smelled the air in the hopes that it bore the salty odour of the ocean, but it smelled only of the cold.

The dawn cracked and hummed and the snow was so fine that it floated above the ground when a breeze stirred. Not a bird passed overhead. The buntings, long-spurs, and terns were gone from the top of the world.

A willow ptarmigan, the chicken of the tundra, clucked behind her and whistled softly as it hunted seeds. The Arctic Circle had been returned to its permanent bird resident, the hardy ptarmigan. The millions of voices of summer had died down to one plaintive note.

Aha, ahahahahahaha! Miyax sat up, wondering what that was. Creeping halfway out of her bag, she peered into the sky to see a great brown bird manoeuvre its wings and speed west.

'A skua!' She was closer to the ocean than she thought, for

the skua is a bird of the coastal waters of the Arctic. As her eyes followed it, they came to rest on an oil drum, the sign-post of American civilization in the North. How excited she would have been to see this a month ago; now she was not so sure. She had her ulo and needles, her sled and her tent, and the world of her ancestors. And she liked the simplicity of that world. It was easy to understand. Out here she under-stood how she fitted into the scheme of the moon and stars and the constant rise and fall of life on the earth. Even the snow was part of her, she melted it and drank it.

Amaroq barked. He sounded as if he was no more than a quarter of a mile away.

'*Ow, ooo,*' she called. Nails answered, and then the whole pack howled briefly.

'I'm over here!' she shouted joyously, jumping up and down. 'Here by the lake.' She paused. 'You know that. You know everything about me all the time.'

The wind began to rise as the sun started back to the horizon. The lake responded with a boom that sounded like a pistol shot. The freeze was deepening. Miyax lit a fire and put on her pot. A warm stew would taste good and the smoke and flames would make the tundra home.

Presently Amaroq barked forcefully, and the pack answered. Then the royal voice sounded from another posi-tion, and Silver checked in from across the lake. Nails gave a warning snarl and the pups whispered in 'woofs'. Miyax shaded her eyes; her wolves were barking from points around a huge circle and she was in the middle. This was strange – they almost always stayed together. Suddenly Amaroq barked ferociously, his voice angry and authoritative. Silver yelped, then Nails and Kapu. They had something at bay.

She stepped on to the lake and skipped towards them. Half-way across she saw a dark head rise above the hill, and a beast with a head as large as the moon rose to its hind feet, massive paws swinging.

'Grizzly!' she gasped and stopped stone-still, as the huge animal rushed on to the ice. Amaroq and Nails leapt at its face and sprang away before the bear could strike. They were heading it off, trying to prevent it from crossing. The bear snarled, lunged forward, and galloped towards Miyax.

She ran towards her tent. The wind was in her face and she realized she was downwind of the bear, her scent blowing right to him. She darted off in another direction, for bears have poor eyesight and cannot track if they cannot smell. Slipping and sliding, she reached the south bank as the grizzly staggered forward, then crumpled to its knees and sat down. She wondered why he was not in hibernation. The wolves had been sleeping all day – they could not have wakened the bear. She sniffed the air to try to smell the cause, but only odourless ice crystals stung her nose.

The pack kept harassing the sleepy beast, barking and snarling, but with no intention of killing it. They were simply trying to drive it away – away from her, she realized.

Slowly the bear got to its feet and permitted itself to be herded up the lake bank and back to where it had come from. Reluctantly, blindly, it staggered before the wolves. Occasionally it stood up like a giant, but mostly it roared in the agony of sleepiness.

Yapping, barking, darting, the wolves drove the grizzly far out on the tundra. Finally they veered away and, breaking into a joyous gallop, dashed over the snow and out of sight. Their duty done, they were running – not to hunt, not to kill – but simply for fun.

Miyax was trembling. She had not realized the size and ferocity of the dark bear of the North, who is called 'grizzly' inland, and 'brown bear' along the coasts – *Ursus arctos*. Large ones, like the grizzly her wolves had driven away, weighed over a thousand pounds and stood nine feet tall when they reared. Miyax wiped a bead of perspiration from her forehead. Had he come upon her tent, with one curious sweep of his paw he would have snuffed out her life while she slept.

'Amaroq, Nails, Kapu,' she called. 'I thank you. I thank you.'

J. B. S. Haldane

MY FRIEND MR LEAKEY

When you are lucky enough to save the life of a genuine magician (not just the conjuring-trick kind), life is bound to become more interesting. So Professor Haldane (the author was a genuine Professor) wasn't really surprised when he went to dinner with Mr Leakey and had his meal cooked by a dragon and served by an octopus. Or when his Christmas stocking walked over and gave him an invitation to spend a day in Java.

In fact, Mr Leakey is a particularly satisfactory sort of friend because his magic is useful, as well as surprising.

* * *

The day after Boxing Day I went round to Mr Leakey's flat

after breakfast. This time the door was opened by Abdu'l Makkar, Mr Leakey's jinn. He was dressed as a footman, with brass buttons, and took my coat and hat to hang them up. The only odd thing about it was that he stood about two feet away and never touched my coat when he was taking it off. It felt rather queer, but I was accustomed to queer feelings in that house.

Mr Leakey greeted me warmly when I went into his room. So did Pompey the dragon, who was sitting on the fire. He started flapping his wings when I came in, which made the fire smoke, but Mr Leakey had only to pick up a magic wand which was lying on the table, and Pompey at once lay down quietly with his head between his paws.

'I thought we might go over to Java for lunch,' said my host, 'but there are a couple of things I want to do this morning. Would you like to come round with me? If not, stay here and smoke a pipe, and I'll arrange an entertainment for you.'

'I'll come out with you, if you're sure I shan't be in the way,' I answered.

'Oh no, I shall be delighted to have you with me, but you may have to become invisible, so you'd better practise here, because it feels rather funny the first time. Put this cap of darkness on, and walk round the room once or twice. If you look down you may feel giddy. So if you find you're losing your balance look straight in front of you.'

He handed me a black cap with a peak to it, about the shape of the paper hats you get out of a Christmas cracker. It was the blackest thing I have ever seen, not a bit the colour of ordinary black cloth or paper, but like the colour of a black hole. You could not see what it was made of, or whether it was smooth or rough. It didn't feel like cloth or anything ordinary, but like very soft warm india-rubber. I put it on, and at once my arm disappeared. Everything looked slightly

odd, and at first I couldn't think why. Then I saw that the
two ghostly noses which I always see without noticing them
were gone. I shut one of my eyes, as one does if one wants to
see one's nose more clearly. I felt my eye shut, but it made
no difference. Of course now that I was invisible my eyelids
and nose were quite transparent! Then I looked to where my
body and legs ought to have been, but of course I saw
nothing. I got a horrid giddy feeling and had to catch hold of
the table with an invisible hand. However I steadied myself
and looked straight in front of me, and quite soon I was able
to walk round the room easily enough.

'Put the cap in your pocket when we go out,' said my host.
'Then when you want to be invisible, put it on under your
hat. It will make that invisible all right, just like it does your
clothes.'

We went out into the street. This time no one was there in
the hall, but my hat and coat just flew off their pegs and put
themselves on to me.

'First,' said Mr Leakey as we got into a taxi, 'I'm going to
deal with a dog who is making a nuisance of himself. He bites
people, and unless I do something about it the police will have
him killed. But I'm going to do something about it. Then I'm
going to make a cheque invisible, and perhaps one or two
other little things. Of course one can't do magic on a big scale
in London. It would attract notice, and people would start
worrying me, which I don't like. But I like to be useful in a
small way. For example I think our taxi-driver would look
better without all those spots. Don't you?'

Certainly the driver had pimples enough on his face to
make an advertisement for one of those wonderful medicines
you read about in the newspapers. Mr Leakey took up his
umbrella, which had such a queer handle that I guessed at
once that it must really be a magic wand, and started twirling

it about. Through the front window of the taxi I could see two large pimples on the driver's neck suddenly fading away, and by the time we got to the address he had been given, his face was as smooth as a tomato, though he never seemed to notice anything happening.

Mr Leakey gave him a coin. ' 'Ere, guvnor, you've given me a farthing,' said the driver.

'Look again.'

'Well, I'm – 'aven't seen one of them since 1914.'

'Of course,' said Mr Leakey to me, as we walked away, 'I've got a magic purse, but you can only get gold out of it, not notes, because magic purses were invented long before printing. It's a nuisance. Before the First World War one could sometimes pay in gold, and no one was surprised, but now most people have never seen a real golden sovereign, or half a sovereign, which is what I gave the driver. Well, there aren't many people about; I think you might put your cap on. Of course it doesn't do to be invisible in a crowd. People bump into you, and get terribly frightened.'

I put my cap on and vanished. Mr Leakey pointed his magic umbrella at himself, and suddenly both he and the umbrella disappeared, except for the very tip of the umbrella, which seemed to go on walking along the street in a series of hops like a bird.

'Now,' he said, 'come after me into this garden, and see me deal with the dog. Shut the gate behind you. Don't stop him if he tries to bite either of us. He won't.'

As I shut the gate a large mongrel dog ran towards us growling. He had an angry but puzzled look, and soon stopped growling to sniff. Suddenly he seemed to make up his mind. I think most dogs, except greyhounds, pay more attention to smells than to what they see. Anyway this dog suddenly ran towards Mr Leakey. I could see where he was, because the end of his magic umbrella was visible. As the dog ran towards him, the end was lifted up, and a tiny puff of purplish smoke came out of it. The dog did not stop, but suddenly looked even more puzzled than before. Then Mr Leakey's left leg became visible from the knee downwards, and very odd it looked. The dog at last saw something to bite, and rushed at the leg snarling. Mr Leakey, or at least his left leg, stood quite still, and before I could stop him, the dog bit it. You know how a dog pulls his lips back when he is angry, so that you can see all his teeth. I could see that this dog had a very fine set. But when he bit Mr Leakey's trouser the teeth didn't go through it. They just bent. 'I've turned them into white india-rubber,' he said, 'all except four molars at the back. They'll be all right for grinding up dog biscuits. Ah, here's his master. I think I'll hide my leg again.' As the dog's owner, a very grumpy-looking man, came out, the leg vanished, but clearly Mr Leakey lifted it up, for he swung the dog up into the air, where he stayed for a time. I never saw a dog looking so funny. He hung in the air with his mouth wide open and all his teeth bent sideways. Then suddenly he dropped off, and went away with his tail between his legs.

The grumpy man stood stock still with his legs wide apart and his mouth opened in amazement. He hardly opened it any wider when he saw the handle of his garden gate turn, and the gate open and shut again behind us as we went out. When we went round the street corner we became visible again, which was rather a relief to me, because it is certainly odd to feel bits of oneself without seeing them. As we got into another taxi Mr Leakey said, 'If that man had any sense, which he hasn't, he'd make a fortune by showing Fido at fairs as The Rubber-Toothed Dog, and charging people sixpence to let him bite them.' By the way, if anyone who reads this does see a rubber-toothed dog at a fair, I wish they'd write to me, because I should like to meet Fido again, and see if he's got accustomed to his rubber teeth, like people get accustomed to false ones.

Cynthia Harnett

THE WOOL-PACK

Cynthia Harnett wrote cracking good stories which are also burst-ing with detail, all of it accurate (her last book, *The Writing on the Heath* took ten years of research). This story is about Nicholas Fetter-lock, a boy living in the fifteenth century. His father is a wool mer-chant, and his adventures happen because of dark and dirty dealings with foreign wool merchants and dishonest servants.

As well as the intriguing plot, this is a brilliant picture of life for a fourteen-year-old in the fifteenth century, which could be very frus-trating, with Nicholas constrained to unquestioning obedience to his parents; which makes it difficult for him to warn his father of the dangers to his trade, or object to an arranged marriage with eleven-year-old Cecily (who turns out to be a very jolly girl).

As a bonus, anyone visiting Burford (Oxfordshire), or travelling to Southampton can still discover many of the places Nicholas knew.

* * *

Now that the excitement of the shearing was over life settled into a dull routine. Master Richard expected Nicholas to make up for lost time, and kept him long hours at his books. Very little else happened. The customary midsummer fair on St John's feast, judged by the standards of Newbury, seemed little more than a glorified market-day, but it served to break the monotony. Mistress Fetterlock, also, disturbed the peace by insisting that Nicholas must write a letter to Cecily. She knew of a messenger going that way and the chance must not be missed.

For hours Nicholas sat in misery at his father's counter, scratching his nose with the end of his quill. When he appealed to Master Richard for help, the priest replied with a smile that love letters were outside his province, and Nicholas should follow the guidance of his heart. But Nicholas's heart offered no suggestions. At last, in despair, he submitted to his mother's control, and wrote at her dictation a letter based on a scribe's collection of model letters. It was full of fine phrases and began by addressing Cecily as his 'Worshipful mistress and most sweet cousin' ('cousin', he was told, being a useful term which could cover any tie). It commended her piously to the care of the blessed saints, told her that he took no pleasure in life until he might be with her again, and that he was her true lover and humble servant.

He grinned to himself as he scattered sand over the ink, remembering Cecily up a tree, Cecily running away to track the Lombards, Cecily stamping her foot at them at the Fair. He sealed the letter with his father's seal – the merchant's mark so despised by Mistress Fetterlock – and then tried to forget it as quickly as possible.

The reply came in less than a fortnight, written in a round, childish hand. He had not known for certain that Cecily could write. After all, many girls were not taught anything but the domestic arts. But flowery as the letter was, he recognized a touch of the real Cecily about it. She called Nicholas her 'well-beloved Valentine' and told him that if only he were satisfied with her she would be 'the merriest maiden alive'. He laughed aloud at that. Of a truth he was very well satisfied.

But he had not yet finished with his letter-writing. One evening Giles took him aside.

'You are a scholar, young master,' he began. 'Could you make a letter for me to your worshipful father?'

Nicholas stared at him. 'Has anything happened that is new?' he cried.

Giles shook his head. 'It is just that Leach is sending away the wool for Calais. Since I found the bearded sarplers I have done all in my power to delay it. I have discovered reason after reason why it could not go, hoping that the master would come back. But now Leach will wait no longer. He is the packer and I cannot stop him. But I shall sleep better o' nights when your father has been told. I am no scholar, Master Nicholas, and I would not trust this matter to a scribe.'

That was true. It would never do to bring a public letter-writer into it.

'I could write the letter,' said Nicholas. 'But how could we send it? My mother's messenger left yesterday. There will not be another this week.'

'I have thought of that,' replied the shepherd. 'There is a man who rides regularly for the Lord Abbot of Gloucester. He is courting my niece, and he will surely call at the barber's tomorrow on his way to London.'

Nicholas sighed. There seemed to be no help for it. And if the letter was to go in the morning there was no time to spare. Giles would have to tell him what to say, so he took the shepherd home with him, praying that somehow they would be able to elude his mother's eye. His prayer was answered, for in the town they met Mistress Fetterlock on her way to Vespers with her primer, her rosary, and, as usual, Bel tucked away under her sleeve. Nicholas sighed with relief. His mother always lingered over her devotions. They would be undisturbed for an hour at least.

The letter itself was not nearly so difficult as the one to Cecily had been. He knew how to address his father; he had been properly taught. And what he had to say was not difficult either. When he had finished his composition he read it over to Giles.

To my worshipful master Thomas Fetterlock Merchant of the Staple, at London in Mart Lane be this delivered.

Right honourable and worshipful father. In the most humble wise I recommend me unto you, whom I beseech Almighty God to preserve in prosperous health and heart's comfort, desiring of you your daily blessing.

Sir, if it pleaseth you to know, your servant Giles commends him to you and hath prayed me tell you that he hath opened diverse sarplers of your Cots wool the which were packed under the hand of Simon Leach your packer and men of his trust. Giles hath found some of these sarplers sorely bearded with refuse, also one with wool fells feigned like good clip. The sarplers have set forth for Calais and he could in no wise hinder them.

Wherefore I humbly beseech you to let me know your pleasure how that you would have matters ordered as shall be for your worship and profit. No more, good father, but Almighty Jesu have you in His blessed keeping. Written at Burford on St Mary Magdalen's day. Anno Hen. VII 8°. By your own Son,

Nicholas Fetterlock

Giles was open-mouthed with admiration, and Nicholas himself felt that he had done well. He folded the letter, kindled a taper with his father's tinder-box, and sealed it with his father's seal. Then he gave it to Giles.

Well, it was done. He wondered if his father would answer it. He counted on his fingers; it would be six days at the very least before he could hear, and then only if his father sent a messenger immediately.

But the answer was more prompt than even he dreamed. On the evening of the fifth day his father arrived home.

*

Coming in to supper in the belief that, as was the recent custom, he would sup with his mother in her bower, it was a shock to find both parents already seated in the dining parlour. Nicholas was red with embarrassment as he made his obedience, but his father did not refer to any business. Throughout the meal he chatted of Calais and London, and the news of the town from each. Nicholas began to wonder if the messenger from Gloucester had been faithless after all. But at the end of supper, as he toyed with his goblet of wine, he smiled at Nicholas.

'You write an excellent letter, my son,' he remarked pleasantly.

'Letter,' said his wife sharply. 'What letter? I did not know that the boy had written to you.'

'A letter of business,' Master Fetterlock told her quietly, 'just from one merchant to another. The matter in it must wait until the morrow. Ay-de-mi, but I'm weary. Wife, with your leave, I'll to my bed.'

Though Nicholas was up early, his father was earlier still, and had somehow caused Giles to be fetched to the counting-house, even at that hour. Nicholas could hear their voices as he passed the door. It was an effort to hold himself in patience for the summons which he knew was bound to come, but actually Giles had left some time before his father called him.

Master Fetterlock, spectacles on his nose, was seated at his counter, which was almost covered by open ledgers.

'Well, my son,' he said. 'It seems that we have much to say to each other. I have told you that your letter pleased me. It was an excellent letter for a boy of your years. You may sit down. There is some deep mystery here, and I would fain solve it.'

He pushed back the books, tilted his spectacles over his forehead and, leaning his folded arms on the table, looked at Nicholas.

'I suppose you are on tenterhooks to know why I went so suddenly away. It is a long story but I will make it brief. I received a summons from the Staple, from the Mayor himself, that I should wait on him immediately at Calais. There were grave matters to answer. Sarplers of my wool, listed as finest Cotswold, had been found in the mart at Bruges half full of rubbish.'

Nicholas nodded gravely. It was what Giles had feared would happen.

'This is no surprise to you, of course,' his father went on. 'I have spoken long with Giles. It was great ill fortune that I did not see him before I left. But it must have been going on for some time. The new wool could not have reached Bruges yet. That means that it is more than the work of some dishonest labourer, and we must get to the bottom of it. Now, look you here. Giles has given me an account of all the fine wool which he has supplied for packing. It is all writ down.'

He pushed over one of the open ledgers and pointed to the neat columns of entries.

'We will say, to make it easy, that there was enough wool for fifty sarplers. Very well. I have written it in my book that fifty sarplers have been dispatched in one direction or another. So far so good. But if some of those sarplers have been bearded with rubbish, there must be a considerable amount of good wool which is missing. Where has that wool gone? That is what we must discover.'

There was a moment's silence. Then Nicholas plucked up his courage. 'Have you asked Master Leach?' he inquired.

His father smiled. 'Of course it is obvious to suspect Leach. But, my son, there may be more in this than we have yet seen, and it might be wiser not to give him warning until we know all.'

'Sir,' said Nicholas. 'There is a matter which I would fain tell you, but I fear that you may chide me again.'

His father frowned. 'I will not chide you. Tell me what you know. Does it concern Leach?'

Nicholas nodded. It concerned Leach and the Lombards. He described how they had asked the way to Leach's house, how he had seen the Lombard at Leach's barn and, last of all, how Cecily had seen Leach in the New Forest.

His father caught him up quickly. 'In the Forest,' he exclaimed. 'Now of a truth that is strange. And they had pack-horses, you say. Clearly they were going to Southampton.' He brushed aside Cecily's word that they were miles from Southampton. That was of no count. They were riding by some devious way, so that they should not be noticed, which made it all the more suspicious. He pushed back his stool and paced up and down deep in thought. At last he stopped and looked directly at Nicholas.

'I have rebuked you for your tomfoolery, boy, but I will admit that I may have been hasty. Messer Antonio is an honest gentleman; yet his secretary may be a knave. Well – prepare yourself for a journey. Tomorrow we ride for Southampton.'

Russell Hoban

THE MOUSE AND HIS CHILD

The really frightening adventures for the clockwork mouse and his child start after they are broken and thrown on a rubbish dump and a dreadful character called Manny Rat mends their motors and makes them his slaves. For even when they escape, they endure imprisonment, war and more slavery.

This is not an easy book, but it's full of surprises and is funny as well. It is not like any other book I've read; you will want to read it at least twice to relish all the strange adventures, as well as the jokes, and be delighted when the child finds his tin-elephant mother and if Manny Rat finally gets his just punishment.

In this particular piece, the father and his child and their friend

Frog are captured by an army of shrews who plan to eat them as rations. (They don't realize that metal will be too tough even for their teeth!)

* * *

'Midnight!' rang the clock on the steeple of the church across the meadow. 'Twelve o'clock and all's peaceful here. Sleep well!'

Out of the light of the moon that floated clear in a cloudless sky, Frog paused under the trees that bordered the meadow. He turned to look back anxiously over the snow behind them, then faced forward again, listening. The mouse and his child walked on a little way, then stopped, unwound. 'What's the matter?' asked the child.

'I hear something up ahead,' said Frog. 'And Manny Rat is close behind us. I've seen him dodging in and out of the trees. If he catches us, I fear our friendship may not survive the encounter.'

'I hear something now,' said the child. It was a far-off, ghostly whistling, and the rhythmic whisper of a distant drum.

'Whatever it is,' said Frog, 'it can scarcely be worse than Manny Rat in his present mood. Let us press on.' He wound up the father, and hopped beside him and the child towards the sound of the drum and the whistling that now drew closer.

In the shadows of the trees ahead a green light, pale and dim, glimmered and was gone. Then it glimmered again. 'Fox fire beacon,' said Frog. He stopped, and knocked the mouse and his child down to stop them too. 'I've seen those before,' he said, 'and I've smelled that same musky scent I smell now. What's in front of us is . . .' He leaped aside as a wood-mouse bolted past, dragging her children with her.

'War!' she cried.

The drumming grew fierce and louder, and the whistling could now be recognized as the shrill singing of piercing little voices accompanied by a reed fife:

> Onward, shrews, for territory!
> Victory crown our might!
> Onward, shrews, for fame and glory!
>   Heroes, to the fight!

'What are shrews?' asked the child.

'They look something like mice,' said Frog, 'but they're short-tailed, sharper-nosed, and smaller – very little and very bloodthirsty. They eat constantly, and when they have a war they eat even more.' The mouse father's motor having run down, Frog stood him and the child on their feet again. The band of shrews was less than a hundred yards away, and the scout who had signalled with the phosphorescent wood moved off to join them. Frog watched the fox fire bobbing dimly, growing smaller in the distance.

'Their eyesight's very poor,' he said; 'they haven't seen us yet. Perhaps they'll go away, and just as well. They're a commissary company, I think, after rations. That's why the mouse was running so hard. In any case, they don't eat tin.'

'Do they eat frogs?' asked the child.

'When they catch them,' Frog replied.

The shrews moved into the moonlight, and the child, looking beyond his father's shoulder, saw the little company, spiky with the tiny spears they carried, clustered black against the snow. The singing had stopped, but the rolling beat of the nutshell drum and the piping of the reed fife continued while the scout made his report.

'Those spears have poisoned tips,' said Frog.

'Be careful,' said the child. 'Don't go any closer.'

'There's no going back, either,' said Frog. 'Here's Manny Rat.'

'Good evening!' called Manny Rat in a hoarse whisper. He had left the elephant in the brush behind him, the better to come upon his quarry in silence. 'Are we doubtful of the future?' he said. 'Do we wonder which way to turn?'

Frog, remembering his promise to travel with the mouse and his child for as long as their destined roads might lie together, decided that those roads must now diverge. Friendship was a noble thing, but life was sweet. Therefore he hopped out of the shadows to meet Manny Rat, hoping to find some soft answer that would turn away his anger from himself at least.

Manny Rat hesitated. The frog was utterly helpless against him, yet the rat became uneasy. He had always feared the fortune-teller a little; he felt him to be not only a prophet of good or bad luck, but its active agent as well. He drew nearer, and staring past the frog, he saw the mouse child staring back at him, the night sky mirrored in his glass-bead eyes. Manny Rat felt himself by some strange magnetism drawn to the father and the son, felt that something was wanted of him, forgot almost that he was there to smash them. He shook his head and picked up a rock. 'Step aside, Frog,' he said; 'I'm going to smash your friends.'

Frog, racking his brain for some way of placating Manny Rat, acted on a sudden impulse. 'Let me read your future,' he said.

Manny Rat held out his palm and laughed. 'Go ahead,' he said. 'I may very well be the only member of the present company that has one.'

Smiling, the frog approached, but he never took the rat's extended paw, nor did he speak the fair words he was shaping. He found himself looking into Manny Rat's eyes, and other words, obscure and cryptic, came into the fortune-teller's mind; against his will his broad mouth opened, and he spoke them: '*A dog shall rise,*' he said; '*a rat shall fall.*'

Manny Rat leaped back as if he had been struck. 'What's that supposed to mean?' he snarled.

Frog had no idea of what those words meant, nor did he care. He wished heartily that he had never set eyes upon the mouse and his child as his mouth opened again and he heard, as from a distance, his voice repeat, '*A dog shall rise; a rat shall fall.*'

'That may be,' said Manny Rat, his fears forgotten in his rage, 'but you'll fall first. You and your windup friends will finish up together. I'm going to tear your throat out.'

'Of course,' said Frog. 'Why not?' He nodded sadly, then turned his back on Manny Rat and looked towards the shrews as they right-faced and prepared to march away. Above the spears a tattered moleskin guidon hung limply in the moonlight. Frog sighed, and wondered what the mole's last thoughts had been.

'Useless to look to them for help,' said Manny Rat. 'If you have any parting words for one another, now is the time to say them.'

'RATIONS!' bellowed the frog. 'FRESH MEAT FOR THE ARMY! RATIONS FOR THE TROOPS! RIGHT HERE!'

'Rations!' came the shrill response across the snow. The compact little mass of black figures grew suddenly large as it wheeled about and sped forward, the spears all pointing in a single direction and the guidon fluttering like hunger's lean banner.

'Stay for dinner, do!' urged Frog as Manny Rat took to his heels, but the thwarted rat made no reply. Running for his life, he vanished in the darkness of the trees as a wave of musk scent surged over the fortune-teller, the father, and the son.

'Uncle Frog!' cried the child. 'The shrews will eat you up!'

'Better they than Manny Rat,' said Frog. Having intended to betray his friends, he had betrayed himself instead, and now, calm and resigned, he waited as the briskly trotting shrews skidded to a halt before him, two or three of the more short-sighted troops bumping into the mouse and his child and knocking them over. All of them were thin and famished-looking, and moved their jaws as if determined to be chewing hard whenever anything should come their way.

'Tough – very hard and tough,' said one, rubbing his nose where he had bruised it on the father's tin.

'Save him for the officer's mess,' said another as he pinched the frog. 'This one's fine. This one's plump and tasty. He smells good.'

'Oh, yes,' said someone else. 'I've had frog. Frog's good.'

A stiff-nosed corporal appeared, looked up at Frog, and took a straw from a mouseskin pouch. 'One frog,' he said, and notched the straw with his teeth; 'two . . . two what?'

'Mice,' said Frog.

'They don't smell like any mice I ever ate,' the corporal said, and bit more notches in his tally. 'Who turned you in anyhow?'

'Destiny,' said Frog.

'You can't trust anybody,' said the corporal. He put away the straw and turned the captives over to a guard. 'All set,' he reported to the sergeant in command of the commissary patrol.

'Let's go then,' said the sergeant. 'And no more fife and drum – we're getting too close to the border.'

'Rations, fall in!' shouted the corporal. The frog and the mouse and his child were hustled to the head of the column. Behind them a little group of captive wood-mice shuffled their feet and wept.

'Shut up,' said the guard to the wood-mice, 'or I'll stick you with this spear and you'll go bye-bye right now.'

'Forrard, hoo!' yelled the sergeant. The scout with the fox fire trotted on ahead; the guidon bearer stepped out bravely under the lean banner; the troops shouldered their spears and marched off with short tails whisking, their massed black shadow keeping step with them across the moonlit snow as they herded their rations back to headquarters.

Anne Holm

I AM DAVID

David had lived all twelve years of his life in a concentration camp, knowing only the grey, hopeless faces of his companions and the harsh bullying of his gaolers. One day, after his only friend dies mysteriously, one of *them* helps him escape. He is told to find his way to Denmark; and he starts out penniless, hungry and ignorant, not knowing how to tell good men from bad, never having seen the spring or heard music or slept in a bed or used a fork, not even knowing how to smile. His journey is a series of hair-raising escapes and amazing discoveries. Warning! If you decide to read this, you'll probably have a jolly good but happy sort of cry at the end!

Here's a book it's impossible to forget. It was first published in

Denmark in 1963. It was translated and published in Great Britain a few years later, and it has been read and loved ever since.

* * *

David ought to have known something was wrong as soon as they had got back to the road; the three people they had met on the way should have aroused his suspicions. People always looked like that where *they* were – like prisoners in a concentration camp, weary, grey-faced, apprehensive; dejected and sorrowful, as though they had forgotten life could be good, as if they no longer thought about anything.

The dog looked at him questioningly and began quietly whimpering. David placed his hand over its muzzle and it stopped, but it continued to look at him. The bush was too thin, its new green leaves too small. David quite forgot how beautiful he had thought spring was, only that morning, with its small, new, bright-green leaves. His one thought now was that you could look through the bush and see him lying on the ground – and he was David, a boy who had fled from *them*.

In their barracks they would have a list of everybody who was under suspicion and should be arrested on sight. *Their* guards always had a list like that. On that list would be found: 'David. A thin boy with brown hair, escaped from concentration camp.' And under the heading 'Recognition Marks' would be: 'It is obvious from the appearance of his eyes that he is not an ordinary boy but only a prisoner.'

If the men had not been talking so loudly, they would have heard him already. They were much too close to him, and he would never be able to get away. Even if he waited until it was dark, they would hear him as soon as he moved.

His flight would end where it began – at the point of a rifle. For he would not stop when they shouted to him. If he stopped they would not shoot, but they would interrogate him instead and send him back to the camp. And there, strong and healthy as he was, he would be a terribly long time dying.

No, when they called to him, he would run, and then the shot would be fired which had been waiting for him ever since that night when he had walked calmly towards the tree on the way to the mine outside the camp. But this time he would not be able to walk calmly away from them. He now knew how wonderful life could be, and his desire to live would spur him on. He would run – he knew it. And it would be a victory for *them*.

David remembered all the pain and bitterness he had ever known – and how much he could remember in such a short time! He recalled, too, all the good things he had learned about since he had gained his freedom – beauty and laughter, music and kind people, Maria, and a tree smothered in pink blossom, a dog to walk by his side, and a place to aim for . . .

This would be the end. He pressed his face into the dog's long coat so that no one should hear him, and wept. He wept quite quietly, but the dog grew uneasy and wanted to whimper again.

David stopped crying. 'God,' he whispered, 'God of the green pastures and still waters, I've one promise of help left, but it's too late now. You can't do anything about this. I don't mean to be rude, because I know you're very strong and you could make those men down there want to walk away for a bit. But they won't. They don't know, you see, and they're not afraid of you. But they are afraid of the commandant because he'll have them shot if they leave their posts. So you can see there's nothing you can do now. But please don't think I'm blaming you. It was my own fault for not seeing the danger in time. I shall run . . . Perhaps you'll see they aim straight so it doesn't hurt before I die. I'm so frightened of things that hurt. No, I forgot. I've only one promise of help left, and it's more important you should help the dog get away and find some good people to live with. Perhaps *they'll* shoot straight anyway, but if they don't it can't be helped: you must save the dog because it once tried to protect me. Thank you for having been my God: I'm glad I chose you. And now I must run, for if I leave it any longer I shan't have the courage to die. I am David. Amen.'

The dog kept nudging him. It wanted them to go back the way they had come, away from the spot where it sensed danger lurking.

'No,' David whispered, 'we can't go back – it's too late. You must keep still, King; and when they've hit me, perhaps you can get away by yourself.'

The dog licked his cheek eagerly, impatiently nudging him again and moving restlessly as if it wanted to get up. It nudged him once more – and then jumped up before David could stop it.

In one swift second David understood what the dog wanted. It did not run back the way they had come. It was a sheepdog and it had sensed danger . . . It was going to take David's place!

Barking loudly it sprang towards the men in the dark.

'Run!' something inside him told David. 'Run . . . run!' That was what the dog wanted him to do.

So he ran. He hesitated a moment and then ran more quickly than he had ever run in all his life. As he ran, he heard the men shouting and running too, but in a different direction . . . One of them yelled with pain – then came the sound of a shot and a strange, loud bark from the dog.

David knew the dog was dead.

Norman Hunter

THE INCREDIBLE ADVENTURES OF PROFESSOR BRANESTAWM

Professor Branestawm wears five pairs of spectacles (or does when he can find them) and is a great inventor. He invents everything from pancake-making machines to burglar-traps, but his inventions usually land him in the most awful scrapes, and sometimes Mrs Flittersnoop, his housekeeper, and his friend Colonel Dedshott get into trouble as well. Luckily, they're used to him.

The author, Norman Hunter, started his career as a professional magician, and this book was one of the very first Puffins. If this kind of fooling takes your fancy, there are eight other books about Professor Branestawm to enjoy after it, not to mention five others, equally wild and funny, by the same author.

* * *

Professor Branestawm rang the bell for his housekeeper, and then, remembering that he'd taken the bell away to invent a new kind of one, he went out into the kitchen to find her.

'Mrs Flittersnoop,' he said, looking at her through his near-sighted glasses and holding the other four pairs two in each hand, 'put your things on and come to the pictures with me. There is a very instructive film on this evening; all about the home-life of the brussels sprout.'

'Thank you kindly, sir,' said Mrs Flittersnoop. 'I've just got my ironing to finish, which won't take a minute, and I'll be ready.' She didn't care a bent pen-nib about the brussels-sprout picture, but she wanted to see the Mickey Mouse one. So while the Professor was putting on his boots and taking them off again because he had them on the wrong feet, and getting some money out of his money-box with a bit of wire, she finished off the ironing, put on her best bonnet, the blue one with the imitation strawberries on it, and off they went.

*

'Dear, dear,' said the Professor when they got back from the pictures, 'I don't remember leaving that window open, but I'm glad we did because I forgot my latchkey.'

'Goodness gracious, a mussey me, oh deary deary!' cried Mrs Flittersnoop.

The room was all anyhow. The things were all nohow and it was a sight enough to make a tidy housekeeper like Mrs Flittersnoop give notice at once. But she didn't do it.

'The other rooms are the same,' called the Professor from the top of the stairs. 'Burglars have been.'

And so they had. While the Professor and his housekeeper had been at the pictures thieves had broken in. They'd stolen the Professor's silver teapot that his auntie gave him, and the butter-dish he was going to give his auntie, only he forgot. They'd taken the housekeeper's picture-postcard album with the views of Brighton in it, and the Professor's best egg-cups that were never used except on Sundays.

'This is all wrong,' said the Professor, coming downstairs and running in and out of the rooms and keeping on finding more things that had gone. 'I won't have it. I'm going to invent a burglar catcher; that's what I'm going to invent.'

'We'd better get a policeman first,' said Mrs Flittersnoop.

The Professor had just picked some things up and was wondering where they went. 'I'll get a policeman,' he said, putting them down again and stopping wondering. So he fetched a policeman, who brought another policeman, and they both went into the kitchen and had a cup of tea, while the Professor went into his inventory to invent his burglar catcher and Mrs Flittersnoop went to bed.

Next morning the Professor was still inventing. It was lucky the burglars hadn't stolen his inventory, but they couldn't do that because it was too heavy to take away, being a shed sort of workshop, big enough to get inside. They couldn't even take any of the Professor's inventing tools, because the door was fastened with a special Professor-lock that didn't open with a key at all but only when you squeezed some tooth-paste into it and then blew through the keyhole. And, of course, the burglars didn't know about that. They never do know about things of that sort.

'How far have you got with the burglar catcher?' asked Mrs Flittersnoop presently, coming in with breakfast, which the Professor always had in his inventory when he was inventing.

'Not very far yet,' he said. In fact, he'd only got as far as nailing two pieces of wood together and starting to think what to do next. So he stopped for a bit and had his breakfast.

Then he went on inventing day and night for ever so long.

'Come and see the burglar catcher,' he said one day, and they both went into his study, where a funny-looking sort of thing was all fixed up by the window.

'Bless me!' said Mrs Flittersnoop. 'It looks like a mangle with a lot of arms.'

'Yes,' said the Professor, 'it had to look like that because it was too difficult making it look like anything else. Now watch.'

He brought out a bolster with his overcoat fastened round it and they went round outside the window.

'This is a dummy burglar,' he explained, putting the bolster thing on the window-sill. 'In he goes.' He opened the window and pushed the dummy inside.

Immediately there were a lot of clicking and whirring noises and the mangle-looking thing twiddled its arms. The wheels began to go round and things began to squeak and whizz. And the window closed itself behind the dummy.

'It's working, it's working,' cried the Professor, dancing with joy and treading on three geraniums in the flower-bed.

Suddenly the clicking and whizzing stopped, a trap-door opened in the study floor and something fell through it. Then a bell rang.

'That's the alarm,' said the Professor, rushing away. 'It means the burglar thing's caught a burglar.'

He led the way down into the cellar, and there on the cellar floor was the bolster with the overcoat on. And it was all tied up with ropes and wound round with straps and tapes so that it looked like one of those mummy things out of a museum. You could hardly see any bolster or coat at all, it was so tied up.

'Well I never,' said Mrs Flittersnoop.

The Professor undid the bolster and put his overcoat on. Then he went upstairs and wound the burglar catcher up again, put on the housekeeper's bonnet by mistake and went to the pictures again. He wanted to see the brussels-sprout film once more, because he'd missed bits of it before through Mrs Flittersnoop keeping on talking to him about her sister Aggie and how she could never wash up a teacup without breaking the handle off.

Mrs Flittersnoop had finished all her housework and done some mending and got the Professor's supper by the time the pictures were over. But the Professor didn't come in. Quite a long time afterwards he didn't come in. She wondered where he could have got to.

'Forgotten where he lives, I'll be bound,' she said. 'I never did see such a forgetful man. I'd better get a policeman to look for him.'

But just as she was going to do that, 'br-r-r-ring-ing-ing-g' went the Professor's burglar catcher.

'There now,' cried Mrs Flittersnoop. 'A burglar and all. And just when the Professor isn't here to see his machine thing catch him. Tut, tut.'

She picked up the rolling-pin and ran down into the cellar. Yes, it was a burglar all right. There he lay on the cellar floor all tied up with rope and wound round with straps and tapes and things till he looked like a mummy out of a museum. And like the bolster dummy, he was so tied up you could hardly see any of him.

'Ha,' cried the housekeeper, 'I'll teach you to burgle, that I will,' but she didn't teach him that at all. She hit him on the head with the rolling-pin, just to make quite sure he shouldn't get away. Then she ran out and got the policeman she was going to fetch to look for the Professor. And the policeman took the burglar away in a wheelbarrow to the police station, all tied up and hit on the head as he was. And the burglar went very quietly. He couldn't do anything else.

But the Professor didn't come home. Not all night he didn't come home. But the policeman had caught the other burglars by now and got all the Professor's and the housekeeper's things back, except the postcards of Brighton, which the burglars had sent to their friends. So they had nothing to do but look for the Professor.

But they didn't find him. They hunted everywhere. They looked under the seat at the pictures, but all they found was Mrs Flittersnoop's bonnet with the imitation strawberries on it, which they took to the police station as evidence, if you know what that is. Anyhow they took it whether you know or not.

'Where can he be?' said the housekeeper. 'Oh! he is a careless man to go losing himself like that!'

Then when they'd hunted a lot more and still hadn't found the Professor, the Judge said it was time to try the new burglar they'd caught. So they put him in the prisoner's place in the court, and the court usher called out ''Ush' and everybody 'ushed.

'You are charged with being a burglar inside Professor Branestawm's house,' said the Judge. 'What do you mean by it?'

But the prisoner couldn't speak. He was too tied up and wound round to do more than wriggle.

'Ha,' said the Judge, 'nothing to say for yourself, and I should think not, too.'

Then the policeman undid the ropes and unwound the straps and tapes and things. And there was such a lot of them that they filled the court up, and everyone was struggling about in long snaky sort of tapes and ropes and it was ever so long before they could get all sorted out again.

'Goodness gracious me!' cried Mrs Flittersnoop. 'If it isn't the Professor!'

Diana Wynne Jones

CHARMED LIFE

Of all the books about witches, those about young ones still learning their craft seem to me to be the most satisfying. This first-rate story is about awful Gwendolen Chant, the witch you love to hate, and it's one you will enjoy more every time you read it.

At the beginning of the book Gwendolen and her young brother, Cat, have been adopted by a famous enchanter called Chrestomanci, who tries to teach Gwendolen how to behave and control her witchcraft. But she goes from bad to worse as she hopes to become queen of all the witches, and doesn't even care if Cat dies in the process.

For other apprentice witches, try *The Worst Witch* stories by Jill Murphy.

* * *

Gwendolen went down to the village to get her dragon's blood on Wednesday afternoon. She was in high glee. There were to be guests that night at the Castle and a big dinner party. Cat knew that everyone had carefully not mentioned it before, for fear Gwendolen would take advantage of it. But she had to be told on Wednesday morning, because there were special arrangements for the children. They were to have their supper in the playroom, and they were supposed to keep out of the way after that.

'I'll keep out of the way all right,' Gwendolen promised. 'But that won't make any difference.' She chuckled about it all the way to the village.

Cat was embarrassed when they got to the village. Everyone avoided Gwendolen. Mothers dragged their children indoors and snatched babies out of her way. Gwendolen hardly noticed. She was too intent on getting to Mr Baslam and getting her dragon's blood. Cat did not fancy Mr Baslam, or the decaying pickle smell among his stuffed animals. He let Gwendolen go there on her own, and went to post his postcard to Mrs Sharp in the sweet shop. The people there were rather cool with him, even though he spent nearly two shillings on sweets, and they were positively cold in the cake shop next door. When Cat came out on to the green with his parcels, he found that children were being snatched out of his way, too.

This so shamed Cat that he fled back to the Castle grounds and did not wait for Gwendolen. There he wandered moodily, eating toffees and penny buns, and wishing he was back with Mrs Sharp. From time to time he saw Gwendolen in the distance. Sometimes she was dashing about. Sometimes she was squatting under a tree, carefully doing something. Cat did not go near her. If they were back with Mrs Sharp, he thought, Gwendolen would not need to do whatever impress- ive thing she was planning. He found himself wishing she was not quite such a strong and determined witch. He tried to imagine a Gwendolen who was not a witch, but he found him- self quite unable to. She just would not be Gwendolen.

Indoors, the usual silence of the Castle was not quite the same. There were tense little noises, and the thrumming feel- ing of people diligently busy just out of earshot. Cat knew it was going to be a big, important dinner party.

After supper, he craned out of Gwendolen's window watching the guests come up the piece of avenue he could see from there. They came in carriages and in cars, all very large and rich-looking. One carriage was drawn by six white horses and looked so impressive that Cat wondered if it might not even be the King.

'All the better,' said Gwendolen. She was squatting in the middle of the carpet, beside a sheet of paper. At one end of the paper was a bowl of ingredients. At the other crawled, wriggled or lay a horrid heap of things. Gwendolen had col- lected two frogs, an earthworm, several earwigs, a black beetle, a spider and a little pile of bones. The live things were charmed and could not move off the paper.

As soon as Cat was sure that there were no more carriages arriving, Gwendolen began pounding the ingredients together in the bowl. As she pounded, she muttered things in a groaning hum and her hair hung down and quivered over the bowl. Cat looked at the wriggling, hopping creatures and hoped that they were not going to be pounded up as ingredients too. It seemed not. Gwendolen at length sat back on her heels and said, 'Now!'

She snapped her fingers over the bowl. The ingredients

caught fire, all by themselves, and burnt with small blue flames. 'It's working!' Gwendolen said excitedly. She snatched up a twist of newspaper from beside her and carefully untwisted it. 'Now for a pinch of dragon's blood.' She took a pinch of the dark brown powder and sprinkled it on the flames. There was a fizzing, and a thick smell of burning. Then the flames leapt up, a foot high, blazing a furious green and purple, colouring the whole room with dancing light.

Gwendolen's face glowed in the green and purple. She rocked on her heels, chanting, chanting, strings of things Cat could not understand. Then, still chanting, she leaned over and touched the spider. The spider grew. And grew. And grew more. It grew into a five foot monster – a greasy roundness with two little eyes on the front, hanging like a hammock amid eight bent and jointed furry legs. Gwendolen pointed. The door of the room sprang open of its own accord – which made her smile exultingly – and the huge spider went silently creeping towards it, swaying on its hairy legs. It squeezed its legs inward to get through the door, and crept onwards, down the passage beyond.

Gwendolen touched the other creatures, one by one. The earwigs lumbered up and off, like shiny horned cows, bright brown and glistening. The frogs rose up, as big as men, and walked flap, flop on their enormous feet, with their arms trailing like gorillas. Their mottled skin quivered, and little holes in it kept opening and shutting. The puffy place under their chins made gulping movements. The black beetle crawled on branched legs, such a big black slab that it could barely get through the door. Cat could see it, and all the others, going in a slow, silent procession down the grass-green glowing corridor.

'Where are they going?' he whispered.

Gwendolen chuckled. 'I'm sending them to the dining room, of course. I don't think the guests will want much supper.'

She took up a bone next, and knocked each end of it sharply on the floor. As soon as she let go of it, it floated up into the air. There was a soft clattering, and more bones came out of nowhere to join it. The green and purple flames roared and rasped. A skull arrived last of all, and a complete skeleton was dangling there in front of the flames. Gwendolen smiled with satisfaction and took up another bone.

But bones when they are bewitched have a way of remembering who they were. The dangling skeleton sighed, in a hollow singing voice, 'Poor Sarah Jane. I'm poor Sarah Jane. Let me rest.'

Gwendolen waved it impatiently towards the door. It went dangling off, still sighing, and a second skeleton dangled after it, sighing, 'Bob the gardener's boy. I didn't mean to do it.' They were followed by three more, each one singing softly and desolately of who it had been, and all five went slowly dangling after the black beetle. 'Sarah Jane,' Cat heard from the corridor. 'I didn't mean to.' 'I was Duke of Buckingham once.'

Gwendolen took no notice of them and turned to the earthworm. It grew too. It grew into a massive pink thing as big as a sea serpent. Loops of it rose and fell and writhed all over the room. Cat was nearly sick. Its bare pink flesh had hairs on it like a pig's bristles. There were rings on it like the wrinkles round his own knuckles. Its great sightless front turned blindly this way and that until Gwendolen pointed to the door. Then it set off slowly after the skeletons, length after length of bare pink loops.

Gwendolen looked after it critically. 'Not bad,' she said. 'I need one last touch though.'

Carefully, she dropped another tiny pinch of dragon's blood on the flames. They burnt with a whistling sound, brighter, sicker, yellower. Gwendolen began to chant again, waving her arms this time. After a moment, a shape seemed to be gathering in the quivering air over the flames. Whiteness was boiling, moving, forming into a miserable bent thing with a big head. Three more somethings were roiling and hardening beneath it. When the first thing flopped out of the flames on to the carpet, Gwendolen gave a gurgle of pleasure. Cat was amazed at how wicked she looked.

'Oh don't!' he said. The three other somethings flopped on to the carpet, too, and he saw they were the apparition at the window and three others like it. The first was like a baby that was too small to walk – except that it *was* walking, with its big head wobbling. The next was a cripple, so twisted and cramped upon itself that it could barely hobble. The third was the apparition at the window, pitiful, wrinkled and draggled. The last had its white skin barred with blue stripes. All were weak and white and horrible. Cat shuddered all over.

'Please send them away!' he said.

Gwendolen only laughed again and waved the four apparitions towards the door.

They set off, toiling weakly. But they were only half-way there, when Chrestomanci came through the door and Mr Saunders came after him. In front of them came a shower of bones and small dead creatures, pattering on to the carpet and getting squashed under Chrestomanci's long, shiny shoes. The apparitions hesitated, gibbering. Then they fled back to the flaming bowl and vanished. The flames vanished at the same time, into thick black smelly smoke.

Gwendolen stared at Chrestomanci and Mr Saunders through the smoke. Chrestomanci was magnificent in dark blue velvet, with lace ruffles at his wrists and on the front of his shirt. Mr Saunders seemed to have made an effort to find a suit that reached to the ends of his legs and arms, but he had not quite succeeded. One of his big black patent-leather boots was unlaced, and there was a lot of shirt and wrist showing as he slowly coiled an invisible skein of something round his bony right hand. Both he and Chrestomanci looked back at Gwendolen most unpleasantly.

'You *were* warned, you know,' Chrestomanci said. 'Carry on, Michael.'

Mr Saunders put the invisible skein in his pocket. 'Thanks,' he said. 'I've been itching to for a week now.' He strode down on Gwendolen in a billow of black coat, yanked her to her feet, hauled her to a chair and put her face down over his knee. There he dragged off his unlaced black boot and commenced spanking her with it, hard and often.

While Mr Saunders laboured away, and Gwendolen screamed and squirmed and kicked, Chrestomanci marched up to Cat and boxed Cat's ears, twice on each side. Cat was so surprised that he would have fallen over, had not Chrestomanci hit the other side of his head each time and brought him upright again.

'What did you do that for?' Cat said indignantly, clutching both sides of his ringing face. 'I didn't do anything.'

'That's why I hit you,' said Chrestomanci. 'You didn't try to stop her, did you?' While Cat was gasping at the unfairness of this, he turned to the labouring Mr Saunders. 'I think that'll do now, Michael.'

Mr Saunders ceased swatting, rather regretfully. Gwendolen slid to her knees on the floor, sobbing with pain, and making screams in between her sobs at being treated like this.

Chrestomanci went over and poked at her with his shiny foot. 'Stop it. Get up and behave yourself.' And, when Gwendolen rose on her knees, staring piteously and looking utterly wronged, he said, 'You thoroughly deserved that spanking. And, as you probably realize, Michael has taken away your witchcraft, too. You're not a witch any longer. In future, you are not going to work one spell, unless you can prove to both of us that you are not going to do mischief with it. Is that clear? Now go to bed, and for goodness sake try and think about what you've been doing.'

He nodded to Mr Saunders, and they both went out, Mr Saunders hopping because he was still putting his boot back on, and squashing the rest of the dead creatures as he hopped.

Gwendolen flopped forward on her face and drummed her toes on the carpet. 'The beast! The beasts! How dare they treat me like this! I shall do a worse thing than this now, and serve you all right!'

'But you can't do things without witchcraft,' Cat said. 'Was what Mr Saunders was winding up your witchcraft?'

'Go away!' Gwendolen screamed at him. 'Leave me alone. You're as bad as the rest of them!' And, as Cat went to the door, leaving her drumming and sobbing, she raised her head and shouted after him, 'I'm not beaten yet! You'll see!'

Norton Juster

THE PHANTOM TOLLBOOTH

It's tremendously exhilarating to come across a book absolutely unlike anything you've ever read before. And this one is funny as well as original. But you need a quick wit and must pay proper attention if you want to get the best out of the verbal jokes.

The story begins when bored Milo, who hates school and thinks education is a waste of time, is given an odd sort of present, a turnpike tollbooth. Once it's built, he goes through it and life is never the same again. For wherever he arrives, he finds peculiar characters who seem to turn ordinary thinking upside-down! Here, for instance, Milo and Tock the dog find themselves in the Kingdom of Dictionopolis, where all the words in the world are grown.

* * *

'I wonder what the market will be like,' thought Milo as they drove through the gate; but before there was time for an answer they had driven into an immense square crowded with long lines of stalls heaped with merchandise and decorated in gaily coloured bunting. Overhead a large banner proclaimed:

WELCOME TO THE WORD MARKET

And, from across the square, five very tall, thin gentlemen regally dressed in silks and satins, plumed hats, and buckled shoes rushed up to the car, stopped short, mopped five brows, caught five breaths, unrolled five parchments, and began talking in turn.

'Greetings!'
'Salutations!'
'Welcome!'
'Good afternoon!'
'Hello!'

Milo nodded his head, and they went on, reading from their scrolls.

'By order of Azaz the Unabridged –'
'King of Dictionopolis –'
'Monarch of letters –'
'Emperor of phrases, sentences and miscellaneous figures of speech –'
'We offer you the hospitality of our kingdom,'
'Country,'
'Nation,'
'State,'
'Commonwealth,'
'Realm,'
'Empire,'

'Palatinate,'

'Principality.'

'Do all those words mean the same thing?' gasped Milo.

'Of course.'

'Certainly.'

'Precisely.'

'Exactly.'

'Yes,' they replied in order.

'Well, then,' said Milo, not understanding why each one said the same thing in a slightly different way, 'wouldn't it be simpler to use just one? It would certainly make more sense.'

'Nonsense.'

'Ridiculous.'

'Fantastic.'

'Absurd.'

'Bosh,' they chorused again, and continued:

'We're not interested in making sense; it's not our job,' scolded the first.

'Besides,' explained the second, 'one word is as good as another – so why not use them all?'

'Then you don't have to choose which one is right,' advised the third.

'Besides,' sighed the fourth, 'if one is right, then ten are ten times as right.'

'Obviously you don't know who we are,' sneered the fifth. And they presented themselves one by one as:

'The Duke of Definition.'

'The Minister of Meaning.'

'The Earl of Essence.'

'The Count of Connotation.'

'The Under-Secretary of Understanding.'

Milo acknowledged the introduction and, as Tock growled softly, the minister explained.

'We are the king's advisers, or, in more formal terms, his cabinet.'

'Cabinet,' recited the duke: '(1) a small private room or closet, case with drawers, etc., for keeping valuables or displaying curiosities; (2) council room for chief ministers of state; (3) a body of official advisers to the chief executive of a nation.'

'You see,' continued the minister, bowing thankfully to the duke, 'Dictionopolis is the place where all the words in the world come from. They're grown right here in our orchards.'

'I didn't know that words grew on trees,' said Milo timidly.

'Where did you think they grew?' shouted the earl irritably. A small crowd began to gather to see the little boy who didn't know that letters grew on trees.

'I didn't know they grew at all,' admitted Milo even more timidly. Several people shook their heads sadly.

'Well, money doesn't grow on trees, does it?' demanded the count.

'I've heard not,' said Milo.

'Then something must. Why not words?' exclaimed the under-secretary triumphantly. The crowd cheered his display of logic and continued about its business.

'To continue,' continued the minister impatiently. 'Once a week by Royal Proclamation the word market is held here in the great square, and people come from everywhere to buy the words they need or trade in the words they haven't used.'

'Our job,' said the count, 'is to see that all the words sold are proper ones, for it wouldn't do to sell someone a word that had no meaning or didn't exist at all. For instance, if you bought a word like *ghlbtsk*, where would you use it?'

'It would be difficult,' thought Milo – but there were so

many words that were difficult, and he knew hardly any of them.

'But we never choose which ones to use,' explained the earl as they walked towards the market stalls, 'for as long as they mean what they mean to mean we don't care if they make sense or nonsense.'

'Innocence or magnificence,' added the count.

'Reticence or common sense,' said the under-secretary.

'That seems simple enough,' said Milo, trying to be polite.

'Easy as falling off a log,' cried the earl, falling off a log with a loud thump.

'Must you be so clumsy?' shouted the duke.

'All I said was –' began the earl, rubbing his head.

'We heard you,' said the minister angrily, 'and you'll have to find an expression that's less dangerous.'

The earl dusted himself, as the others snickered audibly.

'You see,' cautioned the count, 'you must pick your words very carefully and be sure to say just what you intend to say. And now we must leave to make preparations for the Royal Banquet.'

'You'll be there, of course,' said the minister.

But before Milo had a chance to say anything, they were rushing off across the square as fast as they had come.

'Enjoy yourself in the market,' shouted back the under-secretary.

'Market,' recited the duke: 'an open space or covered building in which –'

And that was the last Milo heard as they disappeared into the crowd.

'I never knew words could be so confusing,' Milo said to Tock as he bent down to scratch the dog's ear.

'Only when you use a lot to say a little,' answered Tock.

Milo thought this was quite the wisest thing he'd heard all

day. 'Come,' he shouted, 'let's see the market. It looks very exciting.'

*

Indeed it was, for as they approached, Milo could see crowds of people pushing and shouting their way among the stalls, buying and selling, trading and bargaining. Huge wooden-wheeled carts streamed into the market square from the orchards, and long caravans bound for the four corners of the kingdom made ready to leave. Sacks and boxes were piled high waiting to be delivered to the ships that sailed the Sea of Knowledge, and off to one side a group of minstrels sang songs to the delight of those either too young or too old to engage in trade. But above all the noise and tumult of the crowd could be heard the merchants' voices loudly advertising their products.

'Get your fresh-picked ifs, ands and buts.'

'Hey-yaa, hey-yaa, hey-yaa, nice ripe wheres and whens.'

'Juicy, tempting words for sale.'

So many words and so many people! They were from every place imaginable and some places even beyond that, and they were all busy sorting, choosing, and stuffing things into cases. As soon as one was filled, another was begun. There seemed to be no end to the bustle and activity.

Milo and Tock wandered up and down between the stalls looking at the wonderful assortment of words for sale. There were short ones and easy ones for everyday use, and long and very important ones for special occasions, and even some marvellously fancy ones packed in individual gift boxes for use in royal decrees and pronouncements.

'Step right up, step right up – fancy, best-quality words right here,' announced one man in a booming voice. 'Step right up – ah, what can I do for you, little boy? How about a nice bagful of pronouns – or maybe you'd like our special assortment of names?'

Milo had never thought much about words before, but these looked so good that he longed to have some.

'Look, Tock,' he cried, 'aren't they wonderful?'

'They're fine, if you have something to say,' replied Tock in a tired voice, for he was much more interested in finding a bone than in shopping for new words.

'Maybe if I buy some I can learn how to use them,' said Milo eagerly as he began to pick through the words in the stall. Finally he chose three which looked particularly good to him – 'quagmire', 'flabbergast', and 'upholstery'. He had no idea what they meant, but they looked very grand and elegant.

'How much are these?' he inquired, and when the man whispered the answer he quickly put them back on the shelf and started to walk on.

'Why not take a few pounds of "happys"?' advised the salesman. 'They're much more practical – and very useful for Happy Birthday, Happy New Year, happy days, and happy-go-lucky.'

'I'd like to very much,' began Milo, 'but –'

'Or perhaps you'd be interested in a package of "goods" – always handy for good morning, good afternoon, good evening, and goodbye,' he suggested.

Milo did want to buy something, but the only money he had was the coin he needed to get back through the tollbooth, and Tock, of course, had nothing but the time.

'No, thank you,' replied Milo. 'We're just looking.' And they continued on through the market.

Clive King

THE TWENTY-TWO LETTERS

A	B	G	D		W	Z	Kh	Th

Y	K	L	M	N	S	ain	P	Q

R	SH	T	TS

When we first published this book, we said it was one of the most important we had turned into a Puffin – and a lot of people agreed with us, because it makes such a riveting story out of a historical mystery.

Three brothers, a soldier, a sailor and a trainee scribe, all leave their native town to seek their fortunes and end up in the hands of enemies; none of them can send home news because they have no written language and they cannot use the hundreds of signs known only to scribes. Then fortune decrees that a childish game played between one of the brothers, Aleph, and his sister, Beth, becomes the basis of all language writing systems of the modern world (except Chinese and Japanese).

This story, set mainly in Lebanon 1500 years BC is, of course, imaginary, but the author has researched many facts which make this seem a reasonable sort of explanation of how the alphabet was invented (for no one really knows). He has also written an exceptional adventure story which offers such extras as learning to sail by the stars, training and breaking horses. In this extract Aleph has just been taken prisoner by the Egyptians.

* * *

Aleph was never to remember much about the southward march to Sinai. He was not living, yet not dead; he had no friend, no hopes, and hardly any recollections. Existence was merely a matter of putting one foot before the other in the shimmering heat of the rocky desert, and collapsing into exhausted sleep at the end of each day. The one thing that reminded him that he was a person, with a life of his own, was the companionship of the incongruous bird in its cage, miraculously thriving despite all the rigours of the march. The effort to keep it alive was perhaps the only thing that kept him going. Perhaps it would have been kinder to have let it go before, but Beth's words ran through his head as if they were a solemn vow he had taken. 'Let him go when you get to where you are going.' And while he still had to put one foot in front of another, he had not yet got there.

He was hardly aware of arriving at their destination, a valley like a great open oven among the baking mountains. Scorched slaves toiled in galleries digging out the copper ore and carrying it away in baskets on their heads; others suffered worse torments at the refinery, where the heat of the smelting furnaces was added to the fantastic heat of the sun. He looked dazedly at the infernal scene. Could anyone live long in such a place? Or had he perhaps died already and been sent to a region of eternal punishment?

Yet when he was led to his place of work he found that he was asked to do something even more impossible. He was being asked to work with his brain, although he felt that it had long ago oozed out in sweat through his scalp.

He was received by the chief of the clerks, a dried-up chip of a man. He asked Aleph if he could count and tally in the Egyptian manner and assigned him to the stockpiles of smelted copper from the refineries. The penalty for any deficiency or mistake was to be sentenced to stoking the furnaces. 'They only last a few months there,' said the chief clerk. 'That's why we're short of tally clerks at present.' It was some time before Aleph's slow brain worked out what he meant.

His name had to be registered on a big scroll of papyrus. When he said he came from Gebal, the chief clerk gave him a sharp look from his black gimlet eyes. 'You've got yourselves to thank for this extra work, then, you Canaanites,' he said.

Aleph stood dumb and uncomprehending. The chief clerk went on speaking, not that he cared to enlighten this wretched Giblite, but in this outpost of exile he liked to keep his brain going by talking politics. 'All the news comes here, you know, and none goes out. So there's no harm in me telling you. Tyre, Sidon, Gebal – these places have always belonged to Egypt. But since the revolution you've all wanted to be independent. Especially rude and defiant your King was, they say. That's why Pharaoh wants weapons to arm an expeditionary force. They're going to march up the coast and put things to rights. Going to raze Gebal to the ground and put your lot to the sword, I'm told. And we've got to sweat to make the copper.'

Slowly Aleph began to understand what the chief clerk was saying. It was not enough that he should suffer here but everything he did would be helping to make weapons that might be used against his own family.

'Get on with it, then!' snapped the clerk. 'Don't stand there! You can start at once!'

Aleph turned away, but the chief clerk called after him, 'What's this about a bird you've got? See that it's turned in at the temple, we're always short of sacrificial animals here.'

Aleph walked slowly out of the building to where he had left the pigeon in the cage, and looked at it without feeling. This was the end of his journey, sure enough. This was where he was going to. All he had to do was to open the door of the cage and let the bird go. That it would make his captors angry did not matter; he was glad to be capable of this small gesture, even though it would do him little good. Yet it was difficult to believe the bird would find its way back over all those weary marches to Gebal. Gebal? It existed in another world, and it was in another age that he had said goodbye so casually to his sister, that he had looked down upon the city from the height, that he had looked over the mountain range for the first time, and even felt a childish excitement at the prospect of seeing Egypt. And if her white pigeon were to arrive at the loft, what could it tell Beth of her brother's sufferings? Nothing. And if it could, would that make her happier? Perhaps it was too late anyhow, and Pharaoh's armies had taken Gebal by surprise and put it to the sword.

He picked up the birdcage and walked in a stupor to the sweltering warehouse where he was to work. In a corner was a rough table, papyrus rolls, pens and ink. Other clerks were stacking ingots of copper in piles and morosely tallying them on the strips of papyrus. He looked at the thin papery strips, the pens and the ink; then at the bird. What about the sign-game he had played with his sister? How much of it, he wondered, did she remember?

Perhaps it was not too late to get a message through to Gebal – a message that would tell his sister what had become of him. At the same time it might warn the King of Gebal of the danger that threatened the city. But it was unheard of, to send a message through the air a distance of many weeks' marches. Fearful doubt told him it was preposterous, but he *had* to believe it was possible. It was possible, and that was enough to make him forget the oppressive heat and the hopelessness of his situation.

He must take no risks with his plan, nor arouse any suspicions. He put the birdcage inconspicuously in a corner and set immediately to work with the other clerks, piling ingots, checking and tallying them, packing them in panniers ready to be sent off by ass-train to the armourers in Egypt. It was exhausting work, physically and mentally, yet he kept a corner of his brain alive and apart, and through it paraded the signs that meant nothing in the world to anyone but him and his sister – the twenty-two letters. Could he remember them himself? He said their names over:

    Aleph – the ox
    beth – the house
    gimel – the stick
    daleth – the door
    the little man who said Ha!
    waw – the peg
    zayin – the weapon

(and where was he, Zayin, his elder brother?)

    keth – the hurdle
    teth – the ball of twine
    yod – the hand
    kaph – the palm branch
    lam – the rod

mem – the water
nun – the sea serpent

(and the sailor, voyaging confidently over the seas)

samekh – the fish
in – the eye
pe – the mouth
quoph – the monkey
resh – the head

(and he thought of his father, head of the family)

shin – the teeth
taw – the mark they put on the felled timber
and   ssad – the grasshopper

He recited the list over and over like a magic spell, and it gave him a marvellous confidence. And yet the words were not magic. There was no mystery to them: if you remembered them correctly, they were as sure as counting; it could not go wrong. Just put the first sounds together, and you could make any word in the language.

Of course it wasn't real writing, Aleph still told himself. But he no longer cared what the priests or the gods might think. They could not condemn him to any worse punishment than that he was suffering now; bodily here in Sinai and in his imagination whenever he thought of the Egyptian armies descending upon Gebal.

When the long day's work came to an end and the exhausted workers trailed off to their quarters, Aleph pretended he had a spoilt papyrus to recopy, and stayed behind in the shed with the pens and the ink to write what he had to write. The light was fading, and in addition he was exhausted, but he forced his brain to remain clear and his hand to write neatly and clearly in tiny characters. He knew he must do it that night, for he was sure tomorrow they would take the bird from him. The guards looked curiously at the new slave working overtime, but the last thing that entered their heads was that he was writing a message of vital importance to his sister.

Aleph finished writing and hid the tiny missive safely in his dress. The sun was setting. He could not set the poor bird free unfed and in the dark. He took it to the sleeping quarters, where he presumed there would be food and water for the prisoners; indeed, by the time he got there he found barely enough even for a pigeon. He was desperately anxious lest they should take the bird from him that night. One of the soldiers threatened to do so, but Aleph managed to make it appear that the man was trying to make off with a sacrificial fowl for his own purposes, and the soldiers were just sufficiently respectful to the clerks, slaves though they were, for Aleph to have his way.

In the squalid, stifling sleeping quarters, Aleph spent a restless night during which sheer exhaustion battled with anxiety for his plan, and with desperate dreams in which he was flying over mountains or falling helplessly into deep gulfs.

He was awake before dawn, and in the dim light he managed to wrap the message round one of the pigeon's legs and tie it with a thread pulled from his garment. As the sun rose, and the rest of the workers were roused, Aleph announced that he was taking the bird to be sacrificed.

The temple was near the clerks' quarters. As he approached the priest standing outside he called out: 'I have here a dove for the sacrifice.' And at the same time he opened the cage door and held the bird aloft in his hand. 'See, a snow-white dove!' he cried.

Then, in front of all the guards and priests he pretended to stumble. As he did so he let the bird go. The pigeon was so astonished that it fluttered to the ground. Aleph ran at it shouting and flapping, as if to catch it, and now the bird took fright and fluttered up, up into the air. The priest cursed him for a fool, the soldiers laughed at him, and he stood there and watched the white bird, bright in the rays of the early sun, circling higher and higher into the blue sky.

'Go with the gods to Gebal!' said Aleph quietly. The sun was rising on his right hand, but the pigeon continued to circle above him, until Aleph's heart sank: how foolish it was to expect it to know in which direction its distant home lay. Then suddenly the bird straightened out on a course that lay directly in front of him. Gradually Aleph watched the pigeon dwindle out of sight, to the northward.

Only then did the thought come to him that, even if his message did get through, he would never know. Yet as he returned to the work of the sweltering copper-mine, and day after day passed in relentless routine, a spark of hope kept him alive: the hope that the pigeon might survive the dangers of the desert, and arrive in the pigeon loft in Gebal to tell Beth that he had not forgotten his family; and a fainter hope that Beth might find and understand the message he had carefully composed in their private sign language, that it might even somehow help Gebal in its danger. And deeper still within him was a faith so faint that he did not yet acknowledge it to himself, that his twenty-two letters might be neither a sin against the gods nor a childish game but something for which he, Aleph, might be remembered.

Dick King-Smith

THE SHEEP-PIG

Dick King-Smith's animal stories are unique. He writes about
farmyard animals who develop special talents which change the
way they live, but hardly involve human beings at all.

In *The Fox Busters* he has three flying chicks who beat off a gang
of foxes. In *Daggie Dogfoot* a little pig (or runt) has dogs' paws
which help him swim. In this book, Babe, a piglet won at a fair,
makes friends with Fly the Sheepdog and learns all her tricks. But
Fly thinks all sheep are stupid and treats them disdainfully, whereas
Babe makes friends with them, and on one exciting occasion even
saves them from sheep rustlers. In this piece he's trying to show
the farmer just how helpful he can be, for he wants, above all
things, to be accepted as a 'Sheep-Pig'.

* * *

Fly ran left up the slope as the sheep began to bunch above her. Once behind them, she addressed them in her usual way, that is to say sharply.

'Move, fools!' she snapped. 'Down the hill. If you know which way "down" is;' but to her surprise they did not obey. Instead they turned to face her, and some even stamped, and shook their heads at her, while a great chorus of bleating began.

To Fly sheep-talk was just so much rubbish, to which she had never paid any attention, but Babe, listening below, could hear clearly what was being said, and although the principal cry was the usual one, there were other voices saying other things. The contrast between the politeness with which they had been treated by yesterday's rescuer and the everlasting rudeness to which they were subjected by this or any wolf brought mutinous thoughts into woolly heads, and words of defiance rang out.

'You got no manners! . . . . Why can't you ask nicely? . . . Treat us like muck, you do!' they cried, and one hoarse voice which the pig recognized called loudly, 'We don't want you, wolf! We want Babe!' whereupon they all took it up.

'We want Babe!' they bleated. 'Babe! Babe! Ba-a-a-a-a-be!'

Those behind pushed at those in front, so that they actually edged a pace or two nearer the dog.

For a moment it seemed to Babe that Fly was not going to be able to move them, that she would lose this particular battle of wills; but he had not reckoned with her years of experience. Suddenly, quick as a flash she drove in on them with a growl and with a twisting leap sprang for the nose of the foremost animal; Babe heard the clack of her teeth as the ewe fell over backwards in fright, a fright which immediately ran through all. Defiant no longer, the flock poured down the hill, Fly snapping furiously at their heels, and surged wildly through the gateway.

'No manners! No manners! No ma-a-a-a-a-nners!' they cried, but an air of panic ran through them as they realized how rebellious they had been. How the wolf would punish them! They ran helter-skelter into the middle of the paddock, and wheeled as one to look back, ears pricked, eyes wide with fear. They puffed and blew, and Ma's hacking cough rang out. But to their surprise they saw that the wolf had dropped by the gateway, and that after a moment the pig came trotting out to one side of them.

*

Though Farmer Hogget could not know what had caused the near-revolt of the flock, he saw clearly that for some reason they had given Fly a hard time, and that she was angry. It was not like her to gallop sheep in that pell-mell fashion.

'Steady!' he said curtly as she harried the rearguard, and then, 'Down!' and 'Stay!' and shut the gate. Shepherding suited Farmer Hogget – there was no waste of words in it.

In the corner of the home paddock nearest to the farm buildings was a smallish, fenced yard divided into a number of pens and runways. Here the sheep would be brought at shearing-time or to pick out fat lambs for market or to be treated for various troubles. Farmer Hogget had heard the old ewe cough; he thought he would catch her up and give her another drench. He turned to give an order to Fly lying flat and still behind him, and there, lying flat and still beside her, was the pig.

'Stay, Fly!' said Hogget. And, just for fun, 'Come, Pig!'

Immediately Babe ran forward and sat at the farmer's right,

his front trotters placed neatly together, his big ears cocked for the next command.

Strange thoughts began to stir in Farmer Hogget's mind, and unconsciously he crossed his fingers.

He took a deep breath, and, holding it . . . 'Away to me, Pig!' he said softly.

Without a moment's hesitation Babe began the long outrun to the right.

Quite what Farmer Hogget had expected to happen, he could never afterwards clearly remember. What he had not expected was that the pig would run round to the rear of the flock, and turn to face it and him, and lie down instantly without a word of further command spoken, just as a well-trained dog would have done. Admittedly, with his jerky little rocking-horse canter he took twice as long to get there as Fly would have, but still, there he was, in the right place, ready and waiting. Admittedly, the sheep had turned to face the pig and were making a great deal of noise, but then Farmer Hogget did not know, and Fly would not listen to, what they were saying. He called the dog to heel, and began to walk with his long loping stride to the collecting-pen in the corner. Out in the middle of the paddock there was a positive babble of talk.

'Good morning!' said Babe. 'I do hope I find you all well, and not too distressed by yesterday's experience?' and immediately it seemed that every sheep had something to say to him.

'Bless his heart!' they cried, and, 'Dear little soul!' and, 'Hullo, Babe!' and, 'Nice to see you again!' and then there was a rasping cough and the sound of Ma's hoarse tones.

'What's up then, young un?' she croaked. 'What be you doing here instead of that wolf?'

Although Babe wanted, literally, to keep on the right side

of the sheep, his loyalty to his foster-mother made him say in a rather hurt voice, 'She's not a wolf. She's a sheep-dog.'

'Oh all right then,' said Ma, 'sheep-dog, if you must have it. What dost want, then?'

Babe looked at the army of long sad faces.

'I want to be a sheep-pig,' he said.

'Ha ha!' bleated a big lamb standing next to Ma. 'Ha ha ha-a–a–a–a!'

'Bide quiet!' said Ma sharply, swinging her head to give the lamb a thumping butt in the side. 'That ain't nothing to laugh at.'

Raising her voice, she addressed the flock.

'Listen to me, all you ewes,' she said, 'and lambs too. This young chap was kind to me, like I told you, when I were poorly. And I told him, if he was to ask me to go somewhere or do something, politely, like he would, why, I'd be only too delighted. We ain't stupid, I told him, all we do want is to be treated right, and we'm as bright as the next beast, we are.'

'We are!' chorused the flock. 'We are! We are! We a–a–a–a-a–are!'

'Right then,' said Ma. 'What shall us do, Babe?'

Babe looked across towards Farmer Hogget, who had opened the gate of the collecting-pen and now stood leaning on his crook, Fly at his feet. The pen was in the left bottom corner of the paddock, and so Babe expected, and at that moment got, the command 'Come by, Pig!' to send him left and so behind the sheep and thus turn them down towards the corner.

He cleared his throat. 'If I might ask a great favour of you,' he said hurriedly, 'could you all please be kind enough to walk down to that gate where the farmer is standing, and to go through it? Take your time, please, there's absolutely no rush.'

A look of pure contentment passed over the faces of the flock, and with one accord they turned and walked across the paddock, Babe a few paces in their rear. Sedately they walked, and steadily, over to the corner, through the gate, into the pen, and then stood quietly waiting. No one broke ranks or tried to slip away, no one pushed or shoved, there was no noise or fuss. From the oldest to the youngest, they went in like lambs.

Then at last a gentle murmur broke out as everyone in different ways quietly expressed their pleasure.

'Babe!' said Fly to the pig. 'That was quite beautifully done, dear!'

'Thank you so much!' said Babe to the sheep. 'You did that so nicely!'

'Ta!' said the sheep. 'Ta! Ta! Ta-a-a-a-a-a! 'Tis a pleasure to work for such a little gennulman!' And Ma added, 'You'll make a wunnerful sheep-pig, young un, or my names's not Ma-a-a-a-a-a.'

As for Farmer Hogget, he heard none of this, so wrapped up was he in his own thoughts. He's as good as a dog, he told himself excitedly, he's better than a dog, than any dog! I wonder . . .!

'Good Pig,' he said.

Then he uncrossed his fingers and closed the gate.

Ursula Le Guin

A WIZARD OF EARTHSEA

I think this is one of the best books I ever discovered. Of all the books about magic and wizardry, it is the most satisfactory, for while it has a terrific and often frightening story to tell, it also makes such marvellous sense of the skills and discipline involved in serious magic.

It's the story of a village boy, who seems to be born with unusual magic powers. He lives in an imagined archipelago of islands in an imagined age, and he is sent to be trained as a proper wizard at the College of Roke. But although he is a brilliant pupil, his pride and a brief flash of bad temper cause him to unleash a dreadful force which pursues and nearly destroys him. This episode tells of the quarrel

184

which sparks it off, and the beginning of his suffering. Here he is referred to by his true name, Ged, although his companions think of him as Sparrowhawk.

* * *

Ged said to him, 'What is it you want, then, Jasper?'

'I want the company of my equals,' Jasper said. 'Come on, Vetch. Leave the prentices to their toys.'

Ged turned to face Jasper. 'What do sorcerers have that prentices lack?' he inquired. His voice was quiet, but all the other boys suddenly fell still, for in his tone as in Jasper's the spite between them now sounded plain and clear as steel coming out of a sheath.

'Power,' Jasper said.

'I'll match your power act for act.'

'You challenge me?'

'I challenge you.'

Vetch had dropped down to the ground, and now he came between them, grim of face. 'Duels in sorcery are forbidden to us, and well you know it. Let this cease!'

Both Ged and Jasper stood silent, for it was true they knew the law of Roke, and they also knew that Vetch was moved by love, and themselves by hate. Yet their anger was balked, not cooled. Presently, moving a little aside as if to be heard by Vetch alone, Jasper spoke, with his cool smile: 'I think you'd better remind your goatherd friend again of the law that protects him. He looks sulky. I wonder, did he really think I'd accept a challenge from him? A fellow who smells of goats, a prentice who doesn't know the First Change?'

'Jasper,' said Ged, 'what do you know of what I know?'

For an instant, with no word spoken that any heard, Ged vanished from their sight, and where he had stood a great falcon hovered, opening its hooked beak to scream: for one instant, and then Ged stood again in the flickering torchlight, his dark gaze on Jasper.

Jasper had taken a step backward, in astonishment; but now he shrugged and said one word: 'Illusion.'

The others muttered. Vetch said, 'That was not illusion. It was a true change. And enough, Jasper, listen –'

'Enough to prove that he sneaked a look in the Book of Shaping behind the Master's back: what then? Go on, Goatherd. I like this trap you're building for yourself. The more you try to prove yourself my equal, the more you show yourself for what you are.'

At that, Vetch turned from Jasper, and said very softly to Ged, 'Sparrowhawk, will you be a man and drop this now – come with me –'

Ged looked at his friend and smiled, but all he said was, 'Keep Hoeg for me a little while, will you?' He put into Vetch's hands the little otak, which as usual had been riding on his shoulder. It had never let any but Ged touch it, but it came to Vetch now, and climbing up his arm cowered on his shoulder, its great bright eyes always on its master.

'Now,' Ged said to Jasper, quietly as before, 'what are you going to do to prove yourself my superior, Jasper?'

'I don't have to do anything, Goatherd. Yet I will. I will give you a chance – an opportunity. Envy eats you like a worm in an apple. Let's let out the worm. Once by Roke Knoll you boasted that Gontish wizards don't play games. Come to Roke Knoll now and show us what it is they do instead. And afterward, maybe I will show you a little sorcery.'

'Yes, I should like to see that,' Ged answered. The younger boys, used to seeing his black temper break out at the least hint of slight or insult, watched him in wonder at his coolness now. Vetch watched him not in wonder, but with growing fear. He tried to intervene again, but Jasper said, 'Come, keep out of this, Vetch. What will you do with the chance I give you, Goat-herd? Will you show us an illusion, a fireball, a charm to cure goats with the mange?'

'What would you like me to do, Jasper?'

The older lad shrugged. 'Summon up a spirit from the dead, for all I care!'

'I will.'

'You will not.' Jasper looked straight at him, rage suddenly flaming out over his disdain. 'You will not. You cannot. You brag and brag –'

'By my name, I will do it!'

They all stood utterly motionless for a moment.

Breaking away from Vetch who would have held him back by main force, Ged strode out of the courtyard, not looking back. The dancing werelights overhead died out, sinking down. Jasper hesitated a second, then followed after Ged. And the rest came straggling behind, in silence, curious and afraid.

*

The slopes of Roke Knoll went up dark into the darkness of summer night before moonrise. The presence of that hill where many wonders had been worked was heavy, like a weight in the air about them. As they came on to the hillside they thought of how the roots of it were deep, deeper than the sea, reaching down even to the old, blind, secret fires at the world's core. They stopped on the east slope. Stars hung over the black grass above them on the hill's crest. No wind blew.

Ged went a few paces up the slope away from the others and turning said in a clear voice, 'Jasper! Whose spirit shall I call?'

'Call whom you like. None will listen to you.' Jasper's voice shook a little, with anger perhaps. Ged answered him softly, mockingly, 'Are you afraid?'

He did not even listen for Jasper's reply, if he made one. He no longer cared about Jasper. Now that they stood on Roke Knoll, hate and rage were gone, replaced by utter certainty. He need envy no one. He knew this his power, this night, on this dark enchanted ground, was greater than it had ever been, filling him till he trembled with the sense of strength barely kept in check. He knew now that Jasper was far beneath him, had been sent perhaps only to bring him here tonight, no rival but a mere servant of Ged's destiny. Under his feet he felt the hillroots going down and down into the dark, and over his head he saw the dry, far fires of the stars. Between, all things were to his order, to command. He stood at the centre of the world.

'Don't be afraid,' he said, smiling. 'I'll call a woman's spirit. You need not fear a woman. Elfarran I will call, the fair lady of the *Deed of Enlad*.'

'She died a thousand years ago, her bones lie afar under the Sea of Éa, and maybe there never was such a woman.'

'Do years and distances matter to the dead? Do the Songs lie?' Ged said with the same gentle mockery, and then saying, 'Watch the air between my hands,' he turned away from the others and stood still.

In a great slow gesture he stretched out his arms, the gesture of welcome that opens an invocation. He began to speak.

He had read the runes of this Spell of Summoning in Ogion's book, two years and more ago, and never since had seen them. In darkness he had read them then. Now in this darkness it was as if he read them again on the page open before him in the night. But now he understood what he read, speaking it aloud word after word, and he saw the markings of how the spell must be woven with the sound of the voice and the motion of body and hand.

The other boys stood watching, not speaking, not moving unless they shivered a little; for the great spell was beginning to work. Ged's voice was soft still, but changed, with a deep singing in it, and the words he spoke were not known to them. He fell silent. Suddenly the wind rose roaring in the grass. Ged dropped to his knees and called out aloud. Then he fell forward as if to embrace the earth with his outstretched arms, and when he rose he held something dark in his straining hands and arms, something so heavy that he shook with effort getting to his feet. The hot wind whined in the black tossing grasses on the hill. If the stars shone now none saw them.

The words of the enchantment hissed and mumbled on Ged's lips, and then he cried out aloud and clearly, 'Elfarran!'

Again he cried the name, 'Elfarran!'

And the third time, 'Elfarran!'

The shapeless mass of darkness he had lifted split apart. It sundered, and a pale spindle of light gleamed between his opened arms, a faint oval reaching from the ground up to the height of his raised hands. In the oval of light for a moment there moved a form, a human shape: a tall woman looking back over her shoulder. Her face was beautiful, and sorrowful, and full of fear.

Only for a moment did the spirit glimmer there. Then the sallow oval between Ged's arms grew bright. It widened and spread, a rent in the darkness of the earth and night, a ripping open of the fabric of the world. Through it blazed a terrible brightness. And through the bright misshapen breach clambered something like a clot of black shadow, quick and hideous, and it leaped straight out at Ged's face.

Staggering back under the weight of the thing, Ged gave a short, hoarse scream. The little otak watching from Vetch's shoulder, the animal that had no voice, screamed aloud also and leaped as if to attack.

Ged fell, struggling and writhing, while the bright rip in the world's darkness above him widened and stretched. The boys that watched fled, and Jasper bent down to the ground hiding his eyes from the terrible light. Vetch alone ran forward to his friend. So only he saw the lump of shadow that clung to Ged, tearing at his flesh. It was like a black beast, the size of a young child, though it seemed to swell and shrink; and it had no head or face, only the four taloned paws with which it gripped and tore. Vetch sobbed with horror, yet he put out his hands to try to pull the thing away from Ged. Before he touched it, he was bound still, unable to move.

The intolerable brightness faded, and slowly the torn edges of the world closed together. Nearby a voice was speaking as softly as a tree whispers or a fountain plays.

Starlight began to shine again, and the grasses of the hillside were whitened with the light of the moon just rising. The night was healed. Restored and steady lay the balance of light and dark. The shadow-beast was gone. Ged lay sprawled on his back, his arms flung out as if they yet kept the wide gesture of welcome and invocation. His face was blackened with blood and there were great black stains on his shirt. The little otak cowered by his shoulder, quivering. And above him stood an old man whose cloak glimmered pale in the moonrise: the Archmage Nemmerle.

The end of Nemmerle's staff hovered silverly above Ged's breast. Once it gently touched him over the heart, once on the lips, while Nemmerle whispered. Ged stirred, and his lips parted gasping for breath. Then the old Archmage lifted the staff, and set it to earth, and leaned heavily on it with bowed head, as if he had scarcely strength to stand.

Penelope Lively

THE GHOST OF THOMAS KEMPE

Of course, there are dozens of good tales about ghosts, but I think this one has an extra-special ingredient, for it's not only unusual and scary, but funny.

The hero, James, finds it bad enough getting blamed for things when he deserves it, but when the real culprit has been dead for hundreds of years and is likely to go on doing worse things, it's more than flesh and blood can stand.

What is more, Thomas Kempe, Esq., Sorcerer, wants James to be his apprentice, and every time James refuses or begs to be left alone, the sorcerer throws a temper tantrum and does even more awful things. Of course, James's family know nothing about his problem. Here's Thomas Kempe making his presence felt while the Vicar is paying a visit.

* * *

There were cream splits for tea, which James found very heartening. After a while he felt sufficiently restored to tease Helen about her new dress.

'What's it s'posed to be? I never saw such a weird object. Oh, *I* know – it's a football jersey that someone left out in the rain so it got all soggy and stretched so it wasn't any use any more . . .'

'It's a striped shift. Julia's got one too.'

'It's shifted all right. Shifted in all the wrong directions. Why's it such a peculiar shape – oh, *sorry*, that's you, I thought it was the dress . . .'

'Mum!' wailed Helen.

'Enough!' said Mrs Harrison. 'And finish your tea, please. I want to clear up before the Vicar comes.'

'The *Vicar*?'

'About the choir.'

The Vicar, however, arrived before Mrs Harrison had had time to establish order in the kitchen. Moreover, he was one of those people who like to make it instantly clear that they are unusually accommodating and easygoing, and refused to be steered into the sitting-room.

'Please – I do hate people to put themselves out – just carry on as though I weren't here.'

That, thought James, would be a bit difficult. The Vicar was six feet tall and stout into the bargain. He had already clipped his head on a beam as he came in and was trying desperately to suppress a grimace of pain.

'Oh dear,' said Mrs Harrison, sweeping crockery into the

sink. 'These blessed ceilings. I'm so sorry. Will you have a cup of tea? I'll just make some fresh.'

The front door slammed with a loud bang, making the Vicar jump. 'I never refuse a cup of tea – but please – I don't want to be a nuisance.'

'No trouble,' said Mrs Harrison. 'James, do something about that dog. It seems to have gone mad.'

Tim had gone into the now-familiar routine that indicated, James realized with a sinking heart, that Thomas Kempe was not far away. He grabbed him. The Vicar, too, was looking at him, though apparently for different reasons.

'Dear me, how like the stray who got in and took the joint from our larder last week. Curious to see two mongrels so much alike, eh? Well, well. And how's school, young man?'

'Fine,' said James, 'thanks.' Tim was struggling violently, and lunging with bared teeth at a point somewhere behind the Vicar. The windows rattled. 'These autumn winds,' said the Vicar. 'I always think of those at sea.'

'What?' said Mrs Harrison. 'Oh, yes, yes, quite.' She slammed the lid on the teapot irritably.

The electric light flickered. Upstairs, distantly, came the sound of an alarm clock going off. A cup jinked in its saucer on the dresser.

'Do sit down,' said Mrs Harrison. 'James, pull up a chair for the Vicar.'

James fetched the windsor chair from the corner and placed it by the table. He still had one hand on its arm as the Vicar began to lower himself into it, and so felt the whole thing twitch, stagger, and jerk suddenly sideways, so that the Vicar, prodded violently in the hip, lurched against the table and almost fell.

'James!' said Mrs Harrison angrily. 'Look what you're doing!'

'Sorry,' said James in confusion, straightening the chair. The Vicar sat down, rubbing his hip and also apologizing. Tim began to bark hysterically.

'Put that dog out!' shouted Mrs Harrison.

With Tim outside, things were quieter, except for another bang as the back door, this time, slammed. The Vicar passed a hand across his forehead and rubbed his head, furtively.

'Family life, eh! There's always something going on, what?'

'Never a dull moment,' said Mrs Harrison grimly. 'Milk?'

'Oh – please – yes, if I may . . . So kind of you. I do hope I'm not interrupting. I'm sure you're very busy, like we all are these days, eh?'

'Not at all,' said Mrs Harrison. 'James, pass the Vicar his tea, will you?'

James, with extreme caution, carried cup and saucer across the room. He was standing in front of the Vicar, and the Vicar's fingers were just closing on the edge of the saucer, when the cup jolted, tipped, hung at an angle of forty-five degrees, and turned over. Tea flowed into the saucer, and thence in a cascade on to the Vicar's trousers.

'James!' said Mrs Harrison in a strangled voice.

There was a great deal of mopping and exclaiming. The Vicar apologized, and then apologized again. James apologized. Mrs Harrison's face had taken on that pinched, gathered look that foretold an outburst as soon as circumstances permitted. Finally, the Vicar, dried off and supplied with a new cup of tea, stopped saying how sorry he was and began to talk about choir practices. Mrs Harrison liked to sing sometimes: she said it allowed her to let off steam. Furthermore, she thought it would be a good idea if James sang. James, knowing this, had been hoping to beat a retreat. He sidled towards the door. 'My son,' said Mrs Harrison, glaring at him, 'sings too. After a fashion.'

'My dear boy,' said the Vicar, 'you must come along. We've got some other chaps about your age.'

James mumbled that he'd love to, or words to that effect. He was pinned to the spot now, by a steely look from his mother.

'Splendid, eh?' said the Vicar. 'Tell you what, I'll just jot down the times of our practices, shall I?' He patted his pockets.

Mrs Harrison said, 'James. Fetch the telephone pad, please, and a pencil.'

James opened the kitchen door, which swung shut again behind him, and crossed the hall. The telephone pad had a shopping list on it which said 'Onions, cereals, elastic bands, disinfectant.' Underneath that was a message about an electrician who would call back later, and a picture of a spaceman (drawn by James), and underneath that was a message from Thomas Kempe in large letters, which said, 'I am watchynge ye.'

'Go on and watch then,' shouted James, in a fury. 'See if I care!'

There was a crash. The barometer had leapt off the wall and lay on the floor, the glass cracked. And a series of loud bangs, apparently made by some kind of blunt instrument, such as a hammer, reverberated through the house.

The kitchen door flew open. The banging ceased instantly. Mrs Harrison was standing there saying the kind of things that were to be expected, only slightly toned down in deference to the Vicar, who was standing behind her, with a dazed expression on his face. He had hit his head on the beam again, James realized.

'. . . must apologize for my son's appalling behaviour,' concluded Mrs Harrison.

'Boys will be boys,' said the Vicar, without conviction. 'Eh? And now I really must be on my way. So kind . . . So glad we can look forward to having you with us . . . Do hope I haven't kept you from anything . . .' He edged sideways through the front door, stooping, with the air of a man who wanted only to be unobtrusive and had always wished himself several sizes smaller.

James picked up the barometer and waited for the wrath to come.

Margaret Mahy

THE HAUNTING

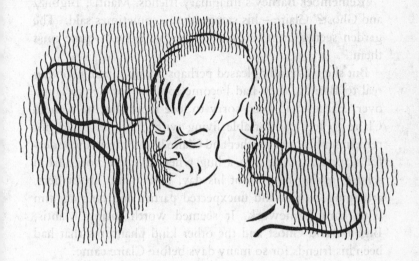

What does it feel like to be really haunted? To be not quite sure whether you are being invaded by someone alive or dead? To have someone else's eyes looking out at you from the mirror, and to be helpless to do anything about it?

This is a chilling tale of a rather weird family with a sinister past. But Barney, the central character, is quite ordinary. He is happy that his father has remarried, for he loves his stepmother Claire and can't remember his own mother, who died when he was born.

This is the beginning of Barney's story, when he realizes he is about to be haunted again.

* * *

When, suddenly, on an ordinary Wednesday, it seemed to

Barney that the world tilted and ran downhill in all directions, he knew he was about to be haunted again. It had happened when he was younger but he had thought that being haunted was a babyish thing that you grew out of, like crying when you fell over, or not having a bike.

'Remember Barney's imaginary friends, Mantis, Bigbuzz and Ghost?' Claire – his stepmother – sometimes said. 'The garden seems empty now that they've gone. I quite miss them.'

But she was really pleased perhaps because, being so very real to Barney, they had become too real for her to laugh over. Barney had been sorry to lose them, but he wanted Claire to feel comfortable living with him. He could not remember his own mother and Claire had come as a wonderful surprise, giving him a hug when he came home from school, asking him about his day, telling him about hers, arranging picnics and unexpected parties and helping him with hard homework. It seemed worth losing Mantis, Bigbuzz and Ghost and the other kind phantoms that had been his friends for so many days before Claire came.

Yet here it was beginning again . . . the faint dizzy twist in the world around him, the thin, singing drone as if some tiny insect were trapped in the curling mazes of his ear. Barney looked up at the sky searching for a ghost but there was only a great blueness like a weight pressing down on him. He looked away quickly, half expecting to be crushed into a sort of rolled-out gingerbread boy in an enormous stretched-out school uniform. Then he saw his ghost on the footpath beside him.

A figure was slowly forming out of the air: a child – quite a little one, only about four or five – struggling to be real. A curious, pale face grew clearer against a halo of shining hair, silver-gold hair that curled and crinkled, fading into the air like bright smoke. The child was smiling. It seemed to be having some difficulty in seeing Barney so that he felt that *he* might be the one who was not quite real. Well, he was used to feeling that. In the days before Claire he had often felt that he himself couldn't be properly heard or seen. But then Mantis had taken time to become solid and Ghost had always been dim and smoky. So Barney was not too surprised to see the ghost looking like a flat paper doll stuck against the air by some magician's glue. Then it became round and real, looking alive, but old-fashioned and strange, in its blue velvet suit and lace collar. A soft husky voice came out of it.

'Barnaby's dead!' it said. 'Barnaby's dead! I'm going to be very lonely.'

Barney stood absolutely still, feeling more tilted and dizzy than ever. His head rang as if it were strung like a bead on the thin humming that ran, like electricity, from ear to ear.

The ghost seemed to be announcing his death by his proper christened name of Barnaby – not just telling him he was going to die, but telling him that he was actually dead already. Now it spoke again.

'Barnaby's dead!' it said in exactly the same soft husky voice. 'Barnaby's dead! I'm going to be very lonely.' It wasn't just that it said the same words that it had said earlier. Its very tone – the lifts and falls and flutterings of its voice – was exactly the same. If it had added, 'This is a recorded message,' it would not have seemed very out of place. Barney wanted to say something back to it, but what can you say to a ghost? You can't joke with it. Perhaps you could ask it questions, but Barney was afraid of the answers this ghost might give him. He would have to believe what it told him, and it might tell him something terrible.

As it turned out this ghost was not one that would answer

questions anyway. It had only one thing to say, and it had said it. It began to swing from side to side, like an absent-minded compass needle searching for some lost North. Its shape did not change but it swung widely and lay crossways in the air looking silly, but also very frightening.

'Barnaby's dead!' it said, 'Barnaby's dead! And I'm going to be very lonely.' Then it spun like a propeller, slowly at first then faster and faster until it was only a blur of silver-gold in the air. It spun faster still until even the colours vanished and there was nothing but a faint clear flicker. Then it stopped and the ordinary air closed over it. The humming in Barney's ears stopped, the world straightened out; time began again, the wind blew, trees moved, cars droned and tooted. Down through the air from the point where the ghost had disappeared fluttered a cloud of blue flakes. Barney caught a few of them in his hand. For a moment he held nothing but scraps of paper from a torn-up picture! He caught a glimpse of a blue velvet sleeve, a piece of lace cuff and a pink thumb and finger. Then the paper turned into quicksilver beads of colour that ran through his fingers and were lost before they fell on to the footpath.

Barney wanted to be at home at once. He did not want the in-between time of going down streets and around corners. There were no short cuts. He had to run all the way, fearing that at any moment he might be struck by lightning, or a truck, or by some terrible dissolving sickness that would eat him away as he ran. Little stumbles in his running made him think he might have been struck by bullets. His hair felt prickly and he wondered if it was turning white. He could imagine arriving at home and seeing his face in the hall mirror staring out under hair like cotton wool. He could imagine Claire saying, 'Barney, what on earth have you been up to? Look at the state of your hair.' How could he say, 'Well, there was this ghost telling me that I was dead.' Claire would just say sternly, 'Barney, have you been reading horror comics again?'

As it happened it was not Claire who met him when he got home but his two sisters, one on either side of the doorway – his thin, knobbly sister Troy, stormy in her black cloud of hair, her black eyebrows almost meeting over her long nose, and brown, round Tabitha, ready to talk and talk as she always did.

'Where have you been?' she asked. 'You're late and have missed out on family news. But it's OK – the family novelist will now bring you up to date.' By 'the family novelist' Tabitha meant herself. She was writing the world's greatest novel, but no one was allowed to read it until she was twenty-one and it was published. However, she talked about it all the time and showed off by taking pages and pages of notes and talking about those, too.

'I stopped to . . .' Barney began. He felt his voice quaver and die out. He couldn't tell Tabitha about his ghost, particularly in front of Troy, who was five years older than he was and silent and scornful. But anyway – Tabitha was not interested in his explanations. She was too busy telling him the family news in her own way.

'We are a house of mourning,' she said in an important voice. 'One of our dear relations has died. It's really good material for my novel and I'm taking notes like anything. No one I know has ever died before.'

Barney stared at her in horror.

'Not Claire!' he began to say because he was always afraid that they would lose Claire in some way, particularly now that she was expecting a baby, which Barney knew was dangerous work. But Tabitha was not upset enough for it to be Claire.

'Great-Uncle Barnaby . . . a Scholar relation,' she went on and then, as Barney's face stiffened and became blank she added, sarcastically, 'You do remember him don't you? You're named after him.'

'I'm going to be very lonely,' said a soft, husky voice in Barney's ear. He felt the world begin to slide away.

'Hey!' Troy's voice spoke on his other side. 'You don't have to be upset. He was old . . . and he'd been ill – very ill, for a while.'

'It's not that!' Barney stammered. 'I – I thought it might be me.'

'Lonely!' said the echo in his haunted ear.

'I thought it *was* me,' Barney said, and suddenly the world made up its mind and shrank away from him, grown to tennis ball size, then walnut size, then a pinhead of brightness in whirling darkness. On the steps of his own home Barney had fainted.

Jan Mark

HANDLES

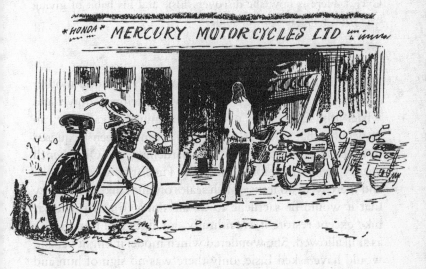

Deciding which of Jan Mark's books I should introduce you to was
fearfully frustrating. Her stories are chiefly about people and the
odd, interesting or alarming things that happen to them because of
their own characters. She is also very good writing about friendship (*Thunder and Lightnings* is about two boys with quite different
homes and, at the beginning, different interests), and she can be
very funny, as in *Hairs in the Palm of the Hand*.

In *Handles* you really have to understand and *like* the heroine.
For it's a book with a lot more about feelings than happenings.
Erica Timperley has one ambition in life – to be a motor mechanic,
and she is looking forward to spending her summer holidays

hanging around gazing at motor-bikes in the multi-storey car park in Norwich. Instead she is sent to stay with fussy Auntie Joan and her awful cousin Robert.

But luck is with her. At the end of the first week, Auntie Joan sends her off to the local town with a letter to an Elsie Wainwright, who turns out to be a young man who works at Mercury Motor Cycles. Here is how she discovers Elsie and his habit of giving everyone a 'handle' (nickname).

* * *

In the middle of the floor, balanced on oil cans, stood another skeleton, the frame of a motor cycle, stripped down and wheel-less. Erica went over and examined it carefully, an inspection that told her that it had recently been lacquered over its dark, red paint and was hardening off. On a bench nearby lay its front forks and tank. The forks were red, too, and there were no ferns or fish scales on this tank. Erica knew that it would be sacrilege to do anything to this particular bike except restore it as faithfully, lovingly and respectfully as skill allowed. She wondered which model it might be, and would have asked Elsie, only there was no sign of him and no sound from behind the counter. He seemed to have vanished, and she feared he had tiptoed out while she was examining the restoration work. Perhaps the counter could conceal the mouth of a burrow (where Bunny lived?) into which Elsie had tunnelled. She looked over the top and saw his back. He was on hands and knees and really did seem to be burrowing, for first one hand, then the other, reached out behind him and deposited something on the floor. A stack of boxes and dirty paper bags was growing round him and he seemed quite happy, like a hamster rearranging its bedding. Erica left him to it and went back to the open double doors to look out over the yard, where Auntie Joan's bicycle was browsing among

the fireweed. It was now half-past nine, and the yard was
waking up.

Along either side more doors were opening, and artefacts
were appearing outside various premises: a stack of pallets by
one, a couple of fibreglass hulls and a canoe outside another;
although there was nothing that could possibly be a birdcycle.
Two vans drove in from the far end of the yard, and here and
there was the tadpole child, darting and skittering. Along the
alley from the street came a frog on a Honda, his four-stroke
nattering back at him from the high walls on either side.
He circled the yard, bouncing loosely over ruts and broken
bricks, before turning back to halt in front of Erica. He
removed the crash helmet that concealed his entire head and
said, 'Elsie about?'

Erica gaped at him. He was wearing a green boiler-suit and
his helmet was green with a wide yellow stripe fore and aft.
Without it he appeared quite normal, a bit spotty perhaps,
but definitely a human being. In it he had looked so like a
frog, with his knees up and his head drawn into his shoulders,
that Erica almost expected him to inflate below the chin and
croak.

'Elsie about?'

'In there.' She jerked her thumb over her shoulder.

The frog climbed off his machine and wheeled it into the
shop.

'Else!'

Elsie's voice from under the counter said, 'That you, Kermit?'

'That is.'

'D'you want a word?'

'Brought the bike along.'

'Wheel her in.'

'Did.'

'Good.'

Erica lolled in the doorway, gazing. Was the frog called Kermit because he looked like a frog, or had he grown to look like a frog because he was called Kermit? He hung his green frog's head over his arm by the chin strap and waddled out, bowlegged, nodding to Erica as he went. His flat-footed boots slapped the muddy ground like flippers. Over by the vans a little voice began to yelp, 'Dad! Dad!' and the child who looked like a tadpole cantered towards him.

'What you doing here, then?' Kermit said. 'Where's your mum?'

'She's over Uncle Alan's, cleaning out.' The tadpole hopped about, arms waving. His mum and Uncle Alan could be anywhere, including on the roof.

'Well, you stick close with her and don't go breaking nothing. And stay you out of Elsie's,' Kermit admonished it.

Elsie's own urgent hissing called her attention indoors.

'Is that the Gremlin?'

'The what?'

'A little lad – big head.'

'That's right.'

'Keep him out of here. Head him off.'

'I don't think he's coming over here anyway. Why d'you call him the Gremlin?'

'Because when he gets into things they go wrong.'

Erica watched the frog part company with his tadpole as they took off in opposite directions, and went back into the shop.

'I thought it looked more like a tadpole,' Erica said.

Elsie straightened up from behind the counter. 'I suppose it would, being Kermit's,' he said. 'Karen – his mum – Mrs Kermit, her brother-in-law runs the fish shop. His old lady's supposed to do the cleaning but she put her back out and

Karen helps him. I always know when Mrs Catchpole's back's playing up if the Gremlin's about.'

Erica wondered if Kermit's Karen's brother-in-law's old lady was his wife, his mum, or just an old lady employed by him.

'. . . and the Gremlin,' Elsie was saying, 'likes coming in here to pass the time. He can't take a hint, that lad. Why don't you go over to Yerbut's and ask him to wire you up? Why don't you drop into Rat's Castle and get Jack to nail you to the wall? Why don't you go back to your Uncle Alan and get deep-fried? But he just hangs around here, prodding. He's got a special long stick, specially for prodding things. "What's this here?" he says. *Prod.* "What's that for?" *Prod.* "What does this do?" *Prod. Clang, splat, kaput!* "It doesn't do anything, *now*," I tell him.'

'Yerbut?' Erica said. She saw from the direction of Elsie's pointing finger that Yerbut's place must be the back premises of Polthorpe Radio Services in the Street.

'He argues,' Elsie said. 'Everything you say to him, he goes, "Yer, but . . ." What else would we call him?'

'But what's his name?'

'Corbet.'

Yerbut Corbet?' The Gremlin went by, his prodding stick at the ready. 'Why doesn't his mum look after him?' Erica said.

Yerbut Corbet? The Gremlin went by, his prodding stick on a bench, out of spares.'

'No, the Gremlin's mum.'

'Look after him? What with, a submachine-gun? She does look after him, according to her lights. She calls it reasoning. "You have to *reason* with them," she says. She's read too many books. "Now then, pet, we don't do that, do we?"

Prod! She'd be all right with a knot in her neck,' Elsie said, reflectively.

Conversation with Elsie was like flicking quickly through a book of pictures that had nothing to do with the words printed underneath. Already the yard was coming to life with strange people; strange people with strange names. Even the buildings were beginning to sound bizarre – Rat's Castle? Erica said quickly, 'Did you find the leads?'

'Leads?'

'Uncle Peter's jump leads that I came for.'

There was a long pause.

'Not as such,' Elsie said, finally. 'They'll be about somewhere. I'll get somebody to bring them round.'

'I could come in for them another time,' Erica suggested, having suddenly realized that there was no longer anything to keep her there, and that unless she thought of a good excuse, there would be nothing to bring her back again. In a few minutes she would be riding away into the green desert of Calstead, never to return.

'You do that,' Elsie said, 'if it's no trouble. You didn't come specially, did you?'

'No, I was shopping. I'm staying in Calstead for the holidays.'

'I thought I hadn't seen you around,' Elsie said. 'And are you enjoying it?' Unlike most people who asked her that, he sounded uncertain.

'Oh yes; ever so,' Erica said. She looked round at the fireweed where the wrought-iron cow was ruminating drunkenly; a cow with a crumpled horn. She moved reluctantly towards it.

'Mind the San Andreas Fault,' Elsie called after her.

'You what?'

'That crack in the kerb on the way out. The Duchess came

in the other day and jammed the front tyre of her Puch in it. Took a long time to lever her out. I told the council but they said it was up to Howlett's.'

'Who's Howlett's?'

'The landlord. Howlett's Industrial Estate.'

Erica looked all round her again. Behind her was Elsie's cavernous shop, in front, the little garages and stables, open windows in back premises, the mud, the fireweed and, somewhere, Rat's Castle. In the distance the Gremlin ran about, prodding and yoiking, Bunny crouched nearby alongside the Duchess's Puch that had jammed in the San Andreas Fault, and a smell of fish hung damply over all.

'Where is that?'

'Where's what?'

'The industrial estate.'

'This is it,' Elsie said.

'But that's only a yard.'

'I reckon you come from the big city, lady,' Elsie drawled. Erica knew sarcasm when she heard it, and flushed.

'I thought there'd be factories.'

'Well, Jack makes pallets – you could call him a factory. And there's the fibreglass boys, and Bill Birdcycle, only he's closed all day Wednesday. He's up at the other end, renovating a wreck. He thinks he might hire it out to television companies who need authentic, historic background material.' Elsie was indicating the distant heap of junk that Erica had seen on the way in.

'Is his name really Birdcycle?'

'No, but he does lousy lettering,' Elsie said, obscurely.

'Can I get out at that end?'

'Follow the track and you'll come into Broad Street. Watch out for Copernicus. See you . . .'

Erica mounted one pedal of the cow with the crumpled

horn and scooted over the mud and bricks, past the open doors, the Gremlin, Bill Birdcycle and his scrap heap. In the middle of the track was a crateous pothole with yellow water at the bottom. Erica wobbled round it and reached the corner of Broad Street. Now she mounted the iron cow and rode back along the side road, turning left into the Street. This time she kept her eyes open and saw the mouth of the alley-way before she passed it, with its swinging sign, the great crack in the kerb that must be the San Andreas Fault, and the glimpse of the strange land beyond; the industrial estate.

So far the journey had been uneventful. The articulated lorry had freed itself after all, she had not got jammed, like the Duchess, in the Fault, and she had managed to avoid Copernicus, whoever he might be.

William Mayne

EARTHFASTS

When I was first made Editor of Puffins (before you were born)
I made a list of authors whose books I would like to turn into
paperbacks – and at the top was William Mayne, but I had to wait
a long time to get permission from his hardback publishers – so he
wrote one especially for us called *A Parcel of Trees*, about a girl who
wanted to own a tiny piece of land. Alas, it is out of print now.
The chief reason I wanted his books was because all his plots are
quite different from anyone else's, and because his characters talk
so interestingly.

Sometimes, as in *Winter Quarters*, which is about circus people,
the characters seem to speak a different language, and sometimes a

family will have a sort of shorthand which may bewilder you at first. But, if you stay with it, you will be well rewarded. His novels are for readers with a good ear and imagination, and when you're hooked, you'll read them more than once.

Earthfasts is the story of a ghost. Nellie Jack John was a drummer-boy in 1742 whose companions dared him to go walking through a secret tunnel in the hillside to see how long they could hear him drumming. He never came out – at least he did, but in the twentieth century, where he is seen by two schoolboys, David and Keith. He can't understand what has happened and says he must go back to his billet as the army is moving out and he'll be late. David, who knows the old legend, but has already touched him and found a solid arm, is worried about how to tell him it's 200 years later.

* * *

The internal buildings of the castle have mostly gone. The keep is there, hollow as a reed, and there are two more dry towers and the skull of a dining hall. There is the stump of a well casing, and the empty socket in the ground where water once lay.

'No guns,' said Nellie Jack John. 'They're off, that's it, and I'll have to follow, and it'll be a whipping.'

'There aren't any guns,' said Keith. 'There haven't been guns here since I can remember.'

'Thou'd not ken,' said Nellie Jack John. 'It's just the soldiers get to see guns. Thou'll be out of the town and never see sike as our artillery.'

'There aren't any soldiers here now,' said Keith.

'Thou's a canny fellow,' said the drummer boy. 'That's what I've said a time or two.'

David was pacing up and down the green grass. Keith knew he was thinking. David had a grave way with him of deliberating and then pronouncing. People would listen to him, boys and masters. He walked up and down now against the distant window of clear sky west over Walker Fell, where the last gleam looked in over Vendale. Then he stood and faced Keith and Nellie Jack John.

'What year is it?' he said.

'Forty-two,' said the drummer boy. 'What year is it wi' thee?'

'The same year as it was yesterday,' said David, before Keith could speak. 'Let's sit on this rock for a bit.'

'Nay,' said Nellie Jack John. 'I'll find my quarters and you fellows can be off. There's only soldiers in here of a night.'

'Is that where you sleep?' said David.

'Aye,' said Nellie Jack John. 'Up in yon wall. They won't let us lads sleep in a tent, because we die off so soon if we do. There was one went a bit back, and that's what they took me for, in his stead.'

They stumbled in darkness towards the tower, which was black against grey sky. There was rough ground underfoot. Though the grass was mown each week there was a great deal of low wall showing the outlines of previous buildings, uncovered by the Ministry of Works and left out for interest. It was something to see for your shilling. Keith barked his shins on one of the walls. He muttered a bit, because he did not like to swear in front of David. If David swore it sounded respectable and necessary. If anyone else swore in front of him it sounded childish and petulant and weak.

'Don't say anything,' said David, softly.

'I didn't,' said Keith, a little surprised that David should think he had sworn. Never before had he said anything for or against swearing. He had always managed to convey his disapproval just by being there, a thing that Keith sometimes resented very much, and at other times marvelled at. David had a presence with him, even when he was doing nothing.

'I don't mean swearing,' said David. 'I mean about him. I know what's happened, and I'll have to tell him in a bit.'

'What happened?' said Keith. 'What do you know? Tell me first, because I don't like being out here in the dark with a sort of ghost.'

'Wait on,' said David.

They followed Nellie Jack John. He was feeling his way up a broken stair towards the tower. David ran up beside him, to stop him when he reached the tower, because he knew that there was no sleeping place there for anyone, and no floor. There was an iron bar, and that was all, and the drop into the cellars of the tower.

Nellie Jack John came to the iron bar, and stopped. He shook the bar. 'What is it?' he said.

'Look,' said David. He brought out a match and struck it. Nellie Jack John shrank away from the sudden flame, and then looked round at what the light of it showed. There was the dark depth below, and beside him the ruined doorway with the wallflowers and herb robert rooted in the cracks of the stone. Above was the roofless tower and the gaping windows. David let the match drop into the windless cellar. The flame went blue as the little stick fell, then landed on the broken stone below, flared up and showed the walls, and then died.

After it none of them could see anything. They could hear each other's breathing, and that was all. Then their eyes could see the sky again, and then the paleness of skin, and eye could see eye.

Nellie Jack John sat down where he was and leaned against the wall.

'Where's my supper at, then?' he said. His mind was not going to believe yet. Keith felt in his pocket for the light unripe nuts he had gathered in Haw Bank. He put a handful down. Nellie Jack John picked them up and felt them.

'Nuts,' he said, and put one in his mouth between his teeth, to crack the shell. 'Nay,' he said, spitting it out. 'That's not ready. Them's not brown-leemers.'

Brown-leemers are ripe nuts, ready to slip shining from their leafy holder and be cracked smartly and be mellow on the tongue.

'It's the time of year,' said David.

'Nay, there's niver nuts in May,' said the drummer boy. 'That's a song t'lasses sing.'

'It is yet,' said David. 'But it isn't May.'

'It was May an hour ago,' said Nellie Jack John. 'I was smelling the blossom when I went in the rock.'

He cracked a nut carefully, and chewed up the kernel. 'My mob's that dry,' he said. 'There's watter in t'cundith.'

'Water where?' said David, now that he came across an unfamiliar word.

'In t'cundith,' said the drummer boy. 'Where t'watter runs.'

'It's all dried up,' said Keith.

'We can't find it in the dark,' said David. 'Where did you go into the rock?'

'I'll not tell you that,' said the drummer boy. 'Ask on.'

David sat beside the drummer boy. 'I'll have to tell you something,' he said. 'You'd better come home with me.'

'Nay, we've to stop in this end of the night,' said the drummer boy. 'Or we'll be whipped.'

'There's nobody here to whip you,' said David.

'They'll not be so far,' said the drummer boy.

'Nellie Jack John,' said David, 'don't you think there's something different about this place now?'

'I do that,' said the drummer boy. 'It doesn't stink so much as it did.'

'And it's fallen in more, and got in a ruin.'

'It has that,' said the drummer boy.

'And there's no folk about. And listen.'

They listened. Keith thought there was no unusual sound. A car started in the market place, went up the steepness in a low gear, and then hurried along King Street to the round-about and along the Reeth road.

'Wild boars,' said Nellie Jack John. 'They come up by the town of a night.'

Then there was a noise in the sky. Keith and David were used to the night flight from Liverpool to Newcastle that went winking overhead in the darkness. Tonight it was just under the cloud, the same old Dakota, lumbering over the hills, echoing over each dale in turn.

Nellie Jack John put a hand on David's arm. 'I don't like that so much,' he said. 'I don't.'

'It was May time when you went in that tunnel,' he said. 'It's September now, turning to October.' Then he told him the year.

The drummer boy looked at him. 'Nay,' he said. 'Thou's chousing me.'

'No,' said David. 'You were two hundred years and more in that passage, just walking through. I know about you. You went in there because they said that King Arthur was asleep under the castle, with his knights and his treasure.'

'I'll not tell you the spot,' said Nellie Jack John.

'But that's what you did,' said David. 'You took the drum, because you were going to play it all the way, and your friends were going to follow on the ground above, to see where the passage went. Then they would dig down and find the treasure.'

'Ay,' said Nellie Jack John. 'It were that.'

'You went in,' said David. 'They heard the drum going for a bit, and then it stopped. And you never came out.'

'I niver stopped,' said Nellie Jack John. 'I played all the time, right on. And I came out.'

'You came out,' said David. 'But two hundreds years later.'

'It can't be so,' said Nellie Jack John. 'It would never be. I niver heard owt like it.'

'If King Arthur can be asleep there all this time, then you can be there a long time too,' said David.

Keith could not bear this story in this place at this time of night.

'Let's go home,' he said.

'Ay,' said Nellie Jack John. 'Give up your tale, and let's be having some ale and be off to bed.'

'It's true, though,' said David. 'This is not 1742. Not seventeen anything, but nineteen something. You were two hundred years walking.'

'I thought I wanted my supper,' said Nellie Jack John. 'But two hundred years is out of all reckoning.'

'It can't be right,' said Keith.

'It's the simplest explanation,' said David. 'You told me just now that the simplest theory was the best one. Try and explain it another way.'

'Yes, but that story about King Arthur,' said Keith. 'You just made that up.'

'I didn't,' said David. 'I can show you it in a book. I thought you would know it too.'

'I never heard of it,' said Keith. 'Why would the drumming stop if he didn't stop doing it?'

'Oh, work it out,' said David. 'Nellie Jack John, you'd better come to my house tonight.'

'Nay,' said the drummer boy. 'If there's nowt here, then I's off home t'i Eskeleth.'

They all sat where they were for a time, letting the idea sink into their minds. But even David's mind, which had been playing with the idea longest, would not take it in. It was not possible by ordinary standards of thought for a boy to walk for two hundred years underground, and then come out. Nor was it possible for two more boys to meet him and talk to him, even fight with him for a moment. There were too many impossible things. But the only explanation was the impossible one.

'I's off,' said Nellie Jack John, standing up and scattering nuts over the others. 'I'll see my lass, Kath, and she'll tell me I's right, and me and t'other fellows will give thee bounce in the morning.'

'No,' said David. 'Come back with me.'

'Nay, I will not,' said Nellie Jack John. 'There's two liars I niver want to meet again without I've a brog wi' me, and then I'll brog them. I'll fend the night by meself, and then we'll see.'

David stood up too. He was prepared to take Nellie Jack John and drag him home, rather than let him wander about in the strange night of a different century, where he would know nothing about so many things. But Nellie Jack John pulled his arm away from David's hand, and ran across the grass of the castle bailey, towards the edge of the rock, tripping and stumbling as he went. They heard his words change to a different sound. When he had come to the edge of the rock, and was casting about for a way to go down, he was no longer speaking and calling them liars and villains and claiming they were mainswearing him, but gasping out sobs. As he went down the rock, clambering and scrambling, his voice grew louder. Anger gave way to fear, and his last cry was one of terror, coming up the rock out of the darkness.

They could not find him in the dark. They climbed down the way he must have gone, and searched the walk below, in case the terror was from falling. But he was not there. Then David went home and brought out a torch, and they looked again. He was not there. In the end David said he certainly had not fallen, and went home abruptly. Keith followed.

Mary Norton

THE BORROWERS

I'm so nutty about the *Borrowers* books that I'd be quite happy
with them alone on a desert island – and it's been dreadfully difficult
deciding which bit will make you go rushing out to find them.
Well, imagine whole families of tiny people living in hiding in
your house, and just popping out every now and again to 'borrow'
things they need, like a safety pin for a clothes line, or a thimble
for simmering soup, or, of course, a few crumbs of pie or even a
couple of peas. No bother to anyone, unless losing a few buttons
and bits of string is upsetting. Only, of course, Human Beans –
that's us – must never see them in case they do them harm, like
awful Mrs Driver, the housekeeper, who tries to exterminate them.

Here are the Clock family (because they live under the grandfather clock) facing a crisis in their lives, because Pod (the father) has been seen by A Boy. Arrietty is his daughter, and Homily is his wife.

There are four other Borrowers books: *The Borrowers Afield*, *The Borrowers Afloat*, *The Borrowers Aloft* and finally, *The Borrowers Avenged*. I think they are classics and will live for ever.

* * *

Arrietty had not been asleep. She had been lying under her knotted coverlet staring up at the ceiling. It was an interesting ceiling. Pod had built Arrietty's bedroom out of two cigar-boxes, and on the ceiling lovely, painted ladies dressed in swirls of chiffon blew long trumpets against a background of blue sky; below there were feathery palm-trees and small white houses set about a square. It was a glamorous scene, above all by candlelight, but tonight Arrietty had stared with-out seeing. The wood of a cigar-box is thin and Arrietty, lying straight and still under the quilt, had heard the rise and fall of worried voices. She had heard her own name; she had heard Homily exclaim: 'Nuts and berries, that's what they eat!' and she had heard, after a while, the heart-felt cry of 'What shall we do?'

So when Homily appeared beside her bed, she wrapped herself obediently in her quilt and, padding in her bare feet along the dusty passage, she joined her parents in the warmth of the kitchen. Crouched on her little stool she sat clasping her knees, shivering a little, and looking from one face to another.

Homily came beside her and, kneeling on the floor, she placed an arm round Arrietty's skinny shoulders. 'Arrietty,' she said gravely, 'you know about upstairs?'

'What about it?' asked Arrietty.

'You know about the two giants?'

'Yes,' said Arrietty, 'Great Aunt Sophy and Mrs Driver.'

'That's right,' said Homily, 'and Crampfurl in the garden.' She laid a roughened hand on Arrietty's clasped ones. 'You know about Uncle Hendreary?'

Arrietty thought awhile. 'He went abroad?' she said.

'Emigrated,' corrected Homily, 'to the other side of the world. With Aunt Lupy and all the children. To a badger's set – a hole in a bank under a hawthorn hedge. Now why do you think he did this?'

'Oh,' said Arrietty, her face alight, 'to be out of doors . . . to lie in the sun . . . to run in the grass . . . to swing on twigs like the birds do . . . to suck honey . . .'

'Nonsense, Arrietty,' exclaimed Homily sharply, 'that's a nasty habit! And your Uncle Hendreary's a rheumatic sort of man. He emigrated,' she went on, stressing the word, 'because he was "seen".'

'Oh,' said Arrietty.

'He was "seen" on 23rd of April, 1892, by Rosa Pickhat-chet, on the drawing-room mantelpiece. Of all places . . .' she added suddenly in a wondering aside.

'Oh,' said Arrietty.

'I have never heard nor no one has never seen fit to tell why he went on the drawing-room mantelpiece in the first place. There's nothing on it, your father assures me, which cannot be seen from the floor or by standing sideways on the handle of the bureau and steadying yourself on the key. That's what your father does if he ever goes into the drawing-room –'

'They said it was a liver pill,' put in Pod.

'How do you mean?' asked Homily, startled.

'A liver pill for Lupy.' Pod spoke wearily. 'Someone started a rumour,' he went on, 'that there were liver pills on the drawing-room mantelpiece . . .'

'Oh,' said Homily and looked thoughtful, 'I never heard

that. All the same,' she exclaimed, 'it was stupid and fool-hardy. There's no way down except by the bell-pull. She dusted him, they say, with a feather duster, and he stood so still, alongside a cupid, that she might never have noticed him if he hadn't sneezed. She was new, you see, and didn't know the ornaments. We heard her screeching right here under the kitchen. And they could never get her to clean anything much after that that wasn't chairs or tables – least of all the tiger-skin rug.'

'I don't hardly never bother with the drawing-room,' said Pod. 'Everything's got its place like and they see what goes. There might be a little something left on a table or down the side of a chair, but not without there's been company, and there never is no company – not for the last ten or twelve year. Sitting here in this chair, I can tell you by heart every blessed thing that's in that drawing-room, working round from the cabinet by the window to the –'

'There's a mint of things in that cabinet,' interrupted Homily, 'solid silver some of them. A solid silver violin, they got there, strings and all – just right for our Arrietty.'

'What's the good,' asked Pod, 'of things behind glass?'

'Couldn't you break it?' suggested Arrietty. 'Just a corner, just a little tap, just a . . .' Her voice faltered as she saw the shocked amazement on her father's face.

'Listen here, Arrietty,' began Homily angrily, and then she controlled herself and patted Arrietty's clasped hands. 'She don't know much about borrowing,' she explained to Pod. 'You can't blame her.' She turned again to Arrietty. 'Borrow-ing's a skilled job, an art like. Of all the families who've been in this house, there's only us left, and do you know for why? Because your father, Arrietty, is the best Borrower that's been known in these parts since – well, before your grandad's time. Even your Aunt Lupy admitted that much. When he was younger I've seen your father walk the length of a laid dinner-table, after the gong was rung, taking a nut or sweet from every dish, and down by a fold in the tablecloth as the first people came in at the door. He'd do it just for fun, wouldn't you, Pod?'

Pod smiled wanly. 'There weren't no sense in it,' he said.

'Maybe,' said Homily, 'but you did it! Who else would dare?'

'I were younger then,' said Pod. He sighed and turned to Arrietty. 'You don't break things, lass. That's not the way to do it. That's not borrowing . . .'

'We were rich then,' said Homily. 'Oh, we did have some lovely things! You were only a tot, Arrietty, and wouldn't remember. We had a whole suite of walnut furniture out of the doll's house and a set of wineglasses in green glass, and a musical snuff-box, and the cousins would come and we'd have parties. Do you remember, Pod? Not only the cousins. The Harpsichords came. Everybody came – except those Overmantels from the morning-room. And we'd dance and dance and the young people would sit out by the grating. Three tunes that snuff-box played – *Clementine*, *God Save the Queen* and the *Post-Chaise Gallop*. We were the envy of everybody – even the Overmantels . . .'

'Who were the Overmantels?' asked Arrietty.

'Oh, you must've heard me talk of the Overmantels,' exclaimed Homily, 'that stuck-up lot who lived in the wall high up – among the lath and plaster behind the mantelpiece in the morning-room. And a queer lot they were. The men smoked all the time because the tobacco jars were kept there; and they'd climb about and in and out the carvings of the overmantel, sliding down pillars and showing off. The women were a conceited lot too, always admiring themselves in all those bits of overmantel looking-glass. They never asked anyone up there and I, for one, never wanted to go. I've no head for heights, and your father never liked the men. He's always lived steady, your father has, and not only the tobacco jars, but the whisky decanters too, were kept in the morning-room and they say those Overmantel men would suck up the dregs in the glasses through those quill pipe-cleaners they keep there on the mantelpiece. I don't know whether it's true but they do say that those Overmantel men used to have a party every Tuesday after the bailiff had been to talk business in the morning-room. Laid out, they'd be, dead drunk – or so the story goes – on the green plush table-cloth, all among the tin boxes and the account books –'

'Now, Homily,' protested Pod, who did not like gossip, 'I never see'd 'em.'

'But you wouldn't put it past them, Pod. You said yourself when I married you not to call on the Overmantels.'

'They lived so high,' said Pod, 'that's all.'

'Well, they were a lazy lot – that much you can't deny. They never had no kind of home life. Kept themselves warm in winter by the heat of the morning-room fire and ate nothing but breakfast food; breakfast, of course, was the only meal served in the morning-room.'

'What happened to them?' asked Arrietty.

'Well, when the Master died and She took to her bed, there was no more use for the morning-room. So the Overmantels had to go. What else could they do? No food, no fire. It's a bitter cold room in winter.'

'And the Harpsichords?' asked Arrietty.

Homily looked thoughtful. 'Well, they were different. I'm not saying they weren't stuck-up too, because they were. Your Aunt Lupy, who married your Uncle Hendreary, was a Harpsichord by marriage and we all know the airs she gave herself.'

'Now, Homily –' began Pod.

'Well, she'd no right to. She was only a Rain-Pipe from the stables before she married Harpsichord.'

'Didn't she marry Uncle Hendreary?' asked Arrietty.

'Yes, later. She was a widow with two children and he was a widower with three. It's no good looking at me like that, Pod. You can't deny she took it out of poor Hendreary: she thought it was a comedown to marry a Clock.'

'Why?' asked Arrietty.

'Because we Clocks live under the kitchen, that's why. Because we don't talk fancy grammar and eat anchovy toast. But to live under the kitchen doesn't say we aren't educated. The Clocks are just as old a family as the Harpsichords. You remember that, Arrietty, and don't let anyone tell you different. Your grandfather could count and write down the numbers up to – what was it, Pod?'

'Fifty-seven,' said Pod.

'There,' said Homily, 'fifty-seven! And your father can count, as you know, Arrietty; he can count and write down the numbers, on and on, as far as it goes. How far does it go, Pod?'

'Close on a thousand,' said Pod.

'There!' exclaimed Homily, 'and he knows the alphabet because he taught you, Arrietty, didn't he? And he would have been able to read – wouldn't you, Pod? – if he hadn't had to start borrowing so young. Your Uncle Hendreary and your father had to go out borrowing at thirteen – your age, Arrietty, think of it!'

'But I should like –' began Arrietty.

'So he didn't have your advantages,' went on Homily breathlessly, 'and just because the Harpsichords lived in the drawing-room – they moved in there, in 1837, to a hole in the wainscot just behind where the harpsichord used to stand, if ever there was one, which I doubt – and were really a family called Linen-Press or some such name and changed it to Harpsichord –'

'What did they live on,' asked Arrietty, 'in the drawing-room?'

'Afternoon tea,' said Homily, 'nothing but afternoon tea. No wonder the children grew up peaky.'

Robert C. O'Brien

MRS FRISBY AND THE RATS OF NIMH

Who would have thought someone could write a story which makes you like rats? Well, this one does. Mind you, they *are* exceptional rats, captured and trained in a science laboratory, fed on drugs to increase their intelligence and life span, and *taught to read*, which is how they make their escape. After two difficult years they have found a safe home.

Mrs Frisby, on the other hand, is a lone, lorn widow fieldmouse, worried to death because her son is too ill to be turned out of his winter home and the farmer is about to start spring ploughing. The owl advises her to ask help from the rats of NIMH, and when they discover who her dead husband was they come to her rescue. Here they are making their plans.

* * *

Nicodemus closed the door behind her, then sat down on one of the benches, facing Mrs Frisby; the others sat down too, Mr Ages stretching his splinted leg in front of him. Nicodemus took the reading-glass from his satchel, opened it, and through it gravely examined Mrs Frisby's face. 'You will forgive the glass and the scrutiny,' he said. 'When I lost my left eye, I also damaged the right one; I can see little close-up without the glass – indeed, not very much even with it.' At length he folded the glass and put it on the table.

'Now,' he said, 'what is it we can do to help you?'

So Mrs Frisby recounted once more the events that had led to her coming there, and at the end repeated what the owl had advised her to say – 'move the house into the lee of the stone.'

She added: 'I don't understand just what he meant by that. Jeremy – the crow – says it means the side where there's no wind. But what good would that do?'

'I think I know what he meant,' said Nicodemus. 'In a broad sense, lee means the sheltered side. A bird, flying over Mr Fitzgibbon's garden, would notice something most of us would miss.'

He reached down into his satchel and took out a sheet of paper and a pencil; he opened the reading-glass again. As he talked, he drew a sketch:

'When a farmer ploughs a field with a big rock in it, he ploughs around the rock – close on each side, leaving a triangle of unploughed land on each end.

'Mrs Frisby's house is beside the rock, and will get ploughed up – and probably crushed, as the owl said. But if we can move it a few feet – so that it lies buried *behind* the rock – in the lee – then she and her children can stay in it as long as they need to.

'From the air, the way the owl sees it, the garden would look like that.' He inspected the sketch through the reading-glass and then placed it on the table.

Mrs Frisby climbed up on the bench and looked at it. It was a rough map, showing the garden, the big stone near the middle, and the way the furrows made by the plough would curve around it, rather like waves around a boat.

'Show me where your house is buried,' said Nicodemus. Mrs Frisby pointed to the spot on the sketch.

'I know where that cement block is,' said the rat named Arthur. 'In fact, I thought about bringing it in, but I decided it was too long a haul. They had it tied on top of the harrow for weight, and it fell off just as they were finishing the garden.'

'Can you move it,' asked Nicodemus, pointing at the sketch, 'to this spot right there, and bury it again?'

'Yes,' said Arthur. 'That shouldn't be hard.'

Mrs Frisby was delighted; looking at the map, it all became clear, and she could see what a beautifully simple idea it was. When Mr Fitzgibbon ploughed, he would go right past their house; they would not have to move until Timothy was well and until the weather was truly warm. She remembered again what her husband had said – how easy to unlock a door when you have the key. She had found the key. Or rather, the owl had found it.

Nicodemus asked Arthur: 'How long will it take?'

'Depends. With a party of ten, a couple of hours. With twenty, maybe an hour.'

'We can spare twenty. But it's still too long.' He looked worried.

So did Arthur. 'Yes,' he said. 'We'll have to work at night – but even so . . . There's just no cover at all. It's wide open.'

'We'll have to take care of Dragon,' said Justin.

'Yes,' said Mr Ages, 'and with this leg, I can't do it. I'd never make it to the bowl, much less get back again.'

Mrs Frisby, looking at their baffled faces, felt her delight subsiding. Obviously something was wrong.

'I don't understand,' she said. 'I know about Dragon, of course, but . . .'

'At night,' said Justin, 'Dragon prowls the farmyard like a tiger. And you don't see him until he's on top of you.'

'Then you can't move my house after all.'

'Well,' Justin said, 'ordinarily . . .' He turned to Nicodemus. 'Should I explain it to her?'

'Yes,' said Nicodemus.

'Ordinarily,' said Justin, 'when we have a long project to do at night – sometimes even by day – we make sure Dragon won't bother us. We put sleeping powder in his food. Mr Ages makes it. It doesn't do the cat any harm; but he stays extremely drowsy for the next eight hours or so. We station a sentry to watch him, and we're free to work.'

'You did it yesterday!' cried Mrs Frisby, remembering the figures toiling with the wire through the grass, remembering how strangely disinterested Dragon had seemed when he saw her. 'I saw the cat sleeping in the yard.'

'Yes,' said Justin, 'but today Mr Ages has a broken leg.'

'Then he can't make the powder?'

'It isn't that,' said Mr Ages. 'I've plenty of powder.'

'The trouble is,' said Justin, 'it's Mr Ages who puts it in Dragon's dinner bowl, inside the farm kitchen. With his leg broken, he can't move fast enough.'

'But why Mr Ages?' said Mrs Frisby. 'Can't someone else do it?'

'I'd be glad to do it myself,' said Justin, 'but I'm too big.'

'You see,' Nicodemus explained, 'Mrs Fitzgibbon feeds the

cat in the morning and in the evening, and his bowl is always kept in the same place – next to a cabinet in one corner of the kitchen. There's a very shallow space between the floor and the bottom of the cabinet. A few years ago when we conceived the idea of putting Dragon to sleep, we cut a hole in the floor just behind the cabinet – if we put it anywhere else they'd see it. To reach the bowl, Mr Ages crawls under the cabinet. When he gets to the edge, he makes a quick dash to the bowl, drops in the powder, and dashes back out of sight. But with a broken leg, he can't dash.'

'We might try leaving some bait outside the house,' said Justin. 'That worked once.'

'Once out of a dozen tries,' said Nicodemus. 'It isn't dependable, and we don't have much time. To be safe, we ought to move that block tonight.'

'If we had some catfood . . .' said Justin, thinking aloud. 'He might eat that, even on the porch, because he knows it's his. Maybe tonight I could go in through the attic and down to the kitchen . . .'

'No use,' said Mr Ages. 'They keep it in a metal cabinet up on the wall. You couldn't get it without a crew. And that would make too much noise.'

'Anyway,' said Nicodemus, 'it would put off moving the block until tomorrow night.'

'Then,' Justin said, 'I guess what we do is stake our scouts wherever we can, try to keep track of Dragon, and hope for the best. Some nights he doesn't go near the garden at all. We might be lucky.'

'Or we might not,' said Arthur. 'I don't like it. We can't dig that block out without some noise, you know.'

Mrs Frisby interrupted quietly. 'There is another way,' she said. 'If Mr Ages can get into the kitchen, so can I. If you will give me the powder and show me the way, I will try to put it in Dragon's bowl.'

Justin said quickly: 'No. It's no job for a lady.'

'You forget,' Mrs Frisby said. 'I'm Timothy's mother. If you and Arthur and others in your group can take risks to save him, surely I can, too. And consider this: I don't want any of you to be hurt – maybe even killed – by Dragon. But even more, I don't want the attempt to fail. Perhaps the worst that will happen to you, with luck, is that you will have to scatter and run, and leave my house unmoved. But then what will happen to us? Timothy, at least, will die. So if there is no one else to put the cat to sleep, I must do it.'

Nicodemus considered, and then spoke:

'She's right, of course. If she chooses to take the risk, we can't deny her the right.' To Mrs Frisby he added: 'But you should know that the danger is great. It was in the same kitchen yesterday, running from Dragon's bowl, that Mr Ages got his leg broken. And it was in doing the same thing, last year, that your husband died.'

Philippa Pearce

TOM'S MIDNIGHT GARDEN

I've chosen this as one of my favourite books because, as well as telling a wonderful story, it explores the mysteries of time travel in a serious and thoughtful way. For Tom – staying with relatives, lonely and bored – doesn't just accept the fact that the dreary back-yard of the house can be transformed into a magical garden at the midnight hour, he keeps trying to work out just how and *when* he is able to move in and out of this fascinating Victorian world. He is also worried in case he gets suddenly trapped and will have to stay there for ever.

Here is Tom on the verge of his first fantastic discovery, when he decides to investigate the grandfather clock which has just struck thirteen!

* * *

Tom put on his bedroom slippers, but decided against his dressing-gown: after all, it was summer. He closed his bedroom door carefully behind him, so that it should not bang in his absence. Outside the front door of the flat he took off one of his slippers; he laid it on the floor against the door jamb and then closed the door on to it, as on to a wedge. That would keep the door open for his return.

The lights on the first-floor landing and in the hall were turned out, for the tenants were all in bed and asleep, and Mrs Bartholomew was asleep and dreaming. The only illumination was a sideways shaft of moonlight through the long window part way up the stairs. Tom felt his way downstairs and into the hall.

Here he was checked. He could find the grandfather clock – a tall and ancient figure of black in the lesser blackness – but he was unable to read its face. If he opened its dial-door and felt until he found the position of the clock-hands, then his sense of touch would tell him the time. He fumbled first at one side of the door, then at the other; but there seemed no catch – no way in. He remembered how the pendulum-case door had not yielded to him either, on that first day. Both must be kept locked.

Hurry! hurry! the house seemed to whisper round him. The hour is passing . . . passing . . .

Tom turned from the clock to feel for the electric-light switch. Where had it been? His fingers swept the walls in vain: nowhere.

Light – light: that was what he needed! And the only light was the moonbeam that glanced sideways through the stairway window and spent itself at once and uselessly on the wall by the window-sill.

Tom studied the moonbeam, with an idea growing in his mind. From the direction in which the beam came, he saw that the moon must be shining at the back of the house. Very well, then, if he opened the door at the far end of the hall – at the back of the house, that is – he would let that moonlight in. With luck there might be enough light for him to read the clock-face.

He moved down the hall to the door at its far end. It was a door he had never seen opened – the Kitsons used the door at the front. They said that the door at the back was only a less convenient way to the street, through a backyard – a strip of paving where dustbins were kept and where the tenants of the ground-floor back flat garaged their car under a tarpaulin.

Never having had occasion to use the door, Tom had no idea how it might be secured at night. If it were locked, and the key kept elsewhere . . . But it was not locked, he found; only bolted. He drew the bolt, and, very slowly, to make no sound, turned the door-knob.

Hurry! whispered the house and the grandfather clock at the heart of it beat an anxious tick, tick.

Tom opened the door wide and let in the moonlight. It flooded in, as bright as daylight – the white daylight that comes before the full rising of the sun. The illumination was perfect, but Tom did not at once turn to see what it showed him on the clock-face. Instead he took a step forward on to the doorstep. He was staring, at first in surprise, then with indignation, at what he saw outside. That they should have deceived him – lied to him – like this! They had said, 'It's not worth your while going out at the back, Tom.' So carelessly they had described it: 'A sort of backyard, very poky, with rubbish bins. Really, there's nothing to see.'

Nothing . . . Only this: a great lawn where flower-beds bloomed; a towering fir tree, and thick, beetle-browed yews that humped their shapes down two sides of the lawn; on the third side, to the right, a greenhouse almost the size of a real house; from each corner of the lawn, a path that twisted away to some other depths of garden, with other trees.

Tom had stepped forward instinctively, catching his breath in surprise; now he let his breath out in a deep sigh. He would steal out here tomorrow, by daylight. They had tried to keep this from him, but they could not stop him now – not his aunt, nor his uncle, nor the back flat tenants, nor even particular Mrs Bartholomew. He would run full tilt over the grass, leaping the flower-beds; he would peer through the glittering panes of the greenhouse – perhaps open the door and go in; he would visit each alcove and archway clipped in the yew-trees – he would climb the trees and make his way from one to another through thickly interlacing branches. When they came calling him, he would hide, silent and safe as a bird, among this richness of leaf and bough and tree-trunk.

The scene tempted him even now: it lay so inviting and clear before him – clear-cut from the stubby leaf-pins of the nearer yew trees to the curled-back petals of the hyacinths in the crescent-shaped corner beds. Yet Tom remembered his ten hours and his honour. Regretfully he turned from the garden, back indoors to read the grandfather clock.

He re-crossed the threshold, still absorbed in the thought of what he had seen outside. For that reason, perhaps, he could not at once make out how the hall had become different: his eyes informed him of some shadowy change; his bare foot was trying to tell him something . . .

The grandfather clock was still there, anyway, and must tell him the true time. It must be either twelve or one: there was no hour between. There is no thirteenth hour.

Tom never reached the clock with his inquiry, and may be excused for forgetting, on this occasion, to check its truthfulness. His attention was distracted by the opening of a door down the hall – the door of the ground-floor front flat. A maid trotted out.

Tom had seen housemaids only in pictures, but he recognized the white apron, cap and cuffs, and the black stockings. (He was not expert in fashions, but the dress seemed to him to be rather long for her.) She was carrying paper, kindling wood and a box of matches.

He had only a second in which to observe these things. Then he realized that he ought to take cover at once; and there was no cover to take. Since he must be seen, Tom determined to be the first to speak – to explain himself.

He did not feel afraid of the maid: as she came nearer, he saw that she was only a girl. To warn her of his presence without startling her, Tom gave a cough; but she did not seem to hear it. She came on. Tom moved forward into her line of vision; she looked at him, but looked through him, too, as though he were not there. Tom's heart jumped in a way he did not understand. She was passing him.

'I say!' he protested loudly; but she paid not the slightest attention. She passed him, reached the front door of the ground-floor back flat, turned the door-handle and went in. There was no bell-ringing or unlocking of the door.

Tom was left gaping; and, meanwhile, his senses began to insist upon telling him of experiences even stranger than this encounter. His one bare foot was on cold flagstone, he knew; yet there was a contradictory softness and warmth to this flagstone. He looked down and saw that he was standing on a rug – a tiger-skin rug. There were other rugs down the hall. His eyes now took in the whole of the hall – a hall that was different. No laundry box, no milk bottles, no travel posters on the walls. The walls were decorated with a rich variety of other objects instead: a tall Gothic barometer, a fan of peacock feathers, a huge engraving of a battle (hussars and horses and shot-riddled banners) and many other pictures. There was a big dinner gong, with its wash-leathered gong-stick hanging beside it. There was a large umbrella stand holding umbrellas and walking-sticks and a parasol and an air-gun and what looked like the parts of a fishing-rod. Along the wall projected a series of bracket-shelves, each table-high. They were of oak, except for one towards the middle of the hall, by the grandfather clock. That was of white marble, and it was piled high with glass cases of stuffed birds and animals. Enacted on its chilly surface were scenes of hot-bloodshed: an owl clutched a mouse in its claws; a ferret looked up from the killing of its rabbit; in a case in the middle a red fox slunk along with a gamefowl hanging from its jaws.

In all that crowded hall, the only object that Tom recognized was the grandfather clock. He moved towards it, not to read its face, but simply to touch it – to reassure himself that this at least was as he knew it.

His hand was nearly upon it, when he heard a little breath behind him that was the maid passing back the way she had come. For some reason, she did not seem to make as much sound as before. He heard her call only faintly: 'I've lit the fire in the parlour.'

She was making for the door through which she had first come, and, as Tom followed her with his eyes, he received a curious impression: she reached the door, her hand was upon the knob, and then she seemed to go. That was it exactly: she went, but not through the door. She simple thinned out, and went.

Even as he stared at where she had been, Tom became aware of something going on furtively and silently about

him. He looked round sharply, and caught the hall in the act
of emptying itself of furniture and rugs and pictures. They
were not positively going, perhaps, but rather beginning to
fail to be there. The Gothic barometer, for instance, was
there, before he turned to look at the red fox; when he turned
back, the barometer was still there, but it had the appearance
of something only sketched against the wall, and the wall was
visible through it; meanwhile the fox had slunk into nothingness, and all the other creatures were going with him; and,
turning back again swiftly to the barometer, Tom found that
gone already.

In a matter of seconds the whole hall was as he had seen it
on his first arrival. He stood dumbfounded. He was roused
from his stupefaction by the chill of a draught at his back: it
reminded him that the garden door was left open. Whatever
else had happened, he had really opened that door; and he
must shut it. He must go back to bed.

He closed the door after a long look: 'I shall come back,'
he promised silently to the trees and the lawn and the greenhouse.

Arthur Ransome

WE DIDN'T MEAN
TO GO TO SEA

Arthur Ransome is the kind of author you either take to your heart,
so that you want to read every one of his books, or else you wonder
why he bothered to write about rather everyday things. There are
adventures, of course, but for the most part his books are all about
quite ordinary children enjoying perfectly possible doings, almost
always to do with sailing or camping. He makes them fascinating
simply because of the way he writes and gets in every tiny detail
without being boring about it.

There are eight books about three different sets of families, all of
whom you get to know extremely well. This book – which is my
favourite – is about the Walker family: John, Susan, Titty and

Roger (who also starred in *Swallows and Amazons*). They have been given permission to join their friend, Jim, on his yacht, but while he's away shopping for provisions, having left the yacht securely anchored in the harbour, a thick fog comes down, the tide comes up, the anchor breaks and they find themselves drifting. Here they are, desperately trying to drop another anchor to stop themselves going out to sea.

* * *

'What's happened?'

'What's the matter?'

Titty and Roger dodged out of the way as John came tumbling up out of the cabin. John did not really know himself, not for certain. But that jerk and then the queer feel of something scraping and then the jerk again had reminded him of a day out fishing long ago when the anchor had dragged because the rope had not been long enough. Then it had not mattered. But now, if the *Goblin* was dragging her anchor in a fog, with a tide under her . . . It didn't really matter Jim Brading being ashore while the *Goblin* was safely anchored where he had left her. But if she dragged . . .? John hurried along the side deck, holding on to a rail on the cabin top that was dripping wet in the fog. That was the worst of it. You couldn't see the shore. You couldn't see anything. Perhaps nothing had happened and she was still in the same place.

'Beu . . . eueueueueueueu . . .'

That was the lightship, somewhere away over the starboard quarter, and it had been somewhere on the port bow. He remembered that the tide had turned, so that now the *Goblin*'s bow would be heading up the harbour. The ebb was racing past her out to sea.

Just as John got to the foredeck, that queer shiver ran through the boat again. He steadied himself with a hand on the winch, half covered with rusty chain. He grabbed the forestay and looked down over the stemhead. The chain was hanging straight up and down. Last time he had seen it it had been leading well away from the stem as the *Goblin* was pulling at her anchor. Something had happened. He knelt as near the stemhead as he could get and leaning over pulled at the chain. It was as if something under water was gently tapping at it. Yes, the anchor was dragging. But surely the anchor had gone down all right, not tangled in the chain or anything like that. Why, Jim Brading had anchored the *Goblin* himself . . . and then Jim Brading's last words flashed into John's mind . . . 'Tide's just turning . . . dead low water . . .' But that was six hours ago. Six hours the tide had been pouring in. The chain that had been long enough to hold the *Goblin* at dead low water was far too short to hold her at high water, at the top of the tide, when the water was more than twice as deep. The anchor must be hardly touching the bottom.

John scrambled to his feet, almost more ashamed than he could bear. Call himself a mate, indeed. He ought to have thought of that ages ago and let out more chain as soon as the fog had come, or even sooner. Jim had said himself he was anchoring only for ten minutes and he had left John in charge. He ought to have been thinking about that chain and the rising tide as soon as those ten minutes were up and Jim had not come back. Jim must have counted on him.

He scrambled to his feet and looked at the chain, which ran from a fairlead at the stemhead to a small windlass. A lot of chain was coiled this way and that round first one and then the other drum of the windlass, like a rope belayed on a cleat. The rest of the chain was in the chain-locker below. John could see where it came up through a chain-pipe in the deck. Well, the first thing to do was to cast off those turns and let out more chain . . . quick. Though there was nothing to be seen but fog, John knew the *Goblin* must be moving. He tugged at the rusty links.

'Is it all right?'

He looked over his shoulder, and saw that there were three faces, dim and white in the fog, looking at him from the cockpit.

'It will be in a minute,' he said. 'I've been an awful idiot. I ought to have let out more chain ages ago.'

'Are you sure you know how?'

'As soon as I've got it loose,' said John.

He spoke cheerfully, while his hands pulled this way and that at the coils of chain that seemed to grip each other and the windlass as if they had been made in one solid piece.

'Can't I help?'

'No,' he panted. 'It's coming now.'

He had freed one coil. The next came unwound quite easily. He slipped another from under the drum on the opposite side. Now it ought to go. There were just two turns round the drum. Surely that drum ought to go round so that he could pay out as much chain as he wanted. How on earth did the thing work?

'Is it all right now?'

'It won't go out.'

'What won't?'

'The chain.'

He hauled some chain up out of the chain-pipe and tried working it round the drum. A foot or so of chain pulled round and went out with a jerk. But he wanted yards and yards out before the anchor could hold again, and they were moving . . . moving . . .

He pulled up more chain out of the chain-pipe, hand over hand as fast as he could get it on deck. Horribly heavy it was. And what was the good of getting it up if it would not pay

out? He must get it clear of that winch in order to be able to
pay it out at all. He got one turn off the drum and as nearly
as possible got his finger nipped in getting off the other. And
just at the very worst moment there came a jerk. John slipped
and grabbed with one hand at the forestay. He never knew
exactly what happened to the other hand. He had been holding the chain with both of them. There was a rattle and roar
as the loose chain he had hauled up on deck went flying out
over the fairlead close by the bowsprit. More chain came
pouring up out of the chain-pipe in the deck and went flying
overboard to join the rest. There was nothing to stop it. It
raced out through the fairlead rattling and roaring, fathom
after fathom of heavy iron chain.

Stop it. He must stop it. Questions darted through his
mind. How was the end of the chain fastened in the chain
locker down below? Was it fastened at all? How long was the
chain? But there was no time to get answers. Somehow or
other, now, at once, he must stop the chain roaring out over
the bows. He jammed his right foot hard down on the leaping
chain. On the instant his foot was torn from under him and
he was flung heavily on his back.

There was a shriek from the cockpit. Desperately he scrambled up again. The chain was still pouring up and overboard.
He had no time to do another thing before he saw the end of
the chain come up out of the chain-pipe and fly out over the
bows with a bit of frayed rope flying after it. The rattle and
roar ended in a sudden silence.

'Beu . . . eueueueueueu . . .' The Cork lightship far away
outside the harbour was still sending its long, melancholy
bleats into the fog. But aboard the *Goblin* Titty was not banging the frying-pan, and Roger was not playing the penny
whistle. They knew that something awful had happened,
though they did not know exactly what. Susan was hurrying

forward along the side deck, holding on to a rail on the cabin top. She had seen John go flying backwards.

'Have you hurt yourself?' she asked.

But John in his horror at what had happened had hardly felt the ringbolt in the deck on which he had come down.

'It's all gone,' he panted. 'All his chain and his anchor. I've let it all go overboard . . .'

'But are you all right?'

'Chain and anchor and everything,' said John. 'Miles of it . . . It's all gone . . .'

'John,' cried Susan. 'We're adrift.' And then, at the top of her voice, she shouted, 'Jim! Ahoy! Jim! Ahoy!'

. . . . . .

'Clang!'

The noise of a deep-toned bell startled them by coming out of the fog astern of them. All the bells that kept jangling aboard the anchored steamships were ahead of them, farther up the harbour.

'What's that?'

'Another boat probably,' said Susan. 'Bang that frying-pan, Titty, or let me have it.'

'She must be at anchor if they're ringing a bell,' said John.

'Clang! . . . Clang!'

John stood up and peered into the fog.

'Listen! Listen! We may hear them talking.'

'Clang!'

'Clang! . . . Clang!'

'It's like the bell we heard this morning,' said Roger, 'on that buoy. You know, when Jim said there wasn't enough of a ripple to set it properly ringing.'

'It can't be anchored,' said Titty. 'It's ever so much nearer.'

'Clang! . . . Clang!'

Roger was leaning out of the cockpit, listening and looking down at the grey water close to the side of the *Goblin*, the only thing there was to see in the fog.

'The tide's not moving as fast as it was,' he said. 'It was swirling past a minute ago.'

'Do be quiet a moment.'

'Clang!'

'The tide's not moving at all,' said Roger.

'What?' shouted John. At first he had hardly heard what Roger was saying. Then, for a moment, he had not realized what it meant. He too looked down at the water. He climbed out of the cockpit and hurried to the foredeck. What on earth was happening now? He watched the anchor rope leading away from the stem. It tautened till it looked like wire. The tide was pouring past, rippling against the *Goblin*'s bows. Suddenly the rope slackened, then tautened, then slackened again. The rippling stopped. It was as if the *Goblin* were anchored in still water.

'Clang!'

'It must be a boat,' said Titty. She beat a hard tattoo on the frying-pan.

'Shall I play my whistle?' said Roger. 'We don't want them running into us.'

John hardly heard them. What *had* gone wrong with that anchor? The rippling against the *Goblin*'s bows had stopped altogether. Yet the tide must be still pouring out of the harbour. That meant that the *Goblin* must be moving with it. Yes. The anchor rope was now hanging straight up and down as the chain had hung before. Desperately he began hauling it in.

'Hi! Susan! Come and lend a hand. Quick!'

'What's happened?' Susan was at his elbow.

'Get a hold of the rope and haul when I do! Now then. Now . . . Now . . . Up she comes.'

'But why?' panted Susan. 'You're not getting up the anchor?'

'Got to,' said John. 'It's not got hold of anything. Something's wrong with it.'

'Clang!'

The noise of the bell was nearer than ever. There was a frenzy of banging on the frying-pan in the cockpit and the first verse of 'God Save the King!' on the whistle. The kedge anchor, not so heavy as the big one that had been lost, came up against the bobstay with a sudden jar.

'Hang on, Susan, while I have a look,' said John. 'It's gone and come unstocked. It's my fault again. The fid's come out. I didn't know how to make it fast. At least I thought I had . . .'

'Clang!'

'Pull now. We've got to get it on deck.'

With an awful struggle they hauled the anchor aboard. Anybody could see why it had not been holding. The fid had come out, the stock had slipped and was swinging loose beside the shank.

'Clang!'

The noise was so near that John and Susan on the foredeck turned to look into the fog even while Susan was holding the anchor and John was working the stock back into place.

'Clang!'

There was a yell from the cockpit. 'God Save the King' came to the end in the middle of a bar.

'John! John! It's here . . .'

Something large loomed out of the fog astern. It was a big red-painted cage, like an enormous parrot cage with a pointed top, built on a round raft. On the top of the cage was a lantern, and, as they watched, they saw a thin line of white light leap up in the lantern, vanish and leap again. It was a buoy. In the cage was something big and black . . . the bell.

'Clang!'

'It's coming jolly fast,' shouted Roger. 'Look at the wash round its bows.'

'It's going to bunt into us,' cried Titty.

'It isn't the buoy that's moving,' said John. 'It's us.'

They swept past it, missing it by only a yard. The heavy hammer in the cage swung against the bell when they were near enough almost to touch the buoy. The melancholy 'Clang!' boomed in their ears. They read the big white letters painted on the side of the cage . . . 'BEACH END'. A moment later the buoy had faded away into the fog, and the next 'Clang!' sounded out of nothingness.

'Oh, John!' gasped Susan. 'That was the Beach End buoy. We're out at sea.'

Joan G. Robinson

WHEN MARNIE WAS THERE

Here's another time-travel book, which is so cunningly wrought
and so careful of detail that you, the reader, will slip in and out of the
centuries hardly noticing when it happens.

The real-life heroine is Anna, a shy, inhibited girl who, when she
wants people to stop noticing her, puts on what she thinks of as her
'ordinary' face. This becomes such a habit that she feels outside of
everyone, even the warm-hearted Peggs family in Norfolk (where
she is sent to recover from her misery at discovering she is a foster-
child). Then, in her loneliness, she finds a charming but mysterious
girl called Marnie who belongs to a different age and who, inciden-
tally, helps her unravel a few mysteries in her own life.

You ought to enjoy everything about this book, and if you do, then try others with the same sort of tantalizing circumstances such as *Charlotte Sometimes* by Penelope Farmer, *The Root Cellar* by Janet Lunn, *A Traveller in Time* by Alison Uttley or *Playing Beatie Bow* by Ruth Park.

* * *

Anna moved nearer and the girl said, still in a half whisper, 'You remember I said last night that you were my secret?'

Anna nodded. 'I knew just what you meant. You're mine.'

'Well, that's it! Don't let's spoil it by gabbling at each other, and asking a whole lot of questions, and arguing, and perhaps end up quarrelling. Let's go on like we are.'

'Yes – oh, yes!' said Anna, then hesitated. 'But I don't even know your name yet.'

'Marnie.' The girl seemed surprised. 'I thought you knew.' Anna shook her head. 'Listen,' she went on, 'there are all sorts of things I want to know about you; why you're here, and where you live, and what you do all day – things like that – and yet, in a way, I don't want to know them at all –' she broke off and laughed quickly. 'No, that's wrong! I *do* want to know. But I want to find them out slowly, by myself, as we go along. Do you know what I mean?'

Yes, Anna did know. This was just how she felt.

'I'll tell you what we'll do!' said Marnie. 'We'll make a pact to ask each other only one question a night, shall we? Like wishes in a fairy story.'

'They're usually three,' said Anna doubtfully.

'All right, we'll make it three. I'll start. Question number one – why are you here at Little Overton?'

This was fun. Anna drew a deep breath and told her about coming to stay with the Peggs instead of going back to school, because Dr Brown had said it would be good for her and she was underweight. And then, because Marnie looked so interested, she told her about not-even-trying, and Mrs Preston being worried about her future. 'But it's not just that,' she said. 'They don't know that I know, but it's because they want to get rid of me for a bit. I'm a sort of worry to them.'

'Oh, poor you! But are you sure? Sometimes it feels like that, I know, but it isn't really true.'

'No, I do know. One day I'll tell you how I know, but not tonight. Is it my turn now?' Marnie nodded. 'How many brothers and sisters have you got?'

'Me?' Marnie was amazed. 'None. Why should you think I had?'

'Do you mean you're the *only one*?' Anna's voice sounded quite shocked. She was disappointed. What about the boys and girls in navy-blue jeans and jerseys? She had been so sure they belonged to The Marsh House too . . .

Marnie gave her a little push with her elbow. 'What's the matter? Aren't I enough for you? – And that's not a proper question, by the way.'

Anna laughed. 'Yes, but I always thought you were a big family.'

'Well, I suppose we are, in a way –' Marnie began counting on her fingers, 'there's me, and Lily, and Ettie, and Nan, and Mother, and Father –' she hesitated – 'and Pluto.'

Something about the way her eyes suddenly darkened made Anna ask quickly, 'Who's Pluto?'

'No, no, you're cheating! It's my turn now. Question two – are you an only, too?'

Anna considered. Did Raymond count or not? He was not really a brother or a cousin or any relation at all. 'Sort of,' she said at last.

'What do you mean, sort of?'

'Now you're cheating! It's my turn. Who's Pluto?'

'Our dog.' Marnie looked suddenly solemn. 'I'll tell you a secret. I hate him really. He'd big and black, and quite fierce sometimes. He lives in a kennel outside most of the time. Father said he'd be good company for me, but he's not. I wanted a kitten, a dear little fluffy kitten that I could nurse on my lap, but Father said Pluto'd be good for guarding the house when he's away. He wasn't so bad when he was a puppy, though even then he was too big and rough, but he's awful now. He eats *raw meat*, think of that! Don't tell anyone, but secretly I'm frightened of him.' She gave a little shudder, then in an instant became gay again. 'It's my turn, isn't it? What's it like, living at the Peggs'?'

Anna opened her mouth to answer and found, to her surprise, that she could not remember. Perhaps it was because she had been thinking about Marnie's answer, and wondering whether it was Pluto she sometimes heard barking in the night. What *was* it like at the Peggs'? Not one single thing could she remember. It had all gone out of her head as completely as if someone had wiped a sponge across a blackboard. Marnie, who had seemed only half real, had now become more real than the Peggs. It was odd.

She glanced across at Marnie, who seemed to have sunk into a dream of her own while waiting. She was sitting huddled in the stern with her feet up and her head bent, her face in shadow.

Anna tried again. She *must* remember about the Peggs, otherwise she would not be able to tell Marnie anything about them. She closed her eyes and saw – faintly at first, then clearly – the scullery, the kettle on the stove, and through the door, Sam's armchair with the broken springs in the corner. The Peggs and their cottage came to life again. Relieved, she opened her eyes and saw – no one. Marnie had gone! She was alone in the boat.

She gave a little cry and sprang up, the boat rocking beneath her. At the same minute, from somewhere behind her, she heard Marnie's voice saying in a startled whisper, 'Anna! What's the matter? Where are you?'

'I thought you'd gone!' said Anna. 'What are you doing out there?'

Marnie was standing on the bank behind her. In her long white dress, with the reeds standing up all round her, and the moonlight shining on her pale hair, she looked more than ever like someone out of a fairy story. She came nearer, and Anna saw that she was looking quite frightened.

'Oh, you gave me a shock!' she was saying. 'You shouldn't have run away. I got out to look for you. I thought you must be hiding in the reeds.' She took hold of Anna's hand to steady herself and stepped back into the boat. 'Don't do that again, Anna – dear.' Her voice was almost pleading.

'But I didn't! I didn't do anything!'

Marnie sat down again and folded her hands in her lap. 'Yes, you did,' she said primly, 'you played a trick on me. It wasn't fair. I asked you a question and you never answered. Instead you ran away and hid –'

'Oh, I remember now!' said Anna. 'But I didn't run away. You asked me about the Peggs and what it was like there. Well, I'll tell you. It's . . .' her voice faltered. 'It's . . .' She had forgotten again. It was extraordinary.

Marnie laughed gaily. 'Oh, don't bother! What do I care about the Peggs? I don't even know who they are. It was a silly question anyway. Let's talk about something real. Have you got a watch on?'

'No. Why?'

'I think we ought to go back soon. It was late when we came out. They might discover I'd gone. Shall I row?'

Anna nodded, and they changed seats and pushed out from the reeds into the stream.

'You didn't have your last question,' said Marnie.

'No, but I wasn't able to answer yours,' said Anna, still wondering.

'Oh, that doesn't matter! I'll ask you another instead. Where do you live?'

'In London,' said Anna quickly. 'Twenty-five Elmwood Terrace.'

Marnie nodded approvingly. 'You were able to answer that one, anyway. Now you can ask your last.'

Anna turned over in her mind which of many questions to ask. Should she ask Marnie about her dress? No, she had probably been to some sort of grown-up dinner party. Or about her family? No, they were only grown-ups after all. But she was still intrigued by Marnie's confession that she was frightened of her own dog. She said, at last, 'Does anything else frighten you – apart from obvious things like earthquakes, I mean?'

Marnie thought seriously. 'Thunderstorms, a little – if they're bad. And –' She turned and looked behind her across the fields to where the windmill stood like a solitary sentinel, dark against the sky. 'That does sometimes,' she said quickly, with a shiver.

'The windmill! But why?'

'Too late! You'll have to save that for next time,' said Marnie, laughing again. Then she added, more seriously, 'I don't think it's a very good game after all. You seemed to ask all the wrong questions. I don't usually think of gloomy things like that old windmill. And I asked a wrong question, too. You couldn't even answer it, and frightened me by running away instead.'

'I wish I knew what you meant about that,' said Anna, still worrying over it. 'Honestly, I never moved.'

'Oh, but you did!' Marnie's eyes were round. 'How can you say such a thing? I waited and waited for you to answer, and then when I looked up you just weren't there. That's why I jumped out.'

'No, it was you!' said Anna indignantly.

Marnie sighed. 'You think it was me, and I think it was you. Don't let's quarrel about it. Perhaps it was both of us.'

'Or neither of us,' said Anna, her anger slipping away. After all, what did it matter? The last thing she wanted to do was quarrel with Marnie. She changed the subject quickly. 'You are lucky to have a boat like this all of your own.'

'I know I am. It's what I always wanted, and this year I had it for my birthday. You're the first person who's ever been in it, apart from me. Are you glad about that?' Anna was.

They drew in to the shore. 'I'll drop you here,' said Marnie. 'Can you paddle now or is it too deep?'

Anna put a foot over the side. The water came up to just below her knee. 'It's all right. For me, that is,' she said, thinking of Marnie's dress.

'What do you mean, "for you"!' said Marnie with mock indignation. 'I'm as tall as you are.' She laughed suddenly. 'Oh, you mean my evening gown! And poor old you in your boys' clothes! Do you wish you were dressed the same as me?'

She's getting at me, thought Anna, and made no reply. But Marnie had turned the boat and was already rowing away, still chuckling.

'Goodbye!' called Anna in a small, forlorn voice – quickly before it was too late.

'Goodbye!' called Marnie, still laughing. She went on chuckling until the darkness had almost swallowed her up, then, just as she disappeared out of sight, Anna heard her call quietly, but quite distinctly, over the water.

'Silly, it's my nightie!'

Antoine de Saint-Exupéry
THE LITTLE PRINCE

Sometimes it's good to read a story which has two layers, one about the characters themselves and what happens to them, and the other about life itself, and how it should be lived. This is such a one.

The author was an airman who died in the war. About this book he wrote: 'Six years have already passed since my friend went away with his sheep. If I try to describe him here it is to make sure I shall not forget him.' If you decide to try this very unusual book, you'll remember the little prince too.

An airman has crashed in the Sahara Desert with only enough food and water for a week. While he tries to mend his plane, he is visited by the little prince, who comes from Asteroid B 612, a small planet where he lives alone with three volcanoes and a flower. He is visiting the other planets looking for a sheep and he asks the airman to draw one for him.

* * *

On the fifth day – again, as always, it was thanks to the sheep – the secret of the little prince's life was revealed to me. Abruptly, without anything to lead up to it, and as if the question had been born of long and silent meditation on his problem, he demanded:

'A sheep – if it eats little bushes, does it eat flowers, too?'

'A sheep,' I answered, 'eats anything it finds in its reach.'

'Even flowers that have thorns?'

'Yes, even flowers that have thorns.'

'Then the thorns – what use are they?'

I did not know. At that moment I was very busy trying to unscrew a bolt that had got stuck in my engine. I was very much worried, for it was becoming clear to me that the break-down of my plane was extremely serious. And I had so little drinking-water left that I had to fear the worst.

'The thorns – what use are they?'

The little prince never let go of a question, once he had asked it. As for me, I was upset over that bolt. And I answered with the first thing that came into my head:

'The thorns are of no use at all. Flowers have thorns just for spite!'

'Oh!'

There was a moment of complete silence. Then the little prince flashed back at me, with a kind of resentfulness:

'I don't believe you! Flowers are weak creatures. They are naïve. They reassure themselves as best they can. They believe that their thorns are terrible weapons . . .'

I did not answer. At that instant I was saying to myself: 'If this bolt still won't turn, I am going to knock it out with the hammer.' Again the little prince disturbed my thoughts:

'And you actually believe that the flowers –'

'Oh, no!' I cried. 'No, no, no! I don't believe anything. I answered you with the first thing that came into my head. Don't you see – I am very busy with matters of consequence!'

He stared at me, thunderstruck.

'Matters of consequence!'

He looked at me there, with my hammer in my hand, my fingers black with engine-grease, bending down over an object which seemed to him extremely ugly . . .

'You talk just like the grown-ups!'

That made me a little ashamed. But he went on, relentlessly:

'You mix everything up together . . . You confuse everything . . .'

He was really very angry. He tossed his golden curls in the breeze.

'I know a planet where there is a certain red-faced gentleman. He has never smelled a flower. He has never looked at a star. He has never loved anyone. He has never done anything in his life but add up figures. And all day he says over and over, just like you: "I am busy with matters of consequence!" And that makes him swell up with pride. But he is not a man – he is a mushroom!'

'A what?'

'A mushroom!'

The little prince was now white with rage.

'The flowers have been growing thorns for millions of years. For millions of years the sheep have been eating them just the same. And is it not a matter of consequence to try to understand why the flowers go to so much trouble to grow

thorns which are never of any use to them? Is the warfare
between the sheep and the flowers not important? Is this not
of more consequence than a fat red-faced gentleman's sums?
And if I know – I, myself – one flower which is unique in the
world, which grows nowhere but on my planet, but which
one little sheep can destroy in a single bite some morning,
without even noticing what he is doing – Oh! You think that
is not important!'

His face turned from white to red as he continued:

'If someone loves a flower, of which just one single blossom grows in all the millions and millions of stars, it is enough
to make him happy just to look at the stars. He can say to
himself: "Somewhere, my flower is there . . ." But if the
sheep eats the flower, in one moment all his stars will be
darkened . . . And you think that is not important!'

He could not say anything more. His words were choked
by sobbing.

The night had fallen. I had let my tools drop from my
hands. Of what moment now was my hammer, my bolt, or
thirst, or death? On the star, one planet, my planet, the Earth,
there was a little prince to be comforted. I took him in my
arms, and rocked him. I said to him:

'The flower that you love is not in danger. I will draw you
a muzzle for your sheep. I will draw you a railing to put
around your flower. I will –'

I did not know what to say to him. I felt awkward and
blundering. I did not know how I could reach him, where I
could overtake him and go on hand in hand with him once
more.

It is such a secret place, the land of tears.

George Selden

THE CRICKET IN TIMES SQUARE

This is one of the first books I turned into a Puffin, and it's still one of my favourites.

Who'd have thought a tiny cricket could so cast his spell over the great Times Square in New York that traffic came to a standstill and everyone stood in silence while he gave them a concert? It all starts unexpectedly when country-born Chester Cricket arrives at Grand Central Railway Station in some picnic rubbish, and is rescued by Mario, the boy on the bookstall. At night when all is quiet, he is befriended and taught city ways by Tucker Mouse and Harry Cat. Soon, with his singing, he is helping Mario's bookstall to become famous, although there are a few minor mishaps such as eating dollar bills (because he thought they were leaves) and causing a fire during his birthday feast.

In this extract he has just come back from Chinatown where Mario has bought him a cricket cage.

* * *

That same night, after the Bellinis had gone home, Chester was telling Harry and Tucker about his trip to Chinatown. The cat and the mouse were sitting on the shelf outside, and Chester Cricket was crouched under the bell in the cage. Every minute or so, Tucker would get up and walk around to the other side of the pagoda. He was overcome with admiration for it.

'And Mr Fong gave Mario a fortune cookie too,' Chester was saying.

'I'm very fond of Chinese food myself,' said Harry Cat. 'I often browse through the garbage cans down in Chinatown.'

Tucker Mouse stopped gaping at the cricket cage long enough to say, 'Once I thought of living down there. But those Chinese make funny dishes. They make soup out of birds' nests and stew out of sharks' fins. They could make a soufflé out of a mouse. I decided to stay away.'

A low rumble of a chuckle came from Harry Cat's throat. 'Listen to the mouse,' he said and gave Tucker a pat on the back that sent him rolling over and over.

'Easy, Harry, easy,' said Tucker, picking himself up. 'You wouldn't know your own strength.' He stood up on his hind legs and looked in through the red painted bars of the cage. 'What a palace,' he murmured. 'Beautiful! You could feel like a king living in a place like this.'

'Yes,' said Chester, 'but I'm not so keen on staying in a cage. I'm more used to tree stumps and holes in the ground. It makes me sort of nervous to be locked in here.'

'Do you want to come out?' asked Harry. He sprung one of

his nails out of the pad of his right forepaw and lifted the latch of the gate to the cage.

Chester pushed the gate and it swung open. He jumped out. 'It's a relief to be free,' he said, jumping around the shelf. 'There's nothing like freedom.'

'Say, Chester,' said Tucker, 'could I go in for a minute? I was never in a pagoda before.'

'Go right ahead,' said Chester.

Tucker scrambled through the gate into the cage and pranced all around inside it. He lay down, first on one side, then on the other, and then on his back. 'If only I had a kimono now,' he said, standing up on his hind legs again and resting one paw on a bar. 'I feel like the Emperor of China. How do I look, Harry?'

'You look like a mouse in a trap,' said Harry Cat.

'Every mouse should end up in a trap so nice,' said Tucker.

'Do you want to sleep in the cage?' asked Chester.

'Oh – could I!' exclaimed the mouse. His idea of luxury was to spend a night in such surroundings.

'Sure,' said Chester. 'I prefer the matchbox anyway.'

'There's only one thing,' said Tucker, stamping with his left hind leg. 'This floor. It's a little hard to sleep on.'

'I'll go over and get a bunch of paper from the drain pipe,' volunteered Harry Cat.

'No, it'll make a mess,' said Tucker. 'We don't want to get Chester in trouble with the Bellinis.' He hesitated. 'Um – maybe we could find something here.'

'How about a piece of Kleenex,' suggested Chester. 'That's nice and soft.'

'Kleenex would be good,' said Tucker, 'but I was wondering –' He paused again.

'Come on, Tucker,' said Harry Cat. 'You've got something on your mind. Let's have it.'

'Well,' Tucker began, 'I sort of thought that if there were any dollar bills in the cash register –'

Harry burst out laughing. 'You might know!' he said to Chester. 'Who but this mouse would want to sleep on dollar bills?'

Chester jumped into the cash register drawer, which was open as usual. 'There's a few dollars in here,' he called up.

'Plenty to make a mattress,' said Tucker Mouse. 'Pass some in, please.'

Chester passed the first dollar bill up to Harry Cat, who took it over to the cage and reached it through the gate. Tucker took hold of one end of the bill and shook it out like a blanket. It was old and rumply.

'Careful you don't rip it,' said Harry.

'I wouldn't rip it,' said Tucker. 'This is one mouse who knows the value of a dollar.'

Harry brought over the second dollar. It was newer and stiffer than the first. 'Let me see,' said Tucker. He lifted a corner of each bill, one in either paw. 'This new one can go on the bottom – I like a crispy, clean sheet – and I'll pull the old one over for a cover. Now, a pillow is what I need. Please look for more in the cash register.'

Harry and Chester searched the compartments of the open drawer. There was a little loose change, but not much else.

'How about a fifty cent piece?' said Harry.

'Too flat,' answered Tucker Mouse.

The rear half of the drawer was still inside the cash register. Chester crawled back. It was dark and he couldn't see where he was going. He felt around until his head bumped against something. Whatever it was, it seemed to be big and round. Chester pushed and shoved and finally got it back out into the dim light of the newsstand. It was one of Mama Bellini's earrings, shaped like a sea shell, with sparkling little stones all over it.

'Would an earring do?' he shouted to Tucker.

'Well, I don't know,' Tucker said.

'It looks as if it was covered with diamonds,' said Harry Cat.

'Perfect!' called Tucker. 'Send it along.'

Harry lifted the earring into the cage. Tucker examined it carefully, like a jeweller. 'I think these are fake diamonds,' he said at last.

'Yes, but it's still very pretty,' said Chester, who had jumped up beside them.

'I guess it'll do,' said Tucker. He lay down on his side on the new dollar bill, rested his head on the earring and pulled the old dollar up over him. Chester and Harry heard him draw a deep breath of contentment. 'I'm sleeping on money inside a palace,' he said. 'It's a dream come true.'

Harry Cat purred his chuckle. 'Good night, Chester,' he said. 'I'm going back to the drain pipe where I can stretch out.' He jumped to the floor.

'Good night, Harry,' Chester called.

Soft and silent as a shadow, Harry slipped out the opening in the side of the newsstand and glided over to the drain pipe. Chester hopped into his matchbox. He had got to like the feeling of the Kleenex. It was almost like the spongy wood of his old tree stump and felt much more like home than the cricket cage. Now they each had their own place to sleep.

'Good night, Tucker,' Chester said.

''Night, Chester,' Tucker answered.

Chester Cricket burrowed down deeper into the Kleenex. He was beginning to enjoy life in New York. Just before he fell asleep, he heard Tucker Mouse sighing happily in the cage.

I.L.T.S.—15

Ian Serraillier

THE SILVER SWORD

This is a true story about almost unbearable hardship and suffering, but it is also hopeful, because all the characters in it are so courageous and determined.

It is the time of the last war, in Poland. Four children are left destitute when their parents are arrested by the Gestapo and their house is blown up. At first they live like rats in bombed cellars, scratching food from dustbins, hiding in daytime for fear of being taken by soldiers. Then Edek, the eldest brother, is caught and taken off to a slave-labour camp. After the Russians arrive the children decide to make the impossible journey to Switzerland, where they hope their parents may eventually return.

Here they are on their way to Berlin, after they have managed to find Edek, ill in hospital, and persuaded the authorities to let them continue their daunting journey.

* * *

There was still something left of the railway station at Posen, and the track had been mended. Of course there was no such thing as a timetable, but some trains – though much delayed – were getting through to Berlin, 250 miles to the west.

In one of these trains, Ruth, Edek, Jan and Bronia were travelling. It was crowded with refugees. They leaned from the windows, stood on the footboards, lay on the carriage roofs. Ruth's family was in one of the open trucks, which was cold but not quite so crowded.

'I don't like this truck,' said Bronia. 'It jolts too much.'

'Every jolt takes us nearer to Switzerland,' said Ruth. 'Think of it like that, and it's not so bad.'

'There's no room to stretch.'

'Rest your head against me and try and go to sleep. There, that's better.'

'It's a better truck than the other ones,' said Jan. 'It's got a stove in it. And we can scrape the coal dust off the floor. That's why I chose it. When it gets dark they'll light a fire and we shall keep warm.'

'The stove's right in the far corner. We shan't feel it from here,' said Bronia.

'Stop grumbling, Bronia,' said Ruth. 'We're lucky to be here at all. Hundreds of people were left behind at Posen – they may have to wait for weeks.'

'Edek was lucky to come at all,' said Jan. 'The doctor wanted to send him back to the Warthe camp, didn't he?'

'He said you wanted fattening up, as if you were a goose being fattened for Christmas,' laughed Bronia.

'The doctor wouldn't have let him come at all, if I hadn't argued with him,' said Jan.

'They wanted to keep us all, didn't they, Ruth?' said Bronia.

'It was because they wanted to look after us,' said Ruth. And she thought with satisfaction how they had stuck to their point and persuaded the authorities to let them go. She smiled as she remembered the conversation she had overheard afterwards between the doctor and Mrs Borowicz, the welfare officer. 'Those children insist on going to Switzerland – it's their promised land – and we've no power to detain them,' Mrs Borowicz had said. And when the doctor had remarked that Edek was too ill and would die on the way, she had disagreed. 'He believes his father's at the other end, waiting. Highly unlikely, of course, but there's a sort of fierce resolution about the boy – about all of them – which saves them from despair, and it's better than any medicine we can give him. Dope and drugs can't equal that. We must let them go.'

Ruth looked at her brother. Bunched up against the side of the truck, he was staring out at the fields as they swept by. It was over two and a half years since she had last seen him. He was sixteen now, but did not look two and a half years older. So different from the Edek she remembered. His cheeks were pinched and hollow, his eyes as unnaturally bright as Jan's had once been, and he kept coughing. He looked as if he could go on lying there for ever, without stirring. Yet at the Warthe camp they had described him as wild.

She looked at Jan. She was surprised how helpful and good-tempered he had been since Jimpy's death in the scrum by the field kitchen. He had kept his sorrow to himself and not once referred to Jimpy since. Ruth could see that he was not entirely at ease with Edek yet. Did he resent his presence? There might be trouble here, for Edek must to some extent

usurp the position that Jan had held, and Jan had a jealous
nature.

She looked at Bronia. The child was asleep, her head in
Ruth's lap, a smile on her face. Was she dreaming about the
fairy-story that Ruth had been telling her, the one about the
Princess of the Brazen Mountains? Perhaps in her dream
Bronia *was* the Princess, flying through the sky on her grey-
blue wings. Then the Prince, who had searched for her seven
long years, would be flying beside her, leading her to his
mountain kingdom where they would live happily ever after.
Fairy-stories always ended like that, and Ruth was happy to
think that Bronia was still young enough to believe that it
was the same in real life.

Ruth sighed. She leaned back, her head against the side of
the truck, and dozed.

And the train, with its long stream of trucks and carriages
all crammed to bursting-point with refugees, rattled and
jolted on towards Berlin.

In the evening the train stopped and was shunted into a
siding. Everyone got out to stretch his legs, but no one went
far away in case it started again. As the night came on and it
grew colder, they drifted back to their carriages and trucks.
Coal dust was scraped from the floorboards and wood collected from outside, and the fire in Ruth's truck kindled. The
refugees crowded round, stretching out their hands to the
warmth.

It was the hour of the singer and the story-teller. While
they all shared what little food they had, a young man sang
and his wife accompanied him on the guitar. He sang of the
storks that every spring fly back from Egypt to Poland's
countryside, and of the villagers that welcome them by placing cart-wheels on the treetops and the chimney stacks for
the storks to build their nests on. A printer from Cracow told

the tale of Krakus who killed the dragon, and of Krakus's daughter who refused to marry a German prince. Others, laughing and making light of their experiences, told of miraculous escapes from the Nazis.

'I had a free ride on the roof of a Nazi lorry,' said one. 'It was eighty miles before I was seen. A sniper spotted me from the top of a railway bridge, but he couldn't shoot straight and I slid off into the bushes. The driver was so unnerved at the shooting that he drove slap into the bridge, and that was the end of him.'

Another told of a long journey on the roof of a train.

'I can beat that for a yarn,' said Edek.

Everyone turned round to look at the boy slumped down at the back of the truck. It was the first time he had spoken.

'I'll tell you if you'll give me a peep at the fire,' he said. 'And my sisters, too. And Jan. We're freezing out here.'

Ungrudgingly they made a way for the family – the only children in the truck – to squeeze through to the stove. Ruth carried Bronia, who did not wake, and she snuggled down beside it. Jan sat on the other side, with his chin on his knees and his arms clasping them. Edek stood up, with his back to the side of the truck. When someone opened the stove to throw in a log, a shower of sparks leapt up, and for a few moments the flames lit up his pale features.

'I was caught smuggling cheese into Warsaw, and they sent me back to Germany to slave on the land,' he said. 'The farm was near Guben and the slaves came from all parts of Europe, women mostly and boys of my age. In winter we cut peat to manure the soil. We were at it all day from dawn to dark. In spring we did the sowing – cabbage crop, mostly. At harvest time we packed the plump white cabbage heads in crates and sent them into town. We lived on the outer leaves – they tasted bitter. I tried to run away, but they always fetched me back. Last winter, when the war turned against the Nazis and the muddles began, I succeeded. I hid under a train, under a cattle wagon, and lay on top of the axle with my arms and legs stretched out.'

'When the train started, you fell off,' said Jan.

'Afterwards I sometimes wished I had,' said Edek, 'that is, until I found Ruth and Bronia again. Somehow I managed to cling on and I got a free ride back to Poland.'

Jan laughed scornfully. 'Why don't you travel that way here? It would leave the rest of us more room.'

'I could never do that again,' said Edek.

'No,' said Jan, and he looked with contempt at Edek's thin arms and bony wrists. 'You're making it all up. There's no room to lie under a truck. Nothing to hold on to.'

Edek seized him by the ear and pulled him to his feet. 'Have you ever looked under a truck?' he said, and he described the underside in such convincing detail that nobody but Jan would have questioned his accuracy. The boys were coming to blows, when the printer pulled Jan to the floor and there were cries of, 'Let him get on with his story!'

'You would have been shaken off,' Jan shouted above the din, 'like a rotten plum!'

'That's what anyone would expect,' Edek shouted back. 'But if you'll shut up and listen, I'll tell you why I wasn't.' When the noise had died down, he went on. 'Lying on my stomach, I found the view rather monotonous. It made me dizzy too. I had to shut my eyes. And the bumping! Compared with that, the boards of this truck are like a feather bed. Then the train ran through a puddle. More than a puddle – it must have been a flood, for I was splashed and soaked right through. But that water saved me. After that I couldn't let go, even if I'd wanted to.'

'Why not?' said Jan, impressed.

'The water froze on me. It made an icicle of me. When at last the train drew into a station, I was encased in ice from head to foot. I could hear Polish voices on the platform. I knew we must have crossed the frontier. My voice was the only part of me that wasn't frozen, so I shouted. The station-master came and chopped me down with an axe. He wrapped me in blankets and carried me to the boiler-house to thaw out. Took me hours to thaw out.'

'You don't look properly thawed out yet,' said the printer, and he threw him a crust of bread.

Other voices joined in. 'Give him a blanket.' 'A tall story, but he's earned a bed by the stove.' 'Another story, some-body! One to make us forget.' 'Put some romance in it.'

The stories petered out after a while. When all was quiet, and the refugees, packed like sardines on the floor of the truck, lay sleeping under the cold stars, Ruth whispered to Edek, 'Was it really true?'

'Yes, it was true,' said Edek.

'Nothing like that must ever happen to you again,' said Ruth.

She reached for his hand – it was cold, although he was close to the stove – and she clasped it tight, as if she meant never to let go of it again.

Dodie Smith

THE HUNDRED AND ONE DALMATIANS

Although this is mainly a book about two clever Dalmatian dogs, Pongo and Missis, the person you'll remember for ever is Cruella de Vil, who must be the most dreadful, heartless villainess of all time; for she kidnaps their fifteen puppies to make herself a fur coat just because she likes to dress in black and white!

However, she reckons without Pongo's keen brain, and his chain of doggy friends, who manage to find where the puppies are hidden.

Whatever kind of book you usually like, this will also satisfy you. And when you've finished it, go out and grab the marvellous sequel called – when you've read this, you'll know why – *The Starlight Barking*.

* * *

From the first, it was quite clear the dogs knew just where they wanted to go. Very firmly, they led the way right across the park, across the road, and to the open space which is called Primrose Hill. This did not surprise the Dearlys as it had always been a favourite walk. What did surprise them was the way Pongo and Missis behaved when they got to the top of the hill. They stood side by side and they barked.

They barked to the north, they barked to the south, they barked to the east and west. And each time they changed their positions, they began the barking with three very strange, short, sharp barks.

'Anyone would think they were signalling,' said Mr Dearly.

But he did not really mean it. And they *were* signalling.

Many people must have noticed how dogs like to bark in the early evening. Indeed, twilight has sometimes been called 'Dogs' Barking Time'. Busy town dogs bark less than country dogs, but all dogs know all about the Twilight Barking. It is their way of keeping in touch with distant friends, passing on important news, enjoying a good gossip. But none of the dogs who answered Pongo and Missis expected to enjoy a gossip, for the three short, sharp barks meant: 'Help! Help! Help!'

No dog sends that signal unless the need is desperate. And no dog who hears it ever fails to respond.

Within a few minutes, the news of the stolen puppies was travelling across England, and every dog who heard at once turned detective. Dogs living in London's Underworld (hard-bitten characters; also hard-biting) set out to explore sinister alleys where dog thieves lurk. Dogs in Pet Shops hastened to make quite sure all puppies offered for sale were not Dalmatians in disguise. And dogs who could do nothing else swiftly handed on the news, spreading it through London and on through the suburbs, and on, on to the open country: 'Help! Help! Help! Fifteen Dalmatian puppies stolen. Send news to Pongo and Missis Pongo, of Regent's Park, London. End of Message.'

Pongo and Missis hoped all this would be happening. But all they really knew was that they had made contact with the dogs near enough to answer them, and that those dogs would be standing by, at twilight the next evening, to relay any news that had come along.

One Great Dane, over towards Hampstead, was particularly encouraging.

'I have a chain of friends all over England,' he said, in his great, booming bark. 'And I will be on duty day and night. Courage, courage, O Dogs of Regent's Park!'

It was almost dark now. And the Dearlys were suggesting – very gently – that they should be taken home. So after a few last words with the Great Dane, Pongo and Missis led the way down Primrose Hill. The dogs who had answered them were silent now, but the Twilight Barking was spreading in an ever-widening circle. And tonight it would not end with twilight. It would go on and on as the moon rose high over England.

The next day, a great many people who had read Mr Dearly's advertisements rang up to sympathize. (Cruella de Vil did, and seemed most upset when she was told the puppies had been stolen while she was talking to Nanny Cook.) But no one had anything helpful to say. And Scotland Yard was Frankly Baffled. So it was another sad, sad day for the Dearlys, the Nannies, and the dogs.

Just before dusk, Pongo and Missis again showed that they

wished to take the Dearlys for a walk. So off they started and again the dogs led the way to the top of Primrose Hill. And again they stood side by side and gave three sharp barks. But this time, though no human ear could have detected it, they were slightly different barks. And they meant, not 'Help! Help! Help!' but 'Ready! Ready! Ready!'

The dogs who had collected news from all over London replied first. Reports had come in from the West End and the East End and South of the Thames. And all these reports were the same:

'Calling Pongo and Missis Pongo of Regent's Park. No news of your puppies. Deepest regrets. End of Message.'

Poor Missis! She had hoped so much that her pups were still in London. Pongo's secret suspicion had led him to pin his hopes to news from the country. And soon it was pouring in – some of it relayed across London. But it was always the same:

'Calling Pongo and Missis Pongo of Regent's Park. No news of your puppies. Deepest regrets. End of Message.'

Again and again Pongo and Missis barked the 'Ready!' signal, each time with fresh hope. Again and again came bitter disappointment. At last only the Great Dane over towards Hampstead remained to be heard from. They signalled to him – their last hope!

Back came his booming bark:

'Calling Pongo and Missis Pongo of Regent's Park. No news of your puppies. Deepest regrets. End of –'

The Great Dane stopped in mid-bark. A second later he barked again: 'Wait! Wait! Wait!'

Dead still, their hearts thumping, Pongo and Missis waited. They waited so long that Mr Dearly put his hand on Pongo's head and said: 'What about coming home, boy?'

For the first time in his life, Pongo jerked his head from Mr Dearly's hand, then went on standing stock still. And at last the Great Dane spoke again, booming triumphantly through the gathering dusk.

'Calling Pongo and Missis Pongo. News! News at last! Stand by to receive details.'

A most wonderful thing had happened. Just as the Great Dane had been about to sign off, a Pomeranian with a piercing yap had got a message through to him. She had heard it from a Poodle who had heard it from a Boxer who had heard it from a Pekinese. Dogs of almost every known breed had helped to carry the news – and a great many dogs of unknown breed (none the worse for that and all of them bright as buttons). In all, 480 dogs had relayed the message, which had travelled over sixty miles as the dog barks. Each dog had given the 'Urgent' signal, which had silenced all gossiping dogs. Not that many dogs were merely gossiping that night; almost all the Twilight Barking had been about the missing puppies.

This was the strange story that now came through to Pongo and Missis: Some hours earlier, an elderly English Sheepdog, living on a farm in a remote Suffolk village, had gone for an afternoon amble. He knew all about the missing puppies and had just been discussing them with the tabby cat at the farm. She was a great friend of his.

Some little way from the village, on a lonely heath, was an old house completely surrounded by an unusually high wall. Two brothers, named Saul and Jasper Baddun lived there, but were merely caretakers for the real owner. The place had an evil reputation – no local dog would have dreamed of putting its nose inside the tall iron gates. In any case, these gates were always kept locked.

It so happened that the Sheepdog's walk took him past this house. He quickened his pace, having no wish to meet either of the Badduns. And at that moment, something came sailing out over the high wall.

It was a bone, the Sheepdog saw with pleasure; but not a bone with meat on it, he noted with disgust. It was an old, dry bone, and on it were some peculiar scratches. The scratches formed letters. And the letters were S.O.S.

Someone was asking for help! Someone behind the tall wall and the high, chained gates! The Sheepdog barked a low, cautious bark. He was answered by a high, shrill bark. Then he heard a yelp, as if some dog had been cuffed. The Sheepdog barked again, saying: 'I'll do all I can.' Then he picked up the bone in his teeth and raced back to the farm.

Once home, he showed the bone to the tabby cat and asked her help. Then, together, they hurried to the lonely house. At the back, they found a tree whose branches reached over the wall. The cat climbed the tree, went along its branches, and then leapt to a tree the other side of the wall.

'Take care of yourself,' barked the Sheepdog. 'Remember those Baddun brothers are villains.'

The cat clawed her way down, backwards, to the ground, then hurried through the overgrown shrubbery. Soon she came to an old brick wall which enclosed a stable-yard. From behind the wall came whimperings and snufflings. She leapt to the top of the wall and looked down.

The next second, one of the Baddun brothers saw her and threw a stone at her. She dodged it, jumped from the wall, and ran for her life. In two minutes she was safely back with the Sheepdog.

'They're there!' she said, triumphantly. 'The place is *seething* with Dalmatian puppies!'

The Sheepdog was a formidable Twilight Barker. Tonight.

with the most important news in Dogdom to send out, he surpassed himself. And so the message travelled, by way of farm dogs and house dogs, great dogs and small dogs. Sometimes a bark would carry half a mile or more, sometimes it would only need to carry a few yards. One sharp-eared Cairn saved the chain from breaking by picking up a bark from nearly a mile away, and then almost bursting herself getting it on to the dog next door. Across miles and miles of country, across miles and miles of suburbs, across a network of London streets the chain held firm; from the depths of Suffolk to the top of Primrose Hill – where Pongo and Missis, still as statues, stood listening, listening.

'Puppies found in lonely house. S.O.S. on old bone –' Missis could not take it all in. But Pongo missed nothing. There were instructions for reaching the village, suggestions for the journey, offers of hospitality on the way. And the dog chain was standing by to take a message back to the pups – the Sheepdog would bark it over the wall in the dead of night.

At first Missis was too excited to think of anything to say, but Pongo barked clearly: 'Tell them we're coming! Tell them we start tonight! Tell them to be brave!'

Then Missis found her voice: 'Give them all our love! Tell Patch to take care of the Cadpig! Tell Lucky not to be too daring! Tell Roly Poly to keep out of mischief!' She would have sent a message to every one of the fifteen pups if Pongo had not whispered: 'That's enough, dear. We mustn't make it too complicated. Let the Great Dane start work now.'

So they signed off and there was a sudden silence. And then, though not quite so loudly, they heard the Great Dane again. But this time he was not barking towards them. What they heard was their message, starting on its way to Suffolk.

Ivan Southall

HILLS END

Ivan Southall writes about Australia and the people who live there and all his books have a vitality and excitement which seem like the essence of the land itself.

Perhaps it is because it is such a huge country with enormous, uninhabited areas and little isolated timber towns, situated across dangerous bush and river, miles from a city, that so many almost true-life adventure stories can be written.

For instance when the rains begin, Hills End can be cut off from the world for two or three months. But on the morning of the annual Picnic Day, when the inhabitants go off to the Stanley races, no one notices that the River Magnus is strangely swollen. And as it happens, seven children don't get into the cars and trucks lined up, full of food for the day's outing. They stay behind because of a quarrel between two boys, and instead go up the mountains to help their school mistress look for some aboriginal cave paintings. So, when the flood comes and Hills End is destroyed, they have to face hunger, thirst, exhaustion and a wild bull!

But danger brings out unexpected qualities in people, and somehow they find ways of surviving while the whole continent has given them up for lost – here they are, having lost their schoolteacher, struggling back to the village where their troubles are only just beginning.

* * *

The children wriggled down the face of the bluff as carefully as they had climbed it those many hours before. It wasn't difficult. They were agile and they were young. What was a test of courage for Miss Godwin was all in the day's play for children.

They *were* frightened, but not of the bluff. Even the torrent foaming across the rock pan had lost its terrors, because their thoughts were reaching out beyond it. It was the unknown that was frightening them now, not the physical dangers before them. A heavy weight seemed to be inside them. They couldn't smile any more or relieve their worries by chattering about other things. Even Harvey couldn't summon his cheeky grin, and little boys like Harvey are not easily squashed. If the aeroplane had not come they might have invented a reason for the things that puzzled them, but not one was too young to understand now. The aeroplane would not have come if everything had been all right.

The fear was, 'If we really and truly are alone, for ever and ever, what shall we do? What will become of us? Where shall we go?'

They crossed the rock pan without harm, sometimes following Adrian, sometimes following Paul, sometimes Frances, or hand in hand through the more perilous and faster-flowing waters. They battled across like little Britons, but they came through safely because the rock pan had ceased to frighten them. They were given the opportunity to learn that fear, not danger, was their greatest enemy. If they had been more awake to the present they might have realized that courage was more than a virtue – they might have seen that courage was common sense. Perhaps they were too young. Perhaps they were too miserable to learn anything.

They struggled into the forest, not knowing that their crossing of the rock pan was something to be proud of. Their spirits were low. Four and a half miles of steamy, sticky, and tangled forest stretched ahead of them. When they had come the day before they had followed the path that had been tramped by erring children for ten years. This afternoon it was there in part only, in places washed away, in places smothered by fallen timber, and in the gullies submerged beneath streams they had never seen flow before. They leapt some of the streams, anxiously waded through some, and scouted others uphill and downhill until they found bridges of broken trees or could climb across overhanging boughs. Soon their clothes were filthy and torn.

At a quarter to four by Adrian's watch it started raining again; steady, solid rain, but not accompanied by the violent winds and thunder of the day before. Hail didn't fall and the rain didn't roar as though its one desire was to destroy them, but in a very short time they were drenched and cold and the forest floor turned into a gloomy vault that was not at all friendly. The light was weird, as though belonging to another epoch in time or perhaps to another world. Once, from a hilltop, they caught a glimpse of the upper reaches of the bluff far behind them, with cloud swirling round it like smoke. It was low cloud such as they saw in the wet season, that sagged out of heavy skies and sometimes stayed on the mountain-tops and in the gullies for days.

They plodded on and on. They knew they were heading in the right direction, but they had long since lost the old path and were gradually forced lower into the valley towards the road, to avoid wash-aways and landslides. There were times they had to wallow calf-deep through mud. They had seen storm damage before, but nothing like this. Never had such a volume of wind, hail and rain struck their mountains so fiercely and in so few hours. Spread over a week the dry land would have absorbed the rain, but too much had come too quickly, and now it was raining again.

Two thousand yards to the south of the town they reached the road. They were very, very tired, but not too tired to read the story it told.

'Golly!' groaned Paul.

It was pitted with deep holes and the wheel-ruts had been cut to ditches by fast-flowing water. And water still flowed, red with earth, in the direction of the invisible township, ever cutting deeper into the surface of the road, until diverted by fallen boulders or snapped trees, or cascaded over the side towards the river. It simply wasn't a road any more.

Frances looked back into the south, and going uphill it was just the same. 'This is awful,' she said. 'Perhaps even the bridge at the crossing is down.'

That wasn't an idle fancy because the river was roaring so much they could hear it above the rain. In two or three places they could see it, swirling high above its banks, thick with mud and rubbish and scum, all fouled up with tangled trees. It looked like some evil red monster writhing.

'I'm hungry,' whimpered Harvey.

'Won't be long now,' said Frances.

'We can't use the road,' said Adrian. 'It'll be safer in the bush.'

'We can't go through the bush either. That's why we're here.'

'You know,' said Maisie quietly, 'if the road was like this yesterday, no one will be in the town at all. They wouldn't have been able to get back.'

'Yeah . . . And I'll bet the bridge has gone. It took four months to build that bridge. I know, because my dad told me. He had to get engineers up from the city, specially.'

'Four months?' wailed Gussie. 'Four *whole* months?'

'That's what it took 'em to build it; but they built it from both sides, stupid. Just because it took 'em four months to build, it doesn't mean we've got to wait four more months until they get here.'

'How long did it take them to put the road through, Adrian?'

Adrian hadn't thought of that. 'I think the Government did it, but I think dad said there'd been a track out this way for sixty or seventy years. Maybe no one made the road. Maybe it sort of grew up.'

'I'm glad the road's gone,' Frances said suddenly.

'What?' shrieked Paul.

'It means that nothing has happened to our families. It means that they're just not here because they couldn't get here, as Maisie said.'

Paul suddenly felt that awful weight that had been bowing him down disappear like magic. And he wasn't the only one. There were wide smiles everywhere, and Maisie and Gussie hugged each other, and Harvey started dancing up and down, and Adrian let out a great whoop of joy.

'But there's something else,' Frances said. 'Butch, Miss

Godwin, Mr Tobias – surely Mr Tobias could have got out
to us on a tractor or a bulldozer.'

Paul snorted. 'Girls! How could anyone drive through this?
They couldn't get a 'dozer up here until the ground dries, and
a tractor wouldn't get ten yards. It'd turn over.'

'Yeah,' said Adrian. 'That's silly, Frances. We couldn't
even get through the bush on foot. Maybe they are trying to
reach us, anyway. They could be out at the bluff now. We
might have passed them. I'll bet that's what's happened.
While we've been trying to get through the bush, they've
been trying to get through the bush, too.'

Paul grunted. 'Could be,' he said. 'Easily enough. We've
been up and down and all over the place. We might have
missed them by a hundred yards or missed them by a mile.
Golly, the way things are Butch and Miss Godwin mightn't
have got back to the township until this morning. I reckon
things are going to be all right. I do, you know. Things are
beginning to make sense.'

'Even the aeroplane?' said Frances.

'Of course. Why not? Adrian's dad would have organized
it. Probably the mob was held up at Stanley. Golly, perhaps
even the picnic was washed out! The storm might have gone
for miles. Adrian's dad would have asked the Air Force to see
if we were all right. That makes sense, doesn't it? Your dad
was an officer in the Air Force. He'd know the right people
to ask, wouldn't he, Adrian?'

Adrian shrugged his shoulders with importance. 'Sure he
would. My dad knows everyone. He even knows a Cabinet
Minister.'

'There you are,' said Paul. 'We've got all worked up over
nothing.'

'I wish I could feel the same way,' said Frances. 'It seems
to fit together too easily.'

'Now who's not facing facts? They're good facts, so you won't believe them.'

'I didn't say I didn't believe them. I'd like to, very much.'

Adrian suddenly had a wonderful idea. 'Tell you what,' he said. 'As soon as we get home we can call up the Flying Doctor Service on the wireless. Then we'll know for sure.'

'Can you work the wireless?'

'Of course I can. I can even send SOS in morse code. What say we send an SOS? Gee, we'd be in all the newspapers then.'

'I think I'd rather talk in ordinary language,' said Paul, 'and be sure they got the message straight. But the blooming old wireless isn't much good. The time when Mrs Matheson thought she had appendicitis your dad couldn't even get through. Couldn't even ask the doctor what to do for her.'

'It was only indigestion. She'd eaten too much.'

'That doesn't make any difference. The wireless wouldn't work.'

'Goodness!' said Frances. 'Talk, talk, talk!'

'Too right,' said Harvey. 'Let's go home. I'm hungry and I know there's a dirty big pie in our fridge.' A sharp frown suddenly lined Harvey's forehead. 'Buzz! He's tied up at his kennel. He wouldn't have had anything to eat since yesterday. Ooh, I hope Mr Tobias remembered.'

'Of course Mr Tobias would remember,' said Adrian. 'He's got a dog himself. He wouldn't have forgotten the dogs. But let's go, eh? And it looks as though we'll have to stick to the bank above the road. And it's gettin' late. It's twenty to five. If it's hard to get through we might be caught in the dark. You don't want to get caught in the dark, do you?'

'Not me,' said Harvey. 'Not with that pie in the fridge.'

*

They weren't caught in the dark. In less than ten minutes the schoolhouse came into view. There always had been a clearing through there, that opened back on the magnificent vista so loved by Miss Godwin. The clearing hadn't gone. It was wider than ever. The howling wind had torn through it, uprooting trees and snapping others like sticks. One had fallen across the schoolhouse and crushed it like a tin can.

Someone gave a frightened cry, because above the schoolhouse, dimly visible through the rain, but stark for all that, was Miss Godwin's cottage. The roof and two walls had gone. It looked like a ruin from a bombed city.

Gussie shivered. 'Poor Miss Godwin!'

'Golly!' Paul squared himself and thrust out his jaw. 'It looks bad. But come on, everyone.'

They hurried across the tangle of the clearing, and the open ground was almost denuded of soil. It looked as though it had been swilled with a fire-hose. In places the runaway soil had piled up against ledges of rock like sand-drifts. It was mud, with texture fine as silk, and very dangerous. They had to keep clear, because immediately their feet touched it they began to sink.

Then, into view, came Hills End, and the rain beat down upon the children.

Their home town was beneath them, in the valley, and they were overcome with horror.

It was Frances who cried out a heart-broken sob, and started running, stumbling, slipping, down the long hill towards the township, and the others followed.

Noel Streatfeild

THE GROWING SUMMER

Noel Streatfeild's most famous book is *Ballet Shoes*, and most girls will know of it, just as they will have heard about *Tennis Shoes* and *White Boots*. She is very good at creating stories about families who in their different ways become very successful at whatever they do. But you'll notice she never writes about people who have all the luck and find extraordinary adventures without trying. Her characters have to work hard to get their different rewards.

The Growing Summer is just a bit different, and has become one of my favourites chiefly because I so enjoy the eccentricities of Great-Aunt Dymphna.

The story begins familiarly. The Gareths – Alex, Penny, Robin and Naomi (in order of age) are packed off to Ireland to stay with an unknown Great-Aunt. They are rather conventional children and are very shocked to discover their Aunt is a bit odd, doesn't seem at all interested in them and answers all their questions with quotes from 'The Courtship of the Yonghy-Bonghy-Bó' by Edward Lear. So they have to look after themselves right from the very beginning, finding out how to cook, and not at all sure where the next meal is coming from. Added to all that, a mysterious boy turns up and asks to be hidden.

Here they are getting their first taste of what life will be like with Great-Aunt Dymphna.

* * *

The first impression of Great-Aunt Dymphna was that she was more like an enormous bird than a great-aunt. This was partly because she wore a black cape, which seemed to flap behind her when she moved. Then her nose stuck out of her thin wrinkled old face just like a very hooked beak. On her head she wore a man's tweed hat beneath which straggled wispy white hair. She wore under the cape a shapeless long black dress. On her feet, in spite of it being a fine warm evening, were rubber boots.

The children gazed at their great-aunt, so startled by her appearance that the polite greetings they would have made vanished from their minds. Naomi was so scared that, though tears went on rolling down her cheeks, she did not make any more noise. Great-Aunt Dymphna had turned her attention to the luggage.

'Clutter, clutter! I could never abide clutter. What have you got in all this?' As she said 'this' a rubber boot kicked at the nearest suitcase.

'Clothes, mostly,' said Alex.

'Mummy didn't know what we'd need,' Penny explained, 'so she said we'd have to bring everything.'

'Well, as it's here we must take it home I suppose,' said Great-Aunt Dymphna. 'Bring it to the car,' and she turned and, like a great black eagle, swept out.

Both at London airport and when they had arrived at Cork a porter had helped with the luggage. But now there was no porter in sight and it was clear Great-Aunt Dymphna did not expect that one would be used. Alex took charge.

'You and Naomi carry those two small cases,' he said to Robin. 'If you could manage one of the big ones, Penny, I can take both mine and then I'll come back for the rest.'

Afterwards the children could never remember much about the drive to Reenmore. Great-Aunt Dymphna, in a terrifyingly erratic way, drove the car. It was a large, incredibly old, black Austin. As the children lurched and bounced along – Robin in front, the other three in the back – Great-Aunt Dymphna shot out information about what they met in passing.

'Never trust cows when there's a human with them. Plenty of sense when on their own. Nearly hit that one but only because that stupid man directed the poor beast the wrong way.'

As they flashed past farms dogs ran out barking, prepared at risk of their lives to run beside the car.

'Never alter course for a dog,' Great-Aunt Dymphna shouted, 'just tell him where you are going. It's all he wants.' Then, to the dog: 'We are going to Reenmore, dear.' Her system worked, for at once the dog stopped barking and quietly ran back home.

For other cars or for bicycles she had no respect at all.

'Road hogs,' she roared. 'Road hogs. Get out of my way or be smashed, that's my rule.'

'Oh, Penny,' Naomi whispered, clinging to her. 'We'll be killed, I know we will.'

Penny was sure Naomi was right but she managed to sound brave.

'I expect it's all right. She's been driving all her life and she's still alive.'

The only road-users Great-Aunt Dymphna respected were what the children would have called gipsies, but which she called tinkers. They passed a cavalcade of these travelling, not in the gipsy caravans they had seen in England, but in a different type with rounded tops. Behind and in front of the caravans horses ran loose.

'Splendid people, tinkers,' Great-Aunt Dymphna shouted. Then, slowing down, she called out something to the tinkers which might, for all the children understood, have been in a foreign language. Then, to the children: 'If you need medicine they'll tell you where it grows.'

Alex took advantage of the car slowing down to mention the cable.

'We promised Mummy we'd send it,' he explained. 'And she's sending one to us to say she's arrived and how Daddy is.'

'Perhaps a creamery lorry will deliver it sometime,' Great-Aunt Dymphna said. 'That's the only way a telegram reaches me. You can send yours from Bantry. The post office will be closed, but you can telephone from the hotel.'

Penny had no idea what a creamery lorry might be but she desperately wanted her mother's cable.

'Oh, dear, I hope the creamery lorry will be quick, we do so dreadfully want to know how Daddy is.'

'Holding his own,' Great-Aunt Dymphna shouted. 'I asked the seagulls before I came out. They'll tell me if there's any change.'

'She's as mad as a coot,' Alex whispered to Penny. 'I should think she ought to be in an asylum.'

Penny shivered.

'I do hope other people live close to Reenmore. I don't like us to be alone with her.'

But in Bantry when they stopped to send the cable nobody seemed to think Great-Aunt Dymphna mad. It is true the children understood very little of what was said, for they were not used to the Irish brogue, but it was clear from the tone of voice used and the expression on people's faces that what the people of Bantry felt was respect. It came from the man who filled the car up with petrol, and another who put some parcels in the boot.

'Extraordinary!' Alex whispered to Penny when he came out of the hotel. 'When I said "Miss Gareth said it would be all right to send a cable" you'd have thought I had said the Queen had said it was all right.'

'Why, what did they say?' Penny asked.

'It was more the way they said it than what they said, but they told me to write down the message and they would telephone it through right away.'

It was beginning to get dark when they left Bantry but as the children peered out of the windows they could just see purplish mountains, and that the roads had fuchsia hedges instead of ordinary bushes, and that there must be ponds or lakes for often they caught the shimmer of water.

'At least it's awfully pretty,' Penny whispered to Alex. 'Like Mummy said it would be.'

'I can't see how that'll help if she's mad,' Alex whispered back.

Suddenly, without a word of warning, Great-Aunt Dymphna stopped the car.

'We're home.' Then she chuckled. 'I expect you poor little town types thought we'd never make it, but we always do. You'll learn.'

The children stared out of the car windows. Home! They seemed to be in a lonely lane miles from anywhere.

'Get out. Get out,' said Great-Aunt Dymphna. 'There's no drive to the house. It's across that field.'

The children got out. Now they could see that the car had stopped at a gap in a fuchsia hedge, and that on the other side of the hedge there was a field with a rough track running across it.

'Where do you garage your car?' Alex asked.

Great-Aunt Dymphna gave another chuckle.

'There isn't what you mean by a garage, but there's a shed in the field. Too dark to put the car away tonight. Shall leave her where she is until the morning.'

Although the children were used to staying in a caravan they were not used to walking about in the country in the night. On caravan holidays they were always in or near the caravan eating supper or doing something as a family long before it was dark. Now they found they were expected to carry their suitcases across a pitch black field to an invisible house, without even a light to guide them. As well there was no Great-Aunt Dymphna to lead the way for, having said the car would wait where it was until the morning, she had vanished across the field, her cape flapping behind her.

'Horrible old beast!' thought Alex, dragging their cases from the boot. 'She really is insufferable.' But he kept what he felt to himself for out loud all he said was:

'Let's just take the cases we need tonight. We can fetch the others in the morning.'

Alex led the way, carrying his and Naomi's cases, Robin came next, Penny, gripping Naomi's hand, followed the boys.

'I don't wonder nobody brings a telegram here,' said Robin. 'I shouldn't think anybody brings anything. I should think we could all be dead before a doctor comes.'

Alex could have hit him.

'Shut up, you idiot. Of course people come, you heard what she said about a creamery lorry, and there must be a postman, everybody has those.'

'If they're real they do,' Robin agreed, 'but I don't think she is real. I think she's a vampire. I shouldn't wonder if she drank our blood when we're asleep.'

Naomi gave a moan and stumbled against Penny. Penny was sick with fear but she was also angry.

'I should have thought, Robin, one way and another things were awful enough without you making them worse.' Then she said to Naomi: 'Don't listen to him, darling, you'll feel quite different after a hot bath and then I'll give you your supper in bed.'

Naomi was clear about that.

'Not if it means my being alone for one single minute you won't.'

'Even if you don't think she's a vampire,' said Robin, 'I vote we keep our windows shut just in case, that's the way they get in.'

Alex put down the suitcases and turned to face Robin.

'Will you shut up. You know you promised you'd obey me.'

Robin was outraged.

'Mummy said I was to do what you and Penny told me, but she didn't say I wasn't to talk.'

Alex's voice was fierce.

'Well, I'm telling you to shut up and that's an order.'

After that, except for angry mutters from Robin they finished crossing the field in silence. It was then they saw a light. It was very feeble but it was a light.

'Thank goodness,' said Penny. 'This suitcase weighs a ton.'

The light was a candle held by Great-Aunt Dymphna.

'Come along, come along. Thought I'd lost you.'

The children followed Great-Aunt Dymphna into the

house and thankfully put down their suitcases. Great-Aunt Dymphna was lighting four more candles, each was stuck to a saucer.

'You can't see much in this light but up those stairs and turn left you'll come to a door, that's the west wing. It's all yours.'

Penny was standing beside Alex, she gripped his hand.

'Ask about supper?' she whispered.

'Thank you very much,' Alex said, trying desperately to sound polite. 'Do we come down for supper?'

'Supper!' Great-Aunt Dymphna sounded as though she was trying out a new word. 'Oh! When you get to the west wing at the end of the passage there are back stairs. At the bottom there is a kitchen, you'll find all you need there. Good night.'

In the flickering light of their candles the children humped their cases up the stairs, which were wide and uncarpeted. At the top of the stairs they turned left as directed and sure enough they came to a heavy door. Alex opened it but when they were all through it closed creakingly behind them. Penny shivered.

'How shall we know which rooms are for us?'

The question answered itself for on the first door they came to a piece of paper was pinned. It said 'Penelope'. They all walked in.

The room was almost bare, it had no carpet, no curtains and no pictures, but there was a large unmade double bed with one pillow, two blankets, two sheets and one pillowcase lying on it. In a corner there was a mahogany cupboard. It was so awful a bedroom Penny said nothing except:

'Let's look at the other rooms.'

Alex's room was next, it was just like Penny's except that his bed was single and one of its legs had a bit broken off it, so the bed was propped up on two books. He had no cupboard but he had a cheap yellow chest of drawers. In Robin's room there was also a single bed and what must once have been a rather grand hanging cupboard but the door was off its hinges. Naomi's room, which was the far side of the bathroom, had a single bed, a rickety chest of drawers, which leant drunkenly against the wall, but she had a picture, it was of the devil pushing a man into a cauldron.

Everything was so truly terrible it was no good pretending it was not so Alex did not try, instead he said:

'Just dump the cases and we'll see what's for supper.'

The mention of supper was too much for Naomi, she sat on the floor and howled.

'I couldn't eat anything. I'm frightened. I won't sleep alone in this horrible room. Nobody is going to make me.'

Penny knelt down beside her and hugged her.

'Of course you shan't sleep alone, you can sleep with me in my bed, it's enormous.'

'She's a witch,' Naomi howled. 'I know she's a witch. Oh, Penny, I'm so frightened!'

'It's all right, Naomi,' said Alex. 'Of course she isn't a witch, you'll be all right in the morning, you're only tired.'

But Naomi would not be comforted.

'If she's not a witch she's a vampire, like Robin said.'

Penny tried to laugh.

'Don't be so silly, darling, there aren't such things . . .'

Then she broke off for at that moment something banged against the window before it flew off into the night.

Rosemary Sutcliff

THE EAGLE OF THE NINTH

Some historical novels can so load you down with dates and facts that it's hard to get interested in the characters underneath. Rosemary Sutcliff's books are never like that. Once you've discovered her, you'll find endless pleasure in such masterpieces as *The Dragon Slayer*, *Blood Feud* and *The High Deeds of Finn Mac Cool*.

From the very first moment, you understand and care about the problems of Marcus, a young Roman centurion who stationed amongst the rebellious British tribes. He is also trying to solve the mystery of the missing Eagle Standard of the Ninth Legion. In this episode he saves a young Briton from death and develops a friendship which transcends tribal antagonisms.

* * *

The next item was a sham fight, with little damage done save a few flesh wounds. (In the back of beyond, circus-masters could not afford to be wasteful with their gladiators.) Then a boxing match in which the heavy cestus round the fighters' hands drew considerably more blood than the swords had done. A pause came, in which the arena was once again cleaned up and freshly sanded; and then a long gasp of expectancy ran through the crowd, and even the bored young tribune sat up and began to take some notice, as, with another blare of trumpets, the double doors swung wide once more, and two figures stepped out side by side into the huge emptiness of the arena. Here was the real thing: a fight to the death.

At first sight the two would seem to be unequally armed, for while one carried sword and buckler, the other, a slight dark man with something of the Greek in his face and build, carried only a three-pronged spear, and had over his shoulder a many-folded net, weighted with small discs of lead. But in truth, as Marcus knew only too well, the odds were all in favour of the man with the net, the Fisher, as he was called, and he saw with an odd sinking of the heart that the other was the young swordsman who was afraid.

'Never did like the net,' Uncle Aquila was grumbling. 'Not a clean fight, no!' A few moments earlier, Marcus had known that his damaged leg was beginning to cramp horribly; he had been shifting, and shifting again, trying to ease the pain without catching his uncle's notice; but now, as the two men crossed to the centre of the arena, he had forgotten about it.

The roar which greeted the pair of fighters had fallen to a breathless hush. In the centre of the arena the two men were being placed by the captain of the gladiators; placed with exquisite care, ten paces apart, with no advantage of light or

wind allowed to either. The thing was quickly and compet-
ently done, and the captain stepped back to the barriers. For
what seemed a long time, neither of the two moved. Moment
followed moment, and still they remained motionless, the
centre of all that great circle of staring faces. Then, very
slowly, the swordsman began to move. Never taking his eyes
from his adversary, he slipped one foot in front of the other;
crouching a little, covering his body with the round buckler,
inch by inch he crept forward, every muscle tensed to spring
when the time came.

The Fisher stood as still as ever, poised on the balls of his
feet, the trident in his left hand, his right lost in the folds of
the net. Just beyond reach of the net, the swordsman checked
for a long, agonizing moment, and then sprang in. His attack
was so swift that the flung net flew harmlessly over his head,
and the Fisher leapt back and sideways to avoid his thrust,
then whirled about and ran for his life, gathering his net for
another cast as he ran, with the young swordsman hard
behind him. Half round the arena they sped, running low;
the swordsman had not the other's length and lightness of
build, but he ran as a hunter runs – perhaps he had run down
deer on the hunting trail, before ever his ear was clipped –
and he was gaining on his quarry now. The two came flying
round the curve of the barrier towards the Magistrates'
benches, and just abreast of them the Fisher whirled about
and flung once more. The net whipped out like a dark flame;
it licked round the running swordsman, so intent on his chase
that he had forgotten to guard for it; the weights carried the
deadly folds across and across again, and a howl burst from
the crowd as he crashed headlong and rolled over, helplessly
meshed as a fly in a spider's web.

Marcus wrenched forward, his breath caught in his throat.
The swordsman was lying just below him, so near that they

could have spoken to each other in an undertone. The Fisher was standing over his fallen antagonist, with the trident poised to strike, a little smile on his face, though his breath whistled through widened nostrils, as he looked about him for the bidding of the crowd. The fallen man made as though to raise his hampered arm in a signal by which a vanquished gladiator might appeal to the crowd for mercy; then let it drop back, proudly, to his side. Through the fold of the net across his face, he looked up straight into Marcus's eyes, a look as direct and intimate as though they had been the only two people in all that great amphitheatre.

Marcus was up and standing with one hand on the barrier rail to steady himself, while with the other he made the sign for mercy. Again and again he made it, with a blazing vehemence, with every atom of will-power that was in him, his glance thrusting like a challenge along the crowded tiers of benches where already the thumbs were beginning to turn down. This mob, this unutterably stupid, blood-greedy mob that must somehow be swung over into forgoing the blood it wanted! His gorge rose against them, and there was an extraordinary sense of battle in him that could not have been more vivid had he been standing over the fallen gladiator, sword in hand. Thumbs up! *Thumbs up!* you fools! . . . He had been aware from the first of Uncle Aquila's great thumb pointing skyward beside him; suddenly he was aware of a few others echoing the gesture, and then a few more. For a long, long moment the swordsman's fate still hung in the balance, and then as thumb after thumb went up, the Fisher slowly lowered his trident and with a little mocking bow, stepped back.

Marcus drew a shuddering breath, and relaxed into a flood of pain from his cramped leg, as an attendant came forward

to disentangle the swordsman and aid him to his feet. He did
not look at the young gladiator again. This moment was
shame for him, and Marcus felt he had no right to witness it.

*

That evening, over the usual game of draughts, Marcus asked
his uncle: 'What will become of that lad now?'

Uncle Aquila moved an ebony piece after due consider-
ation. 'The young fool of a swordsman? He will be sold in all
likelihood. The crowd do not pay to see a man fight, when
once he has been down and at their mercy.'

'That is what I have been thinking,' Marcus said. He looked
up from making his own move. 'How do prices run in these
parts? Would fifteen hundred sesterces buy him?'

'Very probably. Why?'

'Because I have that much left of my pay and a parting
thank-offering that I had from Tullus Lepidus. There was not
much to spend it on in Isca Dumnoniorum.'

Uncle Aquila's brows cocked inquiringly. 'Are you suggesting buying him yourself?'

'Would you give him house-room?'

'I expect so,' said Uncle Aquila. 'Though I am somewhat
at a loss to understand why you should wish to keep a tame
gladiator. Why not try a wolf instead?'

Marcus laughed. 'It is not so much a tame gladiator as a
body-slave that I need. I cannot go on overworking poor old
Stephanos for ever.'

Uncle Aquila leaned across the chequered board. 'And
what makes you think that an ex-gladiator would make you
a suitable body-slave?'

'To speak the truth, I had not thought about it,' Marcus
said. 'How do you advise me to set about buying him?'

'Send down to tne circus slave-master, and offer half of
what you expect to pay. And sleep with a knife under your
pillow thereafter,' said Uncle Aquila.

*

The purchase was arranged next day, without much difficulty, for although the price that Marcus could afford was
not large, Beppo, the master of the circus slaves, knew well
enough that he was not likely to get a better one for a beaten
gladiator. So, after a little haggling, the bargain was struck,
and that evening after dinner Stephanos went to fetch home
the new slave.

Marcus waited for their return alone in the atrium, for
Uncle Aquila had retired to his watch-tower study to work
out a particularly absorbing problem in siege warfare. He had
been trying to read his uncle's copy of the Georgics, but his
thoughts kept wandering from Virgil on bee-keeping to the
encounter before him. He was wondering for the first time –
he had not thought to wonder before – why the fate of a slave
gladiator he had never before set eyes on should matter to
him so dearly. But it did matter. Maybe it was like calling to
like; and yet it was hard to see quite what he had in common
with a barbarian slave.

Presently his listening ear caught the sound of an arrival in
the slaves' quarters, and he laid down the papyrus roll and
turned towards the doorway. Steps came along the colonnade, and two figures appeared on the threshold. 'Centurion
Marcus, I have brought the new slave,' said Stephanos, and
stepped discreetly back into the night; and the new slave
walked forward to the foot of Marcus's couch, and stood
there.

For a long moment the two young men looked at each
other, alone in the empty lamplit atrium as yesterday they
had been alone in the crowded amphitheatre, while the

scuff-scuffling of Stephanos's sandals died away down the colonnade.

'So it is you,' the slave said at last.

'Yes, it is I.'

The silence began again, and again the slave broke it. 'Why did you turn the purpose of the crowd yesterday? I did not ask for mercy.'

'Possibly that was why.'

The slave hesitated, and then said defiantly, 'I was afraid yesterday; I, who have been a warrior. I am afraid to choke out my life in the Fisher's net.'

'I know,' Marcus said. 'But still, you did not ask for mercy.'

The other's eyes were fixed on his face, a little puzzled. 'Why have you bought me?'

'I have need of a body-slave.'

'Surely the arena is an unusual place to pick one.'

'But then, I wished for an unusual body-slave.' Marcus looked up with the merest quirk of a smile into the sullen grey eyes fixed so unswervingly on his own. 'Not one like Stephanos, that has been a slave all his life, and is therefore – nothing more.'

It was an odd conversation between master and slave, but neither of them was thinking of that.

'I have been but two years a slave,' said the other quietly.

'And before that you were a warrior – and your name?'

'I am Esca, son of Cunoval, of the tribe of Brigantes, the bearers of the blue war-shield.'

'And I am – I was, a centurion of auxiliaries with the Second Legion,' Marcus said, not knowing quite why he made the reply, knowing only that it had to be made. Roman and Briton faced each other in the lamplight, while the two statements seemed to hang like a challenge in the air between them.

Then Esca put out a hand unconsciously and touched the edge of the couch. 'That I know, for the goaty one, Stephanos, told me; and also that my Master has been wounded. I am sorry for that.'

'Thank you,' Marcus said.

Esca looked down at his own hand on the edge of the couch, and then up again. 'It would have been easy to escape on my way here,' he said slowly. 'The old goaty one could not have held me back if I had chosen to break for freedom. But I chose to go with him because it was in my heart that it might be you that we went to.'

'And if it had been another, after all?'

'Then I should have escaped later, to the wilds where my clipped ear would not betray me. There are still free tribes beyond the Frontiers.' As he spoke, he drew from the breast of his rough tunic, where it had lain against his skin, a slender knife, which he handled as tenderly as if it had been a thing living and beloved. 'I had this, to my release.'

'And now?' Marcus said, not giving a glance to the narrow, deadly thing.

For a moment the sullenness lifted from Esca's face. He leaned forward and let the dagger fall with a little clatter on to the inlaid table at Marcus's side. 'I am the Centurion's hound, to lie at the Centurion's feet,' he said.

James Thurber

THE WONDERFUL O

James Thurber, who was a very famous American humorist, wrote this story and *The 13 Clocks* when he was supposed to be writing something else because he simply couldn't help himself – that's why they both bubble with gaiety and wit, and why everybody who reads them immediately wants to start all over again.

The 13 Clocks (which is in the same book as *The Wonderful O*) is a rather grown-up fairy-tale with a wicked uncle, a princess in distress and a prince who is set impossible tasks, but it is funny and poetic and full of meaning. You'll especially enjoy the ghastly Cold Duke of Coffin Castle and the Golux.

If you keep a notebook or a dictionary beside you while you read

The Wonderful O, you'll have a fine time learning new words and working out others – in fact, you'll dazzle your friends with your erudition. For it's about two abominable villains, searching for a treasure, who hate the letter O because one of their mothers got stuck in a porthole and had to be pushed out because they couldn't pull her in – anyway, they ban everything on the island of Oonoo which has an O in it. First they take the O's out of all the words, then they start forbidding such things as dogs, cottages, coconuts and dolls. They are just getting round to forbidding mothers when the islanders decide there are four things with an O in them that must not be lost. Three of them are 'hope' and 'love' and 'valour'. The fourth and most important is really the whole point of *The Wonderful O*.

* * *

That night the people of the town and those who lived in the country met secretly in the woods. They had been called together by a poet named Andreus, who read aloud, or tried to read, a poem he had just had printed at the printer's. It was called 'The Mn Belngs T Lvers', but the poetry had died in it with the death of its O's. 'Soon Black and Littlejack,' said Andreus, 'will no longer let us live in houses, for houses have an O.'

'Or cottages,' said the blacksmith, 'for cottage has an O, and so does bungalow.'

'We'll have to live in huts,' the baker said, 'or shacks, or sheds, or shanties, or in cabins.'

'Cabins without logs,' said Andreus. 'We shall have mantels but no clocks, shelves without crocks, keys without locks, walls without doors, rugs without floors, frames without windows, chimneys with no roofs to put them on, knives without a fork or spoon, beds without pillows. There will be no wood for our fires, no oil for our lamps and no hobs for our kettles.'

'They will take my dough,' moaned the baker.

'They will take my gold,' moaned the goldsmith.

'And my forge,' sighed the blacksmith.

'And my cloth,' wept the tailor.

'And my chocolate,' muttered the candymaker.

At this a man named Hyde arose and spoke. 'Chocolate is bad for the stomach,' he said. 'We shall still have wintergreen and peppermint. Hail to Black and Littlejack, who will liberate us all from liquorice and horehound!'

'Hyde is a lawyer,' Andreus pointed out, 'and he will still have his fees and fines.'

'And his quills and ink,' said the baker.

'And his paper and parchment,' said the goldsmith.

'And his chair and desk,' said the blacksmith.

'And his signs and seals,' said the tailor.

'And his briefs and liens,' said the candymaker.

But the lawyer waved them all aside. 'We shall all have an equal lack of opportunity,' he said smoothly. 'We shall all have the same amount of nothing. There must be precious jewels, or Black and Littlejack would not have come so far to search for them. I suggest we look in nooks and corners and in pigeonholes ourselves.' Some of the men agreed with Hyde, but most of them took the poet's side.

'We must think of a way to save our homes,' the poet said. And they sat on the ground until the moon went down, trying to think of a way. And even as they thought, Black and Littlejack and their men were busily breaking open dolls, and yellow croquet balls, and coconuts, but all they found was what is always found in dolls, and yellow croquet balls, and coconuts.

The next morning Andreus was walking with his poodle in a street whose cobblestones had been torn up in the search for jewels when he encountered Black and Littlejack.

'You are *both* pets now,' sneered Littlejack, 'for the O has gone out of poet, and out of trochee and strophe and spondee, and ode and sonnet and rondeau.'

The poodle growled.

'I hate poodles,' snarled Black, 'for poodles have a double O.'

'My pet is French,' said Andreus. 'He is not only a *chien*, which is French for dog, but a *caniche*, which is French for poodle.'

'*Chien caniche*,' squawked the parrot. '*Chien caniche*.'

'Then I will get rid of the other domestic creatures with an O,' cried Black, and he issued an edict to this effect.

There was great consternation on the island now, for people could have pigs, but no hogs or pork or bacon; sheep, but no mutton or wool; calves, but no cows. Geese were safe as long as one of them did not stray from the rest and become a goose, and if one of a family of mice wandered from the rest, he became a mouse and lost his impunity. Children lost their ponies, and farmers their colts and horses and goats and their donkeys and their oxen.

Test cases were constantly brought to court – or curt, as it was called. 'Somebody will have to clarify the law for everybody, or nobody will know where anybody stands,' the people said. So Black appointed Hyde lawyer, judge and chief clarifier. 'The more chaotic the clarification,' said Black, 'the better. Remember how I hate that letter.'

This was right up Hyde's dark and devious alley. 'Chaotic is now chatic,' he said, 'a cross between chaos and static.' He decided that farmers could keep their cows if they kept them in herds, for cows in herds are kine or cattle. And so the people had milk and cheese and butter. He decided in favour of hens and eggs, if hens were segregated. 'Keep them out of flocks,' he said, 'for flocks are not only flocks, but also poultry.'

'We have no corn or potatoes, or cauliflower, or tomatoes,' a housewife said one day.

'In a vegetable garden,' said Hyde, 'the things that grow are ninety-five per cent without an O. I could name you twenty such,' he added cockily, 'and then you'd scream in unison for broccoli. Almost all the fruits are yours to eat, from the apple to the tangerine, with a good two dozen in between. I'll stick to those that start with P to show you what I mean: the pear, the peach, the plum, the prune, the plantain and pineapple, the pawpaw and papaya. But you will yearn for things you never ate, and cannot tolerate – I know you women – the pomegranate, for one, and the dull persimmon. No grapefruit, by the way. I hate its bitter juice. I have banned it, under its French name, *pamplemousse*.'

Another wife took the stand one day to complain of the things she hadn't. 'Cloves and cinnamon,' she said, 'and marjoram and saffron.'

'You still have dill,' said Hyde, 'and thyme and sage and basil, vinegar, vanilla and sarsaparilla, salt and pepper and paprika, ginger and the spices. You can't have coffee, but there is tea; to sweeten it, there's sugar.'

A seamstress raised her hand to ask about the O's in textiles, fabrics and in clothes. 'You're denied a few,' admitted Hyde. 'Corduroy and bombazine, organdy and tricotine, calico and crinoline. But you have silk and satin, velvet, lace and linen, tulle and twill and tweed, damask and denim, madras and muslin, felt and chintz and baize and leather, and twenty more for cool and warm and winter weather.'

Now the boatswain of the crew was a man named Stragg and the cockswain was a man named Strugg, and the former was allergic to roses, and the latter was allergic to phlox. So

Black decided that even the flowers with an O in their names were against him, and he ordered his crew to get rid of roses and phlox in the gardens of the island, and oleanders and moonflowers and morning-glories, and cosmos and cox-comb and columbine, and all the rest with O's.

'But my livelihood is violets and hollyhocks and mari-golds,' a gardener complained.

'Lilies are nice for livelihood,' said Hyde, 'and more alliter-ative. There are also lilacs and the like. I crossbreed certain things myself with more success than failure. Forget-me-nots, when crossed with madwort, lose their O's. I get a hybrid which I call regret-me-evers. Love-in-a-mist, when crossed with bleeding hearts, results in sweethearts quarrels.'

'It's blasphemy or heresy,' the women cried, 'or some-thing!'

'You haven't heard the half of it,' said Hyde. 'Black-eyed susans, crossed with ragged sailors, give me ragged susans. Jack-in-the-pulpit, crossed with devil's paintbrush, should give me devil-in-the-pulpit. And think of the fine satanic chimes that will emerge from hellebore crossed with Canter-bury bells.' At this the women rose in anger and dismay and left the curt without a curtsy.

'Why not get rid of all the flowers?' demanded Black one day. 'After all, there is an O in flowers.'

'I thought of that,' said Hyde, 'but we must spare collective nouns, like food, and goods, and crops, and tools, and, I should think, the lesser schools. I have taken the carpenter's gouge and boards. It still leaves him much too much, but that's the way it goes, with and without O's. He has his saw and axe and hatchet, his hammer and chisel, his brace and bit, and plane and level, also nails and tacks and brads and screws and staples. But all he can build is bric-à-brac and knickknack, gew-gaw, kickshaw, and gimcrack. No coop or goathouse, no stoop or boathouse.'

'I would that I could banish body; then I'd get rid of everybody.' Black's eyes gleamed like rubies. 'No more anatomy, and no morphology, physiognomy, or physiology, or people, or even persons. I think about it often in the night. Body is blood and bones and other O's, organs, torso, abdomen and toes.'

Hyde curled his upper lip. 'I'll build you a better man,' he said, 'of firmer flesh and all complete, from hairy head to metatarsal feet, using A's and I's and U's and E's, with muscular arms and flexible knees; eyes and ears and lids and lips, neck and chest and breast and hips; liver, heart, and lungs and chin, nerves and ligaments and skin; kidneys, pancreas, and flanks, ankles, calves, and shins and shanks; legs and lashes, ribs and spleen –' Black had turned a little green, and then Hyde held up both his hands. 'Brains and veins and cells and glands –'

'Silence!' thundered Black. 'I wish that more things had an O.'

Hyde sighed. 'There is no O in everything,' he said. 'We can't change that.'

'I will not take their vocal chords, or tongues, or throats,' said Black, 'but I shall make these jewel-hiders speak without the use of O in any word they say.'

J. R. R. Tolkien

THE HOBBIT

Hobbits are about half our size. They wear bright colours and no shoes. They have curly brown hair on their heads and feet, clever fingers and deep fruity laughs, especially after dinner (which they have twice a day if they can get it), and they are inclined to be fat.

The hobbit, Bilbo Baggins, who also had a fairy ancestor, doesn't want to be a hero, but is persuaded to go off and burgle a dragon. On his way he meets fearful dangers and such enemies as trolls and giant spiders. Here, in an underground lake, he meets Gollum, the nastiest, strangest, most loathsome creature of all. Yet there is also some fun to be had before he manages to escape with the help of a magic ring.

The Hobbit was the beginning of a much longer work, which is called *The Lord of the Rings* and which is now one of the most famous books to be written in the last fifty years, and Bilbo Baggins will still be delighting readers a hundred years from now.

* * *

Deep down here by the dark water lived old Gollum, a small slimy creature. I don't know where he came from, nor who or what he was. He was a Gollum – as dark as darkness, except for two big, round, pale eyes in his thin face. He had a little boat, and he rowed about quite quietly on the lake; for lake it was, wide and deep and deadly cold. He paddled it with large feet dangling over the side, but never a ripple did he make. Not he. He was looking out of his pale lamp-like eyes for blind fish, which he grabbed with his long fingers as quick as thinking. He liked meat too. Goblin he thought good, when he could get it; but he took care they never found him out. He just throttled them from behind, if they ever came down alone anywhere near the edge of the water, while he was prowling about. They very seldom did, for they had a feeling that something unpleasant was lurking down there, down at the very roots of the mountain. They had come on the lake, when they were tunnelling down long ago, and they found they could go no further; so there their road ended in that direction, and there was no reason to go that way – unless the Great Goblin sent them. Sometimes he took a fancy for fish from the lake, and sometimes neither goblin nor fish came back.

Actually Gollum lived on a slimy island of rock in the middle of the lake. He was watching Bilbo now from the distance with his pale eyes like telescopes. Bilbo could not see him, but he was wondering a lot about Bilbo, for he could see that he was no goblin at all.

Gollum got into his boat and shot off from the island, while Bilbo was sitting on the brink altogether flummoxed and at the end of his way and his wits. Suddenly up came Gollum and whispered and hissed:

'Bless us and splash us, my preciousss! I guess it's a choice feast; at least a tasty morsel it'd make us, gollum!' And when he said *gollum* he made a horrible swallowing noise in his throat. That is how he got his name, though he always called himself 'my precious'.

The hobbit jumped nearly out of his skin when the hiss came in his ears, and he suddenly saw the pale eyes sticking out at him.

'Who are you?' he said, thrusting his dagger in front of him.

'What iss he, my preciouss?' whispered Gollum (who always spoke to himself through never having anyone else to speak to). This is what he had come to find out, for he was not really very hungry at the moment, only curious; otherwise he would have grabbed first and whispered afterwards.

'I am Mr Bilbo Baggins. I have lost the dwarves and I have lost the wizard, and I don't know where I am; and I don't want to know, if only I can get away.'

'What's he got in his handses?' said Gollum, looking at the sword, which he did not quite like.

'A sword, a blade which came out of Gondolin!'

'Sssss,' said Gollum, and became quite polite. 'Praps ye sits here and chats with it a bitsy, my preciouss. It like riddles, praps it does, does it?' He was anxious to appear friendly, at any rate for the moment, and until he found out more about the sword and the hobbit, whether he was quite alone really, whether he was good to eat, and whether Gollum was really hungry. Riddles were all he could think of. Asking them, and sometimes guessing them, had been the only game he had ever played with other funny creatures sitting in their holes in the long, long ago, before he lost all his friends and was driven away, alone, and crept down, down, into the dark under the mountains.

'Very well,' said Bilbo, who was anxious to agree, until he found out more about the creature, whether he was quite alone, whether he was fierce or hungry, and whether he was a friend of the goblins.

'You ask first,' he said, because he had not had time to think of a riddle.

So Gollum hissed:

> What has roots as nobody sees,
> Is taller than trees
>   Up, up it goes,
>   And yet never grows?

'Easy!' said Bilbo. 'Mountain, I suppose.'

'Does it guess easy? It must have a competition with us, my preciouss! If precious asks, and it doesn't answer, we eats it, my preciouss. If it asks us, and we doesn't answer, then we does what it wants, eh? We show it the way out, yes!'

'All right!' said Bilbo, not daring to disagree, and nearly bursting his brain to think of riddles that could save him from being eaten.

> Thirty white horses on a red hill,
>   First they champ,
>   Then they stamp,
>   Then they stand still.

That was all he could think of to ask – the idea of eating was rather on his mind. It was rather an old one, too, and Gollum knew the answer as well as you do.

'Chestnuts, chestnuts,' he hissed. 'Teeth! teeth! my preci-ouss; but we has only six!' Then he asked his second:

> Voiceless it cries,
> Wingless flutters,
> Toothless bites,
> Mouthless mutters.

'Half a moment!' cried Bilbo, who was still thinking uncomfortably about eating. Fortunately he had once heard something rather like this before, and getting his wits back he thought of the answer. 'Wind, wind of course,' he said, and he was so pleased that he made up one on the spot. 'This'll puzzle the nasty little underground creature,' he thought:

> An eye in a blue face
> Saw an eye in a green face.
> 'That eye is like to this eye'
> Said the first eye,
> 'But in low place,
> Not in high place.'

'Ss, ss, ss,' said Gollum. He had been underground a long long time, and was forgetting this sort of thing. But just as Bilbo was beginning to hope that the wretch would not be able to answer, Gollum brought up memories of ages and ages and ages before, when he lived with his grandmother in a hole in a bank by a river, 'Sss, sss, my preciouss,' he said. 'Sun on the daisies it means, it does.'

But these ordinary above ground everyday sort of riddles were tiring for him. Also they reminded him of days when he had been less lonely and sneaky and nasty, and that put him out of temper. What is more they made him hungry; so this time he tried something a bit more difficult and more unpleasant:

> It cannot be seen, cannot be felt,
> Cannot be heard, cannot be smelt.
> It lies behind stars and under hills,
>   And empty holes it fills.
> It comes first and follows after,
>   Ends life, kills laughter.

Unfortunately for Gollum Bilbo had heard that sort of thing before; and the answer was all round him any way. 'Dark!' he said without even scratching his head or putting on his thinking cap.

> A box without hinges, key, or lid.
> Yet golden treasure inside is hid,

he asked to gain time, until he could think of a really hard one. This he thought a dreadfully easy chestnut, though he had not asked it in the usual words. But it proved a nasty poser for Gollum. He hissed to himself, and still he did not answer; he whispered and spluttered.

After some while Bilbo became impatient. 'Well, what is it?' he said. 'The answer's not a kettle boiling over, as you seem to think from the noise you are making.'

'Give us a chance; let it give us a chance, my preciouss — ss — ss.'

'Well,' said Bilbo after giving him a long chance, 'what about your guess?'

But suddenly Gollum remembered thieving from nests long ago, and sitting under the river bank teaching his grand-mother, teaching his grandmother to suck — 'Eggses!' he hissed. 'Eggses it is!' Then he asked:

> Alive without breath,
> As cold as death;
> Never thirsty, ever drinking,

All in mail never clinking.

He also in his turn thought this was a dreadfully easy one, because he was always thinking of the answer. But he could not remember anything better at the moment, he was so flustered by the egg-question. All the same it was a poser for poor Bilbo, who never had anything to do with the water if he could help it. I imagine you know the answer, of course, or can guess it as easy as winking, since you are sitting comfortably at home and have not the danger of being eaten to disturb your thinking. Bilbo sat and cleared his throat once or twice, but no answer came.

After a while Gollum began to hiss with pleasure to himself: 'Is it nice, my preciousss? Is it juicy? Is it scrumptiously crunchable?' He began to peer at Bilbo out of the darkness.

'Half a moment,' said the hobbit shivering. 'I gave you a good long chance just now.'

'It must make haste, haste!' said Gollum, beginning to climb out of his boat on to the shore to get at Bilbo. But when he put his long webby foot in the water, a fish jumped out in fright and fell on Bilbo's toes.

'Ugh!' he said, 'it is cold and clammy!' – and so he guessed. 'Fish! fish!' he cried. 'It is fish!'

Gollum was dreadfully disappointed; but Bilbo asked another riddle as quick as ever he could, so that Gollum had to get back into his boat and think.

No-legs lay on one-leg, two-legs sat near on three-legs, four-legs got some.

It was not really the right time for this riddle, but Bilbo was in a hurry. Gollum might have had some trouble guessing it, if he had asked it at another time. As it was, talking of fish, 'no-legs' was not so very difficult, and after that the rest was easy. 'Fish on a little table, man at table sitting on a stool, and cat has the bones' that of course is the answer, and Gollum soon gave it. Then he thought the time had come to ask something hard and horrible. This is what he said:

> This thing all things devours:
> Birds, beasts, trees, flowers;
> Gnaws iron, bites steel;
> Grinds hard stones to meal;
> Slays king, ruins town,
> And beats high mountain down.

Poor Bilbo sat in the dark thinking of all the horrible names of all the giants and ogres he had ever heard told of in tales, but not one of them had done all these things. He had a feeling that the answer was quite different and that he ought to know it, but he could not think of it. He began to get frightened, and that is bad for thinking. Gollum began to get out of his boat. He flapped into the water and paddled to the bank; Bilbo could not see his eyes coming towards him. His tongue seemed to stick in his mouth; he wanted to shout out: 'Give me more time! Give me time!' But all that came out with a sudden squeal was:

> 'Time! Time!'

Bilbo was saved by pure luck. For that of course was the answer.

Gollum was disappointed once more; and now he was getting angry, and also tired of the game. It had made him very hungry indeed. This time he did not go back to the boat. He sat down in the dark by Bilbo. That made the hobbit most dreadfully uncomfortable and scattered his wits.

'It's got to ask uss a quesstion, my preciouss, yes, yess,

yesss. Jusst one more question to guess, yes, yess,' said Gollum.

But Bilbo simply could not think of any question with that nasty wet cold thing sitting next to him, and pawing and poking him. He scratched himself, he pinched himself; still he could not think of anything.

'Ask us! ask us!' said Gollum.

Bilbo pinched himself and slapped himself; he gripped on his little sword; he even felt in his pocket with his other hand. There he found the ring he had picked up in the passage and forgotten about.

'What have I got in my pocket?' he said aloud. He was talking to himself, but Gollum thought it was a riddle, and he was frightfully upset.

'Not fair! not fair!' he hissed. 'It isn't fair, my precious, is it, to ask us what it's got in its nassty little pocketses?'

Bilbo seeing what had happened and having nothing better to ask stuck to his question. 'What have I got in my pocket?' he said louder.

'S-s-s-s-s,' hissed Gollum. 'It must give us three guesseses, my preciouss, three guesseses.'

'Very well! Guess away!' said Bilbo.

'Handses!' said Gollum.

'Wrong,' said Bilbo, who had luckily just taken his hand out again. 'Guess again!'

'S-s-s-s-s,' said Gollum more upset than ever. He thought of all the things he kept in his own pockets: fish-bones, goblins' teeth, wet shells, a bit of bat-wing, a sharp stone to sharpen his fangs on, and other nasty things. He tried to think what other people kept in their pockets.

'Knife!' he said at last.

'Wrong!' said Bilbo, who had lost his some time ago. 'Last guess!'

Now Gollum was in a much worse state than when Bilbo had asked him the egg-question. He hissed and spluttered and rocked himself backwards and forwards, and slapped his feet on the floor, and wriggled and squirmed; but still he did not dare to waste his last guess.

'Come on!' said Bilbo. 'I am waiting!' He tried to sound bold and cheerful, but he did not feel at all sure how the game was going to end, whether Gollum guessed right or not.

'Time's up!' he said.

'String, or nothing!' shrieked Gollum, which was not quite fair – working in two guesses at once.

'Both wrong,' cried Bilbo very much relieved; and he jumped at once to his feet, put his back to the nearest wall, and held out his little sword. He knew, of course, that the riddle-game was sacred and of immense antiquity, and even wicked creatures were afraid to cheat when they played at it. But he felt he could not trust this slimy thing to keep any promise at a pinch. Any excuse would do for him to slide out of it. And after all that last question had not been a genuine riddle according to the ancient laws.

But at any rate Gollum did not at once attack him. He could see the sword in Bilbo's hand. He sat still, shivering and whispering. At last Bilbo could wait no longer.

'Well?' he said. 'What about your promise? I want to go. You must show me the way.'

'Did we say so, precious? Show the nassty little Baggins the way out, yes, yes. But what has it got in its pocketses, eh? Not string, precious, but not nothing. Oh no! gollum!'

'Never you mind,' said Bilbo. 'A promise is a promise.'

'Cross it is, impatient, precious,' hissed Gollum. 'But it must wait, yes it must. We can't go up the tunnels so hasty. We must go and get some things first, yes, things to help us.'

'Well, hurry up!' said Bilbo, relieved to think of Gollum

going away. He thought he was just making an excuse and
did not mean to come back. What was Gollum talking about?
What useful thing could he keep out on the dark lake? But he
was wrong. Gollum did mean to come back. He was angry
now and hungry. And he was a miserable wicked creature,
and already he had a plan.

Not far away was his island, of which Bilbo knew nothing,
and there in his hiding-place he kept a few wretched odd-
ments, and one very beautiful thing, very beautiful, very
wonderful. He had a ring, a golden ring, a precious ring.

'My birthday-present!' he whispered to himself, as he had
often done in the endless dark days. 'That's what we wants
now, yes; we wants it!'

He wanted it because it was a ring of power, and if you
slipped that ring on your finger, you were invisible; only in
the full sunlight could you be seen, and then only by your
shadow, and that would be shaky and faint.

'My birthday-present! It came to me on my birthday, my
precious.' So he had always said to himself. But who knows
how Gollum came by that present, ages ago in the old days
when such rings were still at large in the world? Perhaps even
the Master who ruled them could not have said. Gollum used
to wear it at first, till it tired him; and then he kept it in a
pouch next his skin, till it galled him; and now usually he hid
it in a hole in the rock on his island, and was always going
back to look at it. And still sometimes he put it on, when he
could not bear to be parted from it any longer, or when he
was very, very, hungry, and tired of fish. Then he would
creep along dark passages looking for stray goblins. He might
even venture into places where the torches were lit and made
his eyes blink and smart; for he would be safe. Oh yes, quite
safe. No one would see him, no one would notice him, till
he had his fingers on their throat. Only a few hours ago he

had worn it, and caught a small goblin-imp. How it squeaked! He still had a bone or two left to gnaw, but he wanted something softer.

'Quite safe, yes,' he whispered to himself. 'It won't see us, will it, my precious? No. It won't see us, and its nasty little sword will be useless, yes quite.'

That is what was in his wicked little mind, as he slipped suddenly from Bilbo's side, and flapped back to his boat, and went off into the dark. Bilbo thought he had heard the last of him. Still he waited a while; for he had no idea how to find his way out alone.

Suddenly he heard a screech. It sent a shiver down his back. Gollum was cursing and wailing away in the gloom, not very far off by the sound of it. He was on his island, scrabbling here and there, searching and seeking in vain.

'Where is it? Where iss it?' Bilbo heard him crying. 'Losst it is, my precious, lost, lost! Curse us and crush us, my precious is lost!'

'What's the matter?' Bilbo called. 'What have you lost?'

'It mustn't ask us,' shrieked Gollum. 'Not its business, no, gollum! It's losst, gollum, gollum, gollum.'

'Well, so am I,' cried Bilbo, 'and I want to get unlost. And I won the game, and you promised. So come along! Come and let me out, and then go on with your looking!' Utterly miserable as Gollum sounded, Bilbo could not find much pity in his heart, and he had a feeling that anything Gollum wanted so much could hardly be something good. 'Come along!' he shouted.

'No, not yet, precious!' Gollum answered. 'We must search for it, it's lost, gollum.'

'But you never guessed my last question, and you promised,' said Bilbo.

'Never guessed!' said Gollum. Then suddenly out of the

gloom came a sharp hiss. 'What has it got in its pocketses? Tell us that. It must tell first.'

As far as Bilbo knew, there was no particular reason why he should not tell. Gollum's mind had jumped to a guess quicker than his; naturally, for Gollum had brooded for ages on this one thing, and he was always afraid of its being stolen. But Bilbo was annoyed at the delay. After all, he had won the game, pretty fairly, at a horrible risk. 'Answers were to be guessed not given,' he said.

'But it wasn't a fair question,' said Gollum. 'Not a riddle, precious, no.'

'Oh well, if it's a matter of ordinary questions,' Bilbo replied, 'then I asked one first. What have you lost? Tell me that!'

'What has it got in its pocketses?' The sound came hissing louder and sharper, and as he looked towards it, to his alarm Bilbo now saw two small points of light peering at him. As suspicion grew in Gollum's mind, the light of his eyes burned with a pale flame.

'What have you lost?' Bilbo persisted.

But now the light in Gollum's eyes had become a green fire, and it was coming swiftly nearer. Gollum was in his boat again, paddling wildly back to the dark shore; and such a rage of loss and suspicion was in his heart that no sword had any more terror for him.

Bilbo could not guess what had maddened the wretched creature, but he saw that all was up, and that Gollum meant to murder him at any rate. Just in time he turned and ran blindly back up the dark passage down which he had come, keeping close to the wall and feeling it with his left hand.

'What has it got in its pocketses?' he heard the hiss loud behind him, and the splash as Gollum leapt from his boat. 'What have I, I wonder?' he said to himself, as he panted and stumbled along. He put his left hand in his pocket. The ring felt very cold as it quietly slipped on to his groping forefinger.

A. Rutgers van der Loeff

CHILDREN ON THE OREGON TRAIL

Lots of us have seen films and read about the famous covered-wagon trains which took early settlers across the wild Indian territory to the American West. This book is based on a true story. It tells how John Sager (aged thirteen), his young brother, Francis, his four sisters, Louise (twelve), Catherine (nine), Lizzy (three), and Matilda (five) and the newborn baby, Indepentia, leave the rest of the wagon train after their parents die. Along with Oscar the wolfhound, Walter the ox and Anna, a cow, they make the truly appalling journey across two rivers and over the Cascade Mountains until they arrive – more dead than alive – in the state of Oregon. Once started you won't be able to put it down!

This extract is taken from the beginning, before they lose their parents. Here, the entire family faces the first of its perils.

* * *

That day began like any other.

At four o'clock in the morning, when the rising sun stood like a red-glowing ball above the grey landscape, the guards fired off their rifles, as a sign that the hours of sleep were past. Women, men and children streamed out of every tent and wagon; the gently smouldering fires from the previous night were replenished with wood, and bluish-grey clouds from dozens of plumes of smoke began to float through the morning air. Bacon was fried, coffee was made by those who still had some. The families which could still cook maize mush for the children thought themselves lucky.

All this took place within the 'corral', that was to say inside the ring which had been made by driving the wagons into a circle and fastening them firmly to each other by means of the shafts and chains. This formed a strong barricade through which even the most vicious ox could not break, and in the event of an attack by the Sioux Indians it would be a bulwark that was not to be despised.

Outside the corral the cattle and horses cropped the sparse grass in a wide circle.

At five o'clock sixty men mounted their horses and rode out of the camp. They fanned out through the crowds of cattle until they reached the outskirts of the herd; once there, they encircled the herd and began to drive all the cattle before them. The trained animals knew what those cracking whips meant, and what was required of them, and moved slowly in the direction of the camp. There the drivers picked their teams of oxen out from the dense mass and led them into the corral, where the yoke was put upon them.

From six o'clock until seven, the camp was extra busy; breakfast was eaten, tents were struck, wagons were loaded, and the teams of draught oxen and mules were made ready to be harnessed to their respective wagons and carts. Everyone knew that whoever was not ready when the signal to start was blown at seven o'clock would be doomed for that day to travel in the dusty rear of the caravan.

There were sixty-eight vehicles. They were divided into seventeen columns, each consisting of four wagons and carts. Each column took it in turn to lead the way. The section that was at the head today would bring up the rear tomorrow, unless a driver had missed his place in the row through laziness or negligence, and had to travel behind by way of punishment.

It was ten minutes to seven.

There were gaps everywhere in the corral; the teams of oxen were being harnessed in front of the wagons, the chains clanked. The women and children had taken their places under the canvas covers. The guide was standing among his assistants at the head of the line, ready to mount his horse and show the way. A dozen young men who were not on duty that day formed another group. They were going out buffalo-hunting; they had good horses and were well armed, which was certainly necessary, for the hostile Sioux had driven the herds of buffalo away from the River Platte, so that the hunters would be forced to ride fifteen or twenty miles to reach them.

As soon as the herdsmen were ready, they hurried to the rear of their herd, in order to drive them together and get them ready for today's march.

Seven o'clock.

An end had come to the busy running and walking to and fro, the cracking of whips, the shouts of command to the oxen, and the bawling from wagon to wagon – in short, to everything which, only just now, had appeared to be complete and utter chaos. Every driver was at his post. A bugle rang out! The guide and his escort mounted their horses; the four wagons of the leading section rumbled out of the camp and formed the first column, the rest took their places with the regularity of clockwork, and the caravan moved slowly forward over the broad plateau, far above the foaming river.

A new, hard day had begun. Particularly hard for the Sagers, who were having to do without the help of Mrs Ford, since she had gone to look after Walton's sick child.

The sun rose high in the sky. It was hot and stuffy under the canvas tilts, which were thick with dust. Towards noon the children everywhere began to bicker and whimper. But in the Sager family's wagon, they had other things to worry about.

John, who had been riding for hours in the blazing sun beside the heads of the foremost yoke of oxen, was given an order by his father, who was sitting on the driver's bench in the front of the wagon.

Immediately he galloped forward.

He had to fetch the doctor.

The doctor was a veterinary surgeon: the emigrants did not have a real doctor with them. But the vet had already done people a great deal of good, and helped them considerably, as well as animals.

John rode with all his might. Why on earth didn't the doctor travel in the middle of the caravan? From his father's face the boy had seen that the matter was urgent.

Meanwhile, Henry Sager had driven his wagon out of the line. He stopped.

'All the children must get out,' he ordered. 'Go and collect buffalo droppings and make a fire. Louise has to boil as much water as she can.'

Before Louise left the wagon, she filled the big kettle with water, scooping it up in a little tin bowl from the barrel in the back of the wagon. She cast a timid glance at her mother, who lay still and white on the tarpaulin. Mother caught Louise's eye and gave her a gentle, encouraging nod. If only that doctor would come quickly!

The doctor came.

With his long legs, he stepped from the saddle into the wagon in one stride. John tied up his horse. Then he wiped the sweat and dust out of his eyes with the back of his hand.

To the children, it seemed to take a long time. The water had already been boiling for quite a while. No one had asked for it yet, and they did not dare to look into the wagon.

In the distance ahead of them hung a thick cloud of dust, behind which the caravan was hidden. They would fall very far to the rear. John looked worried. He knew that that was dangerous – stragglers ran the risk of being attacked; but he said nothing. Now and again his father came out and glanced around, scanned the trail behind them – eight sets of wagon wheels beside each other and thousands upon thousands of hoof marks. But behind, the horizon was clear and empty.

Until John suddenly perceived a tiny cloud of dust.

He started. He knew that that could only mean that Indians were approaching.

'Father!' he shouted.

Henry Sager stuck his head out of the wagon.

John pointed to the east, where the cloud of dust above their own tracks had now grown rather larger.

Father Sager said nothing.

He went back into the wagon with the kettle of boiling water, but came out again a moment later with five rifles and two pistols. John had already pulled his own pistol from its holster. His father gave him a rifle.

'All the children except John and Louise, get under the wagon,' he commanded quietly. But it was easy to see that that calmness of his required all the self-control he had. His strong, wrinkled neck was fiery red, and the veins on his forehead were thick and purple.

'Take these,' he said to his eldest daughter, and Louise stood with three rifles in her arms, staring at the approaching cloud of dust as if turned to stone.

Father put the powder horn, lead, and ramrods down beside her.

John had laid his rifle across the saddlebow in front of him, as he had always seen the trappers do.

But his father said:

'Are you mad, boy? Get down and tie Mary up in front, along with the oxen. Do you want to serve as a target, and be shot out of the saddle?'

Francis pushed the smaller children under the wagon. Catherine began to resist, crying and kicking. 'Stop howling, you little idiot,' Francis snapped nervously, trying to make his voice sound as manly as possible. Matilda and Lizzy thought it rather a nice game; as a rule, they were never allowed to go under the wagon.

Father Sager climbed back in again.

He brought out two empty water casks, and the only bag of flour they had left. He stood the two casks upright beside the wagon, near one of the rear wheels, and laid the sack of flour across them.

'Come to the back here,' he ordered John and Louise. 'And remember – don't stir from cover. We fire along to one side of this, and between the casks . . . Louise, you load the rifles when we've fired them,' he said to her. To John he said nothing; he only looked at him.

A sound came from the wagon. It was like the crying of a tiny baby.

Father Sager gritted his teeth, and behaved as if he had not heard anything. The sound came again, more distinctly this time. Then he looked at his two eldest children; he almost had tears in his eyes.

'May God help us to protect that young life,' he said between clenched teeth. Rather more calmly, he went on: 'If it comes to that, it's not certain that the Indians mean mischief. And our rifles are good, sound ones. John, don't fire too soon, let 'em get close.'

He put his head back into the wagon.

'Don't worry, Doctor – we'll call if we can't manage without you.'

They waited in suspense. It was now easy to see that the cause of the cloud was horsemen – not many, perhaps half a dozen Indians on prairie ponies. They were superior in numbers, but they could not take cover anywhere.

There was no brushwood in which they could ensconce themselves.

'May God help us to protect that young life,' Father had said.

Cynthia Voigt

HOMECOMING

Some of the very best adventure stories are about children who have been left, or abandoned, by grown-ups and have to manage by themselves. This book is about four American children who lose their mother in a supermarket (she leaves them outside and never comes back). They decide it would be best to go and find an unknown aunt who lives in Bridgeport, Connecticut. So they set out to walk, expecting it only to take a few days. Instead, it's two long, hungry, frightening weeks, sleeping in empty houses, fields and picnic parks, catching fish in streams where they can, scrounging left-over sandwiches from picnickers, and even, when six-year-old Sammy gets really hungry, stealing a whole picnic lunch!

Sometimes they manage to earn tips by helping people with bags, and once, when Dicey thinks they will really have to give up, they are helped by some students. But when they get to Bridge-port they find their aunt is dead, and well-meaning helpers try to separate them, so they go on the run again, to find an unknown grandmother (reputed to be mad) on the other side of the state.

This time the journey is even worse, for when they try to earn money picking tomatoes, an awful farmer tries to kidnap them.

* * *

The screen door opened and a man holding a napkin in his hand stepped out. As soon as he appeared, the dog stopped barking and crouched, fawning and whimpering. The man started towards the children.

He was short and slender. He wore overalls and heavy working boots that laced up the front. The shirt under his overalls was dark blue with fancy red and yellow flowers printed all over it. His face was square and blunt; he had grey hair that he brushed back off his forehead and thin, straight eyebrows over cold eyes. He moved towards the Tillermans without hesitating, without hurrying, and stood silent before them. His skin was tanned and leathery. Deep lines ran across his forehead. He reached his napkin up and wiped his mouth.

'Yeah,' he said.

Dicey spoke. 'You have a sign out front, pickers wanted.' She hesitated, but he didn't say anything. 'We – my brother and me – we'd like to apply.' She motioned James to come stand beside her.

The man didn't speak. He studied them, through hard grey eyes.

'We can work hard,' Dicey said.

She waited. He didn't speak.

'What do you pay?' she asked.

'Fifty cents a bushel.'

You could pick lots of bushels in a day. That would be OK. 'Will you hire us?'

'Yes,' he said. 'What about the smaller ones?' he asked Dicey.

'They'll come with us and help,' Dicey said. 'They won't cause any trouble.'

'Name's Rudyard,' he said, 'what's yours?'

'Verricker,' Dicey said quickly. That seemed to be all he wanted to know. Except, 'What's hers?' he demanded, pointing at Maybeth with his head. 'Maybeth,' Dicey said.

Something was wrong here, something she couldn't put her finger on. Well, it wasn't her problem; they would work an afternoon and take their money.

He told them to get up into the back of a dusty old pickup truck the colour of canned peas. He drove them on a flat dirt road that led around the barn and behind it before heading straight up a slight incline, through an overgrown field, to another field. This was a long field of tomatoes. The plants were crowded with weeds, grasses and low vines. You could barely see the rows they had been planted in. But the tomatoes had grown red and plump. They shone out from the weeds like bulbs on a Christmas tree. At one corner of the field, a mound of bushel baskets waited. The Tillermans scrambled down.

Mr Rudyard didn't even get out of the truck. 'I'll be by at dark,' he said. He backed the truck around and drove off. Dicey watched it go into the distance, back to the barn, then around it and out of sight.

'Creepy,' James said.

'You can say that again,' Dicey agreed. 'Maybeth, you OK?'

Maybeth nodded, wide-eyed.

'How long do we have to stay?' Sammy asked.

They all felt uneasy. Dicey tried to reassure them. 'Just this afternoon. Then we'll take our pay and get out of here. OK?'

They got to it. Because they were hungry, Dicey decided they could each eat two tomatoes. That was fair enough, she figured. Then they all worked together, pushing or pulling weeds away from the tomato plants. One would hold back the overgrowth, and the rest would reach in for tomatoes, wresting the fruit from the stems. Their legs and hands and faces were scratched. They had bug bites on every part of their bodies. Dirt was smeared across their faces and arms and legs. They left the filled baskets where they were when they finished with them.

After an hour they had completed one row. Two to a basket, they carried the bushels down to where the pile of empty baskets waited. They had six baskets. 'Three dollars,' Dicey said.

Dicey's back ached from bending over. Her hands stung where small scratches had accumulated. She had never felt such heat before, an air that closed down over her and made it hard to breathe.

'Hot,' James said. 'It's too hot, Dicey.'

'You two take a break,' Dicey said to Sammy and Maybeth. 'Go off and explore a little. Stick together though. When you're rested, come back and help. Remember our name?'

'Verricker,' Sammy said. 'What's that?'

'Our father's name,' Dicey said.

'That right?' James asked. 'How do you know that?'

'So what,' Sammy said. 'I like Tillerman better.'

Sammy and Maybeth wandered off down the edge of the field, going away from the house and the dog. Dicey and James got back to work.

This row took longer. James grew sloppy and Dicey had to nag at him to keep at it and find all the ripe tomatoes that grew on the plants and on the long vines that crawled along next to the dry earth. 'My back hurts,' he protested. 'I'm hot.' His face was streaked with dirt and sweat. His eyes wavered between anger and self-pity. He crouched unwillingly by her side.

'It's only for an afternoon,' Dicey snapped at him.

Sammy and Maybeth returned before they had finished the row. 'There's another field,' Sammy reported. 'And a river. I wanted to go swimming but Maybeth wouldn't.'

'The Choptank,' Dicey said.

'Could we swim across it?' James asked Sammy.

Sammy nodded. Dicey shot a triumphant glance at James. 'It's not wide,' Sammy said. 'I could swim it easy.'

'Can we go now, Dicey?' Maybeth asked.

Dicey almost said yes. They all looked at her, waiting. She shook her head. 'Not before we get paid,' she said grimly. 'Don't worry, we'll be all right. As long as we're together.'

At late afternoon, when the sun was beginning to lower and the mosquitos were beginning to rise, the green pickup truck returned. The children went eagerly to meet it.

Mr Rudyard had the dog in the front seat with him. He climbed down and pulled on a long rope to get the dog to follow him. The Tillermans crowded together. The dog snarled at them.

'There's a bag in the cab,' Mr Rudyard said to Dicey. 'The missus said I had to feed you something.' He walked off, down to the far end of the field.

'What's he going to do?' Maybeth whispered.

'I dunno,' Dicey said. Fear climbed up from her stomach to her throat. A sour, metallic taste was in her saliva and she swallowed it down. She made herself climb up and get the paper bag from the seat of the cab. Mr Rudyard had left the keys in the ignition.

Mr Rudyard tied the dog to a tree, using the end of the long rope. When he came back, Dicey had decided what to do.

'We can't pick any more,' she said. 'We have to go now,' she said.

He looked at her out of cold eyes. Then he said, 'If he runs against that sapling it'll snap.' He got back into the truck and leaned out the window. 'I keep him hungry,' he remarked. He backed the truck around and drove off.

In the silence, Dicey could hear insects humming. 'What does he *want*?' she demanded.

Nobody could answer her.

'We might as well eat,' Dicey said. They all sat down. Mrs Rudyard had packed a tall thermos of milk and a package of tall biscuits slathered with butter and bright strawberry jam. They passed the thermos around. The biscuits looked delicious. Dicey took a bite of one, and her stomach closed against it. She put it down on the wax paper.

Even James couldn't eat. They looked at one another. 'I'm sorry,' Dicey said.

'Well, I don't care, I'm not picking any more,' Sammy announced. He threw his unfinished biscuit into the pile and they scattered around, like fallen blocks. 'And you can't make me,' he said to Dicey.

Dicey couldn't help smiling at him and that made her feel better. 'I won't try,' she said. 'James? What can we do?'

'I'd like to kill him and hit him,' Sammy said. 'He scares Maybeth.' Maybeth had big tears in her eyes.

'There's the dog,' James said, 'and the man.' Absentmind-edly, he picked up a biscuit. He took a bite, then tossed it down again. 'He's crazy, Dicey.'

'Bad crazy,' she agreed. 'Don't get on that truck again, no matter what.'

'He wants us to be scared,' Maybeth said. 'He wants to hurt us.'

Dicey nodded. Her mind was working and working, and she couldn't think of anything. James just stared at her. She picked up her maroon bag from where she had put it beside the bushels. She took out all of the money and jammed it into her pocket, with the jackknife. (With a jackknife, if she had to, she could try to fight the man or the dog.) She stuffed the map into the waistband of her shorts.

'We're going to have to run,' she said. 'When he comes back for the dog. James, you take Maybeth. Maybeth, no matter what, you stick with James.' Sammy could take care of himself. 'Go for the river.'

'What about you?' James asked.

'I'm not sure,' Dicey tried to keep her voice normal. She had gotten them into this mess, and if anyone got caught it should be her. 'I'll do something. You just keep ready to run.'

It was deep twilight, shadowy and still, when the truck returned. The Tillermans sat where Mr Rudyard had left them. The headlights shone on them briefly. He backed the truck so that its back section was where the filled bushel baskets waited and its nose pointed almost straight down the road to the farmhouse. He got out and looked at them.

'You're not much use,' he observed. Maybeth grabbed Dicey's hand as his eyes rested on her. 'I'll just have to teach you. Now, load up,' he ordered. He walked down to the dog, which barked a greeting.

'How does he know we're alone?' James wondered.

'Quiet,' Dicey said. She looked into the cab to see if the keys had been left there. They had. 'OK, now listen. When he's to the dog, tell me. And when I say run, you run, all of you, as fast as you can. You hear?'

They nodded. Dicey got up into the truck. She tried to forget about the man at the far corner of the field. She looked for the key and found it. She turned on the engine. Nothing happened. She looked at the transmission box. A needle pointed to *D*. Quickly, she shifted it to *N*. 'Now Dicey,' James whispered.

She turned the key again, and the engine caught.

Dicey looked back over her shoulder. Mr Rudyard ran towards them, his mouth open in a yell. The dog ran ahead of him, at full cry, but held back by the rope that his master had looped around his shoulder.

'James,' Dicey yelled. 'Now. Run.'

She shifted into *D*, and turned the wheel so it would head straight down the road to the barn. If she got it started, she figured, the incline would keep it going. She pushed on the accelerator and threw herself out of the cab.

The ground surged up to meet her and the cab door slammed against her shoulder. It hurt, but she didn't have time to worry about that. She rolled on to her feet and looked to see her family, waiting, watching her. 'Go!' she shrieked.

Dicey led them into the middle of the tomato field, away from the man and the dog. It was harder running, especially for Sammy with his short legs, but it would be harder for Mr Rudyard too. She let James and Maybeth pass her and slowed until she was behind Sammy too.

They weren't going to go without her. She didn't have time to know how she felt about that. She glanced over her shoulder.

Mr Rudyard was already letting the dog's rope fall from his shoulder as he ran after the truck. He would catch it easily, but how soon? The dog looked after his master for a second and then bent his head to the ground, snuffling something. Probably their scent, Dicey thought, turning her head back and making a burst of speed to catch up.

Across the tomato field, and then across the next field, where young corn made a narrow path for them to follow, they ran. Dicey tried to listen for the sound of the dog behind them, or the sound of the motor coming out of the darkness. But she could hear only their laboured breathing and the stamping of their feet. She charged through the row of brush and small trees that separated the second field from the river, grabbing Sammy's hand, pulling him with her. The earth fell away from beneath her feet and she tumbled into water.

Water closed warm over Dicey's head. She shut her eyes. She held tight on to Sammy's hand. How deep was it?

Her toes touched muddy river bottom and she pushed up. She shot out of the water. It was only up to her chest.

'James? Maybeth?'

'Here,' James spoke just beyond her.

'It's warm,' Sammy said.

In the distance, a truck motor roared.

'Straight across, then right, downstream. OK? Stay close.'

They set out into darkness, paddling quietly across. Through the gentle sounds of water, Dicey could hear their breathing. Dark water was all around them, and the dark land behind, and the dark land ahead. Every now and then she lowered a tentative foot to touch bottom.

The river was no more than fifty or sixty yards across, and it wasn't long before Dicey saw the opposite bank rise over her head, capped by a tangle of undergrowth and trees. She put her foot down again. It sank into mud.

Dicey and James were tall enough to touch bottom, but the water was over the heads of the smaller children. So Dicey and James each carried the weight of a younger one floating beside. They made their way cautiously, silently, quickly, downstream. They didn't speak, not even when they heard the man breaking through the bushes behind them upstream.

Sounds of someone walking hastily through underbrush across the river.

James moved doggedly on. Dicey followed him. They were near enough to get out and run, if Mr Rudyard dove into the water to pursue them. They could hide in the bushes on this side. He didn't have the dog with him.

The sounds ceased, as if someone were standing still to listen. James stopped too, but she pushed him on with an impatient hand.

The water gurgled around them.

The crackling sounds began again, hurrying away.

The darkness around Dicey lifted, as if a blanket had been taken off her head. There was no actual change, of course. Only, the night seemed cool and empty and the clear dark silhouettes of bushes and trees above them seemed to move back to give her more room, and the broad river seemed to float peacefully beside them.

They kept silence for another half hour, working their way downriver. At last, Dicey spoke. 'Let's get out – James? Can you lift Sammy? Sammy? Do you mind being first?'

'Course not,' Sammy said.

James hoisted the little boy up on to the bank. Sammy reached down to help Maybeth scramble up. Dicey pushed James from behind, and he turned around to pull her up, while her feet slipped against the muddy bank, searching for firm holds. They sat, huddling together, shivering but not from a chill.

Dicey turned to look behind them, where flat farmlands stretched off. No windows shone, but she could see a pair of headlights, far off, moving on a straight line. There must be a road.

'Not him,' Dicey said. She kept her voice low. Danger lurked all around them, always, she knew that now. 'It couldn't be him. There aren't but two bridges over the river and they're miles away.'

'What about the dog?' Sammy asked.

'Dogs can't track through water,' James said.

Dicey remembered the dog, snuffling at the ground for their scents. Then she began to giggle. 'It was eating the biscuits!' she cried. 'He couldn't get it to chase us because it was hungry. Doesn't that serve him right.'

This set them all giggling, even Maybeth. They kept their laughter low, and after a while they lay back on the grassy bank and slept, close together.

Jill Paton Walsh

THE DOLPHIN CROSSING

Jill Paton Walsh never writes the same book twice, or anything like it. Every book has different characters and always introduces you to new kinds of worlds. For instance, *A Parcel of Patterns* is woven round how the dreaded plague reaches and nearly destroys a remote village in Derbyshire, and my own favourite, *The Chance Child*, is about a ghost-like child working his way along the waterways and going through the terrible coal and iron mines where six-year-old children are strapped to trolleys and have to crawl through tunnels dragging their loads of coal, and are left to die where they fall.

She has also written two books about World War II. *Fireweed*, which is set in London during the Blitz is about a boy and a girl,

344

both running away, who meet in an air-raid shelter and wander about, foraging for goods and shelter since they have no identity cards or food rations, determined to stay together.

The Dolphin Crossing is an early and universal favourite. It tells of two boys' courage in joining the fleet of ships which crossed the Channel to rescue our soldiers after the evacuation of Dunkirk. If you want to imagine being young during the war, you should read this book, for it's more than just a memorable and horrifying tale from that time, it is a portrait of friendship, and a reminder that when real people take risks, they do sometimes actually get killed.

In this extract, John and Pat prepare for their heroic and terrifying voyage in the *Dolphin*.

* * *

'Have you got boots, Pat?' asked John. It turned out that Pat hadn't any suitable clothes. They went upstairs, and clambered into the loft in which all the contents of boxes and cupboards from the other house had been crammed. John found a pair of his father's sea-boots, a bit big for Pat, but wearable. Then he found his own. Then he found a duffle coat, and an oilskin cape. There was only one sou'wester, but among the folded things in one wooden box he found an old officer's cap belonging to his father, and a blue jacket with gold braid. They were rather loose on him, but they would do. They carted the clothing downstairs, and then John rummaged through the drawers of a tallboy in the living-room, looking for a chart of the Channel. He found one much battered by use.

'I don't think we'll need this,' he said. 'Not if there's as much going on as there has been today. We won't know where the minefields are, so we will have to try and follow someone who knows more than we do; but a chart is a good thing to have, just in case.'

While he searched around, Pat, with nothing to do, sat in the armchair, staring at the pattern on the carpet, and looking tense. John put a hand on his shoulder.

'You go to sleep now, Pat. We'll make up the camp bed for you.'

'Don't think I could sleep, thank you. Me gut's all knotted up. I'll sit here.'

'You'll go to bed, and sleep! I'll get you some aspirin and a hot drink, that helps. Captain's orders.'

Pat grinned stiffly. 'OK,' he said.

When John had settled Pat he went up to his own room, carrying a mug of hot cocoa. Suddenly a flood of affection for the room came over him. He looked at the bright blue bedcover, the little wicker chair, the round picture of his grandmother mounted on black velvet, the ship in a bottle that his father had brought for him when he was very young, and all these things seemed heart-warming, dearly loved, safe and inviting. How comfortable his bed looked! But he didn't get into it at once. He got into his pyjamas, and then sat in his chair, opened his writing case, and took a clean sheet of paper.

Dear Mother, he wrote, *I have gone.* Then he crossed that out and wrote, *Pat and I have taken . . .* Then he crossed that out too, and threw away the piece of paper. He sat thinking. How could he put it, so that she would not be worried about him? There wasn't a way of doing that. She would be terrified. For the first time John wondered whether it was, after all, a noble thing to do. But then, if everyone stayed at home for their mothers' sakes, Hitler would have the world for himself. And then John had begun to learn that his mother wasn't as delicate as she looked. She never fussed about his father.

But still, it was hard to think of a way of putting it. Perhaps he ought to say they had gone fishing for the day, or something like that. Then they would be back before she began to worry. Or would they? Just how long was it going to take? John realized with a lurch of his stomach that it was impossible to imagine being back; his mind wouldn't do it. It ran ahead only as far as getting there, and then it absolutely stopped. He didn't believe they would ever get back. He shook himself, and gulped some chocolate. He was being a fool. Of course they would get back, and they had a good chance of getting some soldiers back with them. That was the point of going. It was just that it was so tremendous that it filled his mind. He couldn't imagine doing anything ordinary, like going off for his Greek lesson, ever again.

No, he couldn't tell a straight lie to his mother. He couldn't even write *Don't worry*. He wrote, *Back as soon as possible, love, John*. He put the note on his chest of drawers, and climbed into bed.

*

The little alarm clock woke him at six o'clock. He was wide awake on the instant, his mind clear. He slipped out of bed and down the stairs to wake Pat. But Pat was awake already, lying looking at the ceiling with very open eyes. He got up as soon as he saw John.

'Get dressed,' said John, and went upstairs to dress himself. On the way he saw through the landing window that the midwife's bicycle was still leaning against the stable wall.

He put on his old trousers, a shirt, a scarf instead of a tie to keep the sharp sea air from blowing down his neck. He tried his father's jacket, and decided against it. It was uncomfortable. He found a thick ribbed dark blue sweater instead. Then he picked up his boots and his father's cap, and tiptoed past his mother's door.

The door was open. He could see his mother fast asleep, curled up like a child, with the blankets pulled up to her chin. He would have liked to go and kiss her, but he smiled at her instead, and very gently closed her door. Then he went downstairs.

Pat was dressed. John looked at him critically, and then found him a scarf to tuck round his neck.

'Mmm. You'll do,' he said.

'We ought to fill up with grub, but we can't cook bacon; the smell might wake your mum. What is there?' said Pat. They looked in the larder. Porridge seemed to be the best bet. Pat made it, while John searched for more. He found a tin of corned beef, and a tin of peaches. They put the peaches on top of their plates of porridge, and ate the corned beef with bread as a second course. When he went to the larder to fetch the margarine for the bread, John saw the second half of his week's butter ration, standing in a little dish. His mother wouldn't let him touch the second half till Thursday; but then, he thought, he mightn't be here on Thursday, and it would be a dreadful pity to waste it. The thought of not being here didn't disturb him in the least this morning; he had got used to it. But he took the butter. He and Pat shared it, spread gloriously thick, smooth and melting in their mouths. They drank plenty of hot coffee.

'Seems a bit mean to leave the washing-up,' said John, 'but I think we'd better go.' They stacked the dirty plates neatly on the draining board, just to show willing.

'Put on that oilskin,' said John to Pat as he put his duffle coat on.

'You're joking; the sun's coming up. Lovely morning it is.'

'Wear it just the same. It's important not to get cold. It will be cold at sea, and it's much easier to stay warm than to get warm again after you've got cold.' Pat made a face at him, and did as he was told.

It seemed odd to John that for once he was the one who knew more about practical details. But of course, he had grown up with boats.

They closed the kitchen door, and walked quietly past the stable, wondering in silence how Mrs Riley was getting on, and took the path to the sea. It was a cool misty morning, with that gold tinge to the haze which means it will be clear and warm later on. There was nobody about. Once they heard a distant chink of milk churns being moved on one of the farms, but they did not see the dairyman, and it gave the day a feeling of something new; something not handled, not breathed, by anyone before them. Lots of little things were happening. A bright globe of dew ran down a slanting blade of grass, to disappear in the general moisture of the ground. A bird hopped three times one way, and twice another, and cocked his head at them before flying off. They heard his wings. Sheep bleated mournfully from nearby fields.

Then they reached the wall, and walked along it, and the world looked different. The sea is always fresh, always empty. A great blank sweep of sky, a great flat plain of grey water, filled up the view, all without detail, all vast. Only the wind happened to anything here, and the myriad featureless wrinklings of the surface of the sea.

The tide was high, and the wind coming off the sea was cold. John shuddered. Crossman was standing in his doorway, waiting for them. He looked tired and harassed. Looking down at the sea, the boys saw *Dolphin* ready launched, tied up to the little pier. She looked quite a different shape in the water – much smaller.

'I've got some things to give you. I've not put them aboard;

you mightn't find where I'd stowed them. Will you step inside?' said Crossman. The boys followed him in.

Crossman's table was covered with carefully laid out things.

'Take stock of what's here, and remember where you stow everything when we take it aboard,' he said. 'Blankets; only two, I haven't more. Food; biscuit and guava jam, army stores stuff. Not tasty, but filling. And two pounds of chocolate. I've only one thermos flask; here, with coffee in it. But I've made some soup, and put it in these stone bottles. I'll show you where to put them under the engine covers so that the engine will keep them warm.'

'We aren't lifting a siege!' exclaimed John, astonished.

Crossman turned to look at him levelly. 'That's just about what you are doing. I've been in this sort of shambles, I tell you. Any men you pick up will be cold and hungry, and you'll need to eat yourselves. Keep this stuff, don't eat it all at the beginning. Now look here; this is a box of bandages, and iodine and such like. Aspirin here. This ointment for small burns – a bad burn shouldn't be touched. There's a pair of scissors too. Twenty cigarettes; I can't spare more. And last thing, this.' He brought from his cupboard a hip-flask of brandy. 'One of you wear this. Don't let a tired soldier get it unless he needs it. *Dolphin*'s in good order. I've filled her main tank, and her reserve tank. I think it would be dangerous to carry spare tins in the cabin.' Crossman stopped. He looked more tired than before. 'I can't think of anything else I can do for you,' he said. 'Give me a hand carrying this lot.'

They walked over the planking of the little pier, laden with all these things. John stepped easily across the gap between the gently bobbing boat, and the solid pier, and Pat and Crossman handed things down to him. He put the food in the galley, stowed the jars of soup against the warm part of the engine under Crossman's instructions, and put the first-aid stuff under one of the bunks.

'You've got enough petrol to keep going till tomorrow night some time,' said Crossman. 'If you don't keep switching her on and off. You shouldn't have to. Don't forget to bail out. I've stowed a pair of oars under the port bunk in case the engine packs up. God help you if that happens.' He took Pat's hand to steady him as he jumped on board. Pat made the jump clumsily, and *Dolphin* tilted sharply under his weight, and then rocked back the other way equally sharply. Pat sat down abruptly on the bench that ran round the cockpit.

'All set,' said John. He looked up at the man standing on the pier. 'Thank you, Crossman,' he said. There was no coldness in his tone now. He started the engine. It spluttered, and then chugged gently. Crossman cast off, dropping the painter on to the foredeck with expert hand. John eased *Dolphin's* nose away from the pier, let out the throttle and took her seawards. He turned to wave at Crossman, but he had turned his back, and was walking home. Then he increased the speed till the foaming water curled up proudly round *Dolphin's* bows, and they were off.

Robert Westall

THE MACHINE-GUNNERS

There are, of course, lots of good stories about the last war, and it's hard to choose between them. For they cover all sorts of problems and adventures that can happen to young people while grown-ups are busy coping with battles and air-raids and rations. I've chosen this book because it shows how foolish and dangerous games about war can become without any discipline.

The place is Tyneside in 1940–41 when bombing raids were commonplace. Young Chas McGill, who has the second-best collection of war souvenirs in Garmouth, is determined that it is going to be the best. He gets his chance when he finds a crashed German Heinkel, with a machine-gun and all its ammunition. He and his gang decide to keep their discovery secret, while the police and the home guard are desperately searching for the gun, afraid that the kids may have taken it, unaware of its power.

Here is Chas, coming across his greatest find.

* * *

Chas cheered up. Two whole slices of fried bread and a roll of pale pink sausage-meat. It tasted queer, not at all like sausage before the war. But he was starting to like the queerness. He ate silently, listening to his parents. If he shut up, they soon forgot he was there. You heard much more interesting things if you didn't butt in.

'I thought we were a gonner last night, I really did. That dive bomber . . . I thought it was going to land on top of the shelter . . . Mrs Spalding had one of her turns.'

'It wasn't a dive bomber,' announced Father with authority. 'It had two engines. He came down on the rooftops 'cos one of the RAF lads was after him. Right on his tail. You could see his guns firing. And he got him. Crashed on the old laundry at Chirton. Full bomb load. I felt the heat on me face a mile away.' Mother's face froze.

'Nobody killed, love. That laundry's been empty for years. Just as well – there's not much left of it.'

Chas finished his last carefully-cut dice of fried bread and looked hopefully at his father.

'Can I go and see it?'

'Aye, you can go and look. But you won't find nowt but bricks. Everything just went.'

Mother looked doubtful. 'D'you think he should?'

'Let him go, lass. There's nowt left.'

'No unexploded bombs?'

'No, a quiet night really. Lots of our fighters up. That's why you didn't hear any guns.'

'Can I borrow your old shopping-basket?' said Chas.

'I suppose so. But don't lose it, and don't bring any of your old rubbish back in the house. Take it straight down the greenhouse.'

'What's time's school?' said his father.

'Half-past ten. The raid went on after midnight.'

War had its compensations.

*

Chas had the second-best collection of war souvenirs in Garmouth. It was all a matter of knowing where to look. Silly kids looked on the pavements or in the gutters; as if anything *there* wasn't picked up straight away. The best places to look were where no one else would dream, like in the dry soil under privet hedges. You often found machine-gun bullets there, turned into little metal mushrooms as they hit the ground. Fools thought nothing could fall through a hedge.

As he walked, Chas's eyes were everywhere. At the corner of Marston Road, the pavement was burnt into a white patch a yard across. Incendiary bomb! The tailfin would be somewhere near – they normally bounced off hard when the bomb hit.

He retrieved the fin from a front garden and wiped it on his coat; a good one, not bent, the dark green paint not even chipped. But he had ten of those already.

Boddser Brown had fifteen. Boddser had the best collection of souvenirs in Garmouth. Everyone said so. There had been some doubt until Boddser found the nose-cone of a 3.7 inch anti-aircraft shell, and that settled it.

Chas sighed, and put the fin in his basket. A hundred tail-fins couldn't equal a nose-cone.

He knew the old laundry would be no good even before he got there. He began finding bits of the plane, but they were only lumps of aluminium, black on the sides and shiny at the edges, crumpled like soggy paper. They were useless as souvenirs – other kids just laughed and said you'd cut up your mother's tin kettle. Unless it was a piece that had a number on it, or a German word, or even . . . Chas sighed at the tightness in his chest . . . a real swastika. But *these* were just black and silver.

The scene of the crash was a complete catastrophe. It was the partial catastrophes that Chas found interesting – picture frames still hanging on exposed walls five storeys up; chimneys balanced on the verge of toppling – whereas the old laundry had been flattened as completely as if the council's demolition gang had done it. Just piles of brick and the bomber's two engines.

One engine was in the front garden of a council house that had its windows out and its ceiling down. The family were scurrying around like ants from a broken nest, making heaps of belongings they had salvaged, and then breaking up the heaps to make new heaps.

. . . . . .

The other engine was guarded by the local policeman, Fatty Hardy. He was wearing a white tin hat with P on it and looking important, but he was still the Fatty Hardy who had chased Chas off many a building-site before the War. Stupid.

This engine was much better than the one in the front garden. It still had its propeller. Though the blades were bent into horseshoes, the middle was unharmed, a lovely shiny egg-shape painted red. Chas nearly choked with greed. If he only had that . . . that was better than any 3.7 inch nose-cone! The whole propeller was loose – it waggled when the wind blew. Chas's mouth actually filled with saliva, as if he could smell a pie cooking.

How could he get rid of Fatty Hardy? An unexploded bomb? Swiftly he bashed his eyes with his fists, throwing handfuls of dust into them until they began to stream with tears. Then he ran towards Fatty Hardy bawling incoherently. As he reached the policeman he put his hand up; school died hard.

'Please, sir, Mum says come quick. There's a deep hole in our garden and there's a ticking coming from it.'

Fatty looked distinctly worried. Airplane engines was airplane engines and needed protecting from thieving kids. But unexploded bombs was unexploded bombs.

'*Hurry*, sir! There's little kids all round it, looking down the hole.'

Fatty grabbed his shoulders and shook him roughly.

'Where, where? Take me, take me!'

'Please, sir, no, sir. Mum says I mustn't go back there, in case it goes off. I've got to go to me gran's, sir. But the bomb's at 19, Marston Road.'

Fatty went off at a wobbling run, his gasmask case flogging his broad bottom. Before he was out of sight, Chas was at the engine. Its realness was overwhelming. There were German words on the cowling. *Öl* was the only one he could recognize. Everything was bigger close to. The twisted prop-blades curled into the air like palm-leaves. The red spinner, which he had thought as carryable as a rugby-ball, now seemed as big as a brewery-barrel. He tugged at it; it came off so far and then stuck. He heaved again at the shiny red newness. It still resisted.

'Nazi pigs!' he screamed, as his hand slipped and the blood came. He picked up a lump of brickwork, four bricks still cemented together, and, raising it above his head, flung it at the spinner. The beautiful red thing crushed in, but it still wouldn't budge. He hit it again. Another great white flaking dent appeared. It was a mess now, hardly worth having. But still it refused to come off.

There was a sudden roar of rage from behind. Fatty Hardy had returned, sweaty face working. Chas ran.

*

He wasn't greatly worried. Hardy was puffing already; he wouldn't last fifty yards. The only worry was the piles of rubble underfoot. If he fell, Hardy would have him. Placing his feet carefully, he ran towards the Wood.

The Wood was in the grounds of West Chirton Hall. At one time, his father said, the people at the Hall had owned everything. But then the factories came, and the council estate, and the owners of the Hall just curled up and died for shame. Now the house itself was just a hole in the ground lined with brick, and a black cinder floor. There was a big water-tank full of rusty water, and nothing else.

The Wood was bleak and ugly too. Grown-ups dumped rubbish round the outside, and kids climbed and broke the trees. But nobody went into the middle. Some said it was haunted, but Chas had never found anything there but a feeling of cold misery, which wasn't exciting like headless horsemen. Still, it was an oddly discouraging sort of place.

Each year the briars grew thicker; even Chas knew only one way through them. He took it now, wriggling under arches of briars as thick as your finger, interlaced like barbed wire. He was safe. Fatty Hardy couldn't even try to follow. He picked himself up quickly because the grass was soaking. The sky seemed even greyer through the bare branches, and he felt fed-up. Still, since he was here he might as well search for souvenirs. Chirton Hall was another place no one ever looked. He'd found his best bit of shrapnel there – a foot long, smooth and milled on the sides, but with jagged edges like bad teeth.

He sniffed. There was a foreign smell in the Wood . . . like petrol and fireworks. Funny, it wasn't Guy Fawkes yet. Some kids must have been messing about. As he pressed on, the smell grew stronger. There must be an awful lot of petrol.

Something was blocking out the light through the branches. A new building; a secret army base; a new anti-aircraft gun? He couldn't quite see, except that it was black.

And then he saw, quite clearly at the top, a swastika, black outlined in white. He didn't know whether to run towards it or away. So he stayed stock-still, listening. Not a sound, except the buzzing of flies. The angry way they buzzed off dog-dirt when you waved your hand over it. It was late in the year for flies!

He moved forward again. It was so tall, like a house, and now it was dividing into four arms, at right-angles to each other.

He burst into the clearing. It was the tail of an aeroplane: the German bomber that had crashed on the laundry. At least, most of it had crashed on the laundry. The tail, breaking off in the air, had spun to earth like a sycamore seed. He'd read of that happening in books. He could also tell from books that this had been a Heinkel He 111.

Suddenly he felt very proud. He'd report the find, and be on the nine o'clock news. He could hear the newsreader's voice.

The mystery bomber shot down over Garmouth on the night of the 1st of November has been identified as a new and secret variation of the Heinkel He 111. It was found by a nearly-unknown schoolboy, Charles McGill of Garmouth High School . . . sorry, I'll read that again, Form 3A at Garmouth High School. There is no doubt that but for the sharp eyes of this young man, several enemy secret weapons vital to the Blitzkrieg would have remained undiscovered . . .

Chas sighed. If he reported it, they'd just come and take it away for scrap. Like when he'd taken that shiny new incendiary-bomb rack to the Warden's Post . . . they'd not even said thank you.

And he wouldn't get in the news. It was a perfectly normal Heinkel 111, registration letters HX-L, with typical dorsal turret mounting one machine-gun . . .

Chas gulped. The machine-gun was still there, hanging from the turret, shiny and black.

E. B. White

CHARLOTTE'S WEB

I must have had hundreds of letters saying, 'There will never be a nicer book than this one,' and they are right. Anyone who has read this very special story will keep it inside themselves for ever.

Charlotte is a spider, Wilbur is a pig, and Fern is the farmer's daughter. They all live happily together, having the most interesting conversations, until there's a rumour of a very dismal future for Wilbur. Charlotte promises to save him, but how? You'll have to get the whole book to find out – and don't worry, even though the ending is rather sad, you won't feel *too* upset.

* * *

Wilbur liked Charlotte better and better each day. Her campaign against insects seemed sensible and useful. Hardly anybody around the farm had a good word to say for a fly. Flies spent their time pestering others. The cows hated them. The horses detested them. The sheep loathed them. Mr and Mrs Zuckerman were always complaining about them, and putting up screens.

Wilbur admired the way Charlotte managed. He was particularly glad that she always put her victim to sleep before eating it.

'It's real thoughtful of you to do that, Charlotte,' he said.

'Yes,' she replied in her sweet, musical voice, 'I always give them an anaesthetic so they won't feel pain. It's a little service I throw in.'

As the days went by, Wilbur grew and grew. He ate three big meals a day. He spent long hours lying on his side, half asleep, dreaming pleasant dreams. He enjoyed good health and he gained a lot of weight. One afternoon, when Fern was sitting on her stool, the oldest sheep walked into the barn, and stopped to pay a call on Wilbur.

'Hello!' she said. 'Seems to me you're putting on weight.'

'Yes, I guess I am,' replied Wilbur. 'At my age it's a good idea to keep gaining.'

'Just the same, I don't envy you,' said the old sheep. 'You know why they're fattening you up, don't you?'

'No,' said Wilbur.

'Well, I don't like to spread bad news,' said the sheep, 'but they're fattening you up because they're going to kill you, that's why.'

'They're going to *what*?' screamed Wilbur. Fern grew rigid on her stool.

'Kill you. Turn you into smoked bacon and ham,' continued the old sheep. 'Almost all young pigs get murdered by the farmer as soon as the real cold weather sets in. There's a regular conspiracy around here to kill you at Christmastime. Everybody is in the plot – Lurvy, Zuckerman, even John Arable.'

'Mr Arable?' sobbed Wilbur. 'Fern's father?'

'Certainly. When a pig is to be butchered, everybody helps. I'm an old sheep and I see the same thing, same old business, year after year. Arable arrives with his ·22, shoots the . . .'

'Stop!' screamed Wilbur. 'I don't want to die! Save me, somebody! Save me!' Fern was just about to jump up when a voice was heard.

'Be quiet, Wilbur!' said Charlotte, who had been listening to this awful conversation.

'I can't be quiet,' screamed Wilbur, racing up and down. 'I don't want to be killed. I don't want to die. Is it true what the old sheep says, Charlotte? Is it true they are going to kill me when the cold weather comes?'

'Well,' said the spider, plucking thoughtfully at her web, 'the old sheep has been around this barn a long time. She has seen many a spring pig come and go. If she says they plan to kill you, I'm sure it's true. It's also the dirtiest trick I ever heard of. What people don't think of!'

Wilbur burst into tears. 'I don't *want* to die,' he moaned. 'I want to stay alive, right here in my comfortable manure pile with all my friends. I want to breathe the beautiful air and lie in the beautiful sun.'

'You're certainly making a beautiful noise,' snapped the old sheep.

'I don't want to die!' screamed Wilbur, throwing himself to the ground.

'You shall not die,' said Charlotte, briskly.

'What? Really?' cried Wilbur. 'Who's going to save me?'

'I am,' said Charlotte.

'How?' asked Wilbur.

'That remains to be seen. But I am going to save you, and I want you to quiet down immediately. You're carrying on in a childish way. Stop your crying! I can't stand hysterics.'

Laura Ingalls Wilder

LITTLE HOUSE
IN THE BIG WOODS

There are nine books about Laura and her pioneering family, with her restless father, always moving on to new places. The Big Woods, in Wisconsin, U.S.A., is where her life begins, but after that she has stories to tell about life on the Prairie, Plum Creek and the Silver Lake, while all the time she is growing up and learning how to cope with new ways of living.

The delight of these stories is that everything Laura Ingalls Wilder writes about really happened, including falling in love and getting married. Here is a very young Laura facing a serious danger . . .

* * *

Laura and Mary had never seen a town. They had never seen a store. They had never seen even two houses standing together. But they knew that in a town there were many houses, and a store full of candy and calico and other wonderful things – powder, and shot, and salt, and store sugar.

They knew that Pa would trade his furs to the storekeeper for beautiful things from town, and all day they were expecting the presents he would bring them. When the sun sank low above the treetops and no more drops fell from the tips of the icicles they began to watch eagerly for Pa.

The sun sank out of sight, the woods grew dark, and he did not come. Ma started supper and set the table, but he did not come. It was time to do the chores, and still he had not come.

Ma said that Laura might come with her while she milked the cow. Laura could carry the lantern.

So Laura put on her coat and Ma buttoned it up. And Laura put her hands into her red mittens that hung by a red yarn string around her neck, while Ma lighted the candle in the lantern.

Laura was proud to be helping Ma with the milking, and she carried the lantern very carefully. Its sides were of tin, with places cut in them for the candle-light to shine through.

When Laura walked behind Ma on the path to the barn, the little bits of candle-light from the lantern leaped all around her on the snow. The night was not yet quite dark. The woods were dark, but there was a grey light on the snowy path, and in the sky there were a few faint stars. The stars did not look as warm and bright as the little lights that came from the lantern.

Laura was surprised to see the dark shape of Sukey, the brown cow, standing at the barnyard gate. Ma was surprised, too.

It was too early in the spring for Sukey to be let out in the Big Woods to eat grass. She lived in the barn. But sometimes on warm days Pa left the door of her stall open so she could come into the barnyard. Now Ma and Laura saw her behind the bars, waiting for them.

Ma went up to the gate, and pushed against it to open it. But it did not open very far, because there was Sukey, standing against it. Ma said:

'Sukey, get over!' She reached across the gate and slapped Sukey's shoulder.

Just then one of the dancing bits of light from the lantern jumped between the bars of the gate, and Laura saw long, shaggy, black fur, and two little, glittering eyes. Sukey had thin, short, brown fur. Sukey had large, gentle eyes.

Ma said, 'Laura, walk back to the house.'

So Laura turned around and began to walk towards the house. Ma came behind her. When they had gone part way, Ma snatched her up, lantern and all, and ran. Ma ran with her into the house, and slammed the door.

Then Laura said, 'Ma, was it a bear?'

'Yes, Laura,' Ma said. 'It was a bear.'

Laura began to cry. She hung on to Ma and sobbed, 'Oh, will he eat Sukey?'

'No,' Ma said, hugging her. 'Sukey is safe in the barn. Think, Laura – all those big, heavy logs in the barn walls. And the door is heavy and solid, made to keep bears out. No, the bear cannot get in and eat Sukey.'

Laura felt better then. 'But he could have hurt us, couldn't he?' she asked.

'He didn't hurt us,' Ma said. 'You were a good girl, Laura, to do exactly as I told you, and to do it quickly, without asking why.'

Ma was trembling, and she began to laugh a little. 'To think,' she said, 'I've slapped a bear!'

Then she put supper on the table for Laura and Mary. Pa had not come yet. He didn't come. Laura and Mary were undressed, and they said their prayers and snuggled into the trundle bed.

Ma sat by the lamp, mending one of Pa's shirts. The house seemed cold and still and strange, without Pa.

Laura listened to the wind in the Big Woods. All around the house the wind went crying as though it were lost in the dark and the cold. The wind sounded frightened.

Ma finished mending the shirt. Laura saw her fold it slowly and carefully. She smoothed it with her hand. Then she did a thing she had never done before. She went to the door and pulled the leather latch-string through its hole in the door, so that nobody could get in from outside unless she lifted the latch. She came and took Carrie, all limp and sleeping, out of the big bed.

She saw that Laura and Mary were still awake, and she said to them: 'Go to sleep, girls. Everything is all right. Pa will be here in the morning.'

Then she went back to her rocking chair and sat there rocking gently and holding Baby Carrie in her arms.

She was sitting up late, waiting for Pa, and Laura and Mary meant to stay awake, too, till he came. But at last they went to sleep.

In the morning Pa was there. He had brought candy for Laura and Mary, and two pieces of pretty calico to make them each a dress. Mary's was a china-blue pattern on a white ground, and Laura's was dark red with little golden-brown dots on it. Ma had calico for a dress, too; it was brown, with a big, feathery-white pattern all over it.

They were all happy because Pa had got such good prices for his furs that he could afford to get them such beautiful presents.

The tracks of the big bear were all around the barn, and there were marks of his claws on the walls. But Sukey and the horses were safe inside.

All that day the sun shone, the snow melted, and little streams of water ran from the icicles, which all the time grew thinner. Before the sun set that night, the bear tracks were only shapeless marks in the wet, soft snow.

After supper Pa took Laura and Mary on his knees and said he had a new story to tell them.

'When I went to town yesterday with the furs I found it hard walking in the soft snow. It took me a long time to get to town, and other men with furs had come in earlier to do their trading. The storekeeper was busy, and I had to wait until he could look at my furs.

'Then we had to bargain about the price of each one, and then I had to pick out the things I wanted to take in trade.

'So it was nearly sundown before I could start home.

'I tried to hurry, but the walking was hard and I was tired, so I had not gone far before night came. And I was alone in the Big Woods without my gun.

'There were still six miles to walk, and I came along as fast as I could. The night grew darker and darker, and I wished for my gun, because I knew that some of the bears had come out of their winter dens. I had seen their tracks when I went to town in the morning.

'Bears are hungry and cross at this time of year; you know

they have been sleeping in their dens all winter long with nothing to eat, and that makes them thin and angry when they wake up. I did not want to meet one.

'I hurried along as quick as I could in the dark. By and by the stars gave a little light. It was still black as pitch where the woods were thick, but in the open places I could see, dimly. I could see the snowy road ahead a little way, and I could see the dark woods standing all around me. I was glad when I came into an open place where the stars gave me this faint light.

'All the time I was watching, as well as I could, for bears. I was listening for the sounds they make when they go carelessly through the bushes.

'Then I came again into an open place, and there, right in the middle of my road, I saw a big black bear.

'He was standing up on his hind legs, looking at me. I could see his eyes shine. I could see his pig-snout. I could even see one of his claws, in the starlight.

'My scalp prickled, and my hair stood straight up. I stopped in my tracks, and stood still. The bear did not move. There he stood, looking at me.

'I knew it would do no good to try to go around him. He would follow me into the dark woods, where he could see better than I could. I did not want to fight a winter-starved bear in the dark. Oh, how I wished for my gun!

'I had to pass that bear, to get home. I thought that if I could scare him, he might get out of the road and let me go by. So I took a deep breath, and suddenly I shouted with all my might and ran at him, waving my arms.

'He didn't move.

'I did not run very far towards him, I tell you! I stopped and looked at him, and he stood looking at me. Then I shouted again. There he stood. I kept on shouting and waving my arms, but he did not budge.

'Well, it would do me no good to run away. There were other bears in the woods. I might meet one any time. I might as well deal with this one as with another. Besides, I was coming home to Ma and you girls. I would never get here, if I ran away from everything in the woods that scared me.

'So at last I looked around, and I got a good big club, a solid, heavy branch that had been broken from a tree by the weight of snow in the winter.

'I lifted it up in my hands, and I ran straight at that bear. I swung my club as hard as I could and brought it down, bang! on his head.

'And there he still stood, for he was nothing but a big, black, burned stump!

'I had passed it on my way to town that morning. It wasn't a bear at all. I only thought it was a bear, because I had been thinking all the time about bears and being afraid I'd meet one.'

'It really wasn't a bear at all?' Mary asked.

'No, Mary, it wasn't a bear at all. There I had been yelling, and dancing, and waving my arms, all by myself in the Big Woods, trying to scare a stump!'

Laura said: 'Ours was really a bear. But we were not scared, because we thought it was Sukey.'

Pa did not say anything, but he hugged her tighter.

'Oo-oo! That bear might have eaten Ma and me all up!' Laura said, snuggling closer to him. 'But Ma walked right up to him and slapped him, and he didn't do anything at all. Why didn't he do anything?'

'I guess he was too surprised to do anything, Laura,' Pa said. 'I guess he was afraid, when the lantern shone in his eyes. And when Ma walked up to him and slapped him, he knew *she* wasn't afraid.'

'Well, you were brave, too,' Laura said. 'Even if it was only a stump, you thought it was a bear. You'd have hit him on the head with a club, if he *had* been a bear, wouldn't you, Pa?'

'Yes,' said Pa, 'I would. You see, I had to.'

MORE BOOKS NOT TO BE MISSED!

You will have guessed that I have far more than fifty favourite books; after all, I picked more than a thousand to turn into Puffins. So lots that are just as good have had to be left out, otherwise this book would have been so heavy you wouldn't have been able to hold it! So here is a list of some other books which I truly hope you will read; put crosses against those which make your eyes open and your ears prick. And don't forget that most of the authors in this anthology have written many other super stories.

ADVENTURE

The Perilous Descent Bruce Carter—Two airmen shot down during the war find their parachutes have taken them to a country miles below the earth, which they help to save before they end up in an even more desperate situation. One ingenious adventure after another, told in diary form, after they managed to get back to civilization. Or have they?

Run for Your Life David Line—The story of an odd friendship, a senior boy unwillingly getting involved with a small Hungarian refugee; together they stop a murder.

Gumble's Yard John Rowe Townsend—Four abandoned children

avoid authority by hiding in a deserted warehouse where they disturb and defeat a gang of crooks. One of the first and best books about modern city life.

ANIMALS

The Runaways Victor Canning—First of a trilogy about Smiler, a boy on the run, and the escaped animals he meets on the way. In this book he meets a cheetah.

Break for Freedom Ewan Clarkson—Another escaped animal, this time a mink who has a difficult time learning to live in the wild.

Joe and the Gladiator Catherine Cookson—A boy and a horse, with no home and no money – but they manage.

Ned Kelly and the City of the Bees Thomas Keneally—Ned shrinks to bee size and lives in a hive for an entire summer. Not everyone's drop of honey, but certainly mine!

The Log of the Ark Kenneth Walker/Geoffrey Boumphrey—Here the authors report what it was like living cooped up in the Ark for those forty days and nights, and how Noah managed to keep the peace. It's a lovely book.

FAMILY

Collision Course Nigel Hinton—A boy gets into dreadful trouble with a stolen motorbike, and has a hard time confessing.
King of the Barbarians Janet Hitchman—Here is another true-life story about the author's growing-up – first in a succession of foster homes and then in Barnardo's, where she got the education she longed for, and learnt to be a writer.

Goodnight Mister Tom Michelle Magorian—William is a miserable, skinny evacuee with a dreadful mother. Mr Tom is a gruff old man who comes to love him (and helps find him when his mother locks him up and he is starving to death).

Auntie Robbo Ann Scott-Moncrieff—A wonderful, zany old lady who runs away with her great-nephew to help him escape from boarding school and a dreadful foster-mother.

I Own the Racecourse Patricia Wrightson—How backward Andy thinks he has bought a racecourse for three dollars, and his friends have to help him out of trouble.

FANTASY

Stranger at Green Knowe Lucy Boston—There are six books about this ancient house, often full of ghosts of past inhabitants, but all the stories are riveting and different. This particular one includes a visiting gorilla.

Hobberdy Dick K. M. Briggs—Dick is a hobgoblin who looks after Widford Manor and its inhabitants, protects poor orphan Anne and saves young Martha from the witches' spell. But the best thing is that you learn about all the other creatures who inhabit the Cotswold night. Written by a professor of fairies.

The Hollow Land Jane Gardam—Anything by this writer is worth reading, but this collection of short stories, funny or frightening, is good to start off with.

Playing Beatie Bow Ruth Park—Another good time-slip story, set in Australia, remarkably well worked out and often very scary.

Marianne Dreams Catherine Storr—A sick girl and boy, strangers to each other, meet in dreams by means of a magic pencil. At first glance this may sound a little too young for you, but it's so brilliantly worked out (and often frightening) that, once read, it won't be forgotten.

HISTORY

Boy with the Bronze Axe Kathleen Fidler—How the Bronze Age developed; riveting in the telling.

Tales of the Greek Heroes Roger Lancelyn Green—This erudite but wonderfully readable author has also taken care of the Trojans, the Norsemen, Ancient Egypt and King Arthur. Not to be missed.

The Namesake C. Walter Hodges—I hope you can find a copy of this somewhere because it's such a very good picture of Alfred the Great (that gentle, scholarly king), and of another Alfred, Alfred Daneleg, his friend and scribe. Try the libraries.

A Traveller in Time Alison Uttley—Penelope finds herself caught up in English history, trying to save Mary, Queen of Scots although, with her modern knowledge, she knows it won't work.

HUMOUR

Grimble and *Grimble at Christmas* Clement Freud—I have a weak spot for this precocious boy, deeply interested in food and invading all his relations' kitchens in turn.

Midnite Randolph Stow—Midnite was a rather dumb seventeen-year-old, but his five animal friends take care of him even when he gets put in prison.

Bottersnikes and Gumbles S. A. Wakefield—Bottersnikes are ugly, lazy and mean and they make slaves out of Gumbles who are a bit silly and giggly and can be squashed into prisons made of jam tins. It takes place in the Australian bush.

SCHOOL STORIES

Terry on the Fence Bernard Ashley—Terry Harmer is bothered by dishonest bullies and gets into deep trouble.

Flood Warning Paul Berna—Schoolboys trapped by a rising flood, and the least likely one manages to save them.

Autumn Term Antonia Forest—If you are keen on school stories, these (there are four) are the best there are, all about the Marlow sisters and what boarding-school life means to them.

The Turbulent Term of Tyke Tiler Gene Kemp—Tyke is good at heart, but championship of backward Danny lands them both in funny, interesting and unexpected trouble.

The Goalkeeper's Revenge Bill Naughton—Short stories, mostly about football, all vivid and exciting. This author wrote a funny grown-up book called *Alfie*.

BIBLIOGRAPHY

Richard Adams, *Watership Down*, Rex Collings, 1972, Allen Lane,
1982 (now Viking), Puffin, 1973

Joan Aiken, *The Wolves of Willoughby Chase*, Jonathan Cape, 1962,
Puffin, 1968

Nina Bawden, *Carrie's War*, Gollancz, 1973, Puffin, 1974

Betsy Byars, *The Eighteenth Emergency*, Bodley Head, 1974, Puffin,
1976

John Christopher, *The Guardians*, Hamish Hamilton, 1970, Puffin,
1973

Susan Cooper, *The Dark is Rising*, Bodley Head, 1973, Puffin, 1976

Helen Cresswell, *The Night-Watchmen*, Faber and Faber, 1969, Puffin,
1976

Roald Dahl, *The BFG*, Jonathan Cape, 1982, Puffin, 1984

Lionel Davidson, *Under Plum Lake*, Jonathan Cape, 1980, Puffin, 1983

Meindert DeJong, *The House of Sixty Fathers*, Lutterworth Press, 1958,
Puffin, 1966

Peter Dickinson, *The Dancing Bear*, Gollancz, 1972, Puffin, 1974

J. Meade Falkner, *Moonfleet*, Edward Arnold, 1898, Puffin, 1962

Nicholas Fisk, *Trillions*, Hamish Hamilton, 1971, Viking Kestrel,
1984, Puffin, 1973

Leon Garfield, *Smith*, Constable, 1967 (now Viking Kestrel), Puffin,
1968

Alan Garner, *Elidor*, Collins, 1965, Fontana Lions, 1974

Jean Craighead George, *Julie of the Wolves*, Hamish Hamilton, 1973,
Puffin, 1976

J. B. S. Haldane, *My Friend Mr Leakey*, The Cresset Press, 1937 (now
Century Hutchinson), Puffin, 1944

Cynthia Harnett, *The Wool-Pack*, Methuen, 1951, Puffin, 1961

Russell Hoban, *The Mouse and his Child*, Faber and Faber, 1969, Puffin,
1976

Anne Holm, *I am David*, Methuen, 1965, Puffin, 1969

Norman Hunter, *The Incredible Adventures of Professor Branestawm*, Bodley Head, 1933, Puffin, 1946

Diana Wynne Jones, *Charmed Life*, Macmillan, 1977, Puffin, 1979

Norton Juster, *The Phantom Tollbooth*, Collins, 1962, Fontana Lions, 1974

Clive King, *The Twenty-two Letters*, Hamish Hamilton, 1966, Puffin, 1966

Dick King-Smith, *The Sheep-Pig*, Gollancz, 1983, Puffin, 1985

Ursula Le Guin, *A Wizard of Earthsea*, Parnassus Press (U.S.A.), 1968 (now Houghton Mifflin Co.), Puffin, 1971

Penelope Lively, *The Ghost of Thomas Kempe*, Heinemann, 1973, Puffin, 1984

Margaret Mahy, *The Haunting*, Dent, 1982, Magnet Books, 1984

Jan Mark, *Handles*, Viking Kestrel, 1983, Puffin, 1985

William Mayne, *Earthfasts*, Hamish Hamilton, 1966, Puffin, 1969

Mary Norton, *The Borrowers*, Dent, 1952, Puffin, 1958

Robert C. O'Brien, *Mrs Frisby and the Rats of NIMH*, Gollancz, 1972, Puffin, 1975

Philippa Pearce, *Tom's Midnight Garden*, Oxford University Press, 1958, Puffin, 1976

Arthur Ransome, *We Didn't Mean to Go to Sea*, Jonathan Cape, 1937, Puffin, 1969

Joan G. Robinson, *When Marnie Was There*, Collins, 1973, Fontana Lions, 1973

Antoine de Saint-Exupéry, *The Little Prince*, Heinemann, 1945, Piccolo Books, 1982

George Selden, *The Cricket in Times Square*, Dent, 1961, Viking Kestrel, 1982, Puffin, 1973

Ian Serraillier, *The Silver Sword*, Jonathan Cape, 1956, Puffin, 1960

Dodie Smith, *The Hundred and One Dalmatians*, Heinemann, 1956, Piccolo Books, 1975

Ivan Southall, *Hills End*, Angus and Robertson, 1962, Puffin, 1965

Noel Streatfeild, *The Growing Summer*, Collins, 1966, Puffin, 1968

Rosemary Sutcliff, *The Eagle of the Ninth*, Oxford University Press, 1954, Puffin, 1977

James Thurber, 'The Wonderful O', Hamish Hamilton, 1958, published together with 'The 13 Clocks' in *The 13 Clocks and The Wonderful O*, Puffin, 1962, Hamish Hamilton, 1966

J. R. R. Tolkien, *The Hobbit*, Allen & Unwin, 1937

BIBLIOGRAPHY 381

A. Rutgers van der Loeff, *Children on the Oregon Trail*, University of London Press, 1961, Puffin, 1963
Cynthia Voigt, *Homecoming*, Collins, 1983, Fontana Lions, 1984
Jill Paton Walsh, *The Dolphin Crossing*, Macmillan, 1967, Puffin, 1970
Robert Westall, *The Machine-Gunners*, Macmillan, 1977, Puffin, 1979
E. B. White, *Charlotte's Web*, Hamish Hamilton, 1952, Puffin, 1963
Laura Ingalls Wilder, *Little House in the Big Woods*, Methuen, 1956, Puffin, 1963

ACKNOWLEDGEMENTS

The editor and publishers gratefully acknowledge permission to reproduce copyright material in this anthology, in the form of extracts taken from the following books:

Watership Down by Richard Adams, published by Penguin Books Ltd; *The Wolves of Willoughby Chase* by Joan Aiken, published by Jonathan Cape Ltd; *Carrie's War* by Nina Bawden, by permission of Victor Gollancz Ltd; extract from *The Eighteenth Emergency* by Betsy Byars, copyright © 1973 by Betsy Byars, reprinted by permission of Viking Penguin Inc., and by permission of The Bodley Head; *The Guardians* by John Christopher, © John Christopher (Hamish Hamilton Ltd), reprinted by permission of the author; Susan Cooper, excerpted from *The Dark is Rising*, copyright © 1973 Susan Cooper (A Margaret K. McElderry Book), reprinted with the permission of Atheneum Publishers, Inc., and by permission of The Bodley Head; *The Night-Watchmen* by Helen Cresswell, reprinted by permission of Faber and Faber Ltd; *The BFG* by Roald Dahl, illustrated by Quentin Blake, by permission of Jonathan Cape Ltd; *Under Plum Lake* by Lionel Davidson, © 1980 by Manningfield Ltd, published by Jonathan Cape Ltd; *The House of Sixty Fathers* by Meindert DeJong, by permission of Lutterworth Press; *The Dancing Bear* by Peter Dickinson, by permission of Victor Gollancz Ltd; *Trillions* by Nicholas Fisk, published by Viking Kestrel; extract from *Smith* by Leon Garfield (Longman Young Books, 1967), copyright © Leon Garfield 1967, reproduced by permission of Penguin Books Ltd; extract from *Elidor* by Alan Garner, © Alan Garner 1965, published by Collins; *Julie of the Wolves* by Jean Craighead George, reprinted by permission of Curtis Brown Ltd, New York, copyright © 1972 by Jean Craighead George; *My Friend Mr Leakey* by J. B. S. Haldane (Cresset Press, 1937), by permission of Century Hutchinson Limited; *The Wool-Pack* by Cynthia Harnett, reprinted by permission of Methuen Children's Books; pp 38–44 from *The Mouse and his Child* by

Russell Hoban, copyright © 1967 by Russell C. Hoban, reprinted by permission of Harper & Row Publishers Inc. and by permission of Faber and Faber Ltd; *I am David* by Anne Holm, reprinted by permission of Methuen Children's Books; extract from *The Incredible Adventures of Professor Branestawm* by Norman Hunter, reproduced by permission of The Bodley Head; *Charmed Life* by Diana Wynne Jones, by permission of Macmillan, London and Basingstoke; extract from *The Phantom Tollbooth* by Norton Juster, © 1961 Norton Juster, reprinted by permission of Random House, Inc. and by permission of Collins; *The Twenty-two Letters* by Clive King (Puffin Books, 1966), copyright © Clive King, 1966, reproduced by permission of Penguin Books Ltd; *The Sheep-Pig* by Dick King-Smith by permission of Victor Gollancz Ltd; from *A Wizard of Earthsea* by Ursula Le Guin, copyright © 1968 by Ursula K. Le Guin, reprinted by permission of Houghton Mifflin Company; *The Ghost of Thomas Kempe* by Penelope Lively, reprinted by permission of William Heinemann Limited; *The Haunting* by Margaret Mahy, by permission of J. M. Dent & Sons Ltd; extract from *Handles* by Jan Mark (Kestrel Books, 1983), copyright © Jan Mark, 1983, reproduced by permission of Penguin Books Ltd; *Earthfasts* by William Mayne, published by Hamish Hamilton Ltd; extract from *The Borrowers*, copyright 1952, 1953, 1980 by Mary Norton, renewed 1981 by Mary Norton, Beth Krush, and Joe Krush, reprinted by permission of Harcourt Brace Jovanovich, Inc., and by permission of J. M. Dent & Sons Ltd; Robert C. O'Brien, excerpted from *Mrs Frisby and the Rats of NIMH*, copyright © 1971 Robert C. O'Brien, reprinted with the permission of Atheneum Publishers Inc., and by permission of Victor Gollancz Ltd; extract reprinted from *Tom's Midnight Garden* by Philippa Pearce (1958), by permission of Oxford University Press; *We Didn't Mean to Go to Sea* by Arthur Ransome (Jonathan Cape Ltd), reprinted by permission of the Arthur Ransome Estate; *When Marnie Was There*, © Joan G. Robinson 1967, published by Collins; extract from *The Little Prince* by Antoine de Saint-Exupéry, copyright 1943, 1971 by Harcourt Brace Jovanovich, Inc., reprinted by permission of the publisher and by permission of William Heinemann Limited; selection from *The Cricket in Times Square* by George Selden, copyright © 1960 by George Selden, reprint by permission of Farrar, Straus and Giroux, Inc., and by permission of Penguin Books Ltd; *The Silver Sword* by Ian Serraillier, reprinted by permission of Jonathan Cape Ltd; *The Hundred and One Dalmatians* by Dodie Smith, reprinted by permission of William Heinemann Limited; extract from *Hills End* by Ivan Southall, by permission of Angus & Robertson (U.K.) Ltd; extract from *The Growing Summer* by Noel Streatfeild, © text Noel Streatfeild 1966, published by Collins; extract reprinted from *The Eagle of the Ninth* by Rosemary Sutcliff (1954), by permission of Oxford University Press; *The Wonderful O* by James Thurber, published by Hamish Hamilton Ltd and by permission of Rosemary A. Thurber, Attorney-in-fact for Helen W. Thurber; *The Hobbit* by J. R. R. Tolkien, published by Allen & Unwin; *Children on the Oregon Trail* by A. Rutgers van der Loeff (University of London Press, 1961), reprinted by permission of Hodder & Stoughton Ltd; Cynthia Voigt, excerpted from *Homecoming*, copyright © 1981 Cynthia Voigt, reprinted with the permission of Atheneum Publishers, Inc., and by permission of Collins; *The Dolphin Crossing* by Jill Paton Walsh, by permission of Macmillan, London and Basingstoke; *The Machine-Gunners* by Robert Westall, by permission of Macmillan, London and Basingstoke; complete text of chapter 7 from *Charlotte's Web* by E. B. White, copyright 1952 by E. B. White, text copyright renewed 1980 by E. B. White, reprinted by permission of Harper & Row Publishers Inc., and by permission of Hamish Hamilton Ltd; text of pp. 102–15 (with one deletion) from *Little House in the Big Woods* by Laura Ingalls Wilder, copyright 1932 as to text by Laura Ingalls Wilder, renewed 1959 by Roger L. Macbride, reprinted by permission of Harper & Row Publishers Inc. and by permission of Methuen Children's Books.

Every effort has been made to trace copyright holders. The editor and publishers would like to hear from any copyright holders not acknowledged.

Text has been omitted in the extracts taken from *The Eighteenth Emergency* by Betsy Byars, *We Didn't Mean to Go to Sea* by Arthur Ransome, and *The Machine-Gunners* by Robert Westall. This is indicated by [. . . . . .]